Praise for Lee Goodman and his stunning debut
INDEFENSIBLE

"Goodman takes the reader by the hand and leads them into a frightening world they will never forget. . . . This book is top-notch!"

—*Suspense Magazine*

"Compelling from start to finish—well-written, populated with intriguing multidimensional characters, and with many plot twists leading to a surprise ending."

—*Library Journal*

"As legal thrillers go, this one is right up there with the best of them. That's not because of its nonstop action, but because of its slow-burn pacing, unpredictable characters, and lots and lots of plot switchbacks."

—*Bookreporter*

"Goodman easily makes the transition to fiction writer, as have his brethren Scott Turow and John Lescroart."

—*Booklist*

"Complex and intelligent, fantastically well-plotted. *Indefensible* is as good as it gets."

—John Lescroart, *New York Times* bestselling author

Indefensible is the kind of gem we all love to stumble on, a novel that delivers its story flawlessly . . . and the result may well prove to be the outstanding debut novel of the year."

—William Kent Krueger, *New York Times* bestselling author

"Lee Goodman is a rare find in a crowded field: a talented writer who knows the true intricacies and ironies of the American criminal litigation system. Be sure to put on your helmet and fasten your 5-point harness. You're in for a wild ride."

—Walter Walker, author of *Crime of Privilege*

INDEFENSIBLE

a novel

LEE GOODMAN

EMILY BESTLER BOOKS

WASHINGTON SQUARE PRESS

NEW YORK   LONDON   TORONTO   SYDNEY   NEW DELHI

WASHINGTON SQUARE PRESS
An Imprint of Simon & Schuster, Inc.
1230 Avenue of the Americas
New York, NY 10020

First Emily Bestler Books/Washington Square Press edition April 2015

EMILY BESTLER BOOKS / WASHINGTON SQUARE PRESS and colophons are trademarks of Simon & Schuster, Inc.

For information about special discounts for bulk purchases, please contact Simon & Schuster Special Sales at 1-866-506-1949 or business@simonandschuster.com.

The Simon & Schuster Speakers Bureau can bring authors to your live event. For more information or to book an event, contact the Simon & Schuster Speakers Bureau at 1-866-248-3049 or visit our website at www.simonspeakers.com.

Interior design by Kyoko Watanabe
Cover design © Jae Song
Cover images © David McLain/Getty Images; © Justin W. Kern/Getty Images

Manufactured in the United States of America

10 9 8 7 6 5 4 3 2 1

The Library of Congress has cataloged the hardcover edition as follows:

Goodman, Lee.
    Indefensible : a novel / Lee Goodman. — First Emily Bestler Books/Atria Books hardcover edition.
        pages   cm
    1. Legal stories. I. Title.
    PS3607.O577I53 2014
    813'.6—dc23   2013032300

ISBN 978-1-4767-2800-1
ISBN 978-1-4767-2801-8 (pbk)
ISBN 978-1-4767-2802-5 (ebook)

For Dana and Isabella

Each lawyer must find within his own conscience the touchstone against which to test [his actions]. But in the last analysis it is the desire for the respect and confidence of the members of his profession and of the society which he serves that should provide to a lawyer the incentive for the highest possible degree of ethical conduct. The possible loss of that respect and confidence is the ultimate sanction. So long as its practitioners are guided by these principles, the law will continue to be a noble profession. This is its greatness and its strength, which permit of no compromise.

—from the Preamble to the ABA Model
Code of Professional Responsibility

PART I

CHAPTER 1

I don't honestly expect to find a body. Someone has to go look, though, and on a day like this—the first Friday in June with the memory of cold winter lost beneath the trilling surface of summer—volunteers abound. *Carpe diem*; I have been offered an excuse to spend a couple of hours in sunshiny woods.

We take the river road to the highway, passing century-old mill buildings. Some are crumbling, encircled by chain-link and razor wire, and others are merely shuttered. They seem to stretch for miles, rotting corpses of an old economy, lining the banks of the Aponak River.

The westbound ramp will clog to a standstill by midafternoon, everyone going to lakes or mountains, but it's early now, and I speed around the curve with tires squealing. On the highway, other travelers are making an early break from the city. Some have windows open, husbands driving while their pretty wives ride shotgun with hair blowing in the wind and flip-flopped feet up on the dash. Kids ride in back with Nintendos and iPhones, ball caps pulled low. A dog in a minivan paints the rear window with slobber as I pull alongside, and a boy presses his face to the side window and watches me. He thinks I'm a criminal because I'm at the wheel of my Volvo wagon doing twenty over the limit with the troopers behind me, blues-and-reds flashing, and behind them is the coroner's van (just in case), its antennas bending in the wind. I slow enough to give the boy a goofy, cross-eyed look, and he responds with a smile so huge and gap-toothed that I'm laughing out loud with my head pressed back against the seat. The boy laughs too, and his mom, fresh from the pages of L.L.Bean's summer catalog, looks over. We exchange knowing parental smiles. Then I speed away.

"Oh God," says my daughter, Lizzy, in contempt of my inexplicably good mood, "you're such a . . . weirdo."

I look in the rearview for a glimpse of her complex smile. Lizzy is fourteen. Everything is a test.

"I've never seen a dead body before," Lizzy says.

"Redundant," I answer. "The word 'body' implies it's dead."

She thinks for a second, then snaps, "That is so not true. Like in health class, they used to say, 'At a certain age, you begin to notice mysterious changes in your body.'" (This last part she squawks in her old-biddy voice.) "So are we all, like, dead?"

"Point taken," I say, "but in any case, you're not going to see any dead body, you're staying in the car. And there might not even be a body." I look at Cassandra, who is in the front seat beside me. Cassandra smiles and says, "I guess we'll see."

If I really believed for a second we'd find a body, I wouldn't have come myself, and I certainly wouldn't have brought Lizzy. Crime scenes aren't places for teenage daughters. But with Cassandra here beside me, I need to pretend there's a possibility. Cassandra is a civilian. I've known her under two hours. She is dressed in olive cargo pants with the cuffs tucked inside white socks. She wears a tight pink tee, which would look silly on a woman her age—early forties—except that she also wears a loose, unbuttoned work shirt over it, changing it from inappropriately adolescent to enticingly youthful. She is a younger version of my ex-wife, Flora, Lizzy's mom.

"We should have brought Bill-the-Dog," I say to Lizzy, "maybe let her run in the woods." I explain to Cassandra that Bill-the-Dog is Lizzy's border collie, a female.

"Oh, sure," Lizzy says in a mocking voice, "Bill could help you dig. Maybe she'd find herself a nice arm or leg bone to chew on."

"Well, I didn't mean let her out at the scene; I was thinking we could stop on the way home. Pick up sandwiches someplace and . . . you know." I stop. The idea is ludicrous: turning a possible crime scene visit and exhumation into a picnic with the witness. I brace myself for the onslaught of Lizzy's ridicule, but in the rearview, I see her watching Cassandra.

"Oh, that sounds lovely, Nick," Cassandra says, "let's do." She turns to look at Lizzy in the backseat. "Is Bill-the-Dog named for Bill-the-Pony? From Tolkien?"

"My mom named her," Lizzy says. "My mom's kind of weird, like she has this sign outside the house: WELCOME TO MIDDLE EARTH."

"Do you have a dog?" I ask Cassandra.

"Definitely," Cassandra says. "Having a dog is one of the best things about being human. One of the ten best."

"And the other nine?"

"I don't know. Love, dancing, good coffee, kids, summer? I never made a list. But if I did, dogs would be on it."

"Jane Austen would be on it," Lizzy says, and I look in the rearview just before her mouth tightens into a disdainful line of pursed lips. But it was there for a second: her metal-mouth smile showing those red-banded braces like a centipede across her teeth.

Cassandra turns again to look at Lizzy and says, "Definitely Jane Austen."

CHAPTER 2

I'd been sitting at my desk reading a state police bulletin about several missing children from Rivertown when Agent Chip d'Villafranca called from the FBI. "Nick, I have a long-shot theory on our college boy," he said. "We've maybe got a body. I mean, we don't *got* it yet, but we're going to *got* it," and he chuckled, because this mangling of tenses was Chip's idea of humor. I like this about him. Maybe he hadn't mastered ironic wit, but at least he's less dour than some other agents at the Bureau who seem to think a sense of humor is vaguely seditious.

"I just got a call from Captain Dorsey at the state troopers," Chip said. "They have a woman, a bird-watcher, who maybe witnessed someone dumping a body out at the reservoir. Dorsey thought it sounded Mob-ish, is why he called me. So if it's a body—big if—maybe your college boy didn't exactly go missing of his own free will. I'm driving over to talk to the bird-watcher. Want to come?"

I did want to. So I went to meet Chip at trooper headquarters, where Captain Dorsey introduced us to Cassandra.

I offered my hand. "Nick Davis, U.S. attorney's office."

We shook. She had a firm handshake, but then she stood awkwardly, uncertain what to do. In her other hand, she held a copy of *Soldier of Fortune* magazine.

"Is that the issue with the article on rose-breasted sap suckers?" I asked.

She laughed. "Officer Dorsey's," she said. "I . . . you know . . . picked it up to read while I waited."

Dorsey took the magazine from her. "I like to stay current on what the wack jobs are up to."

I had met Captain Dorsey only a couple of times, so I wasn't sure whether to believe him. He seemed like the kind who might get more jollies from *Soldier of Fortune* than *Playboy.* He was a G. Gordon Liddy–ish guy with a black bottlebrush mustache and an everybody's-an-asshole look in his eye.

Cassandra and I stood staring at each other, and I couldn't think of anything to say, so I finally said, "Shall we get started?" I sat down, and Cassandra and Chip sat down, and Dorsey sat behind his desk.

Cassandra told us she'd left home about four in the morning, driven to the reservoir, found an access road into the woods, parked, and followed a trail through the pine needles. The sun wasn't up yet, and the thrushes were singing. "Pebbles falling down a drainpipe," she said. "Hermit thrush. Have you heard it? Pebbles in a drainpipe?"

The trail she found skirted the edge of the marsh where she had hoped to see a yellow rail. The yellow rail, she explained, is a bird.

"So just as the trail got where I could see the reservoir through the trees," she said, "I see this big boulder, but when I get close, it turns out not to be a boulder but a mound of dirt. So I go investigate, and there's this hole somebody had dug right in the middle of no place. Kind of oblong. And recent. You can tell: The dirt was all fresh. You could smell it. And footprints all around. But I didn't think much about it, and I'm standing looking at this hole, when I suddenly hear one: a yellow rail. *Tap tap tap.* So I went after it, and I got pretty close. It's a tiny thing, you know, walks, mostly. Flies only when it has to. I stalked it for like half an hour. It was probably luring me away from its nest. It finally flew away, and I waited another half hour to see if it would come back, but it never did, so eventually, I got up and walked back toward the trail, and that's when I heard voices. Two men. And there I am, a woman alone in the woods in the early morning, so even though I figured they were just park rangers or something, I sat down behind a tree and waited. But they didn't sound like park rangers. Too gruff somehow, and laughing, but I couldn't make out anything they were saying. I stayed hidden, and a long time goes by when I don't hear them, so I get up and walk back to the trail. And the hole was gone. It was even hard to find where it had been, like they'd set aside the chunks of topsoil with ferns and everything and just fit it all back in place. And I still didn't think much about it until I'm off looking for warblers and hoping to hear another rail, and I suddenly realize, "Holy shit, they were burying a body."

Dorsey stroked his silly merkin of a mustache. "Ms. Randall, here are the salient points," he said too loudly, as if Cassandra herself were the body dumper. "First, they dug the hole ahead of time. Second, there were two of them. Third, they were quick. Fourth, they were jovial; fifth, they were, as you described it, exacting in covering the area." Dorsey counted out these points on his fingers. "These are the reasons I opted to contact Agent d'Villafranca, because they bespeak a very calculated and dispassionate and professionalistic activity that suggests Mob activity, which then would make it the concern of both state and federal organized crime units."

Apparently, Dorsey was the sort who, the less he has to say, the more words he uses to say it. And he was probably also afraid that, compared to Chip (FBI) and me (U.S. attorney's office), Cassandra might see him as just a floppy-wristed, cross-eyed hayseed of a state cop.

Dorsey wanted to get out to the reservoir as soon as possible.

Chip and I stepped out of the office to confer. "Sounds bogus," Chip whispered. "She seems kind of, you know, skittish."

"Someone burying a cat, probably."

"Or she got disoriented and was looking in the wrong place for the hole."

We paused and considered the situation for several seconds.

"But it's a nice day," I said.

"I wouldn't mind a day out of town," Chip said.

And what I thought but didn't say was that I wouldn't mind a chance to get to know this attractive bird-watcher who wore no wedding band.

We went back into the office. "Tell you what, Captain Dorsey," I said, "I'm kind of curious, too. I'll come along. You can ride with me, Ms. Randall. My daughter, Lizzy, is hanging with me today; she'd probably like some female company." I looked over at Dorsey and Chip. "If that's okay with you gentlemen," I said, making it more of an assertion than a question. I felt guilty, strutting in front of Chip like that. But since Chip had the advantage of youth (his mid-forties to my early fifties), I was using my advantage of rank.

Cassandra stood and waited for us to tell her what to do, and I realized that she was actually quite frightened. I put a hand on her shoulder and said, "How are you holding up, Ms. Randall?"

"I'm okay," she said softly, but then she had her head against my chest, and I had my arm around her in a half-hug, and I felt her ribs under my fingers and smelled her floral shampoo. "If it hadn't been for the yellow rail," she said unsteadily, apparently believing that she might have joined the hypothetical body in the pit if the assassins had found her witnessing the burial. But a second later, she tapped on my chest in a way that said, *I'm fine now*, and she pushed away from me.

Before hitting the highway, I swung back to the office to pick up Lizzy, who just got out of school for the summer and spent all yesterday lying on my office couch reading *Northanger Abbey* and carrying on a whispered conversation with the characters (who irritate her as much as I do).

"Lizzy, road trip," I said.

"Do you have any orange yarn?" she answered, holding a skinny braid where she could see it by looking cross-eyed. She had arranged a biosphere around herself on the couch, the contents of her backpack unloaded onto my office chairs, which were pulled within reach—books, journal, cell phone, water bottle, jog bra, running shoes, granola bars, yogurt, and Gatorade.

From my desk phone, I buzzed Kenny in the law library. "Hey, Kenny, there's something or someone that needs digging up out at the reservoir. Lizzy and I are on our way. Do you want to come?"

"If you need me."

"Not a question of need, Kenny. Opportunity. Think of it as a day's pay for a walk in the woods."

"Okay, if you want me to."

Kenny is my unofficial foster son and our office gofer. He's smart enough to do more—could probably even get a paralegal certificate—but he just clings to his comfortable nonachievement while I persist, like a Boy Scout in the rain, in trying to light a fire under him.

So it's four of us in the Volvo: Cassandra Randall and me in the front, Lizzy and Kenny in the back, off to look for a body in the woods on a beautiful spring day. Kenny dozed off as soon as we hit the highway. In the rearview, I see him slumped in the seat, head lolling.

"My baby brother," Lizzy says of Kenny, who is in his mid-twenties, a dozen years older than she. Lizzy slips a couple of inches toward him so that if his head tips any farther, it will land on her shoulder. "I'm the big sister," she says, "he's my baby brother, and we're in the family car riding to the country with Mom and Dad."

This is typical of Lizzy, pretending to have a normal family. She's never lived in a two-parent home.

CHAPTER 3

At the reservoir district, Cassandra directs me along miles of rural roads to where she'd parked her car this morning. I put two wheels on the shoulder and turn off the engine. Heat waves rise from the asphalt, which is black and silver in the sun, and the sun catches on the wings of butterflies crossing from the weeds on one side of the road to the weeds on the other. My window is open, and for a second I hear the trills and rattles of bugs doing whatever they do on hot woodsy spring days (eating one another and mating, most likely). "How peaceful," I say in the second before the other cars pull up behind and my rearview lights up like the Vegas Strip. The bugs are drowned out by police radios and car doors and the swish-swish jingle of cops scurrying back and forth.

Dorsey immediately has his troopers walking the road in both directions, looking for anything of interest. "How far into the woods?" he asks Cassandra, and she says, "Five minutes. Maybe ten."

"Listen up," Dorsey says to his men. "We'll walk, eyes open for anything obvious, do a good survey before we dig. Leave it all untainted for forensics, in case we actually find something."

I say, "You're the boss, Captain, just tell us what to do." The truth is, I don't know squat about fieldwork and investigation. I'm just a prosecutor and administrator; Dorsey is the one with expertise, manpower, and high-tech laboratories.

Dorsey doesn't acknowledge my comment, but his granite jaw softens.

Six cars are parked behind mine: two marked state police cars, Dorsey's black sedan, the black van, a pickup truck pulling a four-wheeler on a trailer, and the local sheriff's vehicle. The sheriff is standing in the middle of the road in his many-pocketed vest, ready to direct traffic. Never mind that this road probably averages one car a week in the busy season.

"Civilians will wait here," Dorsey orders, clearly meaning Lizzy and Kenny and maybe even me, so I say, "Yes, Lizzy can help direct traffic, can't you, hon?"

"Sure, Daddy!" she says with saccharine enthusiasm, because I'd given her a chance to subtly ridicule the poor sheriff, whose forehead is already beading up with the first drops of sweat.

We start into the woods. Dorsey, Cassandra, Chip, and I walk in front, but the trail narrows immediately, so Chip drops back. Behind him are the uniformed troopers and the four-wheeler pulling a flat trailer with tarps and shovels. Within a couple of minutes, my morning coffee hits bottom, and I dodge off behind a tree while the procession keeps moving. Then I hurry to catch up. Now Chip is between Dorsey and Cassandra, so I step in behind them, and darned if Cassandra doesn't drop back to walk with me. She leans in, puts a hand on my shoulder, and whispers, "I'll be pretty embarrassed if there's nothing here."

She seems at home in the woods, instinctively turning toward birdsong coming from the trees, and regarding flowers and shrubs with a knowledgeable eye.

"There," she says suddenly. Everyone stops. "No, no," she says, "just the bird. Hermit thrush. A pebble in a drainpipe. Listen."

Tinga tinga tinga tinga ting.

It is a descending note. Dorsey tries to catch my eye with a *civilians are such idiots* glance, but I avoid him. Chip tips his head sideways, listening to the bird, and says more to himself than to us, "Drainpipe: exactly. That's brilliant."

We walk in silence until Cassandra tells us we're getting close. She identifies a few landmarks and finally says, "Right here." Dorsey pokes at the ground with a shovel. We establish what seems to be the perimeter of the disturbed area, but it's been skillfully concealed, so we can't be sure. One of the troopers lays out a tarp for the dirt, and they start digging. There is a sudden feeling of solemnity. My sense of adventure dies as the diggers work. The sound of their shovels, the labored breathing as they dig, the notes of another thrush coming from the woods, it all comes together. I understand that there will be a body. Everything has fallen into place too easily for it to be otherwise. The sod has clearly been removed and replaced: The underlying dirt is loose, the grass matted. I look at Cassandra. She is ashen. I have the strange urge to take her hand, but of course I don't. Digging takes longer than I would expect, and there is almost a sense of release when the shovels hit something. Now the men work more carefully, clearing away dirt with hands and trowels, almost lovingly, and the shape of a body takes form in dark relief against the shadowy bottom of the hole.

CHAPTER 4

Dorsey radios back to set things in motion. Troopers string yellow tape. The men clear dirt away from legs and ankles and one of the arms. The other arm is beneath the body, which lies curled on its side because the original hole wasn't big enough to allow a final slumber at full extension. He or she was tossed into the pit like garbage.

I am a federal prosecutor, head of the criminal division of the district U.S. Attorney's Office; I see it all. No, actually, I don't see it all; I prosecute it all. I'm aware of it all. I read crime scene reports and confessions and autopsy results and witness statements. I study eight-by-tens of the most horrible things; I describe the hideous actions of hideous people to juries. I occasionally even attend autopsies. But rarely do I get out to see the actual crime scene. And while this particular incident is probably no great shakes to field-weary guys like Captain Dorsey and FBI Agent Chip, it feels miles more real than what I'm accustomed to.

I feel—what shall I call it?—the chill. And before I know it, like a plant bending to the light or a dog curling up at the fire, I'm warming myself shoulder to shoulder with Cassandra.

"You okay?" I ask her. She nods but says nothing.

After the photographer has documented everything, they pull the arm out from under the body, and with a trooper at each leg and one at each arm, they lift the body from the hole and place it on a tarp. It is scraggly and male and at first looks of indeterminate age, but as dirt falls away from the face, I see he is not bearded and not scraggly. He is youthful, his features gentle, almost feminine, eyes maybe a bit too narrow but offset by a sharp jaw, sculpted nose, and strong cheekbones. His skin is unblemished and smooth except for the whisker stubble. He looks peaceful and asleep, which is comforting, because last time I saw him, he looked like shit, haggard and scared, with eyes bloodshot from a sleepless, tearful night. The college boy.

College boy, whose real name is—was—Zander Phippin, was a shy and likable kid who was selling pot to pay his college tuition. At first he was just selling a few bags on his floor of the college dorm, but when his immediate supplier finished a BA in cultural anthropology and moved away to grad school, Zander stepped up to fill the vacancy. He was in over his head, obtaining his product from some very bad people. When he came to our attention, we let him cook overnight without bail before having a sit-down with him in the morning. The crimes that we could nail him on were minor, good for eighteen months in minimum at most, and normally, we'd have just let the state handle it. But we were itching to get our hands on those suppliers.

Our conversation with him was cordial. His biggest worry was how disappointed his parents were going to be. "They aren't, like, hostile," he said of them. "They just don't know what to do with me. They, you know, had in mind a kid who could read, for one thing, and who wanted to sleep with girls instead of boys, for another."

"Zander has rather pronounced dyslexia," his lawyer said.

He seemed like an average kid, if you can call a gay dyslexic drug peddler average. After graduating from a high school for kids with learning disabilities, he had moved first to Provincetown, then to San Francisco, and finally back home.

"I wanted to try college, get a business degree," he said. "Maybe I would have followed in my dad's footsteps after all." And he began sobbing.

I have a softness for mixed-up boys (evidence: Kenny), so I was glad to have a lifeline to toss him—forgiveness in exchange for cooperation.

Who was the contact? Zander didn't know any names. *How did they communicate?* The supplier called Zander's cell to set up exchanges. *How had they met?* The anthropology student had hooked them up. *Would Zander help us nab the contact?*

"No."

So Chip explained how, even though we knew Zander did nothing but sell pot, he could be charged as a conspirator in the criminal enterprise of his suppliers. Meaning he could be implicated in all of their crimes, including but not necessarily limited to selling crack cocaine, heroin, and methamphetamine, as well as extortion, murder, kiddie porn, and prostitution, to name a few.

"You help us, we'll help you," Chip said to Zander.

The idea was to have Zander inform us of the next exchange. We'd spot the contact, surveil him, pick him up at a later time (to protect Zander), and hopefully work our way up the chain to some bigwigs. Zander would walk away clean. He wouldn't even have to tell his parents.

Zander agreed.

I left him and his lawyer to discuss particulars with Chip, so I wasn't there when Zander walked out the smoked-glass front doors of the FBI building, but I bet he stood breathing in the exhaust-y afternoon air of the city, feeling awed by his freedom. Certainly, he realized it could have gone differently; he could have been up for eighteen months of three hots and a cot at Club Fed just on the possession charges—life if we'd tied him in to a conspiracy. I hope he exulted in however many hours of freedom he got before they picked him up.

CHAPTER 5

At the Drowntown Café near the reservoir, we talk about how to play it. I'm in shirtsleeves, my tie loosened. Dorsey and Chip are still wearing suit jackets, as guys with holsters do in public. Chip's is a belt holster, and Dorsey has a shoulder holster with his jacket semi-intentionally pushed back, making the gun as inconspicuous as a panther in a petting zoo.

It's a huge advantage—finding the body the same day it was ditched, with the bad guys still thinking it'll never turn up. We just have to figure out how to put our advantage to work.

"Dollars to doughnuts," Dorsey says, "we won't find anything on the body. Zilch. Clean as a whistle. You'll see."

I'm feeling on edge. I'm irritated by Dorsey and Chip, and I want to move over one table to where Cassandra and Lizzy sit with Kenny, all of them eating strawberry rhubarb pie. I want to be with them, not with the cops. I recognize how foolish it was to bring Lizzy on this excursion, a lapse of both parental and professional judgment. I've always tried to keep her far from the nitty-gritty of my job, because there are evils afoot in the world that fourteen-year-old girls don't need to know about. It gnaws at me, the stupidity—I feel as though I've ushered her into a sphere of danger. And I know how it happened: I was beguiled by Cassandra. Maybe Lizzy isn't the only one pretending to have a normal family life.

"I don't know," Chip says, "I'm betting we find a calling card: ballistics, DNA, fibers. Something." He has a cup pressed to his face, and I realize I'm doing the same, warming my cheek on willowware, though the room temperature is in the seventies. Dorsey and I have coffee. Chip has herbal tea of some kind that he picked from a wicker basket the waitress brought over. He had engaged her at length about the different qualities of the herbal blends before choosing from the assortment.

"We could get her hypnotized, I suppose," Dorsey says of Cassandra. "Like, maybe she saw their car parked out at the road. Something like that. You know?"

Chip shakes his head and says, "I suppose."

I shrug. Dorsey shrugs. The hypnosis idea is dead. We know she didn't see anything.

At the other table, Cassandra and Lizzy are talking quietly. Kenny is silent.

". . . because she's really no witness at all," Chip says.

"She doesn't exist, evidence-wise. Investigation-wise," Dorsey says.

"Trial-wise," Chip adds.

"Just a bloodhound after it finds a body."

"Let's send her home," Dorsey says, and he's up and at the door, beckoning someone in from the parking lot. A uniformed trooper enters. Dorsey thanks Cassandra for all her help and introduces the trooper, Officer Penhale, who will drive her back to town, where someone at headquarters will take a formal statement.

"I can drive her," I say.

Dorsey's steroidal mustache crinkles. "No, I want to talk this through with you gents. Strategize. How to catch the bad guys, eh? No time like the present, eh?"

"Except that—" I say. And I stop. Everything about the morning has left me shaken, and I just want to hunker down with Lizzy and my new friend Cassandra. But before I figure out how to derail Dorsey's plan, Cassandra is already on her way to the door with Penhale, and Lizzy is on her feet, fingers wrapped around Cassandra's arm. "I'll come, too," Lizzy says, her only concern being that she rides with Cassandra. "Meet you at your office, Daddy."

Though I don't want to let Lizzy out of my sight, I have no good reason to forbid her. "Guess I'll go, too," Kenny says.

Then they're gone, Penhale, Lizzy, Kenny, and the lovely Cassandra. I'm left behind with Dorsey and Chip, wondering how it all got away from me and how, with this turn of events, I can finagle a phone call or, better, a coffee date with Cassandra.

"Here's what I'm thinking," Dorsey says when we're settled back around the table. "We'll put all our manpower into surveillance. Watch the major players. Then we let word out that someone saw it all. See who starts making a move. Dollars to doughnuts, we snare somebody right off the bat."

"What about the witness?" I say, indicating Cassandra with a flick of my head toward the exit door. "Is it dangerous for her?"

"Not dangerous," Dorsey says. "The Bureau will protect her, and there's no way for them to know who she is. Besides, like we said, all she did was find the scene. She didn't actually *witness* anything."

Chip nods his agreement, eyes closed, breathing in the steam of his herbal tea.

Dorsey starts to lay out a strategy for leaking the false info that a witness saw the perps in the woods.

"Not so fast," I say. "If you want to use Cassandra Randall as bait, we need her permission."

"Oh, for crip's sake," Dorsey snaps. "She's not bait. She's nothing. We're making it all up. Ms. Randall doesn't exist."

"I'll talk to her," I say.

Chip raises eyebrows at Dorsey. Dorsey shrugs, opens his notepad, copies down Cassandra's phone number and address, and hands it to me. I stuff it into my shirt pocket. Chip looks at me wide-eyed and laughs. "You sly bastard," he says, eyeing the pocket.

On our way out of the café, Dorsey stops to study one of the old sepia photos on the wall: Workmen are digging in a graveyard; there are dozens of holes already dug, and a wagon is stacked with wooden caskets.

"They dug up all the dead," I tell him, "moved the cemetery to higher ground before closing the dam. Seventy-five hundred of them. Bones, jewelry, trinkets, grave markers. Lock, stock, and barrel."

"You know this because . . . ?"

"Undergraduate history project," I say. "Mom's family had a homestead here, so I took an interest. Big beautiful farm right in the middle of the valley. It's all lake bottom now."

"So this is kind of a tough place to stay buried," Dorsey says, and we both laugh.

CHAPTER 6

Lizzy's breathing is a quiet ocean against the beach. *Haaa . . . saaa . . . haaa . . . saaa . . .*

Through the window, I see pinpoints of light where the moon reflects on the Volvo's chrome and glass.

We're at our cabin up north. After all of today's traumatic events, Lizzy and I loaded the Volvo with beer and Gatorade and groceries and drove the two hours from the city. We arrived late at night, built a fire in the stove, made hot chocolate with marshmallows, and huddled together under a quilt while I read to Lizzy from *Anna Karenina*. When she fell asleep, I tucked the quilt around her and left her in the big bed while I climbed into the cold narrow bunk across the room that is supposed to be hers. This is our routine.

I awaken in the night. The cabin is dark, but I can make out shapes. There is the big four-poster where Lizzy sleeps, and I see the couch and woodstove. I can see the grocery bags we left out on the table when we arrived. In darkness, the bags look solid and weathered, rising above the pine slab like the great stone heads of Easter Island rising from the grass. I see an eye, an ear, and the sad sloping nose. It is Zander Phippin, of course—not that he looked anything like those woebegone heads, but here in the darkness, it is he. His nose, his ears, his head poking up from the dirt with chunks of sod tumbling from his features.

"My own little boy," I whisper. I'm half asleep, and my thoughts are addled. I'm confusing poor dead Zander with another boy. In most matters, I'm a shameless and unimaginative realist, but not so with regard to my own departed son, Toby. I protect my memory of Toby from the weathering elements of logic. Zander is, or was, the same age my son would be now. Toby died in Flora's arms a quarter century ago (in this very room, actually), but I still see him in babies who are around the age he was when he died—nine and a half months—and young men like Zander, who are the age he would be if he had lived.

I snap on the light.

Morning now: It's the sort of morning that makes you wish for nothing beyond the simple pleasure of sitting on the dock, bathed in the indigo and pink of sky and lake. In fact, I'm sitting in my Adirondack chair at the end of the dock with a cup of coffee.

Lizzy comes outside for her run. She's heavy-boned for a runner, but she has her mom's good lung capacity. She stands in front of me, warming up, hopping like a springbuck. The jumping and the spin of her ponytail and the mesh of arms and legs are carefree and exuberant and judgmental and arrogant.

Now she eyes me with a smile that is impish and aware. "She's separated, you know," she says with a sly smile.

"Who is?"

"Duh. Cassandra."

I shrug.

"You like her," Lizzy says.

I wait.

"'Cause she likes you."

"Tell me what you know, babe."

Lizzy stops jumping and jogs once around my Adirondack chair. "I can just tell," she says, and then she is off around the lake. The pastels of morning are fading, loons are swimming, striders striding, fish finning, songbirds singing, and all of it coming together into a pretty convincing dawn-of-creation tableau with the first golden rays tickling the tops of the firs. I have the Adirondack chair oriented to give me the best view of where, in about forty-eight minutes, Lizzy will emerge again from the woods, sweaty and pink and happy.

I dial my voice mail.

Message: "Nickie, it's Flora, I'll see you Saturday afternoon. I'm just calling to say I might be a little late and that I'm bringing my friend Lloyd, I don't think you've met him yet. Nicest man. I know you two will hit it off. We met last month when I had that symposium, you know? Maybe you don't. Bye-bye."

From here on the dock, I can see Flora's cabin through the trees. Our marriage broke up after Toby died, each of us deeming the other guilty of unforgivable acts. But neither of us wanted to give up this cabin on the lake, so we didn't. We swapped the partnership in matrimony for a simple partnership in real estate, satisfying our need to be unmarried without completely letting go.

Our friendly arrangement got *too* friendly a few times, and Lizzy was born eight years after our divorce. Eventually, we divided the land and built the second cabin for Flora.

Message: "Nick, it's Kendall Vance. Listen, I've got this Tamika . . . um . . . um . . . Curtis, Tamika Curtis case. We have to talk. I can't believe for a frigging minute you're serious about this. Call me."

I am chagrined to hear that Kendall has been assigned to the Tamika Curtis case. He is an arrogant defense lawyer who sometimes takes pro bono cases for the federal-defender program. The Curtis case is one of them, because Tamika Curtis's only pot to piss in is the one in her cell. It's typical of Kendall Vance to call me directly instead of talking to whichever assistant is handling the case, because Kendall doesn't want to discuss procedural issues. He wants to harp about the unfairness of the law, the courts, the government, and life in general. He's a Sixth Amendment nutcase (that's the one guaranteeing the defendant's right to counsel) who strains his shoulder patting himself on the back every time he puts a murderer or drug peddler back out on the street. He no doubt wants to make me the great Satan of poor Tamika's miserable existence. *Don't argue with me,* I'll tell him, *your beef is with Congress.*

Which is one of the things I like about my job: There's no room for moral anguish. Somebody else makes the tough choices. I just enforce.

I delete his message.

Message: "Nick, it's Chip. Call me." Chip d'Villafranca, my FBI buddy. I'd like to call Cassandra first, but it's too early to be jingling at the bedside of an almost stranger, so I call Chip. He answers in a laconic Saturday-morning voice, but after a few seconds of small talk, he switches to his badass FBI-agent voice. "I have news," he says. "A person of interest passed through a toll station off the eastbound lane of the pike on the morning in question."

"Meaning what?"

"Meaning the guy was coming from the direction of the reservoir toward town shortly after Ms. Randall's encounter in the woods. The timing is about right."

"Who is he?"

"Avery Illman, aka Scud. A nobody. We've never had direct dealings with him, but his name comes up a lot. Dorsey's putting it together."

"What's the plan?"

"Pick him up today for questioning, then let him go. We won't let on we found the Phippin kid. Then we follow this Scud character around a while, see what turns up, who he talks to. Circle gets wider, we'll bring in a few of his associates for questioning. Let on we have the body, have a witness. Someone will leak something or do something stupid."

"Quick work, Chip."

"It's what they pay us for."

"You're sure this guy Scud, he doesn't live in the west 'burbs, commutes in on the pike, maybe has a girlfriend out there? Something?"

"Girlfriend, who knows. But he lives right in the city. Wife and a stepson. Have you talked to the bird-watcher yet?"

"She's my next call."

"And I suppose you're going to ask me for a workup on her."

INDEFENSIBLE 25

I laugh. "I don't need the FBI. I have a daughter on the case." We both chuckle. Then I switch back to the sorrows at hand: "Who took care of notifying Zander's parents?"

"Dorsey's people. But we haven't interviewed them yet." Chip echoes my mournful tone. "Nothing worse," he says.

"Nothing worse," I agree.

Lizzy is due back in about thirty-five minutes.

I open my billfold to get Cassandra's number, but it isn't there. I must have left it at home, in the pocket of my shirt. No matter: Chip will have Cassandra's phone number in his notes, too, so I call him back, and after some mild ribbing, he gives me the number.

"Hi, you've reached 555-3080," Cassandra's voice says. "Please leave your name and number, the date and time of your call, the purpose of your call, your religious persuasion, political affiliation, NRA membership status, IQ, resting pulse, and whether a spot check of your freezer would reveal fillets of any upper-trophic-level fish, and I'll call you back. Bye."

I hesitate. Her greeting doesn't invite the serious tone of what I want to say regarding the FBI and Zander Phippin. But it does set the perfect tone for me to drop in a breezy, unrefusable invitation for a coffee date. Really, both matters should be addressed to Cassandra herself instead of her message machine.

Click. Too late.

I call back and consider hitting a few of the questions—pulse, 58; the occasional chunk of mahimahi; and a Republican Party affiliation owing to an ironic error many years back, which I've never bothered to correct because it landed me my job. Again, this would all be a suave lead-in to the date question, but in bad taste for the rest. I hesitate.

Click. Too late.

I call back. "Resting pulse and IQ are identical," I say quickly, "but I can't remember the number. Hi, it's Nick Davis with the

U.S. Attorney's Office. From yesterday. Lizzy's father. Listen, I need to speak with you as soon as possible. Please call me immediately. 555-2672."

Done.

I sit back and wait for Lizzy.

CHAPTER 7

From my chair at the end of the dock, I fling coffee dregs into the lake. A fingerling rises to sniff the grounds. Lizzy is overdue by about twenty-eight minutes. Twenty-eight minutes is huge. I stand up, ready to take action. But if I start around the lake in one direction, she may show up from the other. And if I don't find her in a complete circuit of the lake, I've wasted over an hour when I should have called for help. Besides, there are different routes she could have taken, and I might miss her. A lot of the trail is impassable by car, and even a four-wheeler is impractical because of all the fallen trees.

It's too soon to call for help. Any dispatcher will say, *You just keep us informed, okay?* But it isn't too soon. Lizzy is a serious runner, meaning she isn't about to turn a fifty-minute run into, say, a ninety-minute stroll. Therefore, she is either injured or diverted, and I know all about diversions; courtroom dockets are catalogs of hideous diversions. Down in the city, a number of children have gone missing over the past few years.

I sit down in the Adirondack chair and wait. The phone rings, and I snatch it up as if it could be about Lizzy, which is silly because she's not even missing yet. "Nick here."

"Is Lizzy there?"

"Good morning to you, too, Kenny."

"Hi, Nick, it's Kenny. Is Lizzy there?"

"Actually not," I say. "I'm beginning to worry, she went for—"

"Tell her she owes me money," he says, and adds a fiendish chuckle, which, if we were talking in person, he'd emphasize by hunching his back and maniacally rubbing his hands together. He does a pretty good Igor.

"Money? How come?"

"Sheeee'll know." He cackles.

"She went for a run, but she ought to be back by now, and I'm really concerned. I can't imagine what—"

"Ten dollars. We had a bet."

"Half an hour overdue."

"If I could go a whole week without a smoke."

"It's not like her, Kenny."

"And I was thinking I might come up this weekend."

"That'd be great. I'm driving back to town tomorrow, but Flo and Lizzy would love to have you."

"Yeah well, maybe. I'll call back." He hangs up.

Typical Kenny, not getting dragged into my worries. No doubt it's a result of the unpredictable and violent home of his childhood. He always resists drama and emotions, walling himself off from the woes of the world. I wish I had gotten to him sooner. He was a ten-year-old boy in foster care, and I was a fortyish divorced prosecutor with a nine-years-dead infant son. I had the notion of trying to keep some poor kid out of jail instead of continually putting people in. Juvenile services put us together. Now, at twenty-five, Kenny is still a directionless kid, but one with a good heart, and with three people—Flora, Lizzy, and me—who consider him family.

Lizzy is forty minutes late.

As I sit waiting, the sun lights the deck and me in a blaze of daylight. Eyes closed, I hear more of the birds, including the *tinga tinga tinga tinga ting*, which, though I've heard it a million times without really hearing, suddenly feels like a gift from Cassandra.

Along with the warm sunshine, there is something else; something comforting. Wood smoke. I open my eyes into bleached colors that slowly flow back to brilliance. I see the thin line of smoke at half-tree height, threading its way across the dazzling water. A gray smudge, which, if this were a photograph, I'd rub away with my sleeve. I follow it back to the stretch of shore where I know the Sammels' cabin lies hidden in a cove invisible from here. Dink

Sammel is a local. He works for the town, plowing snow in winter and grading the gravel roads in summer. Dink has brothers and cousins and nephews and in-laws I can't keep track of. The cabin, it seems, is available to all comers who can make a reasonable show of relatedness. Recently, I've noticed a kid with curled-in shoulders. I see him walking the road to town, but whenever I offer a ride, he whispers, "No thanks," without bothering to look out at me through his curtain of greasy bangs. He is thin, the way only a meth or heroin user can be. It is more than thinness; it is pale, sallow, ulcerated wastedness. If he spent the night in your home, you'd burn the sheets. I asked Dink about him several weeks ago. "My cousin's stepson," Dink said. "He's okay. I let him use the cabin 'cause, well, he likes his solitude. And he don't mean no harm. You know?"

I know why Lizzy is late. Not details, of course, but enough; I know it with the certainty parents have for things like this. It starts in my chest and flows from there, and I feel the world's recalculated mass.

I rise from the Adirondack chair. I think of Flora. She'll be here in a few hours, and the place will be overrun with cops. I imagine some rookie lifting the tape for her to drive under: *The victim's mother. Let her through.*

Do I believe this? Hard to say. I stand at the end of the dock, staring across to where Sammel's cabin lies hidden in the trees.

"LIZZYYYY," I yell.

Lizzy Lizzy Lizzy, the hills beyond the lake answer, with an infuriating willingness to conceal everything that wants concealing.

"Screw you," I tell the hills. "LIZZYYYY."

Lizzy Lizzy . . .

"Daddy, what's wrong?" She is in the doorway of the cabin, ACE bandage around her left ankle, *Anna Karenina* in her hand, her thumb marking the page. "I thought you knew I was here," she says sweetly.

"Well, I—"

"You were on the phone. I hardly even got started. My ankle again. Can we go to the store for ice? This part with Levin," she says, showing me her book, "it really drags. Don't you think?"

"Sure," I say. "Ice." I turn my back to her and stare out across the lake. Everything goes blurry as my eyes fill.

CHAPTER 8

Southbound on the interstate: I drive toward high-rises that quiver like mirages on the horizon. Other than Lizzy's ankle, this weekend has served its cathartic purpose. Flora and her friend Lloyd and Bill-the-Dog showed up yesterday afternoon. Lloyd seems harmless enough, though dandified. He arrived in green pants and loafers. Mercifully, he never changed into shorts, but he did come outside in a T-shirt once—or rather, a white V-neck undershirt, yellowed at the armpits, revealing a chest and arms that hadn't seen daylight since the doctor smacked his butt.

I haven't reached Cassandra Randall yet, which Lizzy tells me is because Cassandra, like us, was away for the weekend, though Lizzy doesn't know where or with whom. Chip called back to tell me that Scud Illman, our suspect, seems also to have flown the coop for the weekend with his wife and stepson. Everything's on hold till Monday morning.

But Monday starts on Sunday evening, because now, as I pass beyond the last of many cell phone dead spots, my phone chirps its message-waiting jingle.

"Hi, Mr. Davis, it's Cassandra Randall. From, you know, the murder. I'm going out right now, and I probably won't be home till late. You can call late if you want, okay, but otherwise I'll speak to you in the morning? And say hi to Lizzy for me. Okay? Bye."

I press 4 to replay. I hear tension or sadness, except at the beginning. *Hi, Mr. Davis,* and the end, *say hi to Lizzy,* where the voice has a lilt that I find encouraging. Though, I wonder where she's going and why she won't be back until late. I'm about to see if I can catch her before she leaves, but the phone chirps again. Chip calling.

"Nick, we just made contact with the guy I told you about, Scud. Avery Illman. He says he'll talk to us. You want to come, or are you still up north?"

I'm thirty minutes out, so I head right for the FBI building. Chip meets me in the hallway and hands me Illman's file.

"Your basic petty criminal," he says. The skin under Chip's eyes is baggier than it was two days ago. "We haven't told him anything, just that we have a matter we'd like to talk about. He drove over voluntarily. Pretty cool customer. Captain Dorsey will be along in a few minutes. It'll be an odd interrogation. Actually, not even an interrogation, just a chat, because we don't expect any info, and we definitely don't want him to know we found the body. We just want him thinking someone's been blabbing."

"You have a strategy?"

"Aimlessness, incompetence, haplessness," Chip says. "Basically, we could have called him up and said someone mentioned his name. But I want to set the hook deeper. Get him feeling a little threatened so he does the silverback routine: goes out and beats his chest and kicks some ass in the jungle. Then we simply pick up everybody whose ass got kicked, let on we have a body and a witness. Every-one'll sing. We're going to need a goddamn choir director."

"Got anything from the body? Anything from the scene? Autopsy results or anything?"

"No reports yet, but I went down and took a look at the body. It's definitely an execution-type job, but he was roughed up first. Tortured. Nothing in his stomach, so he must have been held a few days, anyway. And he had, like, paint."

"Paint? Where?"

"On his hands. A couple flecks on his face, too."

"What kind of paint?"

"I don't know. Different colors."

Chip shows me to the observation room. It is closet-sized and dim, with a shelf along the windowed wall. The only light in here comes through the one-way glass looking into the interrogation room. The interrogation room has the usual table and chairs, but it also has a bookcase in the corner. I can make out a few of the titles; there is the familiar bright blue binding of an old *DSM III*.

A guy comes in and flips some switches on the electronics.

"Nick Davis," I say, offering my hand.

"Sparky," he says. "You a witness or something?"

"DOJ."

"Yeah, that makes sense. You don't seem all witnessy."

"Witnessy?"

"Jumpy. Nervous, with this 'oh wow' thing going on. And an escort. They always send an agent with the witness." His voice has the barely detectable roundness of someone with a hearing disability.

Through the glass, I see Dorsey and Chip walk into the interrogation room. Dorsey wears a shoulder holster and no suit jacket, but unlike Chip, he's in dress slacks. "Anybody over there?" Dorsey asks, looking toward me through the one-way window. His voice comes through the intercom.

"Nick Davis has joined us," Chip says. "He and Sparky are in the observation room."

"Hi, Nick," Dorsey say, looking toward Sparky and me through the one-way glass.

"Hi, Captain Dorsey."

"They can't hear you," Sparky says. "We hear them, they don't hear us."

"He could join us in here," I hear Dorsey say to Chip. "Nick, you want to join us in here?"

"Um, I don't know," I say, "should I?"

"They can't hear you," Sparky says to me.

"No," I hear Chip say to Dorsey, "having the prosecutor might make the guy more guarded."

"I wonder," Dorsey says. "Might give us a better dynamic." He makes a seesaw motion with his hands. "You know, get something going."

Chip shrugs. "I think it would look more like we have something. We want it to start out like we got squat. Don't you think, Nick?" He looks toward me through the one-way glass.

"Yeah, squat," I say.

"They couldn't hear you," Sparky says. He flips a switch. "There. Intercom. Now they hear you. Can you guys hear us?"

"Hi, Sparky," Chip's voice says through the intercom.

"Guy in here talking to a window," Sparky says.

"So maybe we'll bring you in later, Nick," Chip says. "Can you do the moral-superiority bit?"

I nod.

"They can't see you," Sparky says to me.

"Yeah, that sounds good," Dorsey says. "We'll act like incontinent fools, then Nick comes in all serious."

"Incompetent," I say.

"What's that, Nick?" Dorsey asks.

"Nothing. Never mind."

"So when we want you in here," Chip says, "I'll say to this guy, Scud, I'll say, 'Is it too warm in here?' Then you come in acting like your shit don't stink. Like Dorsey and me are bozos. That'll put Scud on our side, maybe make him just a tad more forthcoming."

"Gee whiz," Dorsey says, stroking his mustache and looking at me/himself in the one-way glass. "Tough order. You think a prosecutor can do that? Act all superior and holier-than-thou?"

Sparky laughs, though it isn't actually a laugh but a hum. Even Chip looks at me (or himself) and laughs. "Just follow our lead." Then Chip brings Scud in. "Got coffee here, or we can get you a Coke or something if you like."

"Free Cokes?" Scud says. "I'll start spreading the word: Bureau's buying!" He cups both hands against the one-way glass and peers in at Sparky and me. "Oh my God," he yells. "It's Director Mueller and the governor in fragrant directo. Sorry, boys, didn't mean to snoop. You two just enjoy yourselves."

Sparky hums.

Inches from my face—hard to believe he can't see a thing, because his eyes seem to find mine—is the killer. Or we assume he's the killer. He is laughing at his own humor, giving me a chance to scrutinize his dental work, which is strangely clear in the dim light.

His front teeth are straight and square, probably the product of some porcelain caps, but farther inside his mouth is a forest of sinkholes and deadfall and rot.

"Let's get started," Chip says.

The guy steps away but watches his reflection a moment, then reaches up to smooth his hair. I almost reach up to smooth mine. Scud Illman has wavy red hair, a Sunday-night shadow, squinted eyes, and freckles. He looks uncool and eager to please; even his joking about the director and the governor seems more awkward than mean.

"Here's the situation," Chip says. "There's a guy we're interested in. Twentysomething named Zander. He sells pot and probably more that we didn't know about. No big deal. But maybe he's connected into something. So we talked to him once, tried to get his cooperation, but right away he lawyers up and won't say a word, and truth is, we don't have squat to make a case for anything but possession. And busting college kids for peddling a couple of joints isn't really what the FBI's all about. So we let him go, figuring he'll stew awhile and maybe we can put something together later." Chip pushes his chair back from the table and takes a pack of cigs from his shirt pocket. He lights up and holds the pack out to Scud.

"Those'll kill you," Scud says. He smirks and Chip smirks, stubbing out his cigarette, because they both know Chip lit up only to get Scud to light up, to make him comfortable and put him off his guard. But comfortable doesn't seem to be a problem for this guy Scud, who is rocking back in his metal folding chair, arms folded on his chest, looking like a day at the beach.

"Anyhow, now the son of a bitch has bolted, and it kind of makes us look bad," Dorsey says. He's imitating Chip's easygoing manner, but it doesn't fit him.

"So?"

"So, we thought you might be able to help us."

"We're reaching out," Chip says, grinning, and the three of them chuckle at the lovely preposterousness of the idea that good guys and bad might put away their differences and pitch in to locate the missing Zander. Sparky hums some more.

"You talking to everybody? Every ex-con who's trying to make an honest go of it?"

"Maybe so," Dorsey says.

"You gotta love these guys," Sparky says, and I do love them: I love their shrewdness and scheming, their elegant understanding of human nature. Interrogation like this is probably harder than cross-examination in court. In cross, they can't get away from you, so you simply wear them down or trip them up. Here you have to outsmart them; just one wrong move, and they clam up or lawyer up, and it's all over.

After several more minutes of aimless questioning, Chip shifts uncomfortably and eyes Dorsey, then leans in toward Scud. "Okay. We'll level with you. We got a little bird who says you or people you associate with were with this kid. Like maybe you even helped him pack his travel bag."

"Normally, we wouldn't give a damn," Dorsey says. "I mean, he's a minnow in the scheme of things, right? But he hurt our feelings, you know? We tried to cut him slack, and now he's screwed us. So if you know anything about this kid . . ."

"You scratch our back, we'll scratch yours," Chip says.

"Maybe my back don't itch."

"Maybe it'll itch tomorrow."

"Who's the bird?" Scud asks.

"Birds don't have names," Chip says. "Suffice it to say, the word on the street is that you're the one to see."

Scud shrugs.

"Do you even know this guy?" Dorsey asks.

"Zander? He go by anything else? I know lots of guys. Zander don't ring a bell."

Chip takes a photo from the file and slides it to Scud, who studies it, making a convincing show. "Nope, don't look familiar."

"Do us a favor," Dorsey says. "If you hear anything, give me a call."

Chip loosens his tie a bit and unbuttons his collar. "Is it hot in here?" he asks.

I walk around to stand outside the door, trying a few facial expressions until I get one that feels convincingly annoyed, then I walk in. Chip and Dorsey both stand. Chip introduces me.

"I've been watching through that window," I say to Scud, "and we got this discrepancy wherein our source says you know quite a bit, Mr. Illman. But you tell us you don't know anything, and we have to figure out who to believe." I turn to Chip. "What have you charged this guy with?"

"Mr. Illman came in voluntarily to help us out. He's not accused of anything," Chip says. "We're just gathering information."

"Looks to me like you ain't gathering shit," I say to Chip. "So, Mr. Illman, we got ourselves a predicament. See, this Phippin kid got himself into some trouble. So first we came down real hard on him, because we figured if we didn't, the press was going to say the kid got special treatment just because he's a lily-white, moneyed boy from a connected family. It kinda makes us look bad, you know? But now he's gone missing, and if he never turns up at all, or turns up dead, know what they'll say? Here's a nice kid from a good family who might have gotten into a bit of trouble, and we screwed him; threw him to the wolves. That kinda makes us look bad, too. Am I right? So you know what, Mr. Illman? You're in a position to do us a huge favor if you know anything, and our intelligence says you might know quite a bit."

Scud shrugs helplessly. I step around to face him across the table. His eyes, like the ends of Dorsey's mustache, are drawn down at the outside as if he's wearing a wry smile. But since this hasn't changed since he walked in, it's probably his natural expression. I suppose, depending on what you do in life, it can either help or hurt to have people thinking you're perpetually amused. I can't pigeonhole the guy, and I wish we could just ask him why he was driving eastbound into the city at about eight-thirty Friday morning. Maybe he has a legitimate reason.

"How old is your stepkid?" I ask.

Eyebrows rise and lower in thought, nose crinkles, eyes narrow, and for a moment they lose their amused cast. He doesn't like the question. He looks at the ceiling, lips mouthing his calculations. We wait. "Eight," he says finally, but his smile isn't back yet.

"What the hell," I say. "I'm just making conversation here, it's not a trick question or anything."

He shakes his head. "I couldn't remember if he'd had his birthday yet, you know. It's this month." The unintentional smile creeps back.

"Eight-year-old boy, eh? Is he a good kid?"

"Yeah, he's a good kid."

I can't think of what else to ask. There's something in my mind, which, when I focus on it, is the recollection that I'm supposed to act annoyed. I don't want to act, because I've got the beginning of something here. A connection. *I had a boy once,* I could say, *lucky you, Mr. Illman: You married into a whole family, that's nice.* But Dorsey and Chip are relying on me, and here I am, thinking this Scud guy is probably not guilty at all. Maybe he manages rental units in one of those rural town-house clusters west of town; had to go unclog a toilet that morning. Or maybe he was dropping the kid at hockey.

I get right up into Scud's face, and I say, "I think you know more than you're telling us, Mr. Illman. I think you know lots more. So Agent d'Villafranca here, and Captain Dorsey and me, we're going to make your life as miserable as we can until you see fit to tell us a few things." I walk out and slam the door.

"You're killing me," Sparky says in the observation room. "That was awesome." He hums.

Chip and Dorsey are all hangdog. "Sorry about that," Chip says.

Dorsey clears his throat and timidly hands Scud a business card. "So if you hear anything, you'll give us a call, okay?"

"Sure," Scud says with his wry, sorrowful smile. "I'll call you."

CHAPTER 9

Scud leaves, and then Dorsey leaves. "How about a drink?" Chip says to me.

"Give me a minute." I go into the men's room to call Cassandra, but she's not in. "Religious persuasion," I say to her answering machine, "I'm an optimist. Call me when you can."

Up in Chip's office, we open a couple of beers. "To your health," I say, and we clink bottles. He nods with a satisfied look, amounting to a whole conversation in itself. He's a year into his divorce, and he hasn't called me for a late-night soul-baring in nearly two months. For a while he was calling almost every night. Lizzy tells me that Chip now calls Flora sometimes in the evening, so I'm assuming she's taken over my role of late-night confidant. Truth is, I kind of miss hearing from him. Sitting here with him now, I can see he's doing well: The end of his belt has gotten longer to where, whenever he stands up, it flops down beside his fly like a vestigial necktie. I'm sure he leaves it long as a way of bellowing to the world, *See how much weight I've lost!*

"You're looking good," I say.

"I'd like to be an animal trainer," he answers. "Think of the purity of that interaction; man and beast. No lies. No shadows on the meaning of words. No punishment. Just positive reinforcement and redirection—that's how they do it, you know. Reinforcement and redirection. I imagine you get into a kind of dance; a blending of the spirits and all that. Doesn't it sound nice?"

It was a bad divorce.

When I leave, he gives me a hug. This is a new habit that started around the same time as the late-night phone calls.

* * *

Monday mornings we have case review in the criminal division. I sit at the head of a conference table with nine other lawyers. I start with the guy at my left. "Whatcha got, Ed?"

Ed Cashdan works in financial crimes. He opens one of his case files, but before he can speak, Tina Trevor, who works in drug crimes and crimes against children, cuts him off. "I've got a hearing in a half hour," she says. "Let me go first. I've got this Tamika Curtis case and—"

"And you were also working on that Phippin case," I interrupt, "so let me just bring you all up to speed on this. Zander Phippin is dead." I brief them on the Phippin murder. "The Bureau is handling this. We'll stay current. But for now, it's hush-hush. Breathe not a word. Tina, I'd like you and Upton for a conference with Agent Chip d'Villafranca at noon."

"So how did this witness find—"

"No questions about the witness. The person's identity and further details are need-to-know only, and you don't need to know. Because even though this individual really only discovered the body, circumstances could lead to a conclusion that he or she is in a position to identify the perps. Then she becomes the target—she or he, I mean."

Tina waits a respectful few seconds, then says, "Now, about Tamika Curtis. She's the last defendant in a meth enterprise. We've got a trial date, and it looks like it's going forward. Kendall Vance is the lawyer."

"Poor you," I say. "Good luck with Kendall. Have you made an offer?"

"The best I can," she says. "We have her, slam-dunk, and I've already dropped a level on quantity."

"Out of the goodness of your heart?"

"No. I mean we could make the case for a full kilo, but it's dodgy, so at this point we're just claiming half a kilo, which, right out of the gate, saves her a couple of years. The base sentencing level for a half kilo is ninety-seven to a hundred and twenty-one months. Eight to ten years, give or take. The mitigators and aggravators are a wash; we bump her down a couple levels as a minor participant in the enterprise, then bump her back up for obstruction."

"Obstruction how?"

"She offered the whole narcotics team blow jobs if they'd forget about it."

One of the assistants whispers, "I should have gone into enforcement," and we all chuckle.

"Plus, she was on probation at the time of the current offense, for another two points. This puts her up in the hundred twenty-one, hundred fifty-one months range. Ten to twelve and a half years."

"Probation for what?"

"Theft," Tina says. "So cutting her some slack here and there, I've gotten her down to seventy-eight to ninety-seven months. Basically, six and a half to eight years. That's a savings of up to four-plus years if she'll plead. I'm being generous here. But Kendall was all pissed. He called me a fascist and ranted about leaving Tamika's three daughters motherless. So I guess I'm going to trial, and all deals are off. Maybe I'll go ahead and make my case for the full kilo. She'll be in for fifteen years and have Kendall to thank for it."

"That probation for theft," I say. "What did she steal?"

Tina flips file pages. "Let's see, it was last December. The officer's report reads: 'The store manager noticed suspect carrying her jacket with something concealed inside. The manager approached defendant, who attempted to flee but was quickly apprehended. On examination, her jacket was found to contain the puppy which defendant had been 'getting to know' in the pet store's preadoptive Getting to Know You Room.'"

"She stole a puppy?"

"Apparently."

"Refresh my memory, Tina. What is Curtis's family status?"

Tina flips to the front of the file: "Twenty-four years old, single, her father is unknown, she lives with her mother. She has three children by three different men."

"Ages?"

"Nine, six, and three."

"Just out of curiosity," I ask, "what day in December was the great puppy heist?"

Tina scans the page again. "December twenty-third," she says. "Why?"

We're all silent for a few seconds.

"Oh, geez," Tina says, "maybe I'll give her a pass on that prior."

Tina is an up-and-comer. She went to the right law school, got the right grades, and clerked in the right courts. She is ambitious. The convictions she wins, the years in prison she totals up, they're rungs of a ladder for her to climb into the stratosphere of legal practice. When I hired Tina, she was kittenish in a Meg Ryan kind of way. But she's taken on a pugnacious and scowly look. Her new hairstyle angles from nearly shorn at the back of her neck into a menacing wedge at her chin. She walks with her hands bunched into fists. I've seen this happen to assistants. Some of them never get the knack of maintaining emotional distance. In trying to get convictions, they begin to absorb the rage and sorrow of the victims. It eats them up. I wish I could think of a reason to fire Tina, because I've become a bit fond of her. I don't want to watch the kittenish Tina morph into the embittered prosecutor.

The idea of Tamika Curtis stealing a puppy for her kids at Christmas has landed us all in a funk. So to lighten things up, I say, "Tina, here's a riddle: What did the Buddhist say to the hot dog vendor?"

Everyone stares at me.

"'Make me one with everything!'" I shout.

The assistants all laugh. Tina laughs. The furrows in her forehead smooth out, and I see the former gentler Tina. Maybe she isn't too far gone.

"Brief us on this meth enterprise," I say.

"Well, it's one of Percy Mashburn's operations. Percy seems to franchise these labs, but we've been unable to reach him. Nobody will finger him. And every time we get something against him, he comes in and gives the Bureau lists of everyone else involved and buys himself a walk. In this case, Tamika's on the bottom. She's the only one left. The only one facing real time."

"Keep the pressure on," I say. "The only way to break these things is to get the patsies to start talking."

"Exactly."

After case review, I call The Man Upstairs: *the* U.S. attorney. My boss, at whose pleasure I serve and who, in turn, serves at the pleasure of the U.S. attorney general, who serves at the pleasure of the president. His office, one floor directly above mine, is a real Taj Mahal. It is a corner office, like mine, but he has appropriated the adjoining office for an anteroom.

The Man Upstairs (TMU) is my fourth U.S. attorney. I've become adept at making myself indispensable because, while it would be difficult for TMU to fire me outright, it would be a small matter for him to ease me back into the ranks of practicing trial lawyers, replacing me with one of his own team.

"Do you expect much press?" TMU asks after I apprise him of the Zander Phippin matter.

"If this comes down the way we hope," I say, "Jonsered will have a very good year." This is a joke I've established between us. Jonsered is a Swedish chain-saw manufacturer. Chain saws cut down trees, trees become paper, paper becomes newspaper, newspapers print news of criminal convictions. Especially convictions in organized crime and drug trafficking. And whenever I can finagle it, TMU gets the credit.

He chuckles. "Always glad to help the Swedish economy."

CHAPTER 10

Upton Cruthers and Tina come into my office at noon. Upton works organized crime and racketeering. We get Chip on speakerphone.

"Dorsey's guys are out in force," Chip says. "They're stirring things up. And we've got an undercover team surveilling Scud. So far, there's nothing interesting from the body of the deceased; bullet fragments, but nothing to match them with. We also have some textile fibers; again, useless until we have something to test them against."

Upton says, "So if the witness heard two voices, and we're assuming one was this Scud guy, any guesses about the other?"

"I wish," Chip says.

"Have you heard from the agents surveilling Scud?"

"I just talked to one. He gave me several individuals we would like to speak with, but we're holding off a few hours. I figure as soon as we make a move, it'll be like, um . . . um . . ."

The line is silent for a second, so Upton says, "Turning over a rock."

"Pardon?"

"Yeah," Tina says to Upton, forgetting to talk loud enough for the speaker phone to pick it up, "turning over a rock. I used to do that with my kids."

"Your kids?"

"Third-graders," she says, switching from a scowly prosecutor into a bubbly third-grade teacher. "When I was teaching, we'd go outside and look for big rocks to turn over, and the bugs all scatter. But you've got a few seconds to catch 'em."

"What the hell?" says Chip from the speakerphone.

"Sorry," I say. "It's my staff. I'll fire them the second we're off the phone."

"I'll hold if you want to do it now."

"So summing up," I say, "your surveillance of Avery Illman, aka Scud, shows promise and has delivered a couple of names, but you're letting it play out several more hours before moving?"

"Correct."

"And the forensic team hasn't yet found anything of obvious interest, but it's still early. So, listen, Tina and Upton are on call for this if you have probable-cause issues or anything else, okay?"

"How much do we know about this guy Scud?" Upton asks.

"I got some stuff on him," Chip says. "I'll put a file together if you want. Give me an hour. How shall we—"

"I'll send Kenny to the FBI building to pick it up," I tell them. We end the call.

Upton stands and takes one slow-motion stride, then swings his leg in an impressive arc, the sole of his well-shined shoe just tickling the carpet on its way through the vertical and up to where it hovers briefly at eye level. He stands watching for a second, then his arms shoot up for the field goal, and he prances around in a circle. "Prediction," he says. "We are about to rain down some major shit upon the disrupters of our urban utopia."

Upton Cruthers was an NFL kicker. "Best job in the world," he tells people. "Money, babes, celebrity, travel, and a bench pass to lots of great games. And all this in exchange for about a half hour's worth of work per year." His professional football career was brief. I've seen footage of the fateful game. It was a playoff of some kind, Upton standing alone on the twenty-second-yard line, watching as the ball wobbled to the left and missed the goalposts by an easy twenty feet. The commentator was apoplectic, the crowd bellowing in rage and grief. A home game, of course. And Upton dejectedly walked off the field.

Upton is my favorite of the assistants. We're close to the same age, and he's a shrewd and confident lawyer, which is no surprise. It must take the same kind of confidence to walk onto the gridiron in the last thirty seconds and to become, with one quick kick, the hero or the goat.

Upton started as an intern during my first year here, and I hired him officially as soon as he was out of law school. He'd already played football for several years by then, so he was older and more worldly than most of the lawyers who come knocking on my door with résumé in hand. I had to pull some strings to get his application approved because DOJ flagged it; Upton had a juvenile record of minor offenses—vandalism, assault, minor-in-possession. That's why we connected from the start, because whatever drove his youthful rebellion had left him feeling like a pretender in the conventional world of law enforcement. And I was fresh from a personal tragedy in my own life, leaving me with a similar sense of separateness. We were both local boys and both kind of surprised to find ourselves representing the government.

After Tina and Upton leave, I call Kenny's cell phone. "Where are you?"

"In my office," he says without irony.

I walk to the law library and find him at his usual table, where he can keep an eye on who's coming and going and where he can chat with the librarian. They're good friends, Kenny and Penny, and I haven't given up hoping they might someday lock the library door and create a little vortex to stir the dust that lies so heavy on all those dreary shelves. They would have to adjust their standards, though; Penny is a potato-shaped young woman hoping for a man of erudition; Kenny is an intellectually incurious young man hoping for a supermodel. But they're both good-hearted.

"Quick job for you, Kenny," I say. "I need you to pick up some documents from Chip over at the Bureau."

"Well, I got all this copying to do," he says, not complaining so much as making sure I don't think that all he does is sit around all day—which is exactly what I think.

"Lizzy's still up north," I say. "I'll probably pick up a pizza and be stony-lonesome tonight, if you want to come over and split it with me."

"You going to rent one of those boring movies you like to get?"

"You mean no car chases or buildings getting blown up?"

"Yeah, right, no chases, no nothing," he says. "*Sex Life of the Oyster; Moss-Growing World Championship.*"

"Yes," I say, "I'll probably rent one of those."

"I don't think so," he says. "Sounds like a yawn-fest."

"Well, I'd love the company." Maybe he'll change his mind at about six-fifteen tonight, grab a six-pack, and drive over to pass the evening with me.

Everyone is excited about this Phippin case: Chip, Dorsey, Upton, me. We're expecting something big. We have a huge tactical advantage because the perps don't know we know. There are four agencies involved: the U.S. attorney's office, the FBI, the state troopers, and now the state attorney general, with dozens of smart people working hard on it, from the forensic scientists on Zander's body, to computer whizzes, to field agents and detectives. This investigation is in the air like ozone before the rain.

Another hour passes with no developments. I walk to the men's room, and I sense staff eyeing me as I pass their cubicles. Also, there are more than the usual number of workers standing in gossipy pods along the hallway. They fall silent as I pass. But on my way back, one young woman, an administrative aide named Kimba, stops me outside my door.

"We're confused," she says with an excited and obsequious tilt of her neck. "Was it your daughter or your ex, or both, who actually witnessed the murder?"

I laugh. "Ahh, the rumor mill." I step back into my office, close the door, and stand for a few seconds in light-headed disbelief. Somehow this has morphed into the misperception that not only was there an actual witness to the gangland execution, but that the witness was either Lizzy or Flora. I make my way to the desk and watch my fingers find Upton's extension on the phone.

"Yes, boss?" His comforting baritone voice fills the room, and my eyes fill with gratitude.

"Upton," I say, "I think I need your help."

CHAPTER 11

It was Upton's idea to put Tina on the whirlybird with me. "You might need a *real* lawyer," he said, making a joke of it to soften me up. What he meant was someone to keep an eye on me, especially if things up north are ugly. The 'copter is Dorsey's, so to speak, a Bell 407 Ranger, chosen over the Bureau's because it was on the pad and ready to fly. It lighted on the roof of the federal building just long enough for Tina and me to sprint in under spinning blades, and then, with one shiver, it was in the air again.

From the air, I watch as we move from the grid of urban streets to the green threads of tree-lined suburban avenues and into the tattered quilting of the outlying farmlands and forests. It is all a work of staggering intricacy.

It makes me sad.

"I've got to get out of this business," I shout to Tina, who sits beside me. Her answer, instead of a shout, is to put her hand on my knee. She means it as a comforting gesture, and it works. She doesn't just pat my knee. She rests her hand there for several seconds. And I feel that much more comforted.

Tina and I sit facing backward, and across from us is a trooper. I put my hand out and yell my name. He does likewise. We shake, but I can't make out his name. And he's hard to get a fix on visually. He wears a Smokey hat and looks like a dentist or bank officer; he has an any-guy look.

I lean toward Tina. "It's Kenny," I yell. She shakes her head and leans in closer. "Kenny," I repeat, not shouting because I'm right in her ear. "He's the leak, probably blabbing to anyone who sets foot in the library, telling just enough for them to make the wrong conclusions."

She nods. Then she has her mouth at my ear: "But he seems so sweet."

"Not malicious," I yell. "Never malicious. Just foolish."

We'll have answers pretty soon. Agents arrived to question the staff before Tina and I were even off the roof. Poor Kenny. I'll have to fire him, and what will he do then? I can probably set him up with something. Maybe a lawn-care business.

The pilot hands me a headset, and I put it on.

"Can you hear me, Mr. Davis?" the pilot asks.

"Loud and clear."

"I'll need you to guide me in once we're close. Think of some-place I can land."

I watch out the window. It's mostly woods, and I catch sight of our shadow riding the contours of the land like a roller coaster.

From way up here, it looks like the mills and factories might still be running, the homes might be kept up, and the jobs might not be gone. We've taken such pains building and improving all of this: society, infrastructure, government, economy. The whole shebang. It ran with the gentle hum of oiled parts spinning at a blur, until everything went to hell in the seventies and eighties. The last of the mills closed, and the disrupters, as Upton calls them—the bad genes, the pathogens, the criminal element without whom it might all be so simple—thrived.

"It should all be so simple," I yell cryptically, and the hand comes back to my knee.

Realistically, there's not much to worry about, because even if Kenny's injudicious blab was early this morning, it needed to work its way along the gossip tree—morphing into the misperception that Lizzy or Flora actually witnessed the grisly deed. Then it had to find its way to whatever hypothetical traitor delivers it to the dark side, and then they, the evildoers themselves, would have to track down Lizzy and her mom—no easy feat, especially with the two of them at the lake for the week. And finally, anyone wishing to pay Flora and Lizzy a visit would have to drive several hours north, because it's unlikely they'd have access to a jet Ranger like we do.

Tina is watching out her window, and I know she's worried, so I lean in close to her and explain my reasoning of how it's all okay.

She gives me a perplexed look for a couple of seconds, then comes back and puts her mouth against my ear. "But Nick, Kenny was back in the office Friday afternoon. Remember? You were gone all day at the reservoir, but he and your daughter came back just after lunch. What if he committed the indiscretions then? They've had all weekend."

The lake surface is pounded into droplets by the blades. Saplings on the shore try to uproot and run. But through the dragonfly eye of the 407, I see no sign of human life around either Flora's cabin or mine. We ascend again, and as we pivot, I catch sight of someone watching from Sammel's dock, far down the shoreline.

We dart over the road. "There's local, just arriving," the pilot says, and we settle down on a Christmas-tree field as two cruisers pull up. One's a trooper, and the other is a local cop. I get in the front seat of the trooper car. "I've been briefed by Captain Dorsey," the driver says, and he sprays gravel pulling back onto the main road, but then turns slowly into my driveway and creeps down the long gravel path. The trooper from the helicopter is in the backseat, and Tina seems to have disappeared.

We stop. "Wait here," the driver tells me as the other trooper walks around the corner of the cabin to the door. The driver and I lean against the car, which idles in the sun. There's no wind, and the black flies find us and add their electric drone to the crackling of the police radio. Everything looks disturbed; leaves and pine needles are stuck to the cabin window, and there's trash in the bushes and against the cabin, and I count three T-shirts, two of Lizzy's and one I don't recognize, thrown into the trees.

"Something's happened," I say.

The trooper I'm standing with answers vaguely: "I'm sure it'll all check out." He wears a brass name tag: J. Voight.

I start for the cabin. Voight catches up and grabs my arm. "Best to wait with me, Mr. Davis."

I twist my arm loose, but I don't make for the cabin.

"Rotor wash," Voight says, waving his hand at the woods and cabin. "The chopper blew things around a bit, that's all it is."

I follow him back to the cruiser. We just stand, waiting, and finally, the other trooper comes out of the cabin and waves me over. "No one's home," he says.

The local cop drives up and parks beside the trooper car. Tina is with him.

"That other cabin?" Voight asks, pointing.

"My ex-wife's."

"Let's take a look."

The two troopers walk over, and I tag along. At the door, one of them stands halfheartedly to one side and knocks. "State police. Anybody home?"

Nothing.

He looks at me questioningly, so before they can object, I open the door and go in.

It's a nice place, with more sunlight than mine. Flora likes pretty curtains and tablecloths, and the woodwork is finished out with gingerbread scrollwork. It smells of incense: typical Flora.

"Everything in order?"

"Well, I—"

There is a rustling. The mound of quilts on the bed heaves, and Flora's friend Lloyd emerges. "Caught me napping," he says, blinking at the two service revolvers leveled at him in the no-nonsense, double-handed grips of my escorts.

"Get your hands out," one of the troopers shouts, which is overly dramatic, since it's hard to imagine anyone less threatening than this pasty-faced guy who keeps blinking even after the shock and bleariness should have passed. He is wearing a white shirt buttoned right up to the neck, and when his hands emerge from the quilts, I'm not surprised to see sleeves buttoned at the cuffs.

"Oh my heavens, don't shoot me!" he says.

"Do you know this individual?" one of the troopers asks.

"Lloyd, where is Lizzy?" I ask.

"I don't . . . ummm, I've been asleep. Isn't she . . . I'd ask Flora."

"Where's Flora?"

"Ummm. Isn't she . . ."

I glance around the room. There are pill vials on the table, and I pick one up. Haldol, which explains the midday nap. I nod at the troopers, and they lower their guns.

"What's going on?" Lloyd asks.

"Probably nothing. We just need to ascertain Lizzy's and Flora's safety."

"Flora did say something about going for groceries."

We escort Lloyd outside, and the troopers confer with the local cop, who is a stubble-headed young man. He goes to his police radio and transmits the details of Flora's car. Then we stand around waiting for the police in town to find Flora at the grocery store. There are six of us: Tina, Lloyd, the two troopers, the stubble-headed local cop, and me.

"How you doing?" Tina asks me.

"Could I wait in the car?" Lloyd climbs into the open trooper cruiser without waiting for an answer. "How do you stand the bugs?" he says, and closes the door.

After about ten minutes, the local police call back on the radio to tell us they've located Flora at Rick's grocery, and Flora says Lizzy is out for a run. The stubble-headed local gets in his car and leaves to circle the lake.

My cell rings. It's Upton. I tell him it looks like everything here is okay, and we'll know for certain in a few minutes.

"That's good," Upton says. "Chip has appointed a female agent to watch over Lizzy and Flora until this is all resolved. She's driving up now."

With the phone at my ear, I walk to the edge of the lake and out onto the dock. I push the Adirondack chair around with my foot to face the shore. I can see Lloyd in the cruiser, watching out the back-seat window with his face pressed to the glass like a little boy. How typical of Flora to find someone in such need of kindness and care. Beside the cruiser, Tina talks with one of the troopers. She laughs, he smiles. The rim of his Smokey hat dips as he nods in agreement with whatever Tina is saying. Tina's still in her court clothes and carrying her ever-present shoulder bag.

I can see both cabins from here, Flora's and mine. "I have to tell you this, Upton," I say. "I'm sure Kenny was the source of the leak. He just doesn't think sometimes."

"It's not Kenny," Upton says. "I had thought so, too. That's where we started the questioning, because he was with you at the reservoir that day. But he checks out. Chip and I did some of the questioning, and I talked to the librarian myself. Penny Russet. She was real contrite; says she cajoled him—that was her word, cajoled—for details. All Kenny would tell her was that he visited a crime scene with you. Period."

Something inside of me gives way, and I slump back into the chair, taking a second to absorb this good news. "Thank God," I say.

"Yes."

"But then who?" I wonder aloud. "Maybe it was out of Dorsey's office. Or Chip's."

"No," Upton says. "We've identified it. It was from this office."

I wait.

"Your daughter," Upton says apologetically.

Of course.

"Apparently, she was traumatized when she got back here Friday afternoon. You were at the reservoir or someplace, and she talked to at least three different people here: Paul Myrtle, Janice Troyer, and Frea Schultz, to be specific. All report her saying, 'Don't tell my dad I told you, but,' and the three of them have strikingly different impressions of the who-what-and-wheres. Then it all went into the gossip machine and, well, God knows."

Now I realize for the first time the magnitude of my indiscretion, bringing Lizzy to the reservoir with me. It's one of those things nobody would give a second thought to until it turned out badly; lousy decision-making by me, head of criminal division.

From my chair on the dock, I see Tina at the door of my cabin.

She's wearing the trooper's Smokey hat now. She signals to ask if she can enter. I nod.

"I wonder if I'll have to step down," I say, thinking aloud, forgetting for a second who is on the phone with me. Upton isn't exactly a therapist or clergyman but, rather, one of my likely successors. And he's ambitious. But his poise is perfect: "Don't be an idiot," he says.

Tina emerges from the cabin carrying her shoes, and I notice her legs have gone from charcoal to flesh-colored. She's wearing the Smokey hat and carrying her shoulder bag.

"One more thing," Upton says. "Scud Illman has slipped surveillance."

"Pardon?"

"Yeah. The agents lost him. We're not sure if he pulled a fast one or if it was a screwup."

CHAPTER 12

I stay on the dock in my Adirondack chair until the local cop who left to circle the lake pulls back into the clearing with someone handcuffed in the backseat.

The officer gets out and walks around the cruiser. He has the head-bobbing strut of a man who has accomplished something grand but is pretending it's no big deal. I walk to the car. Inside, wide-eyed and terrified, is the scrawny, drug-wasted Sammel boy from the cabin up the lake.

"Get him out," I say.

He is pulled from the car and stands in front of me with his hands locked behind his back. From their shadowy sinkholes, his eyes scan the faces in front of him, giving no sign of recognizing me. But there is a barely registerable awakening when he sees Lloyd in the other cruiser, nose against the glass.

"Tell me," I say to the officer. I take a step backward, concerned that if what I'm about to hear is bad, my hands might happily reach out and pop this kid's fucking head off. I am aware of Tina beside me, the Smokey hat gone. She touches my arm.

"Yes, well, circling the lake," the local cop says. "I pulled into the first drive up the road, intending to conduct a visual and to inquire about the girl, your daughter, as to whether anybody who might be home had seen her—"

"Get to the point."

"I knocked at the door of the structure, and I heard a commotion from the rear. I walked around the cabin, and the suspect emerged from an outhouselike structure, very suspicious-looking. I approached the suspect and he was very nervous. I had reasonable suspicion. I asked if he knew Lizzy Davis, and he said yes, and I—"

"Stop," I yell, "just tell me where Lizzy is."

"I don't know, but what I—"

"Where is she?" I say to the kid, taking a step toward him, and Tina immediately has my arm locked in hers and is tugging me backward. The kid in handcuffs blinks at me, bewildered.

"I found this," the stubble-headed cop says, and he holds up a plastic bag, inside of which is a bag of pot with a long string tied to it.

"Where?"

"In the outhouse."

"What the fuck were you doing in the outhouse?"

"Searching."

"For what?"

"As I said, he seemed reasonably suspicious. And I correctly believed—"

"And this has nothing to do with Lizzy?"

"Well, she's why I was—"

"So, the hell with Lizzy and just go dig in this kid's shit pile instead?"

Tina tries to pull me backward. "Let it go, Nick."

Stubby runs fingers through his nonexistent hair.

"Unbelievable," I say to the cop. "You suspend a federal investigation to bust this schmuck for a bag of pot. And with no fucking warrant, no permission to search—"

"Actually, sir, he gave me permission—"

"Bullshit," I scream. "Bullshit, bullshit, bullshit."

"Because I thought—"

"Dereliction of duty," I yell, and before Tina or the troopers can stop me, I snatch the so-called evidence from his hand and toss it to the kid in handcuffs. Of course it hits his chest and lands at his feet. Nobody picks it up. "Uncuff him," I say.

This makes everyone uncomfortable. I have no authority over local or state police. They have a suspect caught in a crime, and while the search was no doubt illegal and any prudent DA would decline to prosecute, that's not a decision for any of us to make.

"I can't do that, sir," Stubby says.

I take a big breath to bellow back into the face of this Johnny Law, but Tina steps between us, her back to me, and she speaks quietly to Stubby's face. "Not a good test case," she says.

"Excuse me, ma'am?"

"Look at him," she says, flicking her head at the handcuffed ne'er-do-well. "You might as well gift-wrap him and send him to the ACLU."

"Ma'am?"

She turns to the kid in handcuffs. "HIV?"

"Leukemia."

"How you doing?"

He shrugs.

I'm stunned. How did I miss it? I gawk at the kid, speechless.

Tina looks at Stubby, then at the two troopers. "Medical use. You hear what I'm saying? And that's without even mentioning the search-and-seizure can of worms."

Stubby looks unsure. He and the troopers go into a huddle, and while we stand waiting to see what will happen next, the rumbling of tires on gravel bursts into the clearing. Flora parks behind the cruisers, and there, beside her on the front seat, fit as a fiddle, sits Lizzy.

"Hi, Daddy," she says, her braces owning the smile like bullfrogs own a pond. In thinking about her the past few hours—my Lizzy, who, for all I knew, had already been whacked by whoever did Zander Phippin—I'd forgotten the braces. The oversight feels tragic. I turn away from her to get everything straightened out in my head.

"What's the matter, Daddy?"

"Nothing," I answer, my voice sounding like it comes through a cylinder. My cell phone is ringing, but I ignore it.

"Oh God," Flora shrieks. She has spotted Lloyd peering out the back window of the state cruiser like a common criminal. He's urgently trying to get out, but the door doesn't open from the inside. Flora runs and opens it for him, then spins and catches me in a look of unmitigated contempt. "What did you do?" she hisses.

I start a babbling explanation, but I'm immediately drowned out by Lizzy, who shrieks, too, but hers is just a wordless scream, as she runs to the kid in handcuffs and attaches herself to one of his arms and cups his cheek in her palm.

"Seamus, oh my God!" Lizzy spins and looks like her mom, giving me the same betrayed expression. "Daddy, what have you *done*?"

"Not me," I protest.

Flora helps Lloyd out of the police car.

Lizzy lays her head on the Sammel kid's shoulder. Stubby snaps into action: "Stay away from the suspect," he says, grabbing Lizzy by the arm and tugging. Lizzy responds by holding tighter to the boy, managing to get her arms around him and locking her grip. Stubby tries to peel her off. "Away from the suspect," he repeats.

"Don't touch my daughter," I tell him, surfacing from the dopey befuddlement of the whole scene. This young goon is manhandling Lizzy, who predictably clings to the wasted boy. The cop doesn't let go.

"Don't touch my daughter," I order again, smarting from Lizzy's and Flora's assumptions that I somehow had both Lloyd and this boy arrested. I grab Stubby to pull him away from Lizzy. Someone stumbles, and the three of them—Lizzy, the Sammel boy, and Stubby—go down in a heap with the boy on the bottom and Stubby squirming around on top of Lizzy. I kneel beside the pile of them, and the crook of my arm finds its target like a heat-seeking missile. I roll, taking Stubby's head and neck with me. The rest of him follows.

Then silence. The screaming stops (most of it, I realize, was Flora's). Lizzy crawls away. I'm sitting in the gravel; Stubby sits between my legs, leaning back against me with my arm circling his throat. He makes gurgly noises, but we sit there together a few seconds longer until I am again aware of shouting, and now Trooper Voight stands nearby with his legs apart and a hand fluttering over the handle of the handgun at his side. "Release the officer," he commands.

I do, but I try to make it look like my own idea. Stubby chokes, coughs, rubs his throat. "You okay?" I ask him.

Flora's hands are pressed to her mouth. In the background, slightly out of the picture, I'm aware of Tina, whose eyes are locked on Voight. Tina's right hand is lifting a standard-issue Glock from the depths of her shoulder bag. Before it's really in view, everything settles. I'm helping Stubby to his feet, Lizzy is kneeling by the Sammel boy, and the trooper has lost interest in me and is also looking at the boy. Tina drops the gun back in her bag.

My cell rings again though it doesn't strike me as the best time to answer. We're all on our feet except the sick boy, who lies in the gravel wheezing. "Daddy, he's hurt," Lizzy says. We crowd around. Lloyd kneels and feels his pulse and looks into the boy's eyes. "Let's get him to the hospital," he says.

"Are you, um, medical?"

"Doctor," Lloyd answers. "Used to be, anyway."

I make eye contact with the trooper who wasn't about to shoot me. He comes over, and we lift the kid up and get him into the cruiser. He flops down in the seat, hands still cuffed behind. "Uncuff him," I say to Stubby. He obeys. Then the cruiser goes out the driveway, Lloyd in back with the kid, lights flashing, *whoop-whoop*ing into the landscape.

Flora, Lizzy, and I get into Flora's car and head for the hospital. My cell rings again. "Davis here," I answer curtly.

"Nick, it's Chip."

"Chip," I say, and it comes out squeaky because my throat catches with affection. Chip's stable and gentle voice is a psychological oasis among lunatic events. "My buddy Chip."

"Bad news, Nick. Cassandra Randall is dead."

PART II

CHAPTER 13

The second Monday in September. It's been a rotten summer, and I'm glad it's over.

I drive through town, watching workers burst from office buildings to speed home and hear about the kids' first day back at school. At an intersection, the light says *walk*, and a damburst of crossers flows into the street. Now the light says *stop,* but they keep coming. I nose through, and in the no-man's-land before the next light, far from any crossing, a guy steps off the curb. He stops me with an upturned hand like a traffic cop as he waits for an opening in the other lane, but no one is as persuadable as I. So I'm stuck waiting until he can spot his chance and bolt. If he'd look at me, I could smile and offer the gift of my patience. By ignoring me, he steals it. Not even a glance in my direction, so in a flash of fury, I add the feeble bleat of the Volvo's horn to the sounds of the afternoon. The crosser sees his opening and runs, but in the air behind him, he leaves the vision of that upturned palm, which, in the moment of its departure, too late for me to stomp the gas and run him down, becomes a single-fingered wave.

Fuck you, too, my friend.

Beyond the business district, I drive past the fenced-off wreck of the old Aponak Mill complex where my dad was a floor superintendent for most of his career. He died of lung cancer three years short of retirement.

Just last week, a couple of kids got inside the fence and spent the afternoon lobbing bricks into the road. No one was hurt, but a few cars got dinged, and the kids earned a trip to juvie on criminal trespass and destruction of property. As I pass now, I see the form of someone in a garbage bag huddled against the fence, a piece of twine tethering his or her wrist to a shopping cart that waits like a loyal steed.

I'm on my way out to Seymour Station to look at another body. This one was found in a freezer. I'm not needed there, but it's a good chance to catch up with Dorsey and Chip. I've scarcely talked to them since June.

There have been no arrests in the murder of either Zander Phippin or Cassandra Randall. The lovely and innocent Cassandra Randall was killed in her home. It was after dark. Someone with an assault rifle shot her through her living room window—a single shot to the head. The shooter apparently waited under a tree across the street from her home. Cassandra's two teenage children were at their father's house, and they came home in the morning to find her there, her hair stuck to the carpet in a hideous mass of dried blood.

We feel pretty certain it was Avery Illman, aka Scud, who killed Zander and probably Cassandra as well, but we've had trouble putting it all together. Of the half-dozen players picked up that day last June, none mentioned Scud's name or admitted knowing anything about Zander Phippin. Maybe they really didn't know, or maybe they were more scared of Scud and his friends than they were of the law. So Chip brought Scud back in and asked him outright: "What were you doing west of town on the early morning of June third?"

His answer, offered with that frownlike smile, eyes drawn down at the corners: "Bird-watching."

If I'd been there in person instead of seeing it four days later on video, I'd have come across the table and twisted his head off.

The agents asked for permission to search Scud's car. "Not without a warrant," Scud answered. Ditto his home. Smug smile.

We weren't able to get a search warrant last June. Upton Cruthers made the request, but instead of signing it, Judge Two Rivers phoned Upton and engaged him in a debate about what does and doesn't constitute probable cause. Apparently, Two Rivers doesn't see probable cause in an ex-con, drug-dealing, midlevel scumbag like Scud Illman driving into town from the direction of a body dumping on the morning in question. Scud Illman is still on the loose, and we're at a dead end. Or we were until Seth Coen was discovered chopped up and packed in his own freezer.

Seymour Station is industrial. I pass a warehouse with dozens of trucks backed up to loading docks like piglets at teats. This is the part of town beyond the car dealerships, but closer in than the rock-crushing plants and junkyards.

The address is a motel-looking place called Seymour Apartments. I don't know much yet. Chip called me and said Dorsey had called him. They believe the deceased might be the second man from the reservoir that day: one of the guys who buried Zander Phippin.

I pull up at the building. There's not much going on outside, just a cop in a raincoat keeping an eye on things, and a few official cars parked in front. "Send him up," Dorsey yells from the balcony. The cop flicks his head toward the stairs. I go up. The photographer and forensics team are there, plus Dorsey and Chip.

"We might have a lead here," Chip says.

"Friggin' time," I say.

"Friggin' time," Dorsey says.

Chip says, "Remember back in June, there was one associate of Scud Illman's we wanted to talk to but we could never find him? Seth Coen. And since we didn't have anything on him, we never bothered asking for a warrant? Well, we've found him."

Dorsey walks me into the bedroom. The forensic team was taking things apart systematically, but you can tell it was a clean and orderly place when they started. Everything is nondescript. Pasteboard dresser, double bed with a dingleberry bedspread, closet with bifolds. Under the window, where you'd expect a desk, there's a chest freezer. Big but not the biggest. Maybe four feet long.

"Mr. Mellon," Dorsey says to one of the guys I assumed was forensics. Now I see he was just standing back out of the way.

"Milan," the guy says. "Spelled like the city."

"What city?"

"Milan."

"I mean—"

"Italy."

"Oh. Mi-*lan*," Dorsey says with a convincing accent. "Amazing cathedral there. Renaissance center of art and culture. Bombed to smithereens during the war. Too bad."

I glance over at Chip to see if he's surprised. I didn't have Dorsey pegged for someone to expound on European history. Chip is oblivious.

"Lousy krauts," Mr. Milan says.

"Actually, the Allies bombed it," Dorsey tells him. "Remember, Il Duce got confused about which side were the good guys. Got cozy with Hitler."

"Anyway, I'm not Italian," Milan says.

"Talk to us about the freezer."

"He was a hunter," Milan says. "He asked permission for the freezer, and I said sure, so long as he takes it away when he leaves. He said he needed it 'cause of his deer meat and fish and ducks. I don't care, so long as they pay rent and don't burn the place down."

"Why in the bedroom?" I ask.

Milan points through the bedroom door, and without looking, I know he's saying the rest of the place is tiny, and this was the only place it fit. "Of course," I say. Milan is a small guy with a squeaky voice and a bald top but plenty of hair on the sides. He's wearing jeans with suspenders and a hooded sweatshirt. He strikes me as the kind of guy who's law-abiding and honest until there's some little provocation not to be. I'm betting if we ran a history, we'd find minor stuff but nothing too recent.

Milan continues, "The last rent I got from Mr. Coen was for June. Then my mother died, and I had to go out of town."

"I'm sorry," Chip says.

"I said I had to go out of town," Milan repeats louder.

"No, no," Chip tells him. "I mean I'm sorry about your mother. Sympathies."

"Yeah . . . well . . ." Milan trails off. Chip and Dorsey and I wait for him to regain composure, then he says, "Stroke."

"Your mom?"

"Healthy as a horse, you know? Then gone. Just goes to show . . ."

We all make sympathetic sounds and wait.

Milan walks in a circle. He says, "So Mr. Coen paid for June, and then I get called out of town and don't get back till late July and my God, when I got back the books were a mess, but oh well. And so I don't even realize he never paid July. But then he doesn't pay August. So I keep trying to get hold of him. Notes on the door and the whole bit. Finally, I use my key and go in, and everything looks clean, no damage, but it's clear he hasn't been around, so I don't worry about it. His deposit covers July and part of August, and there isn't much to haul out of here, just the freezer and some clothes and rotten food in the fridge. Believe me, I've seen worse. At most I'm out a couple hundred. So I fill out the paperwork for the eviction, everything all legal, you know, and that takes a couple more weeks. Yesterday I get the eviction default, so today I come in with garbage sacks and start emptying the freezer, and Jesus, Mary, and Joseph, I almost have a coronary."

"It's all in Ziplocs," Dorsey tells me, "quite tidy."

"And all of it hidden underneath," Milan says.

"Come look," Dorsey says. He lifts the lid of the freezer, but I hesitate, which he notices. "Don't worry, counselor, we've sorted everything into black garbage sacks." He says it with surprising gentleness. "There's nothing grisly to see. Unless you want to."

I walk over. There are several large black bags. "These over here are the body," Dorsey tells me, "and this one here is everything else." He reaches into the "everything else" bag and pulls out a package and hands it to me. It is a clear plastic evidence bag weighing a pound or two; inside is a frozen something expertly wrapped in butcher paper. Someone wrote, "Venison shoulder. June," on the butcher paper. I reach into a black bag and pull out another, this one torpedo-shaped: "Rainbow. March." And another: "Ven. Backstrap. June."

"Are these legit?" I ask.

"Don't know yet," Dorsey says, "we'll let the lab take a look. Anyway, the body parts were all at the bottom, hidden under the frozen game or whatever it is."

"Is the body—the parts—are they wrapped in this butcher paper?"

"No, just bags. I never knew they made Ziplocs that big."

"Is it complete? I mean, if you put the pieces together."

Chip looks at Dorsey. Dorsey shrugs. "It looks about right," he says.

"And do we know for sure the guy in the bags is Seth Coen?"

"If I may," Dorsey says. He reaches into one of the black garbage bags and takes out an evidence bag that was right on top. "One of the smaller packages," he says. It is a Ziploc quart bag with a human hand inside, severed about three inches above the wrist. Something travels down my spine and spreads out and dissipates, but then I'm fine. The hand is covered with frost; Dorsey holds it up and tells me to look closely. I do. I see the green-black ink of a home (or prison) tattoo job. It is a square divided into four smaller squares, like a window made up of four panes.

"Mr. Milan recognized the tattoo," Dorsey says.

"That's right," Milan's high-pitched voice adds from across the room.

I turn away and focus on breathing a moment. Dorsey puts the hand back in the black plastic and closes the freezer.

I say, "I've heard that in medical schools, when they dissect cadavers, hands are the hardest. Emotionally, I mean." I think of Cassandra Randall's slender hands, and quickly, to avoid getting swept back into that mental whirlpool, I say, "So what's the connection?" It comes out loud and aggressive, shouted, really, so I reduce the volume and adjust the tone to something more plaintive and add, "How do you link this guy to Scud Illman and Zander Phippin?"

"It's pretty straightforward," Chip says, pulling on a rubber glove. "One of Dorsey's men found this note and made the association." He flips the sheets of a multicolored note cube by the phone, finds the page he wants, and holds it open for me to read: "Rezavore w/ Scud, tonite. Meet here."

"Simple as that."

"And we know he was an associate of Scud's," Chip says.

"Phone records?"

"We're working on it," Dorsey says. "Dollars to doughnuts, he was on the phone with Scud Illman when he wrote that note."

"Is there any way to date this?" I ask.

"Not sure yet," Chip says. "The other notes here might give us something to bracket it by." He flips through the dozen or so other notes on the pad.

"Here's the deal," I say. "We picked up Zander Phippin on a Tuesday. He spent that night in lockup. We had our little sit-down with him on Wednesday, then we let him go. We became concerned when he hadn't called us back by the next Monday. On Friday we dug him up at the reservoir. So if the phone records show any contact between Scud Illman and this Mr. Coen between Wednesday"—I take out my phone and go to the calendar—"Wednesday, May twenty-fourth, and Friday, June third, then this note, plus phone contact, plus Scud's car being identified at the tollbooth on the day of the body ditching, that makes enough probable cause even for Judge Two Rivers."

My mention of Two Rivers, the woolly-headed Federal District judge, causes Dorsey to exhale contemptuously. Normally, that would piss me off—Dorsey putting himself above a federal judge. But in a collegial gesture that surprises even me, I put a hand on Dorsey's shoulder and drum my fingers. I've begun to think he isn't quite the knuckle-dragger I had him pegged for. Besides, the enemy of my enemy is my friend, as they say, so right now I'm loving the bloviating Captain Dorsey.

"So we can execute a search warrant at Scud Illman's place as soon as we get phone records."

"Make sure Illman's stepkid is in school," I say. "Less trauma."

Dorsey says, "Nick, I'll call you and Agent d'Villafranca when I have an update from forensics. My crew will keep the scene sterile meanwhile. And I'll give you both a shout when I have phone records."

He walks around to the stairway and down to his unmarked sedan. He has to maneuver it around the other cop cars, then he almost backs into a boat on a trailer sticking out from among the few residents' cars in the parking area.

Chip and I stand on the balcony watching. "Pompous . . ." Chip mumbles.

"I don't know," I say. "He's not so bad."

When Dorsey finally gets free of the other vehicles, his hidden blues and reds come on, and he roars out of the parking lot.

Chip looks right at me. "I'm seeing someone," he says, fighting a smile for a moment, then he lets go and it spreads across his face.

"Seeing someone?" I say. "Like a woman?"

"Well, I'm not gay."

"No," I say. "But you might have meant 'seeing someone' as in a shrink."

Chip leaves. I go back inside to see what the forensic team is doing. In the bathroom, some guy in scrubs is spraying luminal and looking for blood residue with a UV light. The room is clean, with no personal effects in sight. I stand in the doorway and watch. The room has a small bathtub with a showerhead but no shower curtain. The bath is walled in cheap ceramic tile. Same with the floor. The vanity is standard stuff from any home supply center. Toilet, too. The only interesting thing I see is that the dangling end of the toilet paper is folded into a point.

"The perp probably took the shower curtain," the forensic tech says. "They do that a lot. It's easier than cleaning it."

"Find anything yet?" I ask.

"Only this," he says. He brings his UV light down close to the floor, and one tiny bit of a shoe print, no bigger than a Ritz cracker, glows green. The tread is a checkerboard pattern, squares only about a quarter inch on a side.

"Is that the only blood you've found?" I ask.

"No," the tech says, shining the light all around the room to show me numerous glowing spots of residual blood, "but that seems to be the only thing usable. No fingerprints, no other shoe prints. Nothing. Whoever did it was pretty careful."

"Excuse me, sir," the photographer says. I move out of the way, and he and the technician go to work documenting the shoe print and the blood spatter.

I leave the apartment and drive back to my office.

CHAPTER 14

*I*t is almost winter, and the trees are stark and colorless. From across the field, I see my ex-wife, Flora, standing at the edge of the woods. She has her back to me, but I recognize her figure and her stance and her long hair. She starts walking away, and I'm desperate to reach her before it's too late. I try to shout, but I have no voice. I try to run, but my legs are leaden. If she disappears into the trees, she will be lost to me. No leaves obstruct my vision, so even now, as she walks into the dark depths and I am in a panic of helplessness to save her, even now I can see her as she becomes smaller and smaller in the distance. She is almost gone, far beyond reach and beyond hope, but just as she is about to disappear entirely, she turns and looks at me like she knew I was here all along, and what I see is that I was wrong; it is not Flora. It is Cassandra. And she is gone.

Morning now. I'm driving Lizzy to school. She has just started ninth grade, though she'd be in tenth or eleventh if Flora and I hadn't resisted all the attempts to advance her. She is beside me, wearing goofy pigtails, filling out subject tabs for her new ring binder, and though I know she has a copy of *Jude the Obscure* in her backpack, she also keeps the pictures of horses she drew when she was eight pinned to her bedroom wall, and she still receives mail from the Chincoteague Pony Centre.

Flora and I share Lizzy 50/50. Except Flora lives out in Turner, where the schools are top-notch, and I live close to town, where they're not, so it ends up being more like 60/40 in her favor. I don't mind the drive to Turner in the mornings, when I take Lizzy to school, because I have her company, and on the return, I just mindlessly embed the Volvo into the glacial flow of traffic and surrender to the Zen of inactivity.

Chip calls on my cell. "I have updates about Seth Coen and Scud Illman," he says.

"Call you back," I say, "give me fifteen. But just tell me first, do phone records reveal contact between our two persons of interest?"

"Affirmative."

"Music to my ears," I say, and I hang up.

"That was about Cassandra," Lizzy says.

"It was not. What do you mean?"

"Your posture changes, and your eyes start moving back and forth, and you think you're being all nonchalant."

"It was something about a freezer."

"I'm sure."

I get off the highway at Turner. The Volvo seems to hum more contentedly here among its own kind. I'm edging forward in a line of cars, all waiting to drop kids in front of the middle school. Lizzy could get out and walk from here, but she waits. She puts the ring binder into her backpack, then sits hugging it to her chest. "Seriously," she says, "it was about Cassandra, wasn't it?"

"Yes."

"Is there news?"

"I don't know, honey, but I'll tell you if something important happens, okay?"

She stares silently out the windshield. I wonder if this could be one of those moments when her shell cracks open and I can catch a view of the workings.

Since Cassandra's murder, Lizzy has been obsessed with running and reading. While she scarcely spoke to either Flora or me all summer, she preferred hanging with me because she and I both experienced the loss of Cassandra. It was a strange loss that is hard to explain to anyone who wasn't there. We knew Cassandra only half a day, but already we had given her a role in our imaginings of the future.

Lizzy hasn't told me this, but I observe it. I know her pretty well. I study her. I know there is a longing inside her, the longing she allowed to awaken in the startling crackle of our morning with Cassandra. It is the idea of a two-parent home and something closer to normalcy than what we've had. Flora loves Lizzy as much as I do, but it's not a simple mother/daughter deal; Lizzy is organized and responsible and prudent—more so as time progresses. Flora is scattered and impulsive and befuddled—more so as time progresses. It's not always clear who is mother and who is daughter. Lizzy takes care of Flora, protects her, worries about her, and whether Liz is aware of it or not, she saw in Cassandra one last chance at finding a woman who could move in with me so that she, Lizzy, could have one last chance to be a normal child before it's too late.

As for me, I had Cassandra confused with Flora from the moment I saw her. And not to put too fine a point on it, I thought I saw a second chance for love. Before it's too late.

Admittedly, it was foolish of us both to be so daring so quickly, to willy-nilly unlock the psychological vault where we've relegated those rambunctious longings. But there was chemistry. *Chemistry!* I felt it with Cassandra; I saw it between Lizzy and Cassandra, and I even felt it surge across the third side of that triangle, something shifting in my relationship with Lizzy.

One of Lizzy's friends raps on the window of the Volvo. The spell is broken. "Goodbye, Daddy," she says. She kisses my cheek and is gone. I pull back into traffic, pick up my cell phone, and dial Chip.

CHAPTER 15

It turns out there were several calls between Scud Illman and Seth Coen during the week in question. That's all we have so far this morning. Body parts haven't thawed enough for an autopsy, and the technicians at the crime lab are just now getting to work. I decide to hold off on the search warrant because it will be some hours, maybe even days, before we know what treasures lie in the bags of evidence gathered in Seth Coen's lonely apartment.

Of particular interest to us—to me—is the muck taken from his boots. If he's been dead all summer, then the sand and mud on the bottom of the boots is most likely a match to the soil at the reservoir eighty miles west of here. If that's the case, and if we can nail down the connection between Coen and Scud, we're almost home. Our other major bit of evidence is the partial shoe print found on the bathroom floor in Seth's apartment. It's a good imprint, and we'll probably be able to match it to some suspect's shoe.

I'm taking more than usual interest in the evidence because I'm going to try this case myself. I don't try many cases anymore; the truth is, I wasn't all that great a trial lawyer to begin with. I just got lucky a time or two. But I want to be the one to get Scud Illman. It can be a capital crime, killing a federal witness. I'll keep Upton Cruthers close at hand, because this would normally be his case, but I want to be the one to avenge Zander and Cassandra.

This morning, as always, my office smells of fresh coffee and of the barely detectable citrus spray they use on the dust rags. The voices of lawyers and support staff, newly arrived and not yet cocooned into brow-furrowing isolation, sound lively and emphatic. Shoes squeak down carpeted hallways, printers hum to life, terminals make their beeping wake-up sounds. I unlock my office, put my briefcase on the desk, and plunk into my chair. On the bookcase, I have pictures of Lizzy, including one in which she and Flora stand arm in arm, smiling the same smile, identical but for the thirty-eight-year age difference. And there is the picture of my son Toby at nine months, taken just a few days before he died. On the wall are my diplomas and bar membership certificates and plaques of appreciation for serving on boards and panels. There are photos of my cabin and some framed yellowed newspaper articles about a well-publicized case I tried when I was the DA up north. And in an elongated frame is a bumper sticker, blue letters on a red background: DAVIS, it says. The "i" is lowercase, dotted with a star; the hollow of the "D" is in the shape of a star. Underneath, in much smaller print, it says, FOR CONGRESS, and it has the year, which is now twenty-three years past. I paid for the printing myself, but before even registering for the race, I decided not to run.

This office is home. I feel good here.

My intercom buzzes, and Janice's voice says, "Mr. Schnair wants to see you."

Harold Schnair is TMU: The Man Upstairs. I go up.

"News, Nick, I've got news!" Harold Schnair says before I'm fully through the door, and he has me by the bicep, steering me to one of two mauve wing chairs in his office. He lets go and pushes me into the seat. He sits opposite, but he springs back up and yells to someone outside the door to bring two coffees. "Oh, and some of those cashews and pretzels," in his Brooklyn accent, which, to my prejudiced ear, always sounds working-class.

Harold's assistant brings two cups of coffee and puts them on a side table. "Black, right?" Harold says. He hands me mine, then sashays back and forth in front of me. I am eye level with his gathering slough of body mass, which, over the decades, has quit his chest and shoulders. From my present view, I'd say it would have fallen clear to his feet except for being stopped at hip level by the hidden belt. His fly is pleated beneath the overhang, and from this unfortunate angle, it reveals a triangle of something that might be shirttail and might be boxers. I'm doing my best not to determine which.

"So," he says.

"So," I answer.

"Interesting piece on the wire today," he says, "the wire" being TMU's term for the Internet. "State court judge in Minnesota or Montana or Missouri—one of those states—he got blown to smithereens right in his own home."

"You mean shot?"

"No. Blown up. Some kind of bomb. They're investigating. What's the latest on the Phippin murder?"

I tell him, which doesn't take long, because I've been sending daily updates. He pretends to be interested. I wrap it up quick. "So."

"So."

"So, Crutchfield has announced his retirement." TMU's lips twitch with a painful attempt to keep from grinning. I wait. Crutchfield is one of the judges on the U.S. Circuit Court of Appeals. Speculation about his stepping down has been rampant.

TMU outwaits me, and I finally say, "Is your name in play?" This is the polite question, not to assume anything. I already know the answer.

He chuckles happily. "Oh, that's rich!" he says.

I do my best to look innocent. Of course his name isn't in play. Nobody would gain a thing getting Harold Schnair appointed to the circuit bench. He's elderly, his health isn't particularly good, and though he's honest, hardworking, and brilliant, his nomination would serve no strategic purpose.

"Pigshit," he says. "I want to retire myself. What the hell am I going to do with a lifetime appointment?"

I wait.

"No, my boy, I'm talking about younger blood. New generation and all of that. Pass the torch, as young Jack said."

"If you're talking about me, Harold, I'm fifty-three. Hardly a new generation."

"But a youthful fifty-three," he says. "Think about it. Who better than you? I know Leslie wants it, that unimaginative pontificating bully"—(he means his predecessor in this office, Leslie Herstgood)—"and other than her, it's just Two Rivers and all the assholes who've spent careers in twentieth-floor glass offices without a clue how the world works. I tell you, you're the one, Nick. You've put in your time, kept a clean nose, made friends, done good work."

"What should I say?"

"Say yes."

"Yes."

"Good. I can't promise you'll get it, but I sure as shit guarantee you'll be on the list that goes to the president. Now scram. I need to get busy." He cackles, then he's at his desk and on the phone before I'm out the door.

Harold Schnair is the fourth TMU since I've had this job, and he is my favorite. I call us friends. He's a loud, witty former city council-man, state prosecutor, and law school dean. He's single and, accord-ing to rumors that he himself encourages, is quite a man about town.

I don't know if TMU is blowing hot air about the circuit court. While there are a thousand reasons I wouldn't stand a chance, there are also a few reasons I would. And what's in it for TMU? He'll probably come up with explanations of devious ways it works to his advantage—how it will realign the political chessboard in his favor—but that's not it. He's almost out of the game anyway. He just wants to make something happen. Somebody's protégé will get the slot, so why not his. He wants to play in one more game, and this should be a good one.

Circuit court judge. That would be okay. The circuits are one step below the U.S. Supreme Court. They don't have trials, it's all appeals. The judges spend most of their days writing decisions in quiet, pan-dered-to eggheadedness. I might like that.

CHAPTER 16

Lizzy is with me this week. On our way to school, I say stupidly, "So how are you feeling about things, Liz?"

"What things?" she says with undisguised annoyance.

"I don't know. Your summer. The ugly stuff. All that."

She exhales loudly, the message being that I might as well flap my arms and jump from the roof. No chance of finding that soft spot today.

We pull up in front of the school. Liz grabs her pack and is out, no kiss, no goodbye, door closed.

I believe that objectively, Lizzy knows there is no connection between her having blabbed about events at the reservoir and Cassandra's death. Through extensive interviews and investigation, we've established that, in errantly telling her tale, Lizzy did not use Cassandra's name nor any other identifying information. And none of the people she spoke with could have passed the information on. So there was definitely a more efficient and malicious snitch, and Lizzy's indiscretion had no real effect. But what the objective self knows and what the mischievous subconscious conjures can be different things indeed.

As for me, it's not a matter of my subconscious inventing facts for the purpose of validating my own feelings of guilt. I know what I know. If I had overruled the idea of dangling Cassandra as bait, albeit anonymously, she might still be alive. And my reason for not objecting: I wanted the excuse to stay in touch with her. Oh, how we are punished for our hubris.

Late in the afternoon, my intercom bleeps: "Kendall Vance on three."

"Take a message, Janice."

And later, "Captain Dorsey of the state troopers, Nick, line three."

I connect. "Gimme some good news, Captain."

"I have info on Seth Coen."

"Hang on." I transfer the call and go into Upton's office. We listen on speaker.

"Three items," Dorsey barks into the phone. "First, we've confirmed that it was Mr. Coen in the freezer. Second, it was all there—he was—the body. Nothing missing. Third, we found Scud Illman's prints in the apartment."

"I love you," I shout.

"Not so fast. The prints were confined to the kitchen area. Apparently, whoever did the dirty work wore gloves."

"So we know Scud was there at the murder, but we can't prove he participated. Right?"

"Wrong. Scud's prints could have been left before, after, or during the murder, but at least we have Coen and Illman verifiably linked. That's something."

Upton has his feet on the desk, rocking in his desk chair. His office is less homey than mine. He has a wall of legal texts and one framed photo from his football years. There is a bookcase behind his desk where he has pictures of his kids and wife. They face me, the visitor, instead of sitting on the desk facing him. It's quite formal that way, but on the desk, as always, is the sports page from today's paper, opened to the scores and rankings, and I see that several items are circled in red.

"What else?" I ask Dorsey.

"The mud from Coen's boots: It's a match with the soil at the reservoir. I have this report from the state lab that talks about feldspars and pollen load composition, blah, blah, blah. Bottom line: It is verifiably from the Slippery River Valley and within a, quote unquote, reasonable proximity of the burial site."

"What the hell is a reasonable proximity?" Upton says.

"It's okay," Dorsey's voice soothes over the phone, "these guys are pros. We've had them on the stand before. I'll talk to them."

"Good. It's all good," I say. "We've got Scud in Coen's apartment, we've got Coen at the reservoir, we've got Scud's car coming back to town that morning. We're almost home. Anything else, Dorsey?"

"Coupla things. The freezer meats, venison, rainbow trout, all of that, they seem to be what the packages say they are. As for the victim, he suffered a single gunshot to the back of the head. Dismemberment took place in the shower stall, by the way. Professional. No usable prints anywhere in the bathroom or freezer area. Hardly even any blood remaining."

"Is that it?"

"Well, that tattoo on Coen's hand. The medical examiner says part of it was recent, and parts were older, like it had been touched up or added to."

"Ever seen it before, Dorsey? Does it mean anything?"

"Like a gang thing?"

"Hold on one," I say. I put Dorsey on hold, beep Tina's extension, and ask her to come in for a minute. Then I put Dorsey back on speaker. Tina shows up. "You ever seen this tattoo?" I ask her, showing a drawing of the four-pane window. Tina's specialty in drug crimes brings her into contact with a lot of gang-type offenders.

"Never seen it," she says.

"Okay, I just thought—"

"It's not like I pay a lot of attention to their artwork."

"We were just—"

"But if you really need to know, I know a guy," Tina says.

"What guy?"

"An offender. Old guy, Fuseli, doing life for a bank withdrawal he tried to make at age seventeen. Felony murder. They left two dead on the floor. He's a mentor now, counsels the newbies, works on paroles. He hates the drugs and gang culture in there, so he's a good contact for what's happening inside. The Bureau uses him. And he's an artist. Most of the body art coming out of there, the good stuff, it's his work. Your guy with the window, Seth Coen, was he in Ellisville Max?"

"No," Upton says, "he was down south in Alder Creek."

"Even so," Tina says, "Fuseli might know if it means anything. Do you have some reason to think it's significant?"

Dorsey says, "I was saying, the ME thinks it was touched up or altered recently. Kind of strange for a guy in his late thirties. So we're curious. But otherwise, no, no reason to think anything."

Tina taps her lips with a finger. I'm still thrown off by her hair—the menacing wedge. At first I thought of Tina as sweet and a bit innocent. Then came her haircut and her perpetual rime of anger. Then we took that helicopter ride together, with her hand resting reassuringly on my knee. Now I don't know who she is.

"Well, if you're interested," she says, "Fuseli would be the one."

We sign off with Dorsey.

"If there's nothing else," Tina says, and she leaves.

Upton and I sit with our feet on his desk. "How are the girls?" I ask.

He exhales and shakes his head.

"What?"

"Like they're juggling grenades with the pins halfway out."

"Growing up?"

"They're babies," he says, "they think it's a big joke. Butt cracks and navels on display. And here." He gestures breasts in his sweet, fatherly inability to use the word.

"You're just old-fashioned," I say. His girls are both in high school, a year apart. In the portraits on his bookcase, they look like porcelain dolls. In real life, they're giggly, and Lizzy isn't crazy about them. Walking mannequins, she calls them, not because they're inanimate but because they're always wearing something fashionable. *Gag me!*

"You wait," Upton says, "you'll have your turn soon enough." He laughs.

I shrug. He's wrong. Lizzy is different.

"And speaking of babes," he says, "you could do worse."

"Worse than what?"

"Heeheehee."

"Tina?"

"I see things."

"Hallucinations," I say, and I feel my face redden. "Let's get a search warrant for Scud's place. We'll execute first thing tomorrow morning when his stepkid is in school."

Upton's cell rings. He looks at the number, and his perpetual grin suddenly looks striven for. He glances up at me: "I have to . . ." Then he answers: "Hello, Mr. Jones . . . well, I'm with a colleague at the moment . . . yes, let's talk later on . . . okay, then." He closes the phone. "Okay, where were we?" he asks.

"Search warrant."

"Right. Tomorrow."

I leave. I'm dying to know what the phone call was about, but since he didn't volunteer anything, I don't ask.

CHAPTER 17

Eight-forty-five in the morning. A few of Dorsey's men cover the back and sides of Scud's house, and three others knock at the front door. The door opens and they go inside.

We wait a couple of minutes, then Dorsey radios that it's all secure, we can go in.

Scud's street is an old GI Bill subdivision of starter homes and finisher homes. Some yards are tidy; some have dead cars rising from the dirt like topiary. Scud's is one of the tidy ones. Flowers are planted along the front wall and the concrete walk. The front door has three glass panes in a stair-step pattern.

The house is bland and spotless inside. The furniture is the kind of generic stuff you buy when you have enough money and don't know what else to buy. The kitchen is small. There are two bedrooms. The dining table is empty, and there are no unwashed dishes in the sink.

In the living room a woman and a young boy sit on the couch. The boy is crying. His mother is on the phone.

"You scared?" I ask the boy, and naturally, he doesn't answer, so I say, "I'd be scared, too. But you know what? These guys, they're just looking for some things. They won't hurt you." I look at the mother, expecting her to tell me to leave him the hell alone, but she seems not to notice I'm there.

"Five of them, I think," she says into the phone.

"What's your name?" I ask the boy, who is looking from his mother to the officer who guards them, then back.

"How the hell would I know?" the mother says into the phone. "Come home and ask them yourself."

An officer in a flak jacket walks through the living room carrying a computer.

"Our computer," the woman says.

"Mommy?" the boy says, looking up at her for comfort, but she doesn't notice him. She's in her late thirties. She isn't sitting on the couch so much as giving up to it; everything about her—shoulders, cheeks, voice—seems to be slumping inward. She's hard to get a fix on. Curled bangs, oversize T-shirt, sweatpants, weary, slow-moving eyes: It all seems to be a husk where she no longer lives. She's watching the officer guarding her.

"How old are you?" I ask the boy.

"Seven."

"Seven! What's your name?"

"Colin."

"Well, Colin, how come you're home today?" He is a sandy-haired boy with the top lip scar of cleft palate surgery. It gives him a quizzical look. Otherwise, he's expressionless. He finally looks at me. He has brown eyes with a spot of green in the right iris.

"I don't feel well," Colin says.

"What grade are you in?"

He doesn't answer.

Dorsey comes in and says, "Ma'am, it's going to be several hours. If you'd like to go anywhere, we can call you a cab."

"I have my car," she says in a blank voice, not looking at him.

"I'm afraid we can't release the car, ma'am."

"It's my car."

"Sorry, ma'am."

She starts crying. I walk into the master bedroom. The officers have the bed apart and the dresser drawers removed, and the closet door is open. The warrant authorizes a search for any weapons and for biological evidence—blood, hair, and any other DNA sources—from any of the three victims (Zander, Cassandra, and Seth Coen) and for textile or chemical evidence, such as fibers of the clothing worn by any of the victims. It also authorizes the search for receipts or documents and for physical or chemical evidence associating Avery Illman with the locations of the murders and/or the disposal of any of the three victims. Essentially, it gives us authority to search everywhere for almost anything.

I go outside to the garage. Upton is there with a couple of officers. The overhead door is closed. The searchers have flashlights and are working their way through cardboard boxes and toolboxes and utility shelves. Everything I see suggests an average and tidy home. In the dim light, there is the smell of gasoline and moldering grass from the mower, with cool cement and mildew. It is a sad smell. I think of Colin with his reconstructed lip and two-tone iris. If, in his adulthood, he ever senses this distinctive smell in some other place, his years here will surge to memory: *the time before Scud went to prison.* I wonder what Colin calls him: Dad? Scud? Avery? Mr. Illman? When I get back to the office, I'll look in Scud's file, see if it tells me how long he's been married to Colin's mother.

Upton sees me. "Nothing obvious yet," he says, grinning as usual, shirtsleeves rolled up to expose beefy forearms.

"What do we want to see before we go to the grand jury?"

"Good question. With three victims, I guess . . . what? Something strong linking him to one of them. Or something less strong linking him to two. Or still less strong linking him to all three."

"If we could link Scud or Seth Coen to the Phippin victim, even without, you know, physical evidence . . ."

"Maybe we'll get lucky. Some kind of pocket litter, maybe, or blood in the trunk of the car, 'cause we won't find the weapon, that's for sure. But if we can put the two of them together at the reservoir—Scud and Seth. Because right now we've got squat."

"Yeah," I say, "but 'squat' is one fingerprint, or drop of blood, or one hair away from conviction."

He chuckles.

"I'm going to try this case," I blurt.

Upton was watching the agents at work, but now he pins me with his openmouthed, jaw-thrusted, Willem Dafoe grin. "Try it yourself?" he says. "Of course you are." He fakes a one-two punch to my stomach and says, "I'll watch your back, man. Count on me."

There is a noise. We all startle. Sunlight blasts in under the overhead door as it automatically rises, and we're blinded by the sudden brilliance. Fingers over my eyes, I make out a car in the driveway. Its front doors open, and two men get out and lift hands into the air. There is shouting. I see an officer with weapon drawn approach from the house. "Drop the weapon."

The men don't respond.

"Drop the weapon," someone yells again. One of the men looks up at his hands, where he and I, and apparently the screaming officer, all see something small and suspicious. The man smiles, and I recognize the red hair and pudgy cynical downturn at the corner of his mouth and eyes. It is Scud. He dangles the item between thumb and forefinger for us to see that it is not a weapon but a remote control for the overhead door. It dangles for a moment, then Scud's fingers open, and as it tumbles, his evil squint finds me, and his eyes and mouth draw down farther in recognition and self-satisfied amusement.

The remote smashes on the pavement, and the door winds back down, and it seems very dark.

Outside, Scud is searched for weapons. I hadn't paid any attention to the other guy, the driver, but now I see it's Kendall Vance, soulless defense attorney to sociopaths and moralizing defender of Tamika Curtis (the meth-lab assistant) and others of her ilk, whom he sees as mewling victims of circumstance, done wrong by society. Scud has apparently retained him as his lawyer. Kendall submits docilely to the pat-down, and then he walks up to Dorsey and says, "I assume you have a warrant?"

Dorsey stands like MacArthur on the beach. "We do."

"May I see it?"

"We presented it to Mrs. Illman inside."

Kendall turns and walks toward the house, but Dorsey says, "I'm afraid you can't enter until we've finished. It will be a while."

They have a brief stare-off, then Dorsey turns away and says, "Back to work, I guess. Mr. Illman, you and your lawyer may observe from the yard. You may not enter the house, nor the garage, nor approach any closer than, let's say, twenty feet while we're conducting our search. If you want to speak with your wife, I'll have her come out, but if she does, she won't be allowed to reenter until the search is finished."

"I'll expect an inventory of seized property," Kendall says.

"Naturally," Dorsey answers.

Kendall looks at me and says, "How you doing, Nick?" Then he looks at Upton and says, "Upton."

"Upton?" Scud says, his face breaking into a grimace of boundless amusement. "Uptown? Uptown Cruthers in the flesh?"

"Do I know you?" Upton asks Scud.

" 'Course not, but we know guys in common. Guys you've put away. You're talked about. Uptown Cruthers. They make jokes. Busting balls. Like they're going to *do* something to you, like they got something over you. Like you're, you know, vulnerable."

"Shut up," Kendall says to Scud. "Don't talk to anyone."

"I mean, I'd never do nothing myself," Scud says. "And I tell them leave the guy alone, he's just doing his job. Right? Friggin' retards, they think—"

"Shut up, Scud," Kendall says.

"—they think they can *influence* things. Like if they—"

"Shut the fuck up."

"—like if they cap the right guy—"

"One more word and you can find a new lawyer."

"Oh, sorry," Scud says, looking at Upton, "I've been advised by counsel to shut the fuck up. Suffice it to say, they're all retards."

Chip, who was has been studying the flower garden, gets right in Scud's face. "Was that some kind of threat?" he asks in a tired voice. "Were you threatening a federal officer?" He outweighs Scud by a hundred pounds, and I wonder, looking into the creases under his eyes, if he has picked this moment to let it all get to him and, with us watching, is about to wrap his beefy fingers around Scud's neck and squeeze.

Scud smiles innocently up at Chip. "'Course not. Just repeating what I've heard on the street. I wouldn't think of—"

"Shut up," Kendall yells. "Let's go. We're leaving."

"Not so fast," Chip says.

"No threat," Kendall says to Chip. "Just bullshit. Street talk. If you had a transcript, no threat. My client and I apologize for any implication to the contrary. Now, unless you plan to arrest him, we're leaving."

"But I live here," Scud says.

"Not today you don't," Kendall snaps. "Come on."

Before Kendall can get Scud into the car, the door of the house opens, and Colin comes out with his mother. They stand in front of the door, the mother with arms crossed and back bent. Maybe she has some scoliosis, or it might just be her surrender to disillusionment. Cheeks, shoulders, eyes, jaw, all like pillowcases hanging limp on the line.

"Honey, did I tell you we were having company?" Scud says.

She ignores him and looks at Dorsey. "How long?"

"At least another hour, ma'am."

"Stupid goddamn—" she says.

"We'll be as unobtrusive as possible, ma'am."

"Good joke."

She eyes us all like she'll lunge for the throat of the first one to make a move. Her eyes jump around and her nostrils widen above the quivering lip. No doubt she's been sitting inside looking for the courage to come out here. Now that she's here, the courage turns out to be hollow, and what fills the space is rage tugging at a fraying tether.

"I'm so sorry, ma'am," Dorsey says with astonishing gentleness, and I realize he's seen what I see—that if we're not careful, we'll have to take this woman out of here in restraints, and who knows what that could trigger from her, from Scud, and from Colin. She scans the group of us but won't look at Scud, and the obvious conclusion is that he's the one she actually loathes, not us.

"Mrs. Illman," I say, following Dorsey's lead, "I'm just about to send someone to Starbucks. What can we get you?"

"Nothing," she says, as I knew she would, but it has the intended effect of knocking her off track.

"Or maybe something for Colin? A soda? A big cookie?"

"Nothing."

"Tell you what," I say, "we'll just get a bunch of stuff, and if Colin wants a cookie or muffin, it'll be here." I watch Colin to see if any of this registers, but he's not letting on.

"Double-shot vanilla latte for me," Scud bellows, but we all ignore him except for Kendall, who looks ready to tackle him.

Dorsey has stepped away and is on the phone. He sees me watching and mouths, "Family services."

Good idea: someone trained in this stuff to get Colin and Mrs. Illman away from the action and keep a lid on things. Scud's wife probably isn't a part of whatever he's into. Not willingly, anyway—no brassy, wrong-side-of-the-tracks, don't-fuck-with-me kind of girl. But she found the backbone to come get in our faces, not to protect Scud or align herself with him, rather, to align *us* with him as intruders, disrupters, violators. In a pathetic way, she is admirable. I wonder how it would affect her if the right woman were here with us, an officer or lawyer. Maybe she wouldn't see herself as so apart from us. Not someone like Flora, whose own "issues" are a bottomless black lake under the most meager crust of ice, and probably not someone like Cassandra, whose sincere warmth would feel patronizing to the suspicious Mrs. Illman. No, the woman who comes to mind, the one most likely to hit the right note, is the gritty but sensitive Tina from my office. As a former elementary schoolteacher, she'd be a good one for Colin, too. But she's not here.

"Come on," Kendall says to Scud, "let's get out of here. Bring your wife and son." He puts a hand on Scud's shoulder and tries to steer him back to the car, and I see Scud check his inclination to swing at the source of this unwelcome touch.

"Bullshit, there's cookies coming. I'm staying," Scud says. He takes Colin's hand, and they walk away from us. Scud kneels down and talks to Colin quietly and brushes hair from his eyes.

Kendall catches my eye and shakes his head in exasperation. This is a smooth move on his part; it puts Scud in the light not of a monster but just an aggravating guy.

"Got your hands full," I say to Kendall.

Chip, who has returned to studying the flower garden, turns and yells, "Who's the gardener here?" Nobody answers, so he walks across the lawn to Mrs. Illman and says, "Nice garden."

"They're his," she says.

"Nice garden," Chip says to Scud, who is standing with Colin and holding his hand.

"Relaxes me after a long day at work," Scud says.

"A day at work?" I hiss. I press to within inches of his vile smirk, and before I know what I'm doing, I have his shirt bunched in my two fists. "And what exactly do you do, Mr. Illman?" I say.

In an instant Dorsey and Chip have separated me from Scud.

"Assault," Scud says.

There is a moment of stillness. Everybody looks at Kendall, who appears not to have noticed.

Upton tugs me toward the car. "Let's get back."

I laugh.

Scud laughs.

I let Upton pull me toward the street. Kendall Vance walks to the road with us. "Infuriating little weasel, isn't he," Kendall says.

"He's a murderer."

"It's my impression, Nick, that you have no real evidence."

"We'll have it soon."

"But what I want to talk to you about is Tamika Curtis."

"Not now. Call me at work."

"I do. You don't call back."

"This afternoon. I'll be in."

I get in the car with Upton and close the door.

We ride without speaking. The person I find myself thinking

about, oddly, isn't Kendall or Scud or Upton but Tina. Tina Trevor, who for some reason surfaced through the drama as the ideal person to get the volatile Mrs. Illman calmed down.

"Well, that was intense," Upton says, breaking into my reverie.

"Upton," I say loudly, "Upton, Uptown. So you have a reputation with the bad boys?"

He laughs and looks at me with a puzzled expression. "Go figure."

CHAPTER 18

riday afternoon: Tina and I are on our way to Ellisville Maximum. She has a deposition scheduled, and I'm riding along to have a chat with Fuseli the tattoo artist/informant/youth counselor. We're in her Toyota Avalon with the stock report on the radio, and our briefcases on the backseat, which looks too clean. It has never seen a child or a dog or even two adults out on a double with Tina and whomever she hangs with.

I remember Cassandra's hair, long and loose. And the funky way she dressed. Tina, by contrast, with her atrocious hairstyle, is wearing her standard gray lawyer uniform.

"Have you read Jane Austen?" I ask.

"Is that by one of the Brontës?"

"What about *Lord of the Rings*?"

"Saw the movies. I don't read much fiction."

We ride on in silence.

At the prison, I wait for Fuseli in a conference room of the administrative complex. He is brought to me in manacles, hands cuffed together and locked to a chain around his waist. His ankles are chained, too, with a few inches of slack for taking tiny steps. The guard parks him in front of me and looks up with questioning eyebrows. I nod. The guard unlocks his hands but leaves his ankles shackled.

"Thanks, Officer, we'll be fine." I skimmed Fuseli's prison file before they brought him in. He's not dangerous. The guard goes out but leaves the door ajar.

Fuseli's name isn't Fuseli. It's Leroy Burton. He is a tall, dissipated white man of forty-seven, but if I were going by appearance, I'd put him past sixty. He is thin and creased, with wispy hair. He sits in one of the padded conference chairs and wiggles around. "Man, don't that feel good," he says in a raspy voice from down in his throat.

The guard comes in and says, "Mr. Norton wants me to ask what you'd like. Coffee, fruit juice, soda?"

"Orange," I say, and I look at Fuseli. It takes him a second, but he finally figures it out, and his eyes go wide in astonishment. "Sprite," he says.

The guard comes back with Sprite and orange soda and two glasses with ice. I had meant orange juice, but I don't say anything. Fuseli pours his soda and takes a sip. "Been a while," he whispers.

"You don't get Sprite?"

"We get Sprite. We don't get waited on."

"Enjoy," I say, and I make a gesture of clinking glasses without really clinking. Fuseli's motions are slow and deliberate, as though he's drugged up, but his whole shtick is that he hates the junk and the gang culture that goes with it. No, Fuseli has two problems that have nothing to do with drugs—first and most obvious, his thirty years in prison with no chance of getting out. I've seen it before. In some guys, the bleakness of prison inhabits the mind like a tumor. It slows everything down.

His other problem is more literal. He has multiple sclerosis.

"So you're the tat man of Ellisville Max?" I say.

He bobs his head.

I say, "I got a question about a tattoo we found on a dead guy. Nobody seems to know anything. I thought you might."

"And you ain't got people to drive out here for you? Or just fax a picture and have the warden ask me?" This is asked not unkindly, and it tells me things about him. He's smart and curious. I wonder what he'd look like if he didn't look so institutional.

"I have an interest," I say.

"You got a photo?"

"Don't need one." I quickly draw the four-part square on a scrap and slide it to him. I don't mention the ME's observation that it was touched up.

"A window?" he says.

"Looks like it."

"Why should it mean anything at all?"

"Maybe it doesn't."

"The dead guy, what's the deal? What do you know?"

"No need to get into all that, Mr. Burton. I'm just curious about the tattoo."

He shrugs.

I wait.

He waits.

I say, "Well, I won't waste your time." I pick up my briefcase.

"That's a good one." He laughs. "Not wasting my time. I like that one. You're a funny man."

"Mr. Burton, do you know anything about the design?"

"I haven't decided yet."

I nod. The last thing I want is to get jacked around by an inmate making himself feel like a big dick by screwing with me. Just another Scud Illman. "Tina told me you were helpful," I say. "She must have gotten you on a good day. I'll tell her and Mr. Norton you're not."

"So send Tina in. I'll talk to Tina."

"But not me?"

"Suppose I know about this tat," he says. "I tell you about it, and you go out of here, use my info, and what do I get? You ain't telling me why the big deal: why a muckety-muck like you drives out here. You ain't telling me who the stiff is or who killed him. Not even a good story. No usable info, no extra privileges. I don't get fifteen minutes looking at Tina's pretty face while she laughs and tells me about some case she's working on, and I don't even get another goddamn soda. You want to tattle to the warden, tattle away. Warden will ask me what gives, and I'll tell him you don't want to pay, and that'll be that. But I can see you're greener than eggs 'n' ham, and you probably don't mean no disrespect, so let's you and me start again."

All this was said in his whispery, nonthreatening voice, but I still considered just walking out. I might have if he hadn't said the part about Tina. It was complicated. The part about listening to her laugh, that was key. He'd shown me a weakness: He'd confessed his sorrows.

"Mr. Burton," I say . . .

"I prefer Fuseli."

I nod. "Fuseli. A kid was selling dope to pay his college tuition. The Bureau determined that his source was a criminal group whose crimes stretch into many other antisocial practices." I lay out a sketchy version of the landscape, leaving out my personal involvement. When I get to Seth Coen's tattoo, I say, "The medical examiner noticed that it was recently altered. It was an amateurish job. We're trying to fill in what we can. Can you help?"

"Why come out here yourself? Why not send somebody?"

We stare at each other across a few feet of conference table. It's a stuffy, windowless room but much nicer than anything Fuseli sees day to day—the Formica conference table has hardwood trim, the padded chairs swivel, and the walls are Sheetrock instead of cinder block.

"Guard," I yell. The door swings open, and two of them come in, ready for action. I hold up a hand. "Could we get another couple of sodas here?" Then I turn back to Burton/Fuseli. "You've received my down payment. From here on, it's value for value."

He considers this. "Tell you what," he says, "you write down six last names on that piece of paper. Five of 'em are guys you know of in prison. The sixth is the dead guy with the tat. Stick him in anywhere. First, last, middle. Don't tell me."

I do as he says, shielding the list with my hand until it's done. Six names, the second is Coen. I slide it over to him. He glances at it. "Coen," he says.

"Impressive. What's the secret?"

He smiles, and immediately, I start to like him. It is an honest and open smile. "Pay up," he says.

I think of arguing, but I don't. I tell him about how Coen was found in a freezer all chopped up. That seems to satisfy him. He taps the drawing of the tattoo. "You think this is significant?"

"I don't think anything."

He nods. He turns the paper over to the clean side and draws a swastika right in the middle with heavy black lines, then he covers it with his palm and traces the outline of his whole hand and slides the drawing toward me. I let it sit on the table between us, reluctant to touch it. I feel something in the back of my throat. I can't think of anything to say.

Fuseli speaks. "They used to have an Aryan problem down at Alder Creek. Vicious bastards. Not enough of them to rule the blacks, but every Jew-boy they get, they branded him. We had one in here once, a nice kid who'd finished his state time and come over here to do his federal. Drug shit. Ain't it always. I worked on some designs with him, how to turn it into something else. Something nice. Finally, we just closed the sides and made a window. I guess that's what the others did once they got away from the Aryans. Simple. Closed up the sides. How long was Coen outside?"

"A couple of years."

"There you go. He got his release, and first thing he does is gets his tat altered. Maybe even does it hisself. I can tell you it was an amateur job, because if it was done right, you wouldn't know it was changed."

Fuseli reached over with the pen and quickly blacked in the four half-sides, turning the swastika into a window. But it was there, the evil disguised as something innocuous—or not just innocuous but spiritual. A window, timeless metaphor for insight and wisdom. It's almost worse in hiding than in the open. Things come into my mind, awful things. Zander emerging from the dirt, Cassandra dead in her home, the hand in the freezer. And my son, Toby. When Toby was alive, there was a kindly and ancient family doctor in the town by the lake. Dr. Wallis. He talked of Toby's illness as a hidden defect, a lurking evil. That's what I see in the altered tattoo, a lurking evil. I'd rather just see the swastika.

"You Jewish?" Fuseli asks. "Looks like you got the wind knocked out."

This embarrasses me. And it impresses me because his voice is earnest and sympathetic. Here he is doing life in prison, and yet he views my momentary show of emotion as an opportunity not to gain leverage or to smirk but to make a human connection—to participate for a second in normal human sadness as we experience it on the outside. I like this guy.

"Just thinking. What about you? You sound compassionate."

"I heard of one guy over there at Alder Creek," he says. "I mean, I never seen him, but this is what I hear: They branded him just like your Mr. Coen. One day he takes a knife and peels the skin right off the back of his hand. You don't need to be Jewish or free to feel for shit like that. It's fucked up. Like this disease I got—"

"MS."

"Done your homework, I see. Well, if I could take a knife and peel if off, I would. Yes, sir."

"Are the Aryans still active over there?"

"You tell me. You're outside, I'm stuck here. But I hear they got broke up. Prison moved a couple. Blacks killed one. Maybe you remember."

We're silent a few seconds, then I say, "You ever hear of a guy named Scud? Scud Illman?"

He shakes his head. "Connected to Coen?"

"Yeah. Small players in a big game. You know anybody inside pulling strings on the outside?"

"Everybody. What strings?"

"Anything. Drugs, mostly."

"Young guys talk to me—guys having trouble adjusting. But see, I'm not in on anything. I sell my tats, I keep to myself."

"But—"

"Ask Tipper, he knows everyone."

"Who's Tipper?"

"Bookie. He was a bookie on the outside, big-time. Bookie on the inside now, small-time. The prison don't care, it's just small change and cigs and favors. Gives us something to do. Makes the ball games on TV more interesting. But Tipper's the one, 'cause everybody wants action, and he's who's got it. So he deals with everyone.

Equal opportunity, you know? Maybe he don't know *all* the secrets, but he sure as hell knows who knows."

"Will he talk to me?"

"He's coming up for parole."

"Tipper. What's his real name?"

Fuseli laughs. "Eggs 'n' ham," he says, "some things you got to find out yourself. Now pay up: How come you, the man, is driving out here yourself to ask me about a tat that probably don't mean shit anyway?"

"Haven't you figured it out?"

"You play 'em pretty close."

We stare at each other. I notice his left hand shaking, which I suppose is from the MS. He sees me watching it. "Lucky I'm right-handed," he says. "I can still do tattoos. For now, at least. That's one thing I got."

"Here's your answer, Mr. Burton: Coen and his associate Scud Illman may have killed someone I know. Two someones. It has become personal."

" 'Zat all you're saying?"

"For now."

"You still owe," he says without anger.

"I'll come back. I'll tell you more when I can," I say. "Promise."

He nods, and we sit silently. His tremor seems to come and go. I notice one of his eyes doesn't always follow the other.

"How come they call you Fuseli?"

Slowly, he pulls up his shirt and reveals an elaborate tattoo across his chest. It's a copy of a painting I recognize: A woman lies stretched on a bed, head dangling backward in death or deathly sleep. Sitting on her chest, as if he owns her, is a demon. In the foreground are prison bars. "*Nightmare* by Fuseli," he says. "I saw it in a book in the library. Copied it."

"The bars are your addition?"

He nods.

It's an impressive bit of body art, especially seeing as he had to do it on himself in a mirror. It tells me more about him, too, because it is an image of horror and sorrow, not of anger: a quietly existential statement about life in prison.

"Talented guy. Smart, too," I say. "How'd you get involved in a double murder?"

He's studying his chest and seems unperturbed by the question. "Never killed anyone," he whispers.

And strangely—because here I am in this world of murderers and thieves and rapists and con men and liars—strangely I believe him.

I wait.

"Read my file," he says.

CHAPTER 19

Tina has a trial tomorrow. I see tension in her face, teeth clenched, eyebrows in a scowl. The car stereo plays harpsichord music as we drive past silver maples whose leaves are already tinged with red. There are just a few settlements between Ellisville and the city, places where dilapidated homes have gathered around a stop sign and a bar. It's all low-value land, too marshy to farm and too far from the city to have residential value.

When we near the outer suburbs, Tina exits where I show her, and we make our way along back roads. I guide her to Flora's two-story shingled Cape. It's a wooded lot on a small pond. There's no lawn, just a carpet of pine needles.

Kenny's truck is here, a Toyota four-wheel-drive pickup with knobby tires and chrome stacks and suspension so high, the running board hits me at midshin. He bought it this summer and keeps a photo of it in his wallet. Kenny likes things with motors. It annoys him that the lake up at our cabin doesn't allow powerboats. He wants to buy a Jet Ski.

Kenny watches TV in the other room while Flora makes dinner. Bill-the-Dog comes over to greet me, then spots Tina and veers off to give her a good sniffing. Flora seizes Tina's hand and holds on while she gazes at Tina with wide, entreating eyes that, in this instance, mean, *Maybe you'll marry my husband and phone me when he's being a jerk, and we'll be best friends, and spend hours talking about him, and about Lizzy, and about buying organic and sustainable groceries.*

The hem of Tina's charcoal skirt is above the knees, which gives Bill-the-Dog an advantage. Since Tina's hands are busy being squeezed by Flora, Bill's head goes under the skirt and, complete with a full-body wag, delivers the most enthusiastic of greetings.

"Oh!" Tina squeaks, but she is heroic: She twists at the waist, maneuvering her hip between Bill's enthusiastic snout and its target while maintaining eye and hand contact with Flora for a few seconds. Then she goes to her knees and pats the ecstatic Bill, who rolls into position for a tummy rub. "Ooooh, such a happy woggy," Tina says.

"This is Bill," Flora says. "Bill-the-Dog."

"Ooooh, such a fuzzy-wuzzy woggy."

I yell up the stairs for Lizzy.

"One minute, Dad."

"Tina has a trial tomorrow."

"I'll hurry."

Flora looks back and forth between Tina and me. "Are you two—"

"Sharing a ride," I say. "We both had business at Ellisville."

Flora has the kettle on. "Preference?" she asks, handing Tina a basket of herbal tea.

"I'm gonna haul some brick for Flora," Kenny yells from the other room.

"Brick?"

"I'm building a patio out back," Flora says. "Won't that be nice?" She puts tea on the table. "Kenny, will you have tea, honey?"

Flora, Tina, and I sit and pour tea. The kitchen smells of curry. There is unshucked corn on the counter.

I go into the other room and sit on the couch beside Kenny and punch him affectionately on the arm, and he punches me back, and we get into a momentary brawl and end up restraining each other, all four hands jumbled into a knot as we sit there trying to get an advantage over each other. It lasts a few seconds before we break apart. But what we were really doing, I think, in a manly, aggressive, competitive way, was holding hands. I get up and turn toward the kitchen.

"Wipe the floor with you if I wanted," he says.

"Crush you like a worm," I say.

On the table in the kitchen, Flora has set out tea for everyone.

"Kenny," I say, "come have tea."

The TV stays on, but he walks in. "Hi, Tina."

"Isn't this nice," Flora says. "All of us here together."

"Lovely home," Tina says.

"You'll stay for dinner," Flora says.

"Couldn't possibly," I say. "Tina has a trial tomorrow."

"Lloyd will be here," Flora adds, as if that should be an inducement.

"I met Lloyd," Tina says. "The doctor."

"Well, he was, but he got disillusioned with Western medicine, and when he used a more ethical approach, it threatened other doctors, so they had him disbarred."

"Wrong word," I say quietly. "Lawyers get disbarred. Doctors get, um, I don't know, something else."

"Because heaven forbid some doctor doesn't prescribe enough pills. Prescribe, prescribe, prescribe. It was all too much for him, and he didn't have enough strength left to fight them. He just let them take his license. But he's been an immense help with my practice."

"You're a doctor?"

"MSW, dear, personal counseling. He's helped me with a more whole-body approach to wellness."

"Lizzy," I yell.

"We're going to dig out all that dirt," Kenny says, pointing out the back door. "Flatten it, you know, put down sand, then brick. Be really nice for barbecues in summer."

"Hi, Daddy," Lizzy says, then she spots Tina and stops to consider the situation.

"Just economizing," I say. "Tina and I both had business at Ellisville."

"They're staying for dinner," Flora says. "Isn't that nice?"

"Not decided yet."

"I've got homework," Lizzy says.

"And Tina's trial. I think we should—"

"I'm ready to go, Daddy."

"How is your friend?" Tina asks Lizzy. "The one with leukemia."

"Seamus. He just e-mailed me that they've found a match for his blood type."

"You could help us dig," Kenny says. "We're starting tonight, me and Flo and Lloyd."

"Love to, Kenny," I say, "but just can't do it tonight. We'll do something soon, though. A dinner or something. Okay?"

I know how much Kenny wants to have us stay and all work on the digging together. He loves these "family" projects. His real family was a train wreck of alcoholism and domestic violence. And even though what Flora and I have to offer is a tepid imitation of normal family life, it's miles closer than anything else Kenny has been part of. In "family" pictures taken during the fifteen years he's been part of our lives, Kenny is grinning like he just won the lottery, always managing to have his arm around one of us. And in the pics from when Lizzy was a baby, it is often Kenny, a cowlick-headed boy of ten or eleven or twelve, who is holding her, making sure he has her facing the camera. I remember how he used to take one of her chubby arms in his hand and flop it up and down. *Wave*, he'd say to her, *wave at the camera*.

"I love your hair," Flora says to Tina. This is a complicated statement. Flora doesn't love Tina's hair because it's the most unattractive haircut in history, and if Flora were being honest, she'd say Tina's head looks like the hind end of a sheepdog shaved for rectal surgery. But Flora isn't lying, either, because she has found Tina's hair so disruptive to her misperception that Tina and I are *together* (meaning Tina and Lizzy will also be *together*) that she has performed an instantaneous rejiggering of everything she's ever thought about hair, and she actually does love it at this moment, on this person. "It's so . . ." Flora says, and she stops to search for a concept. Finally, she makes two fists and jabs them at each other, "Uumph," she says.

And Flora is right. That's exactly what it is.

"Thank you," Tina says.

Tina, Lizzy, and I go out to the car. Lizzy calls Bill-the-Dog, who bounds over, ready for whatever comes next. Bill is officially Lizzy's dog; she usually accompanies Lizzy back and forth between the two homes.

"Wait," I say, remembering Tina's never-used backseat.

"What?" Lizzy and Tina say together.

"Nothing." And we all get in. Lizzy is in back with our shedding, slobbering, unaccountably ecstatic Bill. Tina turns around in the driveway, and I catch sight of the tiny sign near the flagstone walk. It had faded, but now I see it is repainted with pink and orange letters and a trim of green ivy: WELCOME TO MIDDLE EARTH.

CHAPTER 20

The next morning, I drive Lizzy out to school in Turner. Traffic is slow. I get back to the Federal building just as Tina's trial is starting. I turn my cell off and walk into the courtroom to hear opening arguments.

Tamika Curtis reminds me of an animal that has curled up to protect itself after being snatched from home. Tamika *has* been snatched, and thanks to Kendall Vance's bullheadedness, she'll be gone for a long time. Tina made a good offer: seventy-eight to ninety-seven months. Tamika could serve her six and a half to eight years and get out, maybe with some job training, in time to recover her kids from foster care. But Kendall wouldn't go along, arrogant prick. He says he won't let us leave Tamika's daughters motherless. He's taking the case to trial. I can't imagine what he hopes to accomplish, because there's no viable defense. It'll be a bloodbath. It's cruel to raise Tamika's hopes and crueler yet to double her prison time just to stroke his own ego.

Tina gives her opening: "To children, the innocents in the schoolyard, street drugs are the looming death skulking outside the gate." I see Kendall ready to rise in objection, because this kind of stuff—though standard for a closing argument—is on the ragged edge of acceptable openings. Which means everybody does it, but you have to move quickly, jumping to the next point before opposing counsel objects. Tina jumps.

"The evidence will show that the defendant did knowingly and intentionally participate in the manufacture of methamphetamine with the intent to distribute said methamphetamine . . ." And on she grinds, gesturing alternately toward the jury and the defendant at regular intervals, like an industrial robot delivering spot welds.

What the evidence will show is that while some eager-eyed entrepreneurs were in the kitchen cooking up a batch of meth, Tamika Curtis was out front smashing a ceramic cup with a hammer. Meth gets boiled, and some roughage—such as the porcelain chunks that Tamika was providing—helps break up the raw ingredients. For her labors, Tamika was to earn a share of the product, though not the profits from its sale. And though the evidence is sketchier, the government believes she took her runny-nosed children with her to different pharmacies, buying up Sudafed (which provides pseudoephedrine, the key ingredient for meth).

Tina finishes quickly and sits down. Kendall stands. He starts with boilerplate about presumption of innocence and keeping an open mind. He's good. He doesn't lecture—he discusses, informs. "What the evidence will show," he says in a voice weary with the government's preposterousness, "is that some people were manufacturing methamphetamine, and they got caught. The evidence will show that to buy their way out of long prison terms, these criminals had to cooperate. Cooperate! Meaning they had to inform on someone else. But what do you do when everybody has been caught and there's no one left to inform on? What do you do when you've sworn a blood oath not to rat on your friends? (Pause.) You invent someone. (Pause.) And whom do you invent? (Pause.) How about one of the users whose life you've been ruining anyway? Someone you've been selling your poison to all along . . ."

He's smooth. But Tina will win—not because she's better but because Tamika is guilty, we have the witnesses to prove it, and juries like to convict in drug crimes. Tina is a good trial lawyer because she is organized and she prepares diligently. But she lacks Kendall's native understanding of jury psychology, and she lacks his talents as a performer. Tina is a workman in the courtroom; Kendall is an artist.

I go upstairs to my office. I haven't checked in since leaving for the prison yesterday afternoon. Janice hands me a stack of *While You Were Out* slips. I had calls from Special Agent Chip d'Villafranca, Captain Dorsey of the Troopers, Upton (right there in the next office), Kendall Vance (my nemesis), TMU (my mentor), Hollis

Phippin, and Flora. I start with Chip, get his voice mail, leave a quick message, and move on to Dorsey.

"'Bout time," Dorsey says. "I've been trying all three of you. Chip, Upton, and you. I got news and nobody to share it with."

"Got me now, Cap'n."

"Here's the deal. Our search of Scud Illman's home turned up an old rag spattered with blood. We've matched the blood to Seth Coen."

"Beautiful."

"And more. In the garage, they found a cash register receipt crumpled up behind the trash barrels. It was for the purchase of a pack of Camels, time- and date-stamped to two-oh-two A.M. on June third, at the Seven-Eleven right across from Seymour Apartments."

"Oof."

"Dollars to doughnuts, Scud already had Phippin in the trunk, then he drove over to pick up Coen, buys a pack of cigs, then off to the reservoir."

"We've got to find his car. If it's not already smelted."

"Working on it. Let's talk this through with Chip and Upton. I'm meeting Chip at two o'clock at the Rain Tree. Join us. Or better yet, meet me there at one-thirty."

I agree, and we sign off.

On my way out of the building to meet Dorsey, I stop in the courtroom again. Tina has a state trooper on the stand:

". . . and what, if anything, did you see when you entered the kitchen?"

"Well, there was the stove, and there was this big, like, kettle . . ."

The trooper is young. He's good-looking, with a casual overhang of hair, and he looks familiar, but I can't place him. He describes what he saw in the kitchen—an obvious meth-cooking operation. Tina doesn't work him hard on the details. He's obviously not a critical witness. She finishes. Kendall stands up. "I just have a few questions, Officer Penhale . . ."

Penhale. He's the trooper who drove Lizzy and Kenny and Cassandra home from the reservoir that day. That's why he looks familiar. His hair is longer now.

"Do you recognize this woman?" Kendall Vance asks, indicating Tamika Curtis.

"No, sir."

"No? You didn't see her the day you busted the meth lab?"

"No, sir."

Kendall hammers on this for several minutes. He establishes that Tamika Curtis was arrested only after being named by the main guys. The cops never saw her.

I leave to meet Dorsey.

The Rain Tree Grill is in the old Rokeby Mills building on the river. The Rain Tree and a few other businesses, like Liquidation Sales and an army/navy surplus, moved in decades ago, but a few years back the whole complex was bought up, quaint gaslights were installed, and all the tenants except for the Rain Tree were booted to make room for boutiques. I don't see Dorsey, so I sit at the bar. You can smell the charcoal grill, and beer and coffee and clams, and the resin-y smell of unpainted wooden walls. The place has the peaceful feel of midday, when lunch is over and dinner hasn't started. Steve, the owner, rolls up behind the bar.

"What'll it be?" he asks with a smile that says, *I recognize you but can't think how.* The floor behind the bar is elevated for his wheelchair. The other bartenders must find it difficult.

"Coffee."

He pivots and rolls to get it. Steve looks like Charles Manson gone gray: stringy wild hair and a patchy beard but without Manson's burning eyes. Steve gets snappish if you change your order or take an extra few seconds to decide. On the menu and on the sign outside, there's a drawing of an African-looking tree; it rains on either side, but under its sheltering branches stands a crowd of people. "Rain Tree rhymes with Quang Tri," Steve explains to anyone who asks. "Quang Tri is the real name. But if I actually called it Quang Tri, the only ones who'll come are a bunch of fucked-up vets like me, which would please me fine except they ain't got any money to spend. Quang Tri, in honor of my legs, 'cause that's where they're at, bone dust in a rice paddy."

Dorsey shows up, and we get a booth in the corner.

"Chip called. He'll be a couple minutes late," Dorsey says.

"He's usually early."

"How's he seem to you?" Dorsey asks in a significant tone.

I shrug. "Chip-like. Maybe more so than usual. Do you have a concern, Cap'n?"

Dorsey thinks for a few seconds. He strokes his bear rug. "Yes and no."

"Choose one," I say testily. I'm feeling protective of Chip. I know exactly what Dorsey is getting at, but I want him to have to work for it. I've softened on Dorsey a bit, but he's essentially a knuckle-dragger.

"No," he says.

"Good," I say, snipping off that thread of conversation. Of course Dorsey has a concern. Dorsey is an all-business, by-the-book, cut-and-dried, linear-deduction guy. Smart and quick but not creative. You meet a lot of Dorseys in this business, guys born to be pissed off about the world's failure to form straight lines in tidy uniforms. Everything bugs them: nonconformity, quirkiness, laxness, it all brings up their demons. Except Dorsey isn't quite as easily dismissed, because I catch glimpses of an incongruous eagerness in him. Like his enthusiasm about Milan, Italy. I actually have no idea who he is.

"Have you been to Milan?"

He laughs. "Hardly." He goes off to the men's room. I watch him. His back is narrow and straight, but he maneuvers through the room slowly, and I wonder if he's burdened by this thing with Chip. Does he wonder why Chip doesn't like him, or is he afraid Chip could be a security threat? I shouldn't have shut him down so quick.

Truth is, I've been concerned about Chip, too. You give a guy some slack in the wake of a domestic meltdown, but I have to wonder if he has crossed some point of no return; the thing he was saying last summer about becoming an animal trainer, and little things like showing up late at this meeting. Mostly, it's that he seems checked out. Kind of like Flora. Not the guy you want handling critical evidence and sensitive information. Definitely not the guy you want watching your back in the high-adrenaline, life-and-death moments you sometimes see in law enforcement.

The waitress comes with coffee and tops us off. "Anything?" she asks.

"No, thanks," I say.

She starts to leave, but immediately, I say, "Second thought—"

"Make up your mind, darlin'."

"Bowl of clams. Steamers."

Dorsey returns, we don't talk much, then Steve rolls up with the steamers and clasps Dorsey's hand in a thumb-link handshake. "Compadre," Steve says.

"You know Nick Davis?" Dorsey asks.

"Recognize him," Steve says, and we do a quick thumb grapple.

"How's business?" Dorsey asks.

"Same for me as it is for you; economy don't matter, weather don't matter, president and governor don't matter. People still gonna drink coffee and beer and break the law, am I right?"

Steve holds out a fist, and Dorsey bumps it with his own. "Later, gator," Steve says, and rolls away to the far corner table, where half a dozen guys sit drinking coffee. They're all about Steve's age, mid-sixties, but some are more time-worn. In the old days, there was always a plume of cigarette smoke over that table. Steve resisted the smoke-free ordinance as long as possible. He got cited a couple of times and was threatened with shutdown. As it is, he keeps a bench outside for them. Some guys will sit here most of the afternoon, switching between coffee inside and a cig outdoors.

Dorsey takes a clam from its shell, peels the sheath off the siphon, dunks it in the broth, forgoes the butter, then swallows. "Good idea," he says, nodding toward the clams, and goes after another. We work our way through the bowl. Dorsey, I notice, grabs from the bowl without discrimination, while I go after the smaller ones. He pauses and watches me select, dunk in broth, dunk in butter, eat.

"Mmm. Cholesterol," he says about the butter, not to criticize me but to explain himself. He grabs another clam. He wears a wedding ring, and I wonder about his wife. Shy? Intellectual? Homemaker? I can't even guess. Dorsey looks over my shoulder out the window. "We pulled a body out of there a couple of weeks ago."

I turn to see. The window looks out over a defunct power dam in the river, where garbage collects at the edge of the falls. "I heard."

We focus on clams. I see Chip come in. Darn, I think. I don't want to give up the quiet pleasantness of working through a bowl of clams with Captain Dorsey.

CHAPTER 21

I t comes down to motive.

The blood-spattered rag is enough to tie Scud to Seth Coen's murder if we can establish a motive. Why did Scud want Seth dead? The answer, of course, is that Seth helped dispose of Zander Phippin's body, and when the body was uncovered, Scud needed to guarantee Seth's silence. So if we can prove that Scud and Seth actually murdered or at least disposed of Zander, then we also have Scud in Seth's murder.

But so far, our evidence for the Zander Phippin murder—tollbooth records, muddy boots, cigarette receipt, the telephone note in Scud's apartment—is all circumstantial. It's almost enough to convict in Zander's murder, but again, only if we have a strong motive. The motive is simple: Scud was working for whomever Zander was informing against. We just have to prove it.

From our table in the Rain Tree, Chip calls Upton, and they talk it through, then Chip hands the phone to Dorsey, and *they* talk it through. When Dorsey gets off the phone, he says, "We're bringing him in." He punches a number on his own phone. "I want a team to serve an arrest warrant. Possibility of violence," he says.

He gets up and hurries out the door. Chip and I watch him go. We order another bowl of clams.

"So I'm going to a retreat next spring," Chip says partway through the bowl of clams. I could ask him to explain, but I know if I just wait a moment, he'll continue on his own. He does. "It's about archetypal dream analysis."

"Archetypal?"

"You know, the self, the animus, the anima. Very Jungian.

Because dreams are, you know, the only reliable window to the subconscious."

"Oh. Well, that sounds . . ." I eat a clam because I'm not sure how to finish the sentence.

"It's at a little place in Vermont," he says.

"Fun."

"Nope. Wouldn't call it fun. I'd call it supportive. Supportive and enlightening."

Chip is becoming increasingly new-agey. Sometimes he even reminds me of Flora. "Love these clams," I say.

In the courtroom, Kendall Vance has one of the meth makers on the stand. He's a thirtyish guy, and with his black-framed glasses, he looks like a math major. He's wearing a bland suit, but his necktie is bright turquoise.

". . . not how you're usually dressed, is it?" Kendall asks.

"'Scuse me?"

"I mean your suit and tie. Aren't you currently in prison on charges of manufacturing methamphetamine?"

"No, sir."

"Oh, my mistake," Kendall says, eyeing the jury. "The government offered you a plea bargain of simple possession . . ."

"Yes."

"For cooperating?"

"Yes."

"And you haven't been sentenced yet, is that right?"

"Yes."

"So where'd you get the suit and tie?"

"Objection," Tina says, scoring one for the defense. I've seen whole trials, days of testimony, without a single objection. Hearing one just seconds after I walk into the courtroom tells me Tina's being baited into a slap-fest.

". . . government gave me the suit," he says, "but the tie is mine."

I walk through the swinging gate and scribble a note to Tina: "Don't get suckered into unnecessary objections."

Kendall stops whatever he's saying and stares at me. Seconds pass.

"Mr. Vance?" the judge says. (It's not Two Rivers, it's Washington.) "Mr. Vance, are you releasing the witness?"

"How many government bureaucrats does it take to convict this young woman?" Kendall says. He turns fully around to face the courtroom and holds his hands out toward three young girls sitting behind him in the first row. Tamika Curtis's daughters. They're all in tidy white dresses, hair in braided ponytails. One of them, the middle one, wears glasses. They remind me of Norman Rockwell's painting of young Ruby Bridges being escorted to school by four federal marshals—this is certainly intentional on Kendall's part. In the back row, I spot the graying woman in a dingy dress with a rhinestone brooch who is probably Tamika Curtis's mother. Kendall, no doubt, deemed her too ghetto and placed her back out of the spotlight.

"How about it, girls?" Kendall says. "Any notes you want to pass up to your mama?" He looks at the jury. There are two African-American men and one earthy-looking white woman with a braided ponytail. I'm betting Kendall is after eye contact with these three.

"Mr. Vance—"

"Because apparently, it's not enough the government has the laws and the agents and interrogators and all those secret prisons."

"Mr. Vance," Washington says wearily.

I retreat to the rear of the room. I like Washington. He's much older than Two Rivers, no giant of legal reasoning but a competent grocery-store-manager sort.

Kendall shakes his head in disgust. "So tell me, Mr. Mashburn," he says, "what is your understanding of the sentence you might have received if you hadn't cooperated with the government?"

"Objection. Hearsay," Tina says.

I go upstairs and wait for Chip to call and tell me Scud Illman is behind bars.

* * *

At four-thirty Janice buzzes. "Kendall Vance is outside at security. Should they let him in?"

No, I think. "Yes," I say. I go meet him in the hallway and bring him into my office. "Kendall," I say, "are you giving Tina a rough go?"

"You have subject and object reversed." He laughs.

"To what do I owe the pleasure?"

"You told me the other day you'd get back to me. I'm still waiting."

"Oh, cripes, Kendall, I'm sorry. It's been . . . busy."

"I'm teaching a class," Kendall says. "I'd like to invite you to speak. It's the professional responsibility class, evening division."

"Teaching a class. That's admirable." I immediately hate myself for saying it. Kendall's paying clients are scum-of-the-earth career criminals like Scud Illman, whom no ethical person would have anything to do with.

"We must all endeavor to pass our wisdom on to the next generation," he says.

"Are you wise, Kendall?"

"Wisdom is as wisdom does," he answers mysteriously.

"What do you have in mind?"

"Just a discussion. I find it useful to start the semester by getting students thinking about essentials before we get into lawyer advertising, fees, Chinese walls, diligence, confidentiality, and all that happy horseshit. A discussion of morality—legally speaking."

Kendall Vance is a kook, and his teaching a class on professional responsibility is like having someone who thinks he's Jesus Christ teach swimming *(The goal is to simply walk on top of the water, don't allow yourself to sink down into it.)*

"How shall we structure it?" I ask.

"Most basic questions first: I talk about defending the guilty, you talk about prosecuting the innocent."

"I don't prosecute the innocent."

"Of course you don't."

"I don't."

"Good. Then that's what you tell them."

"Be a short discussion."

"Oh, I imagine they'll have some questions. Like, let's talk about prosecuting Tamika Curtis. I've been trying to speak with you about this case for months, but you won't call back. Now we're in trial."

"Wrong guy, Kendall," I say. "This is Tina's case. Talk to her."

"I'm talking to you," he says, trumpeting an end to any pretext of cordiality. "This is bullshit."

"Just doing my job, Kendall. We busted up a meth operation, now people go to jail. That's how it works."

He stares at me.

"Listen," I say in a conciliatory voice, "I'm not the lady with the scales. I learned long ago to do my job and let someone else make the moral judgments. I don't have the stomach for it."

"So said the boys at Nuremberg."

"Go to hell."

"Truth hurts, eh, Nick?"

It's not the first time I've been here with Kendall Vance. Besides his scum-sucking paying clients, he takes a lot of these assigned cases, meaning he ends up with the defendants at the bottom of the food chain—the ones without money and nobody left to rat on. The strange thing about Kendall is that while he'll represent murderers and rapists and drug peddlers and all kinds of sociopaths, he won't represent any defendant in crimes against a child.

"What do you want from me?" I say while he smiles at me bitterly.

"Dismiss it. Go after Mashburn and his buddies with both barrels. Mashburn is the new up-and-comer. He's expanding his turf, diversifying his product line. Convict some criminals for a change, and stop picking on the victims."

I'm stunned by his audacity. "Counselor Vance, if you object to the current state of the law, then go get your self-righteous ass elected to something and change it, but don't come in here blaming me for the way it is. Because the way it is, is the way it is." I glare at him a moment, then shout, "Now get the hell out."

"Sure, Nick, but tell me, are you going to have Tamika's three little girls over to your house on Thanksgiving for the next ten years?"

My office door is open, and people are looking in. Tina appears, which works in Kendall's favor if he can get her rattled. He says, "Tina, come on in. We're just discussing Tamika Curtis and her boss, or should I say her slave master, Percy Mashburn. Tell me, which of them do you think is more evil?"

"You want security?" Tina asks me, ignoring Kendall.

"Just leave, Kendall."

"Or why not spend time looking for the kids who've disappeared from Rivertown?" he says. "Prosecute some perps for a change, and leave the victims alone."

"Oh, for Christ's sake, Kendall—"

Kendall's cell phone rings. He looks at it and steps out of the office.

Janice buzzes me. "Agent d'Villafranca for you, Nick."

I pick up.

"We've got Scud," Chip says. "Picked him up at home, everything smooth."

"At home? Was he alone?"

"The boy was there, but lucky the mother showed up so we didn't have to call Family Services."

"Yeah, lucky."

If I'd known they were taking him at home, I'd have nixed it. The kid seemed fragile: something about the lip scar and the two-tone iris.

"Do you want to come over?" Chip asks.

I do want to go over. Not that there's any official reason for me to be there; I just want to stick my face in front of Scud's homicidal, soon-to-be-convicted—hopefully condemned—smirk and gloat. "I'm on my way, Chip. Do you think he might spill?"

"I think he might."

At the elevators, I find Kendall on his phone, facing into the corner with a hand over his other ear. He's talking quietly, but now he raises his voice. "NO!" he shouts. "Don't say a goddamn thing before I get there."

* * *

On my way over to the FBI building, there's a bobble in the satisfaction I feel at finally having Scud Illman behind bars. It is Kendall's rant about Percy Mashburn. We don't have much info on him yet, but Mashburn's name has come up a lot, and I wonder if Kendall knows a few things about him. Mashburn might be the one to watch. As for Tamika Curtis, of course she's more victim than perpetrator, but she was involved in the meth lab, Mashburn offered her up to us, the FBI cut the deal, and the whole thing landed in a nicely wrapped package on my desk. Congress writes the law, not me and certainly not Kendall. I just enforce.

At the FBI, I find Chip watching as Scud Illman is booked. Scud doesn't seem so cocky anymore. Standing for his photograph and holding up the booking number, he is ashen and his hands tremble. What Scud knows, and what we know, is that he will never again draw breath as a free man. He's wearing a pullover with the sleeves pushed up above the elbows, and on his left forearm, I see the greenish-black tattoo of a dagger with curlicues around the hilt and drops of blood coming off the blade. It's the kind of thing tough guys get when they want a tat but don't have anything to say about themselves or about the world. There are lots of daggers, and mostly, you see them on the left forearm, meaning the guy did it himself out of boredom and in some sad attempt to ink over the niggling realization of his own smallness.

CHAPTER 22

B eyond the last row of seats, the back wall of the lecture hall bends around us like a peach-colored sunset. "I'll teach a course someday," I blurt.

"Absolutely," Kendall says. "The opportunity to give back and to sharpen your mind . . ."

I am pleasantly annoyed by Kendall. He has such an exaggerated sense of altitude on his moral hillock. He talks, and I tune out whatever the hell he's talking about. The class is a law school requirement established in the wake of Watergate, when every lawyer from Nixon on down turned out to be a crumb-bum.

The students come in and Kendall introduces me. I begin my talk with a description of the U.S. attorney's office and its workings. I mention a few interesting cases; I talk about a prosecutor's obligation to society. Kendall gives me a few minutes, then he interrupts: "This being a class on professional ethics," he says, "maybe you could talk about the ethical dilemmas you face."

"Prosecution is luxurious," I answer. "Unlike defense, where every defendant gets a lawyer, I only prosecute those I believe are guilty beyond a reasonable doubt. And Mr. Vance's claims notwithstanding, we don't prosecute the innocent."

"So there are no ethical dilemmas?" Kendall asks.

"No dilemmas like representing guilty and dangerous defendants."

"You dodge. Are there ethical dilemmas in prosecution?"

"No," I say, "no ethical dilemmas. We go where evidence directs, prosecute those we believe are guilty."

I know what Kendall wants; he wants me to pull a chair around backward, sit astride it, and confess my guts out. He wants to hear that I feel anguish over putting people in prison.

Kendall Vance, being a well-known defense lawyer, gets pro-filed in the paper sometimes. I've learned things about him. I've learned that he hates prosecutors; that he has a vendetta, because twenty-plus years ago, my employer, the DOJ, indicted Kendall's father on charges of fraud, racketeering, and tax evasion. "My father didn't have a dishonest bone in his body," Kendall was quoted as saying. But to fight it would have cost Kendall's father a fortune, and if he lost, he risked many years in prison. So Vance Sr. took the government's offer: He paid hefty fines, returned some government grants, and paid back-taxes. No prison. But the dam-age was done, and Vance Sr. suffered the demise of his health, his good name, and his liquidity. At age fifty-nine, with no other risk factors, he died of a stroke. And Kendall, who otherwise might have become a holier-than-thou, moralizing, humorless, ramrod-in-the-butt prosecutor, broke from his social stereotype and became a moralizing, humorless, ramrod-in-the-butt defense attorney. A true believer, the kind who, like I say, will take tens of thousands in legal fees for keeping some scum-sucking sociopath out of prison, then strain a shoulder patting himself on the back for upholding the Constitution.

Now Kendall wants to hear me confess to the anguish of pros-ecuting (or persecuting) all those defendants who really meant no harm. But I have nothing to confess, because the truth is, innocent defendants are rarer than, well, yellow rails. And what other source of moral anguish could there be?

"What about laws you don't agree with?" a student asks. She is sitting forward in her seat, dark hair in a long ponytail, wearing an earth-toned T-shirt with a logo I can't read but which I bet is for some environmental cause. I hadn't really noticed the students until now, but as I make eye contact with this assertive young lefty, the undifferentiated mass becomes differentiated. I do a quick scan. Men and women—some young, some less so. I find myself equat-ing all the women to versions of Lizzy or Flora or Cassandra. For the men, there are Zander and Kenny and the imaginary grown-up Toby, my son.

"Laws are laws," I say, "there is nothing to agree or disagree with."

"But can't you imagine some law you'd have trouble—"

"If you wish to make law," I say, "go into politics."

"Blind obedience," someone calls out, and I reply, "Overstated. Most prosecutions are clear-cut: murder, robbery, extortion, exploitation, fraud, trade in endangered species. You want to take issue with any of those? And if, once in a blue moon, I have to suspend some moral position, and I'm not saying I do, then it's just the price of my privilege to represent all the laws I believe in."

"*Sieg heil!*" This time it is a male voice. I ignore him, but the guy goes on. "Because if you willy-nilly prosecute everyone—"

"I don't willy-nilly prosecute anyone."

"Do you believe in mandatory minimum sentencing?"

"My personal beliefs aren't at issue."

"Moral abdication," the guy says.

"Well," I say, "I guess you can call it what you like."

"What do you call it?" a different voice asks, and I'm about to answer testily that I call it my job, but I catch myself. The students are having fun. I used to like this stuff, but now the questioners just seem naive, and the whole discussion amounts to nothing more than farting in a mitten while there is real-life shit going on in the world. I'm fed up with the snail's pace of this prosecution, and with the timidity of do-nothings like Judge Two Rivers. I scan the students. They are all Zanders and Cassandras, eager to live their lives. They want sunny beaches and red wine and good sex and children and dogs and soft cheese and sleepy Saturday mornings. They want to write letters to the editor and to see them in print, they want to ski at Steamboat, cruise to the Galápagos, make their parents proud, get old. Maybe they want to see a yellow rail. And what do I want? At this moment I want to kill Scud Illman. I think of a death sentence recounted by Dickens—drawing and quartering a prisoner, then eviscerating him and dropping his entrails in the fire.

But there is a question in the air, and I'm expected to address it: *What do you call it?* someone asked. *It.* That endless stream of statutory language, the criminal code of the United States, pattering into our lives as ignorable and continuous as rain on a metal roof. I see Kendall Vance watching me, amused at my silence, because he's a courtroom lawyer and a teacher and an ex–Navy SEAL. And here's me, hapless administrator, proxy for the big bad feds who did Kendall's daddy wrong. I want to say to him, *Let's have it out. You and me. Right here in class.* Proxy to proxy, because if I'm the United States, then Kendall is Scud Illman. The oddsmakers would favor Kendall a thousand to one, because he's probably killed men with his bare hands. He's trained for it: where to jab, squeeze, twist. But at this moment, with a roomful of Zanders and Cassandras, I believe I could come at him like a beast unhinged, a blur, all murderous parts cut loose from reason. And I just might win.

Cut loose from reason.

"The law," I say to the class, and I have to stop and take a deep breath to steady a catch in my voice. "The law is reason. Reason! It is the reins of reason on the horse of emotion. Think about it."

Discussion proceeds. My wave of emotion subsides, and I am again the dispassionate prosecutor. Law *is* the reins of reason. Without it, we would all be vigilantes or victims.

The focus shifts to Kendall. There is one question that defense lawyers always get asked. It comes in a thousand forms and all levels of sophistication. Grade-schoolers ask it and Supreme Court justices ask it: *How can you defend those people?* The discussion bounces around for several minutes, becoming more and more focused, until one student hones it to its essence. He asks Kendall, "Are you ever tempted to do less than your best? To throw the case?"

The question is repulsive to Kendall, and I fear for the student who asked it. He has asked the commando whether treason is a viable option. But commando Kendall maintains his cool. What Kendall says, his voice tense with emotion, is this: "I don't defend criminals, I defend principles. To defy those principles, to turn traitor on a defendant, would violate everything I believe in. I'd rather die."

The conversation moves off this point, and though we transition into a discussion about grand juries and indictments, I'm still thinking through the positions Kendall and I have staked out. To me, a prosecutor, the greatest sin is a failure of objectivity; to Kendall, a defense attorney, the biggest sin is a failure of loyalty.

CHAPTER 23

Wednesday. It's a teachers' in-service day, so the schools are closed. Lizzy is camped out in my office again, surrounded by the paraphernalia of her teenhood. "Go visit Kenny," I say. "I need to make some calls."

I call Hollis Phippin. "We've made an arrest. Scud Illman, the suspect I told you about. We took him yesterday."

"How does it look?" Hollis asks. His diction is razor-sharp. This is the third time we've spoken, and I'm still surprised by how firm his voice is. I expect to hear grief on the surface just as, when I met him at Zander's memorial, I expected a graying wreck of a man leaning heavily on a cane. He was none of that. He remained stoically at the side of his devastated wife, receiving sympathies, giving quiet instructions to the caterers.

"It looks very good," I tell Hollis. I brief him on the evidence, keeping the doubt to myself, but he spots it.

"Sounds thin," he says.

"It is. But it's early. We'll convict him, Hollis, you'll see."

Hollis is right, though. The case isn't clear-cut, and unless we come up with more physical evidence, it relies too heavily on the Bureau's ability to put together a show of Mob involvement. Unfortunately, our best case against Scud isn't for Zander's murder, it's for Seth Coen's murder. But as of yesterday, when I saw that tattoo of a dagger on Scud's arm, I've begun to think our best evidence, the bloody rag, is no evidence at all.

When I hang up, I decide to go and resolve what's bothering me. Lizzy and I drive to the FBI building, and Chip meets us at security and takes us into his office. The place is just like the U.S. attorney's offices. Special agents are in the windowed offices, support staff in cubicles. We leave Lizzy in the office, and Chip walks me down to the evidence room in the basement. I sign the required registers, then a couple of minutes later, I'm holding a plastic bag marked with identifying notations. Inside is a dirty, crumpled rag spattered with Seth Coen's blood.

Our assumption has been that, for all his painstaking care in cleaning the bathroom where Seth Coen was dismembered, Scud forgot to dispose of the rag he used for wiping blood spatter from his own face. Somehow, instead of being tossed into a landfill with all the other bloodied clothes, this rag was crumpled into a pocket and later ended up in the laundry area of Scud Illman's home.

I'm wearing surgical gloves. I open the evidence bag and take out the rag. It is speckled with rusty droplets of blood, which, according to our DNA analysis, belonged to Seth Coen. But more prevalent than the blood are large green-black splotches of ink. It is just what I expected to find and hoped I wouldn't. I can hear my heart pounding in my ears, and for an insane instant, I think of what I could do to redeem this worthless soiled rag. Smuggle in an otherwise clean hankie spattered with blood of my own. Do the switch. DNA analysis has already been run, it's unlikely they'll do it again. We just need a rag with blood spatter and no ink; how simple it would be. Yet through the raging disappointment and criminal temptation, I envision the scene. It is incongruously tender: Scud Illman and Seth Coen, sitting at the kitchen table in Scud's house. Maybe Scud's wife sits with them; maybe Scud's stepson, Colin, watches TV in the living room. They put a towel on the table, and Seth lays his hand on it. *It's been a few years,* Scud says as he prepares the needle and ink. Seth is only a few days out of the oppressive prison culture, and here's Scud offering this act of generosity. First, for no particular reason, Scud traces the design with his forefinger, and maybe that gentle, even affectionate contact makes their nerves tinge with unaccustomed emotion. It quiets them. Now Scud, needle in hand, closes the sides of that wretched brand, and as he works, he rests his free hand on Seth's arm.

Two misfits, Seth and Scud. Scud keeps a rag on hand, blotting the droplets of blood that surface on Seth's skin as the swastika is closed up, dot by dot, until, to the casual observer, it's just a window. When they're done, Scud crumples up the blotter rag and tosses it into his laundry pile.

TMU pushes an index finger against his lips. "It's dicey," he says, rocking in his desk chair. Though he is my mentor in career matters, I'm usually his adviser on prosecutorial details. Today I'm here asking him what to do. There was barely enough evidence as it was, but without the bloodied rag, we have nothing linking Scud to Seth's murder and barely anything linking him to Zander's.

"What do you think we should do?" TMU asks.

"Release him."

TMU nods. "We have to protect your position."

"My position?"

"The circuit bench. Cut your losses now. You don't want to lose this one in trial." He nods in agreement with himself.

I shift on my feet in a way that asks whether he is done and I can leave. He ignores it. "Could the guy be innocent?" he asks. He stares at me with lips pressed tight. I stare back, and we hold for a few seconds, then he explodes in delighted self-amusement. "Got you," he says, and finally, I relax enough to sit down in one of his wing chairs.

Good joke, the idea of Scud's innocence. What TMU means, in his avuncular way, is that our error—if it was an error at all to arrest Scud when we did—was merely a strategic one. The question isn't whether he's guilty. Of course he's guilty. The question is how best to convict him.

"Is it really so clear-cut?" TMU asks, meaning the rag. It's tempting to keep quiet and let a jury decide whether Scud Illman used it to wipe the blood droplets from Seth's tattoo or the splatter from a dismembered corpse. "I mean, we don't need to do the defense's job for them. Right?"

I shake my head. "Too risky."

"Okay," he says approvingly, "take care of it."

And with that, we're back to our usual roles: me advising, TMU deciding.

Scud is transported back to the FBI building. Kendall meets us there. Lizzy waits in Chip's office. Sparky gets set up. We ask Scud the questions obliquely, and he delivers a narrative of doctoring Seth Coen's tattoo to disguise the swastika, just as I imagined. "Did he pay you?" I ask Scud, for no other reason than that I want to know.

Scud looks up at me. The smirk is nearly absent from his unfortunate features. " 'Course not," he says. "There's some things you don't charge a guy for. 'Specially a friend."

Chip, Dorsey, Kendall, and I go into a conference room. It's agreed. We'll release him. Kendall is gracious.

On our drive over to the Rain Tree for a late lunch, my phone rings and I see it's Kendall. I answer.

"You did the right thing," he says.

"No right or wrong," I say. "We do what the evidence requires."

"Anyway. Listen, I need to talk to you. Can I swing by your office? It won't take long."

"Talk now."

"Better in person."

"Yeah, well, my daughter and I are going out to lunch."

"Teachers' professional day? Me, too. How old's yours?"

"Fourteen."

"Mine's sixteen. Where are you going?"

"The Rain Tree," I say before it occurs to me to obfuscate.

"Meet you there," he says, and he hangs up. I'm not sure what just happened, whether I invited them to join us or not. I don't want him there, and Lizzy certainly won't. She's about twelve years beyond the point where I could shove her in front of any little boy or girl her age and expect enthusiasm. I should warn her, but I don't feel like suffering her annoyance, so we ride along quietly, Lizzy in her own world and me in mine.

Kendall comes in the door of the Rain Tree, and immediately, I see there'll be no problem with Lizzy resenting the intrusion. The grinning teenager who follows Kendall has Down syndrome, and at this moment something I know about my own daughter breaks through from my subconscious into full recognition. Namely, Lizzy is all about compassion. It's what motivates her.

Kendall introduces his daughter as Kaylee.

"Where do you go to school, Kaylee?" Lizzy asks.

"No school today!" Kaylee answers, beaming at Lizzy through thick glasses.

"Are you at work with your dad?"

"He's working. I'm just with him."

"Me, too. I'm staying with my dad today, too."

"Because there's no school!"

"Right. I've got an okay dad. Do you have an okay dad?"

Kaylee turns and studies Kendall. "Sometimes," she says, and we all laugh.

The waitress comes. Kendall says he and Kaylee aren't staying, he just wants to chat for a couple of minutes. Lizzy asks for children's place mats and crayons, and when the waitress brings them, she and Kaylee get busy coloring. The mats have a drawing of the Rokeby Mills building with the river and flowers and the Rain Tree Grill with people standing in front. There is one figure in a wheelchair.

"I love to color," Lizzy says.

"Me, too," Kaylee says.

"What's this about?" I ask Kendall, resisting the impulse to act like he and I are best buddies because our daughters are coloring together.

"Scud Illman knows people," Kendall says. "I don't know how much is trash talk. He likes to act important, like nothing goes on in this city that he doesn't know about."

Kendall and I are leaning in toward each other so the girls can't hear. It's cozier than I want to be with an opposing counsel—or at least cozier than I like being with Kendall Vance. I don't mind whispered conversation, but when my vision goes blue with the smell of the guy's Aqua Velva, it's too much.

I straighten up. "Yeah, well. This isn't a matter of trash talk. It's premeditated you-know-what." I glance at the girls.

"No, no," Kendall says. "What do you think, that I'm here to convince you my guy didn't do it? Fu— Screw that. That's not why I'm here. Listen to me. Forget Scud Illman—"

"Forget him? What the hell?"

"*Arguendo,* counselor. For what I'm here to talk about, forget him. Okay? He's a mouthpiece, that's all. I thought you might want to hear what he's saying."

"What's he saying?"

"That there're things going on."

"Things?"

"Like maybe the locals think they're in Colombia or Sicily."

"That's vague, Kendall, let me get it straight: Your client says that—"

"No. He doesn't say, he intimates."

"Your client intimates there are plans—"

"No plans. Just chatter. Noise. A surge of."

"Intimidation or retaliation, or just obstruction?"

He shrugs. "I don't know what to call it. Scud says things like this: 'So I hear from an associate of mine whose name will remain nameless that some guy whose name I don't know but who my associate calls Bulldog, he hears from him that some guys are feeling cramped and want to clear a little space around themselves.'" Kendall uses a whispery, sinister voice for imitating Scud. "Another time he might say, 'Schnair is bad news for people trying to do business in this town, but the times, they are a-changing.' See what I mean? Nothing to really get your teeth into. Just background. Like when you were searching his home, he said to me, 'So that's the famous Uptown Cruthers,' and I asked him what's so famous about Upton, and Scud says, 'Nothing yet. But I've heard talk about guys wanting to make him famous, if you know what I mean.'"

I glance over at the girls. They're oblivious to us. Kaylee has her mouth half open and her tongue spread flat across the bottom lip, eyelids squinted down in fierce concentration as she outlines the wheelchair in silver. Lizzy leans toward Kaylee and whispers some bit of praise for Kaylee's work.

"Why are you telling me this? Why not the Bureau? And aren't you violating confidentiality?"

"I'm telling you because he asked me to," Kendall says.

I exhale contemptuously.

"It's true. Scud always says, 'And you can tell that to Nick Davis.' 'You can tell Nick Davis that I hear from an associate of mine whose name shall remain blah, blah, blah.' See, I think you have it all wrong, Nick. Scud isn't bragging or threatening. He wants you to know that he might be useful."

"What are we talking about, Kendall?"

"I guess that's still up in the air, isn't it?" he says. "We were thinking maybe you guys would like an informant on the street. Someone to let you know just what's going on, what's what, and who's who. Somebody who knows the life."

"Scud isn't the kind of guy we're interested in working with."

"He could be like that Maxy character from way back."

"What do you know about Maxy?"

"Nothing. This is all just a thought. Though I've heard rumors lately that Maxy is back and stirring up trouble."

"Yup, and I spotted Elvis this morning."

"Just repeating what I hear, counselor. But back to Scud Illman: Talk it over with the Bureau. Call me."

I'm repulsed by the thought of flipping Scud Illman to our side. I'd like to get away from Kendall, but Lizzy and I are here for lunch. It's Kendall and Kaylee who are squatting. I straighten up, putting a few more inches between us.

The girls are still coloring. Lizzy is painstaking, Kaylee less so.

Liz looks at Kaylee's picture and says, "Oooh. I like that green in the sky."

"When does Tamika Curtis resume?" I ask.

"First thing tomorrow," he says, "and you know, counselor, you're really on the wrong side of that one."

I ignore him, and we wait a few seconds for the unpleasantness to pass. Then I say, "What's your impression of that trooper Tina had on the stand—Officer Penhale?"

"He strikes me as kind of a weasel. What's your interest?"

"Just curious."

I shouldn't have asked Kendall's opinion. As soon as he gives it, I dismiss it. Defense lawyers are suspicious of cops.

My own interest in Penhale is that he was there that day. He met Cassandra and drove her home from the reservoir. In the question of who leaked Cassandra's name, everyone's a suspect.

When I get back to the Federal building, I pop into TMU's office to brief him on my talk with Kendall. I laugh bitterly at the idea of using Scud as an informant. TMU doesn't laugh with me.

CHAPTER 24

Friday morning. Printers humming, fresh coffee. The cleaning staff came through last night, and the place is sparkly. Tonight Lizzy will stay with Flora out in Turner, so I'll be on my own—a thought that blossoms with possibility as I pass Tina's door with my cup of coffee. She's studying some file with an intensity that surrounds her like quills on a porcupine. But I brave it. "How's Curtis going?"

"Is that a joke?"

"What's the problem?"

"Kendall. He's got a string of bogus rebuttal witnesses a mile long. Judge Washington disqualifies most of them, but each one gives Kendall a chance to speechify about the unfairness of it all. It's a smokescreen defense, and Washington's letting him get away with it. Should have been a two-day trial. We're up to four with no end in sight."

"Is he going to put on a defense?"

"God knows."

"Anything I can do?"

"Yeah. Go away."

The blossom of possibility wilts.

TMU calls me. "Nick, Special Agent Neidemeyer wants a conference on the Avery Illman character."

"Can you stall him?"

Neidemeyer is the section chief. He runs the FBI office here. A conference can only mean that the Bureau is considering offering Scud a deal.

"What's to gain by delaying?" TMU asks.

"Conviction, that's what. I don't want this guy getting immunity.

Believe me, Harold, he's not a guy you want to be doing business with."

"Yeah, well, look, Neidemeyer has a lot of manpower invested in this investigation, and it's not paying off. He could solve it in a second, bring Illman inside, make a couple of big arrests with Illman's help, and maybe close a file."

"Just delay, Harold, okay? Maybe we'll find Illman's car."

"From what I hear, Nick, the car's probably a two-foot block of steel on a freighter to Shanghai."

"Delay, Harold."

"I'll do what I can, Nick, but think days, not weeks. Are you free for lunch later?"

"Sure."

"Good. We'll order sandwiches. Join me in my office."

He hangs up. The idea of immunity is nuts. Scud is a guy who'll try anything to improve his position. This informant angle doesn't surprise me. What's next? Dorsey and Chip both have their people beating the bushes. We're all aching to bring Scud down. Problem is, we haven't been able to place him inside of anything significant or with anyone important. His criminal record is for diddly one- and two-person operations. He did seven years for armed robbery of a liquor store and another four years for assault with a dangerous weapon: To wit, he took a shovel to the head of a coworker on a construction project. He got lucky on that one, because the guy whose skull he creased was an illegal alien, and the sentencing judge, whose politics inhabit a region beyond Pluto, seemed to think Scud deserved some kind of medal.

Everything else in his record is small stuff. Misdemeanors, dropped charges, and investigations without indictment. No doubt he does little jobs and low-risk work, but except for Zander Phippin, it doesn't look like he's cracked the big time.

Zander Phippin was a big-time hit. The state narcotics team determined that most of the pot running into the city was from a single source. It's worth millions, and Zander, having moved up in the scheme of things, was just below the break between little guys and big guys. Zander and everyone below him was small-time: naughty but not bad. Above Zander, though, were real criminals: big-time dealers, murderers, and racketeers. That's why we wanted his help; that's why they needed him dead. It was very much a big-time hit.

A half hour after my conversation with TMU, Dorsey calls. "We've got Scud Illman's car," he says.

The car, a five-year-old Sentra, was under a tarp behind a barn forty miles north of town. "The couple who owns the barn are clean," Dorsey says. "Scud gave them a story about going off to work in the oil fields in Kuwait."

This is why Scud is bush-league. If he were the kind of guy who could really get things done, the car never would have turned up.

"What have you found?" I ask.

"Lots. Blood in the trunk. We've sent it to the lab. There's a problem with the tires, though. They don't match any of the impressions we took at the reservoir. We went to every pullout on the east side that day last summer. We got dozens of treads. This car doesn't match any of them."

"Sure," I say, "but that's consistent with how clean the whole job was. Everything was swept."

"Exactly," Dorsey says. "Treads or no treads, you can't argue with a trunk full of blood. Dollars to doughnuts, it's Phippin's blood. Who needs a splattered hankie now?"

"How did you find the car?"

"The old guy who owns the barn got suspicious and called in the plate."

"Lucky break."

He laughs. "That's police work, Nick," and he hangs up. It's the first time he's called me Nick.

TMU has corned beef, and I eat a salad while rain pounds at the window. "You're on the list," he says, casually tucking a napkin into his shirt collar. "Now the fun starts." The list he refers to is the list of nominees for the circuit court position. "Of course, Crutchfield isn't actually leaving till March, so anything can change."

With his first bite of sandwich, a glob of mustard lands on the napkin that forms a ledge over his belly.

"You're a dark horse, naturally."

"Naturally."

"Heavy hitters on the list. Leslie Herstgood, Two Rivers . . ."

"Give me a break."

"I know. Snowball in hell, right? But the same factors favoring you, favor Two Rivers."

"Being?"

"It's a small, rural, out-of-the-limelight region. The president can make a feel-good appointment without giving anything up. Two Rivers feels good as a minority appointment and a paean to the Defendants' Rights crowd. Then, when Two Rivers starts issuing flaky dissents, the president acts betrayed and gets a walk on his next reactionary appointment to one of the urban circuits, or even the Supreme." Harold opens up his sandwich and spreads horseradish.

"What about me?" I ask. "Why am I a feel-gooder?"

"Serious?"

"Yes."

"You're a dedicated prosecutor who, over the decades, has molded his office into a clean, mean, convicting machine, staying on as guardian of the public trust instead of chasing big bucks into the offices of some white-shoe firm. We can get the newspaper to run a profile, dredge up the country-lawyer stuff. The everyman hero."

I laugh. It's the triumph of perception over reality. But from here in TMU's office, I can see the river and the Rokeby and other brick mills all closed up, and I think, Why not? I *have* been here. When I came on as head of the criminal division, the city was still reeling, making itself believe some factory or new industry would open again. But in the realignment of economic reality, new versus old economies, the end of welfare, the rise of the tech age, rise of meth, rise of crack, the prizing apart of the economic strata, who has been here to keep the peace?

Me.

I've never spoken this, and I feel silly even thinking it, but it's a pretty good song and dance for whoever wants to plead my case.

"How can I improve my odds?"

TMU chuckles. "Keep convicting people. And if anybody talks to you, do the country-lawyer thing that worked for you up north. Your résumé can't compete with the likes of Leslie and Two Rivers, and you haven't written much. You're a blank slate. We draw what we want. What I want, what will get you the bench, is the hayseed lawyer who's all dedication and folksy wisdom with no venal ambitions of your own. Go be it."

Captain Dorsey calls again after lunch. "Nick, get this," he says, brimming with excitement. "We've got a match to the tire treads of Scud Illman's car, but it's from a parking lot on the west side of the reservoir. That's almost a two-hour drive from where we found Zander Phippin."

"The west side?" I say, baffled. This makes no sense. The reservoir fills a narrow north/south valley in an area of few roads. While the reservoir itself averages under a mile across, it can take hours to drive from one shore to the other. "They must have been scouting for where to dig."

"Exactly. Dollars to doughnuts, they encountered someone over there and decided it was too crowded, drove over to the east side."

"West side," I say. "I'm surprised you even took tire prints there."

"We didn't," Dorsey says. "It was the rabbit fuzz."

"Pardon?"

"Game warden. Someone was jacking deer over on the west side, so at the same time we were taking tire prints on the east shore, the game warden was taking them on the west. The lab made the connection. They compare tire prints as a matter of protocol."

"Lucky. But if the blood in the trunk checks out, it's all beside the point. Goodbye, circumstantial, hello, direct physical."

"And goodbye, Scud," Dorsey says.

I buzz Upton and ask him to come talk to me. Usually, I just walk into his office, but once in a while, I make him bow to the king.

"What's up?" he says, appearing in my doorway in his studied, jacket-off, tie-loosened way.

I brief him on the new developments. He makes his way to a chair and settles in.

"What's wrong?" I ask.

"Nothing."

"You look like I just ran over your dog."

"Domestic. Pay it no mind."

"Shall I take you out for coffee? Get the lowdown?"

"Heehee." He chuckles without joy. "I'm booked. But if you're really aching for some vicarious woe, maybe next week."

"Pick a day and pencil me in. Are we talking marital or parental woe? I'm experienced in both."

"Next week."

He stands to leave, but I stop him. "About Scud," I say.

"Yes. Good news," he says without feeling, and I see that poor Upton is really into it, whatever it is.

"This time, when we lock him up," I say, "we're not letting him out again."

Upton drops back into the chair. "I hear talk of immunizing him?"

"Yeah. Can you believe it? It's bullshit. We've got a career criminal on first-degree capital murder, and the Bureau wants to offer him something. The guy's a con man."

"I don't know," Upton says. "Everything indicates he's small change, but maybe he can lead us someplace."

"Not you, too."

"Eyes on the ball, boss."

"Capital murder is the ball," I snap, "and besides, he can't provide anything valuable."

"The Bureau seems to think otherwise."

"Well, when blood results come back from Scud's car, the Bureau can kiss my ass, 'cause I can put Zander Phippin in the trunk of Scud's car, I can put the car at the reservoir, I can put Seth Coen at the reservoir, and I can put Scud with Seth Coen."

"What if Scud loaned Seth the car?"

I stop. I try resolving this question, and I can't.

"That's right," Upton says, "we haven't put Scud himself at the reservoir. I think we should consider using him."

I stare at him. Something's amiss. Upton is the scrappiest one of the bunch. Sometimes I have to keep him on a leash, but here he is, sounding like someone's grandmother. Maybe he's sore that I took over the case. Or maybe he senses change on the wind and he's positioning himself. TMU and Judge Washington are both getting old, and I might be going off to the circuit bench. Jobs are opening up. It's not in Upton's interest to piss off the Bureau. He and I are good friends but not close friends. Allegiances shift. I need to be wary of him for the time being.

"True enough," I say with false cheer that I'm sure he sees through. "Let's see what the lab says about the blood. Then we'll have a powwow and hammer this out."

Upton leaves, looking as miserable as when he came in. Something's clearly out of wack. He doesn't seem at all interested in seeing Scud convicted, and lately, his formerly indelible smile has become cheek-bitten. Something is eating him, and it seems connected to this case. I don't believe it has anything to do with some problem he's having at home.

CHAPTER 25

Lizzy and I are driving north. I left the office late and rode the glacial traffic to Turner, picked up Liz, went grocery shopping, and now we're driving into the night. The wipers are *smack-smack*ing and the defogger is blowing, and I'm driving slowly because it's a real rainstorm and visibility is lousy.

"Potato salad or coleslaw?" Lizzy asks. She wears a headlamp and is dishing dinner from half-quart takeouts while I drive.

"Potato."

She hands me a plate. I set it on my thighs.

"Any news?" she asks.

"Yes. We'll have an arrest again any day. Maybe any minute. We're waiting for blood results."

"Cassandra's?"

"No."

"The guy in the woods?"

"Yes."

Silence. Then, "I never believed in capital punishment."

"I know."

"But this one. When you've met somebody . . ."

"I know."

Silence again. Then, "I never understood what you do before."

"This isn't really what I do, sweetheart."

"Of course it is," she says. "You just usually do it more from behind a desk."

More silence. Later, this time in a lighter voice, "That lawyer who works for you . . ."

"Many lawyers work for me."

"You know. Tina."

"Yes. What about her?"

"I don't know."

"Did you like her?"

"She likes dogs."

I thought of suggesting to Tina that she might enjoy getting out of town and driving up to spend Saturday with Lizzy and me at the lake. But with Tina breathing fire over Kendall's antics in the Tamika Curtis case, I thought better of it.

The road is smooth and winding. My headlights cut a narrow cone into the darkness, and Arthur Rubeinstein caresses out a hypnotic piano sonata on the stereo. Lizzy is silent, and I think she's asleep, but then she says, "There are three kinds."

I wait.

"There're the ones where you know right away. Like Anna K. and Vronsky. Or Romeo and Juliet. And then there're the ones where, like, never in a million years, thank you very much! And then there're all the ones in the middle: maybe yes, maybe no."

"You're a pretty wise girl."

"Cassandra was the first kind. And so was Mommy."

And they all end tragically.

"Mom has told me," Lizzy says. "She says if it hadn't been for baby Toby . . ."

"Yeah, well . . ."

Silence.

Lizzy says, "I hope I only have girls."

This makes me wonder how much Flora has told her about Toby. More than I have, certainly, but less than everything. I say, "Times have changed, babe: amnio and everything. You can tell a lot before they're born; make your decisions."

Quiet.

"Anyway," she says, "the lawyer, Tina, I figure she's in the 'it could go either way' group. And that's okay with me."

"Lizzy! She just works for me."

"No, Dad. She doesn't *just* work for you."

Quiet again. She curls into the seat, and a minute later, I hear the rhythmic breathing, and she is gone. I wonder how much longer she'll be content to spend weekends at the lake with her dad.

Later. My cell rings. I see it is Kendall. I could ignore it, but he probably wants to tell me how impressed he was with Lizzy and how much Kaylee liked her. I answer. "Hi, Kendall."

"Listen," he growls, then he says something about Scud Illman, but I can't make it out. He sounds wrong; his voice is gravelly and choked. I ask him to repeat it. "Scud Illman didn't kill anyone," he says.

I hadn't pegged Kendall as a drinker, and I haven't heard anything about it on the grapevine, but in an instant everything I think about him changes. The swagger, the calculating professionalism, the sanctimony: They're all cover for a soul in pain, and it must be getting to the critical point for him to let his guard down like this—to call opposing counsel after-hours, not with a legal argument or new evidence but with some empty claim of innocence.

"Kendall," I say as compassionately as I can, "Kendall. Friend. It's okay. You're doing a good job for him. Better than he deserves, no doubt. And Tamika Curtis. Man! I'm betting the jury will hang on that. Yes, sir! So why don't you go get some sleep, and we'll talk in the morning. Okay?"

"What have you got against Scud? Why are you so convinced?" he moans.

"Kendall . . ."

"It wasn't me. Why are you convinced it was me? I'm just a guy trying to feed my family, same as you. So leave me the fuck alone."

Something is amiss. This isn't Kendall. "What do you know?" I ask to keep him talking.

He says something, but the cell connection is poor, and I miss it. "Couldn't hear you," I say.

"I'm innocent," he yells. "I'll tell you. Tell you everything. I know everything. Jesus H. I know and I'll tell, but everybody says it's your call."

"Everybody who?"

"Upton, for one. And my worthless lawyer, for another."

"Scud," I say, "did you steal Kendall Vance's phone?"

"I borrowed it."

"You shouldn't be talking to me."

"Then who the hell should I talk to? I need immunity."

"I'm hanging up now."

"No! Listen to me." He's sobbing. "There's things I know."

"What do you know?"

"I know who I fucking work for, for one thing."

"Who do you work for?"

He answers, but again the cell phone blinks out. "Scud, who do you work for?"

"Mercy," he begs in his garbled, drunken voice.

"Mercy? What mercy did you show Zander Phippin or Cassandra Randall?" I say quietly, not intending him to hear.

"I need immunity," he sobs. "I mean, Seth was going to tell you, but he wasn't a two-time loser. No skin off his ass. But I can't do the time, man. Let me talk. I'll talk your fucking ear off. Upton said he'd take care of it, and now he says no."

"Upton? How do you know anything about Upton?"

"We do some business?"

"What the hell . . ."

"You got to fucking protect me, man." He breaks down. I wait. He composes himself. "Will you?" he asks.

"Will I what?"

"Give me protection? Immunity?"

"It isn't that simple, Mr. Illman, and even if it were, no, I wouldn't agree."

"You son of a bitch," he screams, "I know you. I know where you live, I know your car, I know that little sexpot daughter of yours."

Now he has my attention. I reach over and put a hand on Lizzy's knee. "Daddy," she says without waking up.

"Scud," I say, "you're drunk, and you're saying things you shouldn't say. Here's what I want you to do, okay? You know what I look like, right? We've met, right? So I want you to picture my face. Right now. Close your eyes and picture my face. Okay? You got me? Scud, have you got me?"

"Yeah," he says warily.

"Good. Now look at my right eye. See my right eye?"

"Yeah."

"Okay, now make it wink. Did it wink? Scud, did you see me wink at you?"

"What's this about, asshole?"

"Answer the question, scumbag, did I wink at you?"

"Okay, asshole, so I tell you I saw it. I saw you wink. Now what?"

"That's great," I say gently. "You've seen the future. Because when you're strapped to the gurney and they open the curtains for the happy spectators who've come to see you die, you look over, and I'll be right there in the front row, and you watch. When they hit the button, you watch me. I'll wink. And that'll be the last thing you ever see in your miserable excuse for a life. Our inside joke, okay?"

We're off the highway, winding through the hills alongside the Aponak River, which is swelling and rushing with all the runoff.

I hang up and pull off the road into a wayside. There is a sheltered picnic table. I leave the car running and stand under the shelter. The air is cold.

I call Upton and get his voice mail. Though I was calm and rational with Scud, as I say the words "threatened my daughter" on Upton's voice mail, the idea of it spreads through me like an electrical jolt. "Threatened her," I say again, and I hear the note of hysteria rising in my voice. "I'll kill him," I say, my voice trembling. "If he ever comes within ten miles of Lizzy, I'll kill him with no more thought than squashing an ant. I'll wipe him off my shoe like dog shit."

I hang up. The frustration of getting Upton's voice mail and not Upton himself fuels this rage. I call Chip. He answers, and as I repeat the story, I can see Lizzy in the car. In her sleep, the incipient adulthood disappears from her features, and she is again my blameless child. She looks so much like Toby. Her cheeks and forehead are smooth and free of cares, and her slightly parted lips silently speak of a child's vulnerability. She sleeps so soundly because in her child-like way, despite the horrors of Cassandra's murder and Zander's exhumation, she still unconsciously assumes that the ferociousness of Flora's and my love for her is an invincible swaddle that will keep her safe. There is nothing I wouldn't do to protect this child.

"Calm down, Nick," Chip says. "Take some breaths."

I yell—no words, just sound. *Aaaaaaa,* in revolt against the idea of anything that would trespass on her perfect innocence.

"Take a breath."

"Don't tell me to calm down," I yell. "I don't care if I spend the rest of my life in jail. I'll finish him."

"Breathe with me, Nick," Chip says. "Breathe slowly: in, and hold, and out, and hold, and in, and hold."

Because Chip is so calm, and because I trust him, especially knowing that he is emerging from his own dark night of the soul, I do breathe with him, and the mindless rage and hysteria start to diminish.

Chip is silent. My ragged breathing smooths out. I am embarrassed.

"It's okay, Nick," he says in his laconic way. "It's okay."

"Yes."

"Scud just committed a federal crime, didn't he? By threatening you, I mean. We'll go pick him up. Do you want protection meanwhile?"

I think about this. The moment of hysteria has passed, leaving me a little dopey. I know Scud isn't really a threat to Lizzy or me. Besides, he has no idea where we are. "No," I say to Chip, "Lizzy and I are on our way to the lake. And he was just spouting."

"You're sure?"

"I'm sure," I say. "And Chip, that stuff I said about killing Scud . . ."

"What's that, Nick? I remember nothing of the sort."

"Thanks," I say.

"Do this," Chip says. "Let's make a record. Call me back, and I won't answer, and you get my voice mail and recite the exact particulars of your conversation while it's fresh. We've got the son of a bitch."

I ask Chip to inform Kendall of Scud's new crime, and of the whereabouts of Kendall's cell phone, then I settle back in for the drive.

Two things are bothering me. Not Scud's threats—I don't take those seriously. He's the kind of guy who considers intimidation and threats of violence to be standard conversation, right along with "What's happening?" and "How's the weather out your way?" Not that I'm excusing it, especially since he committed the unforgivable sin of bringing Lizzy into it, and especially since he's done his homework on me with the intent of getting some leverage. One thing that bothers me is what Scud said about Upton—that they talk and they're involved in something together. I decide to keep this to myself and talk to Upton about it later. But the main thing bothering me is that when he sobbed out his innocence, when he begged for mercy, he *sounded* innocent. I kind of wanted to believe him. If it weren't for the blood in his car and the tire prints at the reservoir . . . Hell, maybe he *did* loan the car to someone. Maybe I should at least have the conversation with him about immunity.

He'll get locked up over the weekend on charges of threatening a federal officer. By Monday or Tuesday, we'll have blood results. Then we'll talk, get a feel for what he can tell us and how involved he is. I'm available to be convinced. And at some point, when he's out of view of the security monitors and of his lawyer, I'll slam an elbow into his nose or a knee in his groin, and while he writhes on the floor, I'll lean close and whisper that if he ever mentions my daughter again, I'll kill him.

I get back in the Volvo. "Daddy," Lizzy says, sounding more asleep than awake, "Daddy, are we in danger again?"

CHAPTER 26

Lizzy and I planned to stay up north through the weekend, but it continued raining, and we both got cabin fever. Also, I decided to take care of a few things in the city, so we just stayed Friday night and drove back on Saturday. I dropped Lizzy in Turner and went home alone. Now it's Monday morning—humming printers, gossip at the watercooler. My to-do list is long. I've been letting things slide. Scud Illman has gotten the better of me. I need to have a steadier hand on the helm. Act judicious.

Tina is just arriving. I stand in her doorway with my coffee, shoulders squared, voice casual and supportive. "Good morning, how are we doing with Tamika Curtis?"

"We? We have been keeping an effing finger in the effing dike of Kendall Vance's effing histrionics is how *we* are doing." She drops her briefcase on the desk and flops into the chair. "I tried calling him all Friday. Finally, some friend of his answered. Said Kendall was away."

I laugh.

She eyes me suspiciously. "What?"

"Did you talk to the friend?"

"Briefly. He was quite charming."

"Yes," I say, "I talked to him, too. He's a prince of a fellow. Did you happen to tell him who you are?"

"Of course."

"Anything notable in the conversation?"

"Well, he asked me out on a date, but it was just, like, banter. Not for real."

"Oh, you seductress," I say, putting a legal pad on her desk. "Here, write down every detail you can remember of the conversation."

"Why?"

"Because you wooed the murdering extortionist Scud Illman, who stole his lawyer's cell phone."

I go back to my office and dial the Bureau. Chip isn't in, but I get his fellow agent, Isler. He says Scud is still at large. They've been looking for him all weekend.

I take some deep breaths and remind myself: Steady hand on the helm. I realize I didn't get an answer from Tina about Tamika Curtis, so I get up and go back in. She's writing on the pad, as I asked her to. I wait.

Tina's office is tidy but impersonal. She has some peaceful farm-and-mountain prints on the wall, by the regional artist Sabrina, whose work (often in triptych) hangs in half the dentists' offices in the state. On Tina's desk are just two photos—one of her parents and one of Tina and a dog. To see these, I have walked around behind her, and she doesn't seem to mind. She stops writing to think for a moment, arches her back, and swings her head so that if she had hair of any length, it would toss in carefree waves. Looking around the room, I notice the absence of diplomas and bar certificates, and I read this as a good sign, indicating that the office, this job, is not her whole being.

She keeps writing.

"I'll be back," I say, and I leave with no idea what is happening in the Curtis case.

I check Upton's office. He's not in. I call his cell. He doesn't answer. I call his home; Cindy says he worked all Sunday, then phoned last night to say he was going to sleep on his office couch.

I call Dorsey and learn the blood results aren't back from Scud's car. There are messages on my desk from TMU and Hollis Phippin, but right now I don't want to deal with either of them. It's 10:55 A.M. I call Flora's office and get voice mail. "It's me," I say, "can you call me between sessions?"

I try the Bureau again. Still no Chip. Isler says they're worried that Scud might have fled. Scud's wife claims she hasn't seen him, and he isn't at any of his usual haunts. They've been looking for him since I reported his threats on Friday night.

Flora calls back. "Are you okay, Nick?"

"Umm. Working too hard. As usual. Just needed to hear a friendly voice."

"Lizzy had a nice time with you this weekend."

"Did she? I can never tell."

"You worry too much, Nickie."

"How's your patio coming along?"

She laughs. "It started wonderfully. But you know Kenny. He's got it all dug up, and I haven't seen him for days."

"I'll kick him in the butt."

"Please do."

"How's your friend Lloyd?" I ask.

"Having a hard time this week. But he always snaps out of it."

"What is it with him?"

"Off the record?"

"Of course."

"OCD, certainly, but I don't have the whole picture yet. There's more. He's a good man."

I nod. I'm looking at my old photo of Flora with Toby. I like catching her between clients, because for just a few minutes, I can hear that old Flora, the one in the photo from before Toby's death.

"Lizzy likes your new friend," she says.

"Tina? She just works for me."

"That's not Lizzy's impression. But I have to go, my patient is waiting."

"Does it ever get to you, Flo?"

"What, Nickie?"

"Listening to people's misery all day."

"Come have dinner with us tonight. Can you?"

"That sounds nice."

"Bring Tina if you like. Bye, dear."

I feel better for the two seconds it takes me to remember that by dinnertime, flaky Flora will be back on the scene.

It took a few years after Toby's death before Flora and I learned who we should be to each other. But now we share one daughter and one horrible secret, so relegating each other to the painful past is out of the question. At first we were wary and hostile, but Flora increasingly buried her deadly shards of memory beneath pillowy layers of intellectual laxity. She has become a believer in all things pseudo-spiritual and—in my thinking—kooky. I actually worried for a while about her taking Lizzy and disappearing into the lavender reality of some cult. My emotional response to Flora, as she made this sad transformation from a sharp and capable woman into a vulnerable searcher, was to feel protective of her. I guess she noticed the sputtering decline of my fury (at least the part of it directed toward her), because to my surprise, she responded with trust and affection.

After my conversation with Flora, I walk down to the library to look for Kenny. He isn't there. I go back toward my office, but then I veer into Tina's doorway, intending to ask about Tamika Curtis. The legal pad has been pushed aside, and I pick it up. "Are you done here?"

"I wrote down everything I can remember," she says. "I, um, read it over, and now it sounds, um, flirtatious. But he's a joker. You know?"

"Tina?"

"Yes."

"Let's have lunch," I say, trying so hard to make it businesslike that my voice sounds to me like a rusted gate.

She nods. "Okay."

Tina and I go to the Rain Tree. So far today, my new steady hand on the helm has accomplished nothing. I haven't reached Chip, Scud has disappeared, Upton is incommunicado, there are no results from the blood in Scud's car, I'm dodging TMU and Hollis Phippin because there's nothing to tell them, Kenny seems not to have bothered coming to work and hasn't called in sick, and the Tamika Curtis jury, Tina finally told me, is probably hung.

We sit by the window, looking out through the rain toward the dam. The river is nearing flood stage, and it surges over the lip of the dam in a foamy brown cascade. Two city police cars are parked at the picnic area on the far side. My cell rings.

"Sorry," I say to Tina, "I've got to . . ." I answer.

"Are you sitting down?" Dorsey says. Then he waits, like I'm really supposed to answer.

"Yes, Dorsey, I'm sitting down."

"Good. Because we've got results from the blood in Scud Illman's car. You ready?"

"Yes, Dorsey, I'm ready."

"Well, I should tell you. They kept going back to the car for more samples. Kept looking for something else. Okay? A different result. Okay? But it's all the same. Same, same, same. And it's not Zander Phippin, and it's not Cassandra Randall, and it's not even Seth Coen."

"Tell me."

"You know of a guy named Odocoileus?"

"Odocoileus?"

"Yeah, Odocoileus virginianus?"

"What the—"

"Ha! Got you. White-tailed deer. Scientific name, *Odocoileus virginianus*. Those assholes weren't burying Zander Phippin, they were poaching deer. It's all deer blood."

I stare out at the river. Why didn't Scud just say so? Who wouldn't take the rap on a misdemeanor hunting violation to clear himself of suspicion in a capital murder? As I form the question in my mind, I already know the answer. It fits together perfectly. Scud and Seth are both convicted felons. Scud is a two-time loser. Deer poaching may be a state misdemeanor, but being a felon in possession of a firearm is itself a felony, which, under the state's three-strikes law, would land Scud in the slammer for somewhere between twenty-five years and life.

"You okay, Nick?" Tina asks.

We're five months into an investigation of the murder of two federal witnesses, and our whole case has just crumbled, leaving us without a single lead. Except we do have a lead: We have Scud, who genuinely seems to know something that he wants to tell us.

"Find Scud," I say to Dorsey. "Find Scud and find Chip. We'll immunize Scud on the felon-in-possession violation. He knows something, Dorsey. I'm sure of it. He'll talk. He's aching to talk. Forget about the threats to me. Scud is our new best friend. Go get him."

I end the call and try Chip again. No answer. I try Upton. No answer.

"What is it?" Tina says.

I forgot about her. She's there across the table, and as luck would have it, she's about the only person in the world I can explain all of this to. So I do. And she listens. I get into details I don't intend to, like my feelings about Zander—how he was just a terrified kid; how I've strangely superimposed on him the grown-up persona of my departed son, Toby. I tell Tina about the chemistry with Cassandra, and Lizzy's feelings for Cassandra, and how much I'd love for Lizzy to have a stable mother figure ("Let's say role model," I correct myself, embarrassed). I confess to Tina about having gotten too close to the case and maybe not exercising the best judgment. We sit talking for over an hour, until the lunch crowd disappears and we have the place to ourselves. I finish the tale with the part about Scud calling me and begging for help. "I asked who he worked for," I tell Tina, "and all he'd say was 'mercy.'"

"You sure it was 'mercy'?"

"I think so, why?"

"Maybe he said Percy. Percy Mashburn. He seems to be the new meth king. He's who Tamika Curtis was working for."

"You think Mashburn could be running Scud?"

"Might bear looking into."

"Maybe so." I look out at the river. Things have gotten too complicated. I'm having trouble keeping it all clear in my head.

"That's a lot on your plate," Tina says, reaching across the table to pat my hand, and I wonder if she might rest her hand on top of mine, and I wonder if I might turn my hand over and take hold of hers. But we don't, and then the moment is lost, and I am tingly with the almost-ness of it. It's better this way, though. We're colleagues at lunch: supervisor and subordinate. I should ask her to dinner. Dinner is outside of work. Lunch isn't.

We order more clams. My fingers get pruny from all the peeling and dunking, and I worry that she might see the wrinkles and mistake it for age. I've got twelve years on her.

"I've always liked this place," she says.

I could invite her to Flora's with me tonight. It's probably odd, taking someone to dinner at the ex's for a first date, but they've already met, and Tina wouldn't mind. She likes Lizzy. She liked Flora. She liked Bill-the-Dog.

Maybe I will. Her hair really isn't all that bad.

"Something's going on," Tina says.

More police have arrived across the river. I see the coroner's van. They've strung yellow tape along the shore.

The feminine hand that was resting on the table, the hand whose comfort and warmth pulled at me with throat-tightening gravity, now goes into Tina's coat pocket and emerges with glasses. She puts them on, and the hand returns to the table.

Trooper cars have arrived at the scene. We're close enough to make out forms and actions but too far to see faces.

"Drowning, I guess," Tina says.

"Something sad," I say.

Across the room, the vets sit at their table drinking coffee in solemn unity. I see Steve wheeling across the room to join them; Tina and I are at the table where Lizzy and Kendall and Kaylee and I had lunch, and I remember how casually, how nonsignificantly, Lizzy put her arm across Kaylee's shoulders. And just like that, I'm holding Tina's hand across the tabletop.

Four cops are lifting a body up the bank, and gawkers watch from behind the tape. Between police and rescue, there are half a dozen vehicles. It's a light show.

A tall, slender figure separates from the crowd of officers. A man in a suit, not a uniform. He has his back to the river, and I see him lift his hand to his ear. He paces. Then he turns to face us, and I can see that his mouth looks all black. The bear rug: Dorsey's silly mustache, and I'm reaching for my phone before it rings. And of course it does ring.

"Nick Davis here," I say in as level a voice as I can.

"Nick, it's Dorsey."

"Hi, Dorsey."

"Listen, I'm down by the river across from the Rokeby Mills building, and I—"

"Yeah, I see you, Dorsey, I'm at the Rain Tree."

He pauses and waves vaguely in our direction.

"Yeah, hi," I say. "So I assume there's a reason you're calling me?"

"Well, it seems we got a floater here."

"So I see."

"And um . . ." He pauses, and I watch as his black raincoat works its way into the mass of rescue workers and police around the gurney. "Well, Nick, we can call off the search for Scud Illman, because I just found him."

CHAPTER 27

There's nothing at all connecting Scud Illman to Zander Phippin and Cassandra Randall anymore. The deer poaching explains away the last of it. The Bureau and the state police recognize this. Scud's only remaining interest to Dorsey and Chip is as the fourth murder victim.

But in my mind, he's so intertwined with Zander and Cassandra that I need to take pains to separate him. All the loathing I've felt has no object; it is a flopping fish tossed onto the sand. Its context has abandoned it. So I've decided to prove for myself whether it is possible that Seth and Scud could have poached a deer on one side of the reservoir on the same night they buried Zander Phippin on the other.

It is late at night. I buy coffee at the 7-Eleven across from Seymour Apartments. The register receipt reads 11:47 P.M.

The roads are empty. I drive west, skirting the reservoir to the south, then I leave the highway and turn onto County Road D, paralleling the west shore. I see deer; white tails appear like ghosts before dissolving into the black curtain of woods. But one doe freezes, proverbial deer in the headlights, her eyes burning green. It would be easy to step from the car and shoot, but I drive past, and as the headlights move off her, I see the flash of her tail.

Following my map, I arrive at the dirt road leading toward a cul-de-sac where, last June 3, a game warden found gut piles from two midnight deer poachings. I follow a gravel drive for several hundred yards until my lights shine on a picnic table and a campfire grate and a small pay box where boaters are supposed to leave a five-dollar fee for using the boat ramp. Now it is 1:43 A.M.—an hour and fifty-six minutes since I bought coffee across from Seth's apartment. The moon sparkles on the surface of the reservoir, and I can make out the opposite shore barely a half mile away.

I return to the hardtop and follow county roads around the reservoir toward the opposite shore. As I get into the unmarked roads of the more forested eastern shore, I'm tempted to call this off and turn back toward the highway. I'm nearing the spot where someone dumped poor Zander Phippin; the woods are getting thicker with ghosts. I wish I'd brought somebody with me as company, but whom—?

Cassandra—I picture us walking in the woods that day last June, but I change it: There is no corpse to dig up. Just the two of us, her cargo pants swishing, her hand clutching mine. But Cassandra is dead.

Toby—mid-twenties now. Lanky like his mom, messy hair, physically fit, a girlfriend at home, but he's happy to drive around in the woods with his dad, talking about who knows what; maybe grad school, or politics, or girls. Whatever: It's the company that matters. But Toby is dead.

Or Flora, the old Flora; witty, sharp, intellectual. She's gone, too.

More literally, I thought of asking Kenny, but he's not the kind to bask in the quiet pleasantness of familiar company and the woods at night. He has decided to buy a Jet Ski, and it's all he talks about now.

I also thought of Tina or Chip or Upton, but my mission—measuring time and distance where time and distance are already known—is so illogical, I don't want to involve my sober-minded associates. I thought of Lizzy, too. She would be perfect, but keeping her up on a school night to spare myself the hectoring of all my ghosts wouldn't be good parenting.

I am alone but for these ghosts, so I ask them the obvious question: Who wanted Scud dead? The obvious answer is that whoever killed Zander and Cassandra wanted Scud dead, because he was probably about to rat them out. Though it might be true, it's an unsatisfying answer. A dead end.

"Who else wanted Scud dead?" I ask my passengers.

"Doc Wallis," Toby yells. I ignore him, because Dr. Wallis has been dead almost as long as Toby.

"You wanted him dead," the youthful Flora says to me in the voice I remember from eons ago—insightful and ironic and teasing all at once. I ignore her, too.

"Everyone wanted him dead," Cassandra says.

"Can you be more specific?"

"Of course not," she answers. "I don't even know who killed *me*."

They're no help, these uninvited passengers. I silence them, but they're restive, and after a few uneasy miles, Zander blurts, "My father wanted him dead."

"Yes, but . . ." I answer, and that's all I can think of. But what? But nothing. Hollis Phippin, successful, intelligent, well spoken, a man of action. He did want Scud dead. He told me so. Crap.

At 3:09 I arrive near where I parked the day we found Zander. I turn around and drive back toward the highway.

Three hours and twenty-two minutes since I bought coffee. Last June 3, Scud bought cigarettes at 2:02 A.M. Adding their travel time, the earliest Scud and Seth could have arrived near Zander's grave is 5:24 A.M., and that's if they never stopped. So if Cassandra Randall first heard them in the woods at about 6:15, which is what she told us, it means they had about fifty-one minutes to shoot two deer, gut them, and toss them in the car at the picnic area over on the west side, then on the east side to carry or drag the body into the woods, to dig the hole for Zander, pitch him in, and start filling the hole up before Cassandra came along and heard them. Impossible.

Or maybe not. What if they hadn't planned to shoot any deer? No skulking in the woods or staking out a game trail, no quartering, even: They see two deer in the headlights, jump out, shoot. Seth was a hunter. He could have gutted them in minutes. Let's say the whole process takes fifteen minutes. That leaves only thirty-eight minutes to dig Zander's grave. Impossible.

Or maybe not. What if it was already dug?

Possible. Now there are two problems: First, if they already had a grave dug for Zander on the east shore, what were they doing on the west shore?

Second problem: All the evidence we had linking Scud and Seth to Zander's burial—the tollbooth record, the blood, the tire print, the cigarette purchase, the phone note in Seth's apartment—is perfectly explained by the deer poaching. There are no loose ends. Attributing the evidence to the established fact of two felons out poaching a couple of deer, there's nothing left. Scud becomes no more a suspect than anybody else who was out and about that night in June. Less, actually.

Bottom line: Scud and Seth could have poached a deer and buried Zander Phippin all in the same night. But they didn't. The contortions of logic and logistics overwhelm the sliver of feasibility. It's back to square one.

I drive to the highway. Darkness is peaceful now. My dead and departed passengers stayed behind at the reservoir. I wanted it to be Scud, but I'm glad it wasn't. The deer hunting changed my thinking. Not that I'm in favor of poaching (I'm not even a hunter). No, it's the pathetic and redeeming humanness of their mission. Two guys, rejects and lowlifes, team up for an illegal and unsportsmanlike venture away from the neon glow, into the startling blackness of woods. Hoods, criminals, city rats, drawn to the tepid wilderness of the reservoir district. I know the feeling, that urge to fan the primeval spark, nurturing the forgotten connection to the earth: man's longing for self-sufficiency.

We're all the same.

CHAPTER 28

The music is zippy; Scud hoists himself up on some flotsam in the rain-swollen river and hops to the shore.

"Who killed you?" I ask.

He grins his squinty grin, and he is just about to tell me . . .

"Nick," Tina asks, "are you okay?"

My office. Tina is in the doorway.

"Are you on the phone?" she asks.

Apparently, I am on the phone, my head pillowed against the receiver, my elbow propped on the desk, and the on-hold music in my ear.

"I'll come back later," Tina says.

I hang up. "No. Stay."

"Are you okay?"

"I fell asleep."

"On the phone?"

"I was up all night."

"Have you had coffee yet?"

"I don't think so."

She leaves. Then she's back with two cups of coffee. "How you doing, boss?"

"This'll help." I sip the coffee and say, "Mmm," just to say anything, because she has settled down across from me.

"Up all night doing what?"

I tell her about driving to the reservoir.

Janice buzzes. "Agent d'Villafranca for you, Nick."

I put him on speaker. "Hi, Chip."

"Nick, did you just call me?"

"It's possible."

"Beg pardon?"

"I have Tina with me here."

"Hi, Tina."

"Hi, Chip."

I say, "I think it's safe to assume that Scud killed Seth Coen to keep him quiet. They were out poaching deer. Scud was a two-time loser; Seth wasn't. When the shit hit the fan, Seth probably wanted to cop to the felon-in-possession charge to remove suspicion on the murder charge. Scud couldn't allow that because he'd be in on three strikes."

"Nice theory."

"Do you have any evidence from Scud's body?"

"Dorsey's department," Chip says. "The state has the body. They worked the scene."

"I have a name to suggest," I say. "Hollis Phippin has motive, and he's capable."

Tina's eyes widen in surprise, then she nods in agreement.

"Talk to Dorsey," Chip says.

So I do. I hang up with Chip and dial Dorsey's office.

"Dorsey," Dorsey says.

"Nick here. I have a theory on who killed Scud. I'm thinking you might want to interview Hollis Phippin. He's smart, he's a doer, he has motive. He even said something to me about killing Scud himself if he had to . . ."

"Nick—"

"I mean, I'd hate like hell to see him go down. You've got to admire it, really. But that's why we have laws, am I right? I feel responsible. It was me who—"

"Nick—"

"—lost objectivity."

"Nick," Dorsey says, "I've got the ballistics report here. Listen to me. Seth Coen and Scud Illman were killed with the same gun."

Tina and I look across the desk at each other as implications stream from this tidbit of data. "Self-inflicted?" she whispers. This makes sense, considering the state Scud was in when he called me on

Kendall's phone. He'd gotten himself in too deep, the pressure was too much: sayonara. But in this case, it's impossible: Not too many guys off themselves with an executionlike hole in the back of the head and then tumble into the river.

"It doesn't rule Hollis out altogether," Dorsey says. "Like maybe he confronted Scud, got the gun away from him. We'll talk to him."

"Sure," I say, "but keep me out of it. Have you found anything at the scene?"

"No, so far we don't even know where he was killed. I've got investigators searching the picnic areas and waysides for anything interesting."

"Well, keep me informed." I end the call because something just occurred to me. "Tina, go brief Upton," I say to get rid of her.

When she's gone, I call Kendall Vance's office and leave a message saying I need to speak with him immediately and away from the office.

Janice buzzes while I'm waiting for Kendall to call back. "Nick, I have the file you wanted."

"What file?"

"It was several weeks ago. You wouldn't believe what I had to go through. Because it had been archived, but then they'd pulled it for digitizing, but they hadn't digitized it yet, so it was in this never-never status where nobody could find it, and finally, I went over there to look for it myself, but they wouldn't let me take it until they actually did get it digitized, so now I've got it."

"What file?"

"Burton."

"I don't remember Burton."

"Well, you asked," she says.

I go out and take it from her. Leroy Burton. It's a case that was closed almost thirty years ago. Fuseli! The tattoo guy. I'd forgotten.

I silence my cell phone so it won't ring while I'm with Kendall. We meet at the Sahara Café, a tiny falafel joint in the old town.

"I don't have much time," Kendall says, "but you sounded desperate."

"I just thought we should talk," I say. "You lost a client. What must that be like?"

He shrugs.

"So I guess he was innocent," I say. "Of the murder, anyway."

"Innocent or not," Kendall says, "I figured he was going in for life, but your case kept unraveling, and it started looking like I could get the son of a bitch acquitted. I never expected that."

"You sound like you wanted him convicted."

Kendall shrugs. "Scud was bad news, but it's not my fault if you guys can't put a case together."

"I'm wondering if you know anything. Anything nonprivileged. Something to help us sort this out."

"Are you kidding me?"

"I just thought—"

"Forget it, Nick. I don't know anything, and if I did, it would be privileged."

"He's dead."

"Privileged, counselor."

I sip my coffee. It's in a squat porcelain cup. I wipe the grounds off my front teeth with a napkin.

"If that's all you wanted . . ." Kendall says.

"Businesswise, sure. That's everything. But you know, Lizzy might like to see Kaylee sometime."

"Kaylee would like that." His tone softens.

"Crap!" I say. "Speaking of Lizzy, I was supposed to call her. Twenty minutes ago. Excuse me a minute." I stand and reach into my jacket pocket. Then I pat all my pockets. "Crap crap crap. Kendall, I left my phone at the office. Lemme use yours a minute." He reaches into his jacket and hands me his cell phone. I avoid his eyes. "Thanks, be right back."

It's a tiny restaurant. I latch the bathroom door behind me, sit on the lid, then navigate Kendall's phone to the log of numbers dialed. My heart pounds in my ears; I could be disbarred for this. I'm about to violate Kendall's privacy, and worse, the attorney/client confidentiality he had with Scud.

But Scud is dead, so why shouldn't the attorney/client thing die, too? (Never mind that the Supreme Court already nixed this logic: Ken Starr went to the Supreme Court to get Vince Foster's lawyer to surrender his notes. The court said forget about it.)

It was last Thursday afternoon when Kendall called me from his cell to arrange lunch at the Rain Tree when Lizzy met Kaylee. So Scud must have lifted the phone sometime between then and Friday evening, when he called me. That's the closest I can pin it down. At the other end, Kendall got the phone back from Scud late on Friday night. So I'm interested in all calls made between Thursday afternoon and Friday night.

On my own phone, I call voice mail and start reading the log from Kendall's phone. There are eleven calls, including the one Scud made to me. I'm done in under a minute. Now I dial Flora's office on Kendall's phone, just in case he's the suspicious sort who might look to see whom I called. I talk to Flora's voice mail a minute or two, then I flush and bring Kendall his phone back. "Thanks," I say, "gotta run."

"So you arranged this urgent meeting just to ask if I have any intel on who did Scud Illman?"

"Um. Yes."

"Why you? Why not Chip or Captain Dorsey?"

He seems honestly perplexed, so I say, "I'm a lawyer. I'm more sensitive to the question of your residual loyalty to Scud. I mean, we don't want it to get all *legal*, do we?"

"Meaning?"

"Meaning if the Bureau or Dorsey figures you know something, they'll try to compel you. It'll make bad feelings and bad law. I'm trying to work around that."

"Okay, Nick, I'll tell you what I know," he says sarcastically. "I know that Scud Illman was a little player with big enemies. Other than that, I know what you know. Squat. Maybe less."

"Will you make a statement?"

"No, I won't make a goddamn statement. What the hell would happen to my practice? My client gets whacked, then I'm snuggling with the feds, tutoring them on who's who in the city. You'd be pulling me out of the river next."

He's not shouting, but this is too loud for the tiny restaurant. People are eyeing us. Not customers, because we're the only ones, but the owners who work in an open kitchen behind the counter: a middle-aged Lebanese couple and their twentyish daughter.

I pat my palms against the air. "Down, boy, I just want to find who killed him."

"Who the hell cares," he snaps, "good riddance."

"Kendall, settle . . ."

"Scud Illman was scum. Finding whoever killed him won't get you any closer to what you really want."

"It *is* what I want."

"No, it's not. You want to know who killed Phippin and Cassandra and who runs the crime in this city. That's what you want to know."

I stare at him. The café owners have given up trying to look busy.

Kendall slumps. "Listen," he says quietly, "you've never done any criminal defense, have you?"

"No."

"Well, it takes its toll. You feel responsible. But Scud played with a tough crowd, so like that sheriff says, 'Let the dead bury the dead, Mr. Finch.'"

I feel a moment of fondness for Kendall. A lot of us started our legal careers with misty-eyed visions of *To Kill a Mockingbird*—Atticus Finch's noble deeds—but we ended up with the likes of Scud Illman. I say, "So we should get our girls together sometime. Lizzy and Kaylee." I stand up abruptly.

"Wait," he says, "do you have suspects? Info flows both ways, Nick. Right?"

"I hear the Bureau is bringing in Hollis Phippin for questioning."

His face contorts. "The kid's father?"

"Yes."

"And you'd prosecute?"

"Not me personally. Someone would."

He looks at me vacantly a few seconds, then says, "I just figured you guys would convict Scud. Of course he told me he didn't do it, but I never believed him. I figured you'd try him, I'd defend him, you'd win; goodbye, Scud. But you guys kept screwing up, and there were all these holes in your case, and you couldn't even get any charges to stick."

"He sounded scared on the phone."

"Of course. They were after him. He'd become too hot."

"How'd you get your phone back?"

"Special Agent d'Villafranca called me at home, told me about the cell phone and how he threatened you. I immediately call my cell phone, and damned if Scud doesn't answer. I laid right into him about stealing my phone, and we arranged to meet at the Toadstool. I didn't expect him to show, but . . ."

"Where's the Toadstool?"

"West of town on 156, about twenty miles. So damned if Scud didn't show up. Right on time, too. Gave me my phone, all sheepish. I told him to turn himself in on this bullshit about threatening a federal officer. He said he'd think about it. And that's the last I saw of Scud Illman."

"Did he say where he was going after that?"

"No. I left, he stayed."

"You might be the last one who saw him alive."

"Except for whoever killed him."

"Right. Except for whoever killed him."

Kendall looks tired. His commando bearing has slumped into a sunken-necked, bent-backed weariness. He leans heavily on his elbows, and I see how earnestly he wears that confession about the burdens of criminal defense. Again I feel unexpectedly fond of him. It is Kendall's job to defend the indefensible, forgive the unforgivable, and in this instance anyway, grieve for the tragically flawed journeyer whose cause he took up. I mumble niceties, trying to penetrate his sudden gloom, but I'm unsuccessful. As I go out the door, Kendall barely looks up from the blackness of his coffee-cup reflection.

Back at my office, midafternoon: Janice is away from her desk, so I slip in quietly, close the door, and pretend I'm not here. I play the voice mail I left for myself, writing down the numbers dialed from Kendall's phone. I fax the list over to the Bureau, and a half hour later, they fax it back with the numbers identified. Calls were made to:

1. A landline listed to Kendall and Linda Vance. This is probably Kendall calling his wife before Scud took the phone.
2. A landline listed to the law office of Kendall Vance. Kendall calling his office.
3. A landline registered to the law office of Newman, Welch, and Zemp. Kendall calling a colleague.
4. A landline registered to Avery Illman. This is Kendall calling Scud at home, or Scud calling his wife on the newly pilfered phone.
5. A prepaid cell phone traced to the name Maxfield Parrish, which is certainly an alias. The call lasted twenty minutes and was placed at 5:41 P.M. on Friday.
6. A cell phone belonging to Upton Cruthers. This is disturbing. The call lasted thirty-four minutes and was placed at 7:52 P.M. Upton never told me that he, too, got a call from Scud last Friday. It gives some credibility to Scud's claim that he and Upton had something going.
7. A landline registered to Bernier Construction, Inc. Nine minutes.
8. A cell phone belonging to Nick Davis. Me. The call lasted thirteen minutes.
9. Maxfield Parrish again. Seventeen minutes.
10. Bernier Construction again. Eight minutes.
11. Home of Kendall and Linda Vance again.

The only calls of interest, besides the one to Upton, are those to Maxfield Parrish and Bernier Construction. I call Chip and ask him to see what he can find out, though I don't tell him where the numbers came from. I have a sick feeling after seeing the calls Kendall made himself. I have violated my colleague; it goes against everything about attorney confidence.

Midafternoon, the office is quiet, and I didn't sleep last night. My office couch beckons, and I obey.

CHAPTER 29

Morning: Upton, Tina, and I stop at JoMondo's for coffee.
"Upton," I say, "when was the last time you spoke with
Scud before he died?"

"I don't think I ever spoke with him."

"You spoke with him at his house the day we executed the search."

"Right. Except for that. Never."

"Count your blessings," I say.

Something is strange. Somebody called Upton from Kendall's
cell phone last Friday and talked for almost half an hour. Upton says
he never got a call from Scud. I'm certain the call was made while
Scud had Kendall's phone, but just to be sure, I ask Upton, "Have
you spoken to Kendall Vance lately?"

"No, why?"

"No reason."

We get our drinks and walk toward the FBI. Between office
buildings, I glimpse the mills down on the river; always the mills,
the givers and takers away. The mills are the rich uncle who, when
he lies waxy in open casket, is revealed to be penniless. And you still
owe for the undertaker. This is a city of failed nineteenth-century
industry trying to bootstrap itself into a twenty-first-century world.
Over the past quarter century, our statistics have been grim: child
neglect, abuse, assault, DWI, poverty, alcoholism, drug use. We've
made the charts, and though we're climbing our way out of the hole,
it's a long climb.

The FBI conference room is full. It's a bland room in a bland
building. The most notable detail is an old sign on the wall that
someone printed out in large font: MAXY DID IT. This is a joke. Maxy
was an informant who disappeared a decade ago and whose name

has taken on the air of mystery and myth. Perps claim he's active. Unsolved hits get blamed on him.

There are a couple of lawyers here from the state attorney general's office, and Chip's colleague Isler is here with several agents and technicians I don't recognize.

"Whose meeting is this?" Isler asks.

"Mine," I say. "I want to make sure we all know what everybody else knows. We got four murders. Let's start with Phippin."

"Chip will be along in a minute," Isler says. "Let's wait."

So they stand around talking about other things while I go over my notes and we all wait for Chip. They talk about a "small cluster" of disappearances over in Rivertown. A few kids have gone missing. The problem with these small-cluster cases is that you never know if they're just coincidence or if something evil is afoot. But Rivertown is a pretty rough area, so they may be runaways. "Has there been another?" I ask.

One of the state cops answers, "Not since the Tesoro girl, but she was the third in quick succession."

"You guys got anything?"

"Cold as ice."

Chip comes in and sits. "Sorry," he says, not sounding sorry at all.

"Shall we begin?" I say. "Let's talk about the Phippin boy."

"A dealer," Isler says, "small potatoes. He was independent. The big boys wholesaled to him." He is slender and unimposing, but as soon as he opens his mouth, the nerdiness disappears.

"How do you know where he got his leaf?"

"State lab traced it. DNA or something."

"Any reason to think this Phippin deal is something other than what it looks like?"

"No."

"And what's it look like?"

"A simple execution," Dorsey says, "but seeing as how he'd been dead at least a day when we found him, maybe whoever killed him isn't who buried him. Maybe the burier was some grunt finishing someone else's dirty work."

The idea is new to me but it makes sense; upper management takes action, the janitors clean up. "Prospects?" I ask.

"We're dead-ended on forensics right now. Ballistics can't match the gun to anything. We've identified oil paint on Zander's hands and face—artist's oil paints—but it leads us nowhere and probably has nothing to do with the crime. He was obviously held without food, tortured for two to four days. He had abrasions on his wrists from being cuffed to something. That's what we've got. For any more, we'd need to get an informant or find evidence we missed. Or get lucky."

"Possible informants?"

Dorsey and Chip discuss this. They ask their respective staffs, kick it around. I'm aware of Tina at the table. She's quiet because this meeting doesn't really involve her; I invited her as a courtesy. If she weren't here, I'd probably let Chip run things. I'm strutting.

"We're working some prospects," Dorsey says.

"Moving on. Cassandra Randall."

"A professional job," Isler says, and he describes the difficulties of the shot, made at some distance and through a window. "We've sent the bullet fragments to the national lab."

"Anything else?"

Dorsey answers. "A neighbor walking home that night noticed a car parked on the street nearby. White and nondescript. Probably a rental. We've narrowed it to three possible models. We're working the rental data from every outlet in the city."

"You are?" I say, surprised. "But she was shot last June."

"Yeah, but until this week, we thought Scud was our guy."

"So you never—"

"Give me a break," Upton says. "You heard Isler, it was a professional job. It took planning and talent. Scud didn't have that kind of savvy."

This stops the conversation dead. For one thing, Upton's outburst bristles with contempt and emotion. For another, the question of turf can be a powder keg to a multiagency investigation. The best way to blow it all up is to start criticizing everyone else's work. It's not like Upton, and it adds to my growing certainty that he has an agenda of his own.

"Maybe he did, maybe he didn't," I say. "Other leads?"

Silence.

"Prospects?"

They kick it around. The conversation reduces to the bleak facts that, other than Scud, who is dead and probably wasn't capable of the job, we don't have a suspect for who killed Cassandra—and other than an unidentified white rental car that's probably unrelated, we don't have the remotest shred of a clue.

"Moving on," I say. "Seth Coen."

"We're still assuming Scud Illman killed Coen," Dorsey says.

"What do we know about Coen?"

"A loner. We can't get a feel for him. He did time for manslaughter, and he went on trial once for armed robbery, but the case had problems, and it got dismissed. Other than that, it's misdemeanors. He fought in the first Gulf War and showed up here afterward."

"Where's he from?"

"Downstate. The only person we connect him to up here is Scud, and barely that. Scud was into all kinds of crap, but it seems Coen stayed pretty much out of it."

"How'd he support himself?"

Dorsey shrugs. "He drove a delivery van sometimes. Not too often."

"Got anything else?"

"He had health problems. The medicine cabinet was full of prescription meds."

"What problems?"

"We're working on it."

"Did he have family?"

"A sister someplace."

"Let me know when you have something. Moving on to Scud Illman."

"You know everything we know," Chip says. "He was a wannabe.

It looks like he tried legitimate work a time or two, took business classes at community college, worked construction, toyed with photography. He kept ending up with bad boys. I have this probation report . . ."

This is all a waste of time. We have no strategy, no leads except for the bit about the white rental car. Nothing of interest. Murders like Zander's and Cassandra's are the hardest to solve. They're dispassionate crimes: killings without rage or greed or impulse or psychosis. Killings that are all in a day's work.

The other two, the murders of Seth Coen and Scud, are a little different. The way Seth was butchered, along with the sloppiness of leaving a shoe print, suggests something less professional. The Bureau isn't sure what to make of Scud's murder. So far we haven't even found the scene of the crime. We need a lucky break.

Dorsey is talking about the gun that killed both Seth and Scud, so I tune back in.

". . . possibly got in a tussle with Scud, took the gun away, and shot him."

"Or maybe whoever killed Scud had stolen the gun outright ahead of time," I say. "See, the thing is—" I stop.

"The thing is what?" someone says.

"Nothing. Never mind."

I was going to say it could have been someone who knew Scud, knew he had the gun, knew where he kept it, and went and got it for the specific purpose of killing Scud. Something in me tells me to keep my mouth shut. My thinking is . . . It didn't start as a thought, it started as a drop of adrenaline when my subconscious outpaced the march of logic. Maybe Scud's wife used the casual violence of her criminal husband's illicit doings to camouflage a domestic homicide. I remember her on the day we searched her house; disgust oozed out every pore of her outraged face. Was Scud's gun hidden in the house that day, or maybe buried in the yard, or stashed at a friend's? No matter. If she knew of the gun, she could retrieve it. Then it would be a simple matter to come up with the excuse, lure him to a secluded spot, shoot him, dump the body somewhere along the river's unhurried path. Maybe she even affected a twinkle in her eyes, a "come hither" smile as she suggested a drive, just the two of them, to one of those isolated parks.

This wisp of an idea takes root and grows into something surprising. The beleaguered Mrs. Scud probably had more motive and opportunity than God, but other people also had motive to kill the nettlesome Scud. And where motive leads, opportunity has a way of following. Maybe Scud had the gun at home the day we searched his house and grounds. Maybe it was in the living room or kitchen, where the ubiquitous and mysterious Officer Penhale, in blue surgical gloves, poked through drawers and under couch cushions. Penhale easily could have pocketed the gun. Or it could have been in the bedroom, where my friend the disturbingly quirky Chip d'Villafranca went in ahead of the search team to have a look around. Or in the garage, where I found my other friend, my confidant and ally Upton Cruthers, lingering in the dim light while troopers rummaged utility shelves.

Lots of people would love to get their hands on a gun not traceable to them. I acquired one once myself.

Dorsey says my name; I focus on the conversation. "At Nick's suggestion," Dorsey is saying, "we interviewed the Phippin boy's father. We weren't able to clear him in the Scud Illman murder. He was alone and without an alibi during the critical time. His wife was visiting her sister. Mr. Phippin admitted with regard to Scud Illman that he wanted to, quote, 'expunge that little shit from God's green earth.' He's got plenty of money to have hired the job; alternatively, he seems to have the wherewithal to do it himself. So we're keeping him on the list. We're doing a workup on him."

"Other theories?" I ask.

The discussion is aimless. I wait several minutes for something interesting to surface. Nothing does.

"Okay, then," I say. I put the files back in my briefcase and stand up. People head for the door. "Tarry a moment," I say to Dorsey, and when we're alone, "How much do you know about your man Penhale?"

"Competent. Not outstanding. Why?"

"Opportunity," I say. "I'm thinking of the leak: Cassandra Randall's identity. Penhale drove her home that day we were all out at the reservoir. He seems to show up a lot of places."

Dorsey strokes his mustache. "I'd hate it to be one of mine, but I see your point," he says.

We haven't talked about the leak in a long time. The assumption has been that when we got Scud in our grip, he'd offer up the snitch as a bargaining chip to keep himself off death row. Now, with Scud dead and no longer suspected of killing Zander, finding the snitch might be our only route back to the killer.

I leave Dorsey and go find Chip outside the conference room. "Any info on those two names I gave you, Bernier Construction and Maxfield Parrish?" I ask.

"I haven't had a moment, Nick. How about I get back to you this afternoon?"

"Something else," I say. "Your audio/video nerd Sparky, have you looked at him?"

"Looked?"

"As the snitch."

"Sparky?" Chip is about to protest. The idea rankles. None of us wants to think it's one of our own. In his face, I see the brief battle between Chip the big teddy bear and Chip the jaded federal agent. The agent wins. "Sparky," he says. "I see your point."

"Let me know if you find anything," I say.

In an instant, Chip's manner changes. He loses his nonchalance. "But come on down to my office," he says. "I need to speak with you about something."

This is strange, and I'm immediately wary. He's glancing around nervously and trying too hard to seem normal. Whatever it is, I don't want to get pulled in.

"Can't right now, buddy," I say. "I'm already late for my next, um, meeting."

"Oh. Well, call me as soon as you can. Okay?"

"Okay-dokay," I say, and I hurry away.

* * *

I'm not an investigator, I'm an administrator, but I need to go out and start peering under a few more stones on my own, because I heard impatience from both Dorsey's and Chip's teams. Their outrage has decayed into weariness. No longer are these killings an opportunity for that quick high-profile arrest, no promotions in the offing, no media heroes. The case is already a failure; one killing became two, became three, became four. Four murders but without the cachet of a serial killer on a rampage. There is no terrorized public, no sensationalism, no news cameras waiting at the steps. These cases offer the possibility of only minor success but huge failure. The killings are separate enough that solving one still leaves three unsolved. Why bring attention to that? With the death of our main suspect, we could let the investigation itself die a quiet death. Just pretend they were solved. Case closed, because officially, politically, no good can come of it. Which means I might be on my own.

I start with Seth Coen. I don't have much on him, just an old sentencing report and prison records. We must have more but I don't know where it is.

Seth's only conviction was for manslaughter. A guy in a bar menaced him with a knife and wound up dead. The record makes reference to the victim's size and strength (muscle-bound; bodybuilder) and to Seth's lack of size (diminutive). The victim was drunk; it is unclear whether Seth was, too. It is also unclear whether the big guy intended actual harm or if he was flashing his blade for effect, but the cost to him was a savage and "lightning-quick" knife in the throat (according to a witness's statement), inserted with a forward plunging motion and withdrawn in a lateral slicing motion (per the medical examiner's report). The knife work was vicious, competent, and intended to kill. For Seth, the cost was a sentence of twenty years in Alder Creek maximum. I wonder if his skill with a blade kept him safe there, because from the sound of him in these reports, he would have been an appealing target for the bad boys in lockup. Maybe the Aryan who branded him with the swastika kept him on as a pet. Seth was paroled at twelve years for good behavior.

The manslaughter conviction was about three years after Seth got out of the army. He was a sniper in Kuwait during the first Gulf War, deployed under a year, end of story. His prison medical files are extensive. During his years inside, he complained of, among other things, fatigue, confusion, blurry vision, chest pains, and headaches. The prison docs referred to him in their notes as a hypochondriac, complaint-prone, and fragile.

As a whole, the record of Seth's life reduces to a sad profile of human futility: He fought in a war, survived, got in a fight, went to prison, got branded with a swastika, got out of jail, moved into a skuzzy apartment, ended up in a freezer. The only "friend" or acquaintance we're aware of is the lowlife Scud Illman, who, we believe, ended the friendship by putting a bullet in Seth's head. Seth seems to have made a lasting impression on no one and left no one behind.

CHAPTER 30

With Tina beside me, I spin down the ramp of the parking garage. Out on the road, I signal my turn onto the highway, but she yells, "NO," and I swerve back, thinking I'm about to hit something.

"I have to change clothes," she says.

"You look lovely."

"Look at me. A dull gray court suit is lovely?"

"You look fine."

"Turn up there." She directs me to her apartment. "Come in if you want, or just wait. I'm quick."

I wait. It's exactly the kind of place I'd expect her to live. A brick town house, once millworkers' housing, now upscale. She *is* quick, back in a couple of minutes wearing jeans and a silky white blouse with a scarf.

"*Now* you look lovely."

"Too late. Your credibility is shot."

We get on the highway toward Turner.

"So about Tamika Curtis," she says. "The jury is officially hung, and I'm wondering if we should drop this one."

I don't answer. I see patches of gold in the dark green hillsides, birches among the evergreens, leaves turning.

"I mean, she wasn't that involved," Tina says, "and there are those three little girls . . ."

I shrug. "Your call, Tina. What should we do?"

She doesn't answer. She looks through my CDs while I scan for some news on the radio. We ride in silence, then she says, "I don't know if she needs to be in prison just for trying to score a little meth for herself. Percy Mashburn and his gang turned her into a user before she was even sixteen. Kendall is right: It's effing nuts. We give Mashburn a walk in exchange for him turning over all his subordinates."

"What's become of my take-no-prisoners trial lawyer?"

"I tried her once. I was a good soldier, did my best. But Kendall Vance did better. So let's call it a day."

"Okay."

"I know the law, Nick, and nowhere does it say that after getting a hung jury, you have to keep going after this woman who's never caught a break in her miserable life and who keeps having babies with different men, hoping she'll find some guy who likes her enough to stick around. The law doesn't say that Tina Trevor and Nick Davis have to harass her lousy ass till there's nothing left of her."

"Who are you trying to convince here, Tina?"

Silence again until I pull into Flora's drive. Middle Earth. Bill-the-Dog comes woofing out with her tail going in circles. Tina laughs happily and opens the car door, and as she gets out she says, "Maybe I should have effing stayed in the effing classroom where I effing belonged. But don't fire me, okay, boss?"

There are eight of us for dinner. Flora's friend Lloyd is here, Lizzy has her friend Homa, and Kenny has a girl named Amber who, except for the white cowboy boots, looks surprisingly conventional for his taste. He usually likes women with big makeup and clothes that fit like sausage skin.

"How do you know Kenny?" I ask Amber.

"Um."

"At her job," Kenny says, "I seen her and asked her out."

"Where do you work?"

"Um. Jungle-Land Pets."

"I'd love to work at a pet store," Tina says.

Amber stares at her shoes.

"Kenny," I say, "why were you in the pet store?"

"Buying mice. For my snake."

"When did you . . ."

"It's a boa. This guy I know was moving, so he gave it away, and I took it. Aquarium and everything, and it's like six feet long and eats mice, 'cept I bought too many, 'cause it only eats, like, a couple a month. So I put the rest in the freezer, but it's not as cool to feed him the dead ones, so I'll keep those for emergency food. I think I'll buy him a rat next."

"We have rats," Amber whispers.

"We're almost ready," Flora says, taking Amber's hand. "I'm just *thrilled* you could join us. Kenny's told us *all* about you."

I glance at Lizzy, who's glancing at me. We both know Flora has confused this new girl Amber with some girl named Brita who none of us ever met because, despite Kenny's vigorous campaign, she dodged him for weeks and finally threatened to get a restraining order if he didn't stop calling.

Flora leans close to Kenny and says, "She's lovely."

Lizzy and Homa get dinner on the table. They've been friends since grade school. Homa has dark skin and striking black eyebrows. We all sit, and Flora says, "Let's thank the goddess." She takes Lloyd's hand on one side and Homa's on the other. Lloyd has Tina on his other side.

"Goddess of plenty . . ."

I notice Kenny groping for Lizzy's hand, but she has it wrapped around her water glass and isn't letting go.

". . . and the joy of our togetherness . . ."

Lizzy looks pissed.

Tina's thumb does a caress on the back of my hand. I wonder if it's inadvertent. She has Amber on her other side.

". . . enfolded in the womb of our earth. Amen."

"Excuse me," Lloyd says. He goes into the kitchen to wash his hands.

"I wish Chip could have joined us," Flora says. "I invited him, but he couldn't make it."

"Too bad," I say. I'm not sure what to make of this. Chip has always just been my professional buddy. I knew he was talking to

Flora sometimes in the wake of his divorce, but I didn't know they had a real friendship. It makes sense, though. When an FBI agent thinks of becoming an animal trainer, speaking wistfully of blending spirits with the animals, he has apparently glimpsed a skewed reality in which Flora is a regular visitor.

"Kenny," I say, "I see you haven't dug out that area for the patio. What's up?"

"Boulders," he says. "That mound right there. I thought it was dirt. But it's one big rock. And there's another over there."

"What's next?"

"I know some guys. They got a backhoe, but they're busy. They say they can fit me in next week."

Bill-the-Dog comes over and nuzzles Flora. She subtly drops a piece of fish off the table.

"Mom!" Lizzy snaps.

"Oh, for goodness sakes," Flora says, and drops another bit of fish to assert herself. Bill-the-Dog gobbles the treats and, in her enthusiasm, gives Lloyd a quick lick on the hand.

"Excuse me," Lloyd says, and goes into the kitchen to wash his hands.

"Do you have a pet of your own, Amber?" Tina asks.

"Um. The house where I live has a cat," Amber says. Amber has sandy hair and a youthful look, with full cheeks and sleepy eyes.

"I've been comparing the different Jet Skis," Kenny says.

Tina says, "Homa: That's an interesting name."

"Iranian," Homa says. "It's a bird. A bird like the phoenix. It's a good omen."

"We sell birds," Amber whispers.

"It's a lovely name," I say, and Tina gives me a sideways kick under the table because I said "lovely," which she must have decided signals insincerity.

"Birds *are* good omens," I say. "We thought of naming you after a bird, Lizzy. Remember, Flo?"

"No."

"Phoebe."

"No," Flora says, "I don't remember. In fact, I don't remember consulting you at all. We weren't married, so it wasn't really your decision, was it?"

"Mom," Lizzy says threateningly.

"What, dear?" (Innocent.)

"Of course, we could have gone with Ptarmigan or Wren or Robin," I say, to lighten things up.

"Cuckoo," Kenny says.

"Or Yellow Rail," I say. "Yellow Rail Davis."

"Daddy," Lizzy says. She looks crushed, and I feel terrible, because I forgot that we know about yellow rails only because of Cassandra, so they're *not* omens of good luck, at least not to Lizzy and me.

To change the subject, I say, "Kenny, tell us about your Jet Ski."

Kenny talks about horsepower and acceleration. Lizzy, I notice, is rolling her eyes as conspicuously as possible. Then she blurts, "Kenny, none of us gives a crap about your stupid Jet Ski."

"Elizabeth," Flora says.

Something is odd. Lizzy is rarely childish, and I've never seen her be like this toward Kenny, whom she usually tries to mother.

Lizzy and Homa get into a conversation of their own. I can't believe I brought Tina into this. It started with my feeling low and calling Flora that day last week. She asked me to dinner. I had to cancel. Reschedule. People got invited. Then it was a dinner party. I lean over and whisper to Tina, "It's like that rule of trial law, isn't it? If there's something that weakens your case, make sure the jury hears it early so they don't feel tricked."

She smiles. "Don't be silly. This is *lovely*."

"And Flora gets into a mood sometimes," I whisper.

"She's your ex. Wait'll you meet mine."

"Tina," Kenny says, "I hear you got a hung jury this week."

"Yeah, Tamika Curtis. Nick and I were talking about it when we got here. About whether we should retry her."

"What'd she do?"

"She helped make some meth," I say.

Tina says, "She's a user; she helped out in exchange for some product. She has three little girls."

"Are you going to try her again, Daddy?" Lizzy asks.

I shrug, not wanting to get into it with this crowd.

"But Daddy!" Lizzy says. "Three little girls. And you want to put her in jail?"

"Elizabeth," Flora says, "your father likes putting people in jail. He tried to put me in jail once, didn't you, dear?"

"Oh, for Christ's sake."

Everyone, even Kenny, has sense enough not to go anywhere near this comment.

Now dessert.

Now tea.

Now Tina and I are in the car, and before we're even out of the driveway, she says, "Oh my God, what's the deal between Lizzy and Kenny? She seems to hate him."

"No, she loves him like a brother. I don't know, maybe she's mad because he's boinking Amber."

"So?"

"Apparently, Lizzy thinks he's taking advantage of Amber. Amber is slow."

"I noticed. But they seem to like each other."

"I guess you'd have to know Kenny better."

"Is he a heartbreaker?"

"Wrong word."

"Exploiter?"

"Maybe."

Silence. Neither of us mentions Flora's comment that I tried to put her in jail. But I know Tina is sharp and inquisitive, and I'm dreading her question about it.

She doesn't ask.

When we're almost back to town, I say, "Okay, you want to hear it?"

"Yes," she says, "tell me."

Toby, my infant son, had learned to sit up on his own. He sat up, then he fell and bumped his head. No big deal for a normal kid, but for one with hemophilia A, it's life-threatening. We'd been to the hospital a lot with Toby. They knew us; they knew Toby. Dr. Wallis would meet us there. He was ancient—his eyebrows reminded me of weeds erupting through the cracks in a playground. He'd trained as a doctor in the thirties and developed his ethic (if you could call it that) in the post-industrial brave new world where, a continent away, plans were in the works for an untainted race.

"The hidden defect," Dr. Wallis called it. I remember our first appointment after Toby was born. "Such a short and painful life he'll have," the doctor said, and the eyebrows dipped, convincing us that his grief was almost as great as our own. This was his theme every time we sped those forty miles to the hospital. A short and painful life. "With any mercy, it won't draw out too long."

There was no Internet then. We lived in the north woods, near a town where the public library was the size of a one-car garage. Dr. Wallis was beloved in town. *Trust Doc,* everybody said.

We brought Toby to the city. *Not so short, not so painful,* they said, but back home, under Doc's compassionate honesty, Flora was convinced that the urban doctors were too timid to deliver honest news.

Flora had always been a searcher. Intelligent but mistrusting of her own instincts, as some girls are raised to be. She was a disciple in search of her guru. In the early months of Toby's life, Flora lived in a state of fear and exhaustion and desperation. Increasingly, through Toby's short life Flora found her answers in the bottomless compassion of Dr. Wallis's sad eyes.

Toby fell over and bumped his head, as babies do, and Flora, giving the gift that Dr. Wallis had said only she could give, didn't call an ambulance or rush him to the hospital. Instead, she sat him on her lap and rocked him on his way to a happier place.

As for me, I'd only recently taken over as district attorney and didn't even have an assistant yet. I worked ceaselessly. I'd entrusted Toby to Flora, who'd been trusting Dr. Wallis. It never occurred to me *not* to trust Flora. I should have seen it in her, though—her vulnerability. We thought the disease was the evil, but it turned out the real evil was Dr. Wallis, who beguiled Flora. You can be vigilant against foreign evils, but it is the evil under your own roof that escapes notice. Flora might as well have opened our door to an ax murderer, inviting him in to slay us all. With Toby dead, with grief amuck in my soul, I focused my fury on Flora. I did what I do best: I prosecuted.

Failing to provide a seriously ill child with medical care is a crime: I charged Flora with criminal neglect and involuntary manslaughter, but the case didn't last long. The state attorney general's office took over and quickly dismissed the charges. "We can't win this, Nick," the AG told me on the phone. "Remember the religious exemption. If she was treating him with prayer, then the law doesn't require her to call a doctor."

"She's never prayed a day in her life," I answered.

"If she *says* she was praying . . ."

"Put her on the stand, she won't lie."

"Think about it," the AG said. "This isn't something you want to be involved in. Think about your future."

"Fuck my future."

"Then let me put it this way. It's not something I want the Department of Law involved in. We're not prosecuting."

Maybe I could have forgiven Flora if it had been more clear-cut, if she'd been more clearly wrong, if she'd been more decisively coopted into Dr. Wallis's cruel view of humanity. But as the attorney general argued to me that day, nobody could say for sure that Toby would have lived if he'd made it to the hospital. People remind me of this as if it's supposed to be a comfort, as if it vindicates Flora's decision, but I see it differently. The uncertainty has left an emotional labyrinth with no exit. I don't know whether I'm supposed to forgive her for essentially killing our son, or for failing to believe in miracles.

CHAPTER 31

I'm not wearing a tux. TMU pretends to be angered, but he doesn't care, because it's not that kind of city. The mayor is here (red bow tie, no tux), and the governor was invited, though he won't show. It's an invitation-only reception, but anybody who wanted an invite got one.

We're upstairs above the Rain Tree in what was recently the abandoned and cavernous production floor of Rokeby Mills. Now it's a convention center. The side facing the river is all windows, framed in the bright trim of local pines. The room is multilevel: You step down into the several wombish semicircles with built-in sofas for looking out at the river as you sip cocktails in a happy glow of economic upturn and architectural preservation. You go up a step to the bar and buffet areas. Standing here, I can see the North Woods brewery down on the floodplain where, just five years ago, four hundred golden Guernseys wallowed.

TMU insisted I come. He wants me out shaking hands and, with any luck, getting my smiling mug in the news. He has also brought along Pleasant Holly, my equivalent in the civil division of our office. Pleasant is pleasant. She has been on the job only about six months, but so far, we're all impressed. Tina is here, too. I invited her, but she's circulating in the crowd while I'm staying close to the bowl of shrimp.

Hollis Phippin is here. I catch sight of him standing in one of those lounges by the window. I'd like to pretend I don't see him, but he's already spotted me, so I walk over to say hi.

He grabs my hand and shakes robustly. "I have to admit, I'm kind of flattered, Nick," he says.

"How so, Hollis?"

"That the FBI finds me a credible suspect in Scud Illman's murder. Did you know they came by for a conversation?"

"I heard something about that." To change the subject, I say, "Are you connected to the Rokeby project, Hollis?"

"Oh, you know," he says, "everyone's involved somehow; it's not that big a town." The cheerfulness leaves his face in a flash. "Tell me what you think, Nick. Is the one who killed Zander still out there?"

"We believe so, Hollis."

"And the Illman character, couldn't he have shot my son and a deer in the same night?"

I tell Hollis about my midnight drive to the reservoir.

There is a commotion: Two of the regulars from the vets' table down in the Rain Tree roll Steve in his wheelchair off the escalator. All three are laughing. Steve's helpers are in coat and tie. One looks respectable. The other has a face of busted capillaries and big blackhead-infested pores, and he beams his yellow-toothed smile at the watching crowd. "Damn near let him roll back down." He laughs, then he and Steve do a quick high five, and Steve rolls over to the no-host bar.

"It's all in violation," Hollis says. "The elevator won't get installed for at least six months. Maybe a year. The place shouldn't even be open. You could shut us down, you know, Nick. I think you should. Shit, Steve there, he could sue . . . HEY, STEVE!"

Steve doesn't hear him.

Apparently, Hollis downed a few more drinks than I realized. He turns back to me. "Tell me which is worse, Nick. Us putting millions—twenty-two-point-five million, to be exact—into this worthless pile of bricks, and leaving out the elevator so American heroes whose legs got blown off by Richard Nixon can't get in without their drinking buddies pushing them up the escalator. That or my son, Zander, selling a little pot. Which is worse?"

"Well, Hollis, I—"

"I'll tell you which. The pot. You know why? I'll tell you why. Because boys are supposed to come to their rich daddies for tuition.

Do you know why Zander didn't come to me for tuition, Nick? Do you?"

"No, Hollis."

"Because I'm an asshole. So if you want to know who killed Zander, Nick, I'll tell you. I killed him. I didn't kill Scud Illman, though I appreciate the vote of confidence. Tell you what, though. When you do figure out who pulled the trigger, you let me know. I'll try to justify the confidence you guys have in me, okay? I'll go blow his fucking head off. Now, if you'll excuse me, I'm going to go find Steve and tell him if he wants to sue me and all the other assholes involved in violating his rights, he can count on my support."

Hollis walks away. His suit is conservative and distinguished, with perfect pant cuffs and just a touch of narrowing in the waist. From behind, he looks youthful except for the graying hair. He stumbles sideways, recovers, and disappears into the crowd.

I get another drink and go stand beside Tina. She tugs at my sleeve affectionately. "There you are."

"Here I am."

"You having fun?"

"I like shrimp, and I like beer. You?"

"I hate artichoke dip."

"We could leave."

"Soon."

TMU finds us. "Excuse us, Tina, I need Nick for a minute," and he steers me by the elbow to the coat alcove. I expect a strategy session about my prospects for making the short list. But when he turns toward me, his face has lost its clownish rumple. His eyes are fierce. He says, "I asked you if there were skeletons, Nick. You assured me there weren't."

"There aren't."

"There are," he says, "because I'd call being sued for malicious prosecution a skeleton, wouldn't you?"

I don't answer. I stare into his wounded eyes—watery old-man's eyes, eyelids red and creased with the wear of his seven-plus decades, but still accusing, still sure. I have the pleasant notion of smashing his self-righteous glare with murderous fists—letting his despicable smugness ooze out across the floor in rivulets of blood. Of course it isn't my beloved mentor Harold Schnair who stands before me, but Dr. Wallis himself. I see Doc's sad eyes, Doc's smugness, Doc's face that I would happily pound into unrecognizable pulp. How fitting that, having taken my wife and son, Dr. Wallis will take from me the seat on the U.S. Circuit Court of Appeals.

"Let's hear it," Harold says. "Maybe we can do some spin."

When I was a district attorney up north those many years ago, I was generally immune from being sued by anyone I prosecuted. Malicious prosecution is a lawsuit brought against a prosecutor by a defendant. Usually, such cases are dismissed outright. In fact, the disgruntled defendant usually can't find a lawyer willing to sue, because the cases are losers. You have to show that the prosecutor was not just wrong but that he was twisting the system to his own purposes. So long as any charge I filed was supported by a shred of evidence, then the people I prosecuted, guilty or innocent, couldn't touch me.

What happened was that after Toby's death, I charged Dr. Wallis with conspiracy to commit child abuse and manslaughter. Normally, to arrest a respectable geezer like the doctor, you'd approach him after-hours and ask that he accompany you to the station for booking and bail. It is discreet and respectful. But he deserved no respect. I brought in the troopers because the sheriff wouldn't do it. We took the doctor from his office in the middle of town, in handcuffs, at midday.

There was no question about what he'd done: He'd convinced an anguished mother not to seek medical help for her desperately ill son. He proudly admitted it. I could even show a pattern of behavior. Other parents of chronically ill or disabled kids told similar stories. My case failed on the question of whether what he did was illegal. The judge, a cautious man whose own kids had been delivered by the doctor, said Dr. Wallis did nothing illegal. He said Doc gave medical advice as best he could. Whether or not it was good advice didn't concern the court. The charges were dismissed immediately, and then Dr. Wallis had the audacity to turn right around and sue me for malicious prosecution. He wanted $5 million or alternatively, one dollar and a public apology. Naturally, the state wanted me to apologize, because they'd be on the hook for $5 million, as well as having to defend me. I refused.

Ultimately, the doctor and the state settled. I wouldn't have anything to do with it.

I tend to look back on it as *my* victory because, though Dr. Wallis had his loyalists in town, many of the younger and more educated families in the area quit the doctor and had their medical files sent over to the new clinic at the hospital forty miles to the south. When the state licensing board performed an investigation of its own, they decided in a split vote that he was fit to practice.

So when TMU asked me if I had any skeletons in the closet, I didn't even think of this.

"I guess it's not so bad," TMU says when I finish explaining. "You didn't lose, you settled. And if it becomes an issue, it's got fabulous spin potential: senile old doctor; aggrieved father defending the rights of sick children, inept small-town court system. We can make you a regular folk hero . . . again."

Harold has his joviality back. He is convinced that I didn't deceive him on purpose.

At the elevator, Tina takes my arm. We descend and drive toward our office. "What if you get this thing?" she says, meaning the seat on the circuit court.

"Don't be ridiculous," I say. I'm not being honest, because professionally I've always had good luck, and I *expect* to get the appointment. It would be consistent. Jobs have fallen into my lap, things have come along at the right time. One thing that came at the right time was Dr. Wallis's stroke. It was a couple of weeks after they settled the lawsuit: a massive stroke, dead within days. It was good timing because it saved me from killing him, which I wanted to do. The criminal justice system had failed me—ironic, seeing as I *was* the system in my little corner of the woods—so I decided to resolve things. Because TMU's analysis is wrong: There was nothing senile about Dr. Wallis.

The question isn't so much whether Toby would have survived if Flora had rushed him to the hospital. I've looked into it, and I believe he would have. The bigger issue for me was that Dr. Wallis wanted a world without boys like Toby. He didn't believe in medical heroics and in nurturing the weak. He believed in removing them. No, he wasn't senile. He was cogent, he was sharp. He was a monster.

Shortly after Toby's death, an untraceable handgun found its way into my possession, and my toes wiggled over the cliff edge of criminality. Then the doctor died of natural causes, and though I had wanted to kill him, no crime was committed (except for how I got the gun, which, in the scale of things, was tiny).

Most guilty thoughts never give rise to action. For a prosecutor, guilty thoughts without a guilty act are irrelevant. The only way to survive this work is to lean in to it, eyes on the soil, and trudge. It's not my job to ask *how come* when crimes don't get committed, just as it's not my job to ask *how come* when they do; woe unto the prosecutor who keeps his own set of scales. I'm a lawyer, and my client is the government. It is a government of laws, and I'm an obeyer of laws. I've sworn an oath. And though I once had guilty thoughts of killing Dr. Wallis, it spawned no guilty act. No crime was committed.

Now eyes on the soil. Trudge.

Tina and I take my Volvo back to the office so she can get her car. "Where's Lizzy tonight?" she asks.

"Flora's," I answer. Other than that, we ride in a silence made notable by throat clearings, yawns, and my mumbled responses to small traffic events. ("Oh shoot," I whisper when the stoplight up ahead goes yellow.)

It is in the air. *It.* Two adults arriving at the same place in life at the same time.

"Mmm," she says, her head resting back against the seat, eyes closed for a few seconds. What she means by "Mmm" is that the car is warm, the tummy is full of shrimp and beer, the hour is late, the night is long, and the soul—aching to believe in something that, time and again, has been proved impossible—is willing to take a chance.

We idle at the intersection. This thing with Doc Wallis: I'd like to tell Tina about it, but anything I say would leave too much unsaid. I don't have the clarity to find words right now. I wish the light would just stay red.

"It's green, Nick," she says.

"So it is." I pull into the empty parking garage, spin up to our floor, and pull in jauntily beside her car. "That was fun," I say. "I wish I didn't have so much work to do before tomorrow."

Off we go in separate directions, she to her home, me to my office.

They say grief can quickly corrode all the supports that keep a marriage upright. It's common for couples to split following the death of a child. Is it also common, I wonder, for the divorce to fail as monumentally as the marriage did? Because Flora and I have failed at our divorce: We're twenty-plus years out, and both of us are single. Flora lives in a second childhood of discombobulation and fiercely guarded naiveté. And me; well, didn't I just send Tina packing for no good reason? Go figure.

Alas, Flora and I are much too entangled to get far apart. I need her near me because I keep hoping she'll forgive me for trying to throw her ass in jail. It's the same for her: She sticks around hoping I'll absolve her for not trying to save our son. The confounding truth is that we're both barking up the wrong tree. The forgiveness each of us craves, which we probably will never get, would come not from the other but from ourselves. I'm afraid that the result of all this is that as the years go by, we're more and more like an old married couple, except for the fact that we're not so old, not married, and not a couple.

CHAPTER 32

It's late. I make a complete survey of the criminal division offices to ensure that I'm alone. I am. In my office, I check my voice mail. The only message of note is from Chip: "Nick, you promised me the other day that you'd call. I really, really need to speak with you, preferably here at my office. Call."

I delete the message. Chip was acting strange the day of the meeting over in the FBI's conference room. I'd rather not talk to him until I've done a little poking around.

I walk out of my office and close the door. I'll miss this office if TMU does maneuver me onto the circuit court bench. I wonder who will replace me. Either they'll hire from outside the office, or Upton will get the job because none of the other assistants has the gravitas to land the seat. Tina, for example: smart, ambitious, good at what she does, but what she does is try cases. Same with the others. Only Upton, in his invisible way, has made himself seem "greater than." And TMU likes Upton. It's a natural fit.

My master key opens all office doors. It opens Upton's. At his desk, I flip on the lamp, sit in the chair, and rock. I've read stories about the FBI profilers. They like to immerse themselves in the what and where of the crime. So that's what I'm doing here, I'm immersing.

"What's going on, Upton?" I ask the empty room. I get up and look at his stuff. On a plastic stand on the bookshelf, he has a football signed by all his teammates. It's from some game he won with a field goal of I-forget-how-many yards, but it was a lot. There are the pictures of his girls, and of his wife, Cindy.

His bookshelves have the usual assortment of law books and trial technique manuals and law reviews. There's a small section of general reading: novels and political history and travelogues. We all have this. I call it the "I'm a whole person" shelf, but I bet if I slipped a twenty between any two of these books, I could come back a year from now and retrieve it. So just for kicks, I do. I slip it between *Moby Dick* (classic leather-bound reprint with gilt lettering) and *The Wealth of Nations* (probably from his college days) and continue my tour, working my way past more law books, then the wall of diplomas and awards, and around to the desk. Nothing.

Next, file cabinets. I slide one open, and it's packed end to end with case files. It would take a team of trained agents to hunt for something nefarious here. I close it, look in the next drawer— ditto—and the next.

Now the computer. Like most of the rest of us, Upton leaves it on at night with his main programs running. I check the recent documents. Nothing. Braving the same tingle I felt at snooping on Kendall's cell phone, I open Upton's e-mail file and quickly get in the rhythm of scanning through. They're all work-related: messages from defense attorneys, court clerks, judges' clerks, investigators, expert witnesses, press inquiries. And personal e-mails that, as far back as I look, are of no consequence. I don't read any of these, just scan.

My failure to find any dirt is good. I don't want to find dirt on Upton. I don't even want to be doing this. I don't want to be in his office. I don't want to be a sneak and a snoop. I don't want to find out Upton is on the take, and I really don't want to find out he sold Cassandra to her assassins. I don't want to have snooped in Kendall's cell phone. I don't want to doubt Chip. I don't want to be sucked into the gaping void of Hollis Phippin's grief.

But here I am. My suspicion of Upton started not with suspicion but with concern. He seems different; his head hasn't been in the game. And then when he was so willing to consider flipping Scud, making him an informant, essentially turning our backs on the murders of Zander and Cassandra, it got me wondering if something was seriously wrong because Upton isn't one to offer a sweet deal for somebody he thinks is guilty. He is a prosecutor's prosecutor. He speaks jokingly about his contempt for the "disruptors" of our "urban utopia," but it isn't joking. Upton is a true believer in the ideal of a shining city on the hill and is unapologetic about bringing the full weight and fury of the legal system down on the heads of any who would corrupt that vision. So I'm baffled by his sudden interest in immunizing Scud for two capital murders. Something stinks.

Scud Illman claimed he has dealings with Upton; the phone record bears that out; Upton denies the conversation. Even if nothing else turns up, that phone call alone is staggeringly inappropriate. Enforcement should never speak privately to a defendant or suspect who is represented by counsel; an assistant U.S. attorney should never wantonly conceal information from a superior; a lawyer should never go sticking his nose into someone else's case without reporting it. These aren't just little niceties Upton has violated; these are bedrock rules of criminal prosecution.

I abandon my computer search and go back to being Upton: I sit, absorb. The computer screen clicks back to black. No screen saver.

Ethically, my searching this office isn't as bad as searching Kendall's phone. In fact, if I find real dirt on Upton, it would even be admissible in court. But I feel scummy, and in an instant, all my certainty fades. Upton is my friend and trusted colleague. And even if he's into something, I'll never find it. "The hell with this," I say aloud.

I stand up to leave. Not just to leave but to be done with it all, because it pisses me off that I've come in here and snooped. I'll just call Upton. I'll cop to having peeked at Kendall's phone log (Upton won't care) and demand to know why he and Scud were having a tête-à-tête. I step around Upton's desk and catch sight of a photo of his teenage girls, a few years older than Lizzy, and I feel what guys our age feel at the encroachments of age. Upton is still strong, sharp, and powerful, but we've both found ourselves beyond the crest—which, it turns out, doesn't tower high above the landscape. It doesn't shimmer magically in the rare air of enlightenment. It's just a little hill. Another time I might reflect wistfully on all of this, but what occurs to me now is that Upton and I grew up in the era of hard copies. And Upton, I know, is even less comfortable in the electronic world than I am. Forget about hidden or encrypted files, I ought to rifle the desk drawers.

And there it is. Center drawer, laid on top, unfolded and unsigned, addressed to TMU: ". . . with great regret that I resign . . . embarrassment I've caused you or this office . . . inappropriate actions . . . indiscretions of youth . . ."

Standard stuff for resignation in disgrace but with no clue what the disgrace is. It isn't as simple as Upton being our snitch, because that's a criminal matter, and it would mean long prison time. He would leave here in bracelets, not with some polite letter of regret.

The letter is dated last Friday, Scud Illman's farewell day on earth.

I leave the letter where it is, close the drawer, turn off the desk lamp, and walk away. On my way out, though, in the now dim light, I eye Upton's "I'm a whole person" shelf. What are the chances we'll both be here in a year? Or a month? Or a week? I can't guess, but I'm not betting on the status quo. I go and retrieve my twenty dollars from between Melville and Smith.

CHAPTER 33

I hadn't planned to be a prosecutor. Criminal defense or environmental law would have been more my thing, but fresh out of law school and with a pile of debt, I took the first good job I found: assistant DA, up north.

Flora and I lived in the cabin. I used to keep my suits at the office so they wouldn't smell of wood smoke. I'd been in the job only a short time when my boss died of octogenarianitis. When Toby died, I lost my focus and was about to resign ahead of being fired when a dilapidated home in the county burned to the ground. It turned out the owner had recently increased his insurance to well above the value. I charged him with arson and insurance fraud. He somehow got enough money together to hire a flamboyant lawyer from the city who made the trial into a public spectacle, attempting to turn things around and put the town itself on trial because of the recent mill rate increase. It was a good strategy, poorly executed. The news stations took an interest, and I found myself cast as the country lawyer going up against the big-city smoothie. It was in my favor that the defendant, Jimmy Luther, was an obscenity-spewing loser. In news interviews, he couldn't keep track of whether he was saying he hadn't burned the house or that he'd been justified in doing it. He also had a well-publicized history of domestic abuse.

Conversely, I looked young and jaunty on camera. I had a conspiratorial smile, which made viewers feel smart, and I had a voice "like hot buttered rum" (according to some TV people I spoke with). I tried the case recklessly, and in interviews, I fell naturally into a Will Rogers role of innocent country boy with brilliance born of a pure heart. The other guy's flamboyance failed to cover his ineptitude, and I won easily.

"Don't act so surprised," Flora said of my newfound fame. We were on stools at the lunch counter in town. She was out of our cabin for good but hadn't switched from wearing jeans to dressing in long gossamer skirts and crystal necklaces. "I always knew you could be *smart* if you'd stop fretting about every goddamn pebble in your way and *do* something. Anyway, congrats."

The arson case got me enough attention that when, in an unrelated case, I brought murder charges against the husband of a "suicide" victim, the news stations were all over it. We even got some national mention. It was an easy case. The cause of death was an overdose of MS Contin (a morphine-related painkiller), but there was also residue of the drug in the empty beer cans, and in the leavings of the McDonald's burgers, and in the grounds left in the coffeemaker, and even on the victim's toothbrush. There was residue on the bathroom sink where her husband had crushed the pills. He claimed he'd gotten drunk and passed out, and by the time he woke up, she was dead. But his prints were everywhere on the pill vial and the beer cans and the burger wrappers and the coffeemaker. I argued that he'd gotten her drunk enough to be persuadable, fed her a bunch of pills straight, plus burger, beer, and coffee, all laced with more of the drug. He'd recently upped the life insurance and had an affair in the background. The guy was convicted, and suddenly I was a household name in our little corner of the woods. Invitations to do public service announcements and personal appearances followed.

I liked my shot at fame. Our Republican congressman had announced his retirement, so I decided to get away from the small town, the cabin in the woods, and the site of Flora's and my misery. I mentioned around that I was thinking of a run. Word reached the party—the Republican Party—and some men visited to say they'd already picked the congressman's replacement, but if I would be willing to step aside, they could promise me something nice. Otherwise, they'd crush me in the primary and snuff any future I might have within the party. This was all communicated subtly, the overriding message was that I was an up-and-comer with lots of promise, and they were thrilled with my success and would like to be part of my future. We talked about what they could offer that would fit my talents and interests. They would work on it and call me back. I didn't tell them I had planned to run as a Democrat.

A few days later, they had a firm offer: assistant U.S. attorney, chief of the criminal division. It was already greased for me. I could spend a few years there, get experience, and make a name.

I accepted, and here I still am, twenty-plus years later.

Any notion I'd had of playing God in my role as a prosecutor—of defining criminality and being the one to make moral distinctions— it ended with Flora and Toby and Dr. Wallis. Doc, with his concealed belief in eugenic culling, was—in my view of the world—evil but apparently not criminal. Flora was arguably criminal but not evil. And if I'd killed the doctor, as I wanted to, what would I have been? Criminal, certainly, but what else? Evil? Immoral? Or heroic?

Navigating the reefs and channels of all this morality is beyond me. Make me the helmsman, not the captain. Tell me what to do and I'll do it, but let someone else chart the course; I don't have the stomach for it.

I slept in my office and was up and out before the place came to life. Now in the town of Ellisville, I stop for breakfast and—craving a bit of comfort to wedge between me and the world—I call Tina.

"Hullo," she answers crisply. She knows it's me but pretends not to.

"Hi," I say, "it's Nick," and I wait to see if she wants to add something, like how glad she is that I've called. She doesn't. I could blurt out a hurried, self-analytical apology for my anticlimactic snuffing of last night's romantic possibilities, but I'd find myself entangled in the briar patch of stupid word choices and ambiguous meanings. Better to keep my trap shut and launch corrective action later, so I switch tactics. I say, "I informed TMU that we won't be retrying Tamika Curtis."

"I'm pleased with your decision," she says.

"Yes, you made quite a convincing argument last night."

"Glad you think so."

Then there is silence, so in a call-ending tone, I say, "I won't be in till late."

"I'll spread the word," she answers, all business.

Fuseli the tattoo artist told me of another con, a guy named Tipper who knows things. He was a bookie who got too ambitious. His real name, I learn, is Larry Green. He was convicted on mail fraud, extortion, and attempted bribery of federal regulatory officials.

The guards sit him in the same chair where the dissipated Fuseli told his tale. Tipper's eyes are tired, with pleats of flesh stretching down his cheeks and disappearing into a graying jungle of beard. He is a bland guy who speaks quietly. I tell him as much of my story as he needs to know.

"Can you help me with my parole?" he asks.

"If you were to be very helpful, Mr. Green . . ."

He shrugs. "I don't know shit, but if I was you, I'd go ask Platty."

"Who?"

"Guy on the outside. Connected. We did business. Tell him I sent you, and he might have something for you. Platypus, that's what he goes by. I don't know where he's hanging out these days, but try the Elfin Grot."

"Elfin Grot. What is that? It sounds familiar."

"A bar in Rivertown."

"Of course," I say, thinking aloud. "Upton has mentioned it. A place where deals get made."

Tipper was slouched over the table; now he straightens some.

"So this Platypus: What's he into?" I ask.

"Nothing. Just information."

"I don't know, Larry, giving me the name of one guy on the outside who probably doesn't know squat isn't all that helpful."

"I'd really like to get out of here," he says. "Really like to get a friendly word on my parole. And maybe I don't got much to offer about what you was asking about, but maybe I got something else might be of interest to you. How about that? How about I give you this freebie—some info you might find useful. Right?"

"Useful is useful, Mr. Green. I'm not buying information, I'm merely saying that if you proved helpful, I might be moved to put in a word."

His eyes are alight with something. "You just said something about a guy named Upton. Is that Upton Cruthers?"

I nod.

"Upton. Uptown Upton. Uptown Cruthers. I'd forgot he was in with the feds."

"You know him?"

"I used to do business with him. Lots of business. When I was making book. He'd bet on anything. Fucker'd bet on pro wrestling, and nobody bets on wrestling, 'cause it ain't real. But Uptown would bet. Had a problem, if you know what I mean. He got in over his head a few times. Had to get visited by some guys, okay? But this was just while I knew him. There was rumors, though."

"What rumors?"

"From before. Way back. Like some debts he owed got canceled because he helped out."

"Helped how?"

"Remember, I ain't involved in this shit, okay? Some guys want to improve the odds, it's all on them. I just take the action. Most times I don't even know about it beforehand. 'Course, in my business, you learn to spot it. You get a few Big Louis types putting money on the same outcome, then you notice the QB gets sacked an extra time or two, pass gets completed when it should have been blocked, that shit. Or maybe some kicker misses an easy three-pointer. You got me?"

"This is bullshit," I say.

He shrugs.

"You're telling me Upton sold games?"

Tipper shakes his head. "Not that simple. You can't buy a game from a guy who makes that kind of money. You got to persuade."

"Persuade how?"

"Different for everybody. Maybe a ballplayer likes his nose candy too much; maybe another guy's got some old girlfriends who weren't exactly eighteen or weren't exactly willing. Shit, a football team ain't a church choir. You got guys with vulnerabilities and some big money changing hands. Let's say you got a big game coming up: You go to the files, find three or four players with issues, guys on the favored team, pay 'em a visit. Maybe one of 'em's a kicker who likes to gamble, and maybe he's betting on his own games. There you go. That's money in the bank. You haven't guaranteed anything, but you've sure as hell changed the odds."

"Who knows about this?"

"Everybody knows."

"I mean about Upton."

"Everybody and nobody. Everybody knows he was vulnerable. But whether your man Uptown got an actual visit from someone expressing an actual interest in the outcome of an actual game, nobody knows. He's been gone a long time. Guys die. Guys forget. What good is having dirt on a player who hasn't suited up in twenty years? Am I right?"

"But if someone wanted to hold something over him . . ."

Tipper shrugs.

"Why are you telling me this?" I ask, suddenly pissed off by the whole thing.

"Just trying to help," Tipper says.

"Bullshit," I answer furiously. "You accuse an assistant U.S. attorney of . . . well . . ."

I stop myself. This guy isn't a witness; I don't have him on the stand. I'm not trying to debunk his story in front of a dozen persuadable John Q's. He's just a tipster, and my moment of rage is exactly what it is: a moment of rage from the frustration of not having a clue what to do next.

CHAPTER 34

Rivertown isn't a real town, it's just part of the city that started out as squatters' shacks in the early days and has remained an economic sinkhole. Houses are small and decrepit, with rotting porches and abandoned cars. But driving through, I see a new restaurant with a spiffed-up stucco facade and decorative lamps on either side of the door. The Dromedary, it's called. I guess times are changing.

"The Platypus?" I ask a woman on the street. She looks at me blankly and doesn't answer.

Oops. Platypus is the contact. Elfin Grot is the place. I ask someone else for the Elfin Grot and get directions. Just around the corner.

It is a bowling alley–shaped place: The bar and stools take up most of the width, leaving a narrow corridor that stretches from the small window on the street back into the hidden, smoky distance. The bartender is a woman. She studies me a second, then yells at the three guys on barstools, "For the millionth time, put out the goddamn cigarettes." They ignore her.

I laugh. "No," I say, "I'm not public health, I'm just looking for someone."

She reaches under the counter, takes out a lit cigarette, inhales deeply, and blows smoke out nose and mouth. "Who?"

"Platypus."

"Platty don't come around much now."

"Where can I find him?"

"Who are you?"

I hand her a card.

"Looks serious," she says.

"How do I find him? What's his real name?"

"He don't have a name."

I wait. She keeps washing glasses. The place is dim and thick with smoke. The stench of spilled beer is an ecosystem where these four organisms—bartender and three patrons—exist. Barnacles: The patrons look inert to the casual glance, but with more scrupulous observation, a subtle rhythm is revealed as they respirate and ingest. And the barkeep, she darts around with perplexing busyness.

"Do *you* have a name?" I ask her.

"I might."

"And it would be?"

"Go ahead and guess," she says. "I'm betting you'll get it first try."

"Huberly."

"There now, you got it."

One of the barnacles laughs, and I sit down on the stool beside him. Huberly was my freshman dorm in college. I'm always reminded of it by the reek of beer and cigarettes. My barstool neighbor is of some non-Caucasian mix, and I sense he's inconvenienced by my presence.

"You drinking?" Huberly asks.

"North Woods amber."

"Bud, Miller, or PBR."

"Okay, Granddad on ice," I say, then wave a hand at the barnacles and add, "Set them up again."

"A philanthropist."

The barnacles make grunts and shifts of posture that I interpret as thank-yous.

"So how can I find this guy Platypus?"

"Is it about his granddaughter?"

"I don't know about any granddaughter."

Huberly considers me a few seconds. She's sixtyish and looks like she has squeezed every ounce of attractiveness from a tired body. She has purplish hair and a shirt with lacy cuffs, and she's strikingly, clinically thin. I'm sure she's been targeted over the years by legions of alcohol-bolstered would-be mates, and she seems like she'd be adept at the parry and thrust of those negotiations. "You could come back tomorrow night," she says. "Like, say, at nine o'clock. Because what I'll do for you is I'll mention around that you'll be here. And these guys"—she indicates the barnacles—"Curly, Larry, and Moe here, at some point they'll get their fat asses off the stools for one reason or another, and chances are they'll mention how some suit was in here buying rounds and looking for Platty, and word gets around. You know?"

I give Huberly twice the cost of the drinks. "Nine o'clockish," I say, and walk out into the fresh air.

At home, dinner is a beef roast that has spent the day in the slow cooker filling my house with its burgundy-soaked, vegetable-assisted fragrance.

"Smells good, Dad," Lizzy says. We put plates on the table, olive bread, olive oil, and a salad of prewashed, precut, premixed greens. Lizzy selects the carrots, potatoes, and onions from the slow cooker, avoiding the actual roast. We pretend her vegetarianism isn't violated by eating vegetables that have simmered all day in the blood of a bovine. Usually I cook a more Eastern, garbanzo-ish meal, even for myself, but sometimes my inner carnivore stirs to life.

"You're quiet," she says.

"I'm thinking about work. Have I told you about the circuit court?"

"Only eighty-seven times. What are you brooding about?"

"I'm not brooding."

"Is it Tina?"

". . . No."

"You hesitated."

"Did not. It's confidential. Classified. I've got a . . . a problem at work," I say, recognizing that with sad pauses and a woeful voice, I'm begging her to keep asking. Lizzy has more common sense than anyone. No surprise that I find myself manipulating her to drag it out of me.

"Tell," she says.

"Hypothetically," I say, "hypothetically and confidentially. I've encountered evidence . . ." I stop. She's just fourteen. Already she's too involved in this, and here I am about to bring her further in because I need to get it off my chest and there's nobody else I know and trust enough except TMU, and I can't go to TMU, because that's the whole game—whether or not to throw Upton to the wolves.

"Evidence of what?" Lizzy asks.

"Evidence of lax standards at Turner Middle School. Moral standards, academic standards, fashion standards, problems with personal grooming."

"Daddy . . ."

"Our informants tell of actual handholding in the hallways, exposed belly buttons, butt cracks on display."

"Shut up, Daddy."

"Piercings, tattoos."

"Shut up, Daddy."

"A's given out to pretty girls who haven't earned them. And the reading of age-inappropriate literature. Books about adultery and . . . and more adultery."

"Are you awfully pleased with yourself, Daddy?"

"And we're going to raid the place."

"Let me know when you're done."

I go into the kitchen for a bottle of wine and two glasses. I pour myself a glass, then ceremoniously, I pour her about an inch.

"What's this for?"

"You're so grown up for fourteen. Wise beyond your years, responsible, disciplined, all of that. So I'm giving you this taste, illegal though it is, of adulthood. Because it's harmless. Here's to you, babe." I clink her glass.

"Daddy?"

"What?"

"You're a jerk. And you're avoiding the subject. I know you. You're supposed to be telling me about work."

"No, sweetheart, I'm definitely *not* supposed to be telling you about work. Drink your wine. That's the only taste of adulthood you're getting tonight."

"Fine," she says, genuinely pissed off, "and you know I'm a vegetarian, how come you're making me eat this garbage?" She pushes her plate away with an exaggerated motion, takes her salad bowl and the wine, and heads up to her room.

My Lizzy. As if Cassandra's murder hasn't been traumatic enough for her without me unloading on her. This thing with Upton: I need to talk to someone, but it has to be in complete confidence, and it has to be someone compassionate, who understands the law and enforcement and the stakes I'm dealing with. What I need, I realize, is not a fourteen-year-old girl. I need a lawyer.

CHAPTER 35

Kendall Vance writes precise letters that don't touch one another: "Conversation with Asst. U.S. Atty. Davis." It's the top line of a canary-yellow legal pad. On the next line, he letters the date.

"Can I see that?" I say, reaching across his desk. I pull the pad toward me, tear off the top sheet, crumple it, and pitch it over my shoulder.

"I see," he says.

"Just a discussion."

"Concerning someone I represent?"

"Indirectly."

"One moment," he says. He goes to his outer office and comes back with two cups of coffee. His is in a ceramic cup that I recognize as one the local public radio station sends when you pledge over fifty dollars. My coffee is in a paper cup, which seems a bit déclassé for a high-profile criminal attorney. "Now, don't keep me in suspense," he says, settling back behind his desk.

I tell him why I'm here. He already knows a lot of the story from his representation of Scud. I fill in details, though I fudge about my snooping in his, Kendall's, cell phone. "I became aware," I say, which is classic testimonial language for something you don't want to discuss. "I became aware that Upton conversed directly with Scud on at least one occasion, and yet when I asked Upton if that was the case, he denied it."

I tell Kendall about there being a leak in enforcement, and about the resignation letter I found in Upton's desk drawer, and about my conversation with Tipper, the con who told me about Upton's gambling. Kendall doesn't interrupt, but occasionally, I see him eye the yellow pad, wishing, no doubt, he could jot something down. A few times I get close to things I don't want to put out there—my other-than-professional interest in Cassandra, my almost blabbing this whole sorry mess to Lizzy, the sadness I felt when Scud's stepson, Colin, had to sit through the search of Scud's house. But every time I'm tempted to crack that valve, I see Kendall's eyes peering at me with such intensity that he looks nearly cross-eyed. Kendall is no confessor, no confidant. That's why I'm here: In legal matters, Kendall checks his feelings at the door, and he has the intellectual complexity of the *Boy Scout Handbook*. I want someone who, if A=B and B=C, can conclude, without getting mired in the math of his own emotional or ethical universe, that A=C. Because right now I can't.

Maybe it's dicey talking to Kendall. I chose him for a few reasons: First, he might know things about this case that I don't—things Scud might have told him. He wouldn't actually tell me any of it, but he might lead me in a useful direction. Also, though I don't particularly like Kendall, I know he won't play games, he won't intentionally lead me in the wrong direction. Too many defense lawyers are tweedy, muddle-headed moral relativists. Not Kendall. He knows the federal system, and if he has a conflict, he'll tell me. He won't try to screw with me just because I'm a prosecutor.

I weave my story out until I talk myself to a standstill.

"What was Upton's reaction when you said you were going to handle the Scud Illman prosecution yourself?" Kendall asks.

"Surprised."

"Disconcerted?"

"Who knows."

Kendall nods. "Your suspicions: Do you have a theory?"

"Perhaps," I say, "but at three-twenty an hour, I'd rather hear from you."

He laughs. "Professional courtesy, Nick," he says. "Let's say this first meeting is gratis."

I nod graciously. "Still, let me have your unvarnished impressions."

"Realizing that my impression is informed by the details you chose to provide, here is what I hear. I hear that Upton Cruthers has or had a gambling problem and that this knowledge, combined with observations of your own and information you've obtained, leads you to suspect that Assistant U.S. Attorney Cruthers may have been blackmailed, that the blackmailer was Scud Illman, and that Scud was trying to get Upton to sabotage your investigation and prosecution in the murders of Zander Phippin and/or Cassandra Randall."

"Yes," I say, "but there's more, isn't there?"

He missed a lot of it. Or maybe not. Maybe I held back too much in the telling, or maybe I've made a fundamental error in coming here. I'm wanting to talk about this the way I would with my stable of prosecutors and/or some agents at the Bureau. Kendall might be too much the defense attorney. Do all roads lead to innocence in his world? Is he incapable of seeing major crimes if he can see minor ones instead?

I stand and wander the room. I study his wall of fame. All prominent lawyers seem to have one. Plaques and certificates of appreciation: Big Brothers and Big Sisters board of directors; State Commission on the Causes and Treatments of Post-Traumatic Stress Disorder; Disability Law Center Board of Directors. Additionally, he has been pro bono counsel to the Center for Children's and Infants' Rights, and he is a volunteer mentor at the local Veterans' Reentry Program. He's been involved in some good things, which, dammit, forces me to further reconsider my contempt for him again.

"Okay, taking it a step further," Kendall says. "I hear that you're wondering how far Upton went to protect his secret. Like whether it was Upton himself who leaked Cassandra Randall's identity to the bad guys?"

"It has occurred to me."

"And his polite resignation letter was an attempt to put some worms back in the can. Like maybe if he got out ahead of Scud—or whoever was blackmailing him on the gambling—he could keep the snitching secret?"

"Sure," I say. "He knows he's about to get outed by Scud, so he snatches the ball. He cops to the gambling to, quote, clear his conscience, and he denies he ever threw a game. I had already taken over Scud's prosecution, so the question of whether Upton obfuscated on that is moot. Worst case: He loses his job. In all likelihood, Harold and I refuse to accept the resignation, and Upton gets out of it clean."

"What do you believe?" Kendall asks. "Is he the snitch or not?"

"It's still more complicated than that, isn't it?" I say.

"Meaning what?"

Kendall hasn't caught up with me. It's so obvious, I can't believe he's missed it. He just waits, so I feed it to him: "If someone's blackmailing you, Kendall, what are your options?"

"Pay or don't."

"Or?"

He shakes his head, confused.

"Oh, for Christ's sake, Kendall, you whack them. Isn't it kind of coincidental that Scud got killed late in the evening of the very day Upton wrote but apparently decided not to deliver his resignation letter?"

He stares at me, disbelieving.

"Why not?" I say.

"It's just . . ."

"Why the hell not? You find out a guy isn't who you think he is, where do you stop? He'd do this but not that; or he'd do this and that but not the other thing. Fuck it all, if a guy's dirty, he's dirty. And which is worse anyway, snitching secrets that get bystanders like Cassandra Randall killed, or putting a slug into some lowlife like Scud Illman? Personally, I might respect him if all he did was pop the likes of Scud; save everybody a lot of trouble. But snitching, that's a different matter. If Upton sold out Cassandra, I'll make it my life's work to see that . . ."

I stop. I was shouting. Kendall is surprised. He looks terrible, and I want to goad him—this lily-livered defender of hoodlums, gangsters, psychopaths. Here he is, struck speechless by the idea of a murderer among our brothers in the law. I don't say anything. We watch each other across the desk until it gets awkward. Finally, I say, "Anyhow, that's why I'm here."

"I see."

"'Cause I need to believe one thing or another before I do anything."

"Of course."

"And I needed to talk it through with someone who knows the landscape; to hear my thoughts out loud."

"Of course."

"Because if I'm wrong, well, a guy never recovers from an accusation of murder or conspiracy, no matter how innocent he is."

Kendall seems to be shrinking as we talk. He is pale and unsteady in his speech. The idea of Upton as a murderer has completely undone him. "Is there physical evidence of any kind?" he asks. "Anything usable from the scene of Scud's murder?"

"We haven't even figured out where Scud got whacked."

"Should be easy enough," Kendall says. "Guy gets shot in the head and dumped in the river, you just work your way upriver till you find something."

"You'd think," I say, "but the troopers haven't found squat."

"Have them keep looking," he snaps, and for an uncomfortable few seconds, neither of us speaks. Then he says, "Upton might be up to some shenanigans of some kind, but he sure as hell didn't kill Scud."

"You're naive."

Kendall leans back in his chair, hands folded across his stomach, and stares at me, unblinking. He doesn't say anything, but the silence is thick with meaning: He represents criminals accused of unspeakable acts. He's privy, in the sacrosanct attorney-client confidentiality, to details of these crimes that are more horrible than any jury will ever know. He is anything but naive.

"I'm sorry," I say, "of course you're not naive, but you may be mistaken. In any case, I wouldn't think of exposing Upton to suspicion without more evidence."

"Quite right," Kendall says, "to say nothing of what it would do to your own career."

He's right. Timing matters. If my name gets attached to this thing, regardless of whether Upton is guilty, that'll be the end of my shot at the circuit bench.

"So tell me," Kendall says, "why aren't you speaking to Harold Schnair?"

"Several reasons," I say. "For Upton's sake, I'd like to keep it as contained as possible until something is decided. For Harold's sake, I don't want to burden him with a crisis until I can recommend something. And just between you and me, counselor, I'm trying to avoid looking indecisive. Oh, and one more reason—Harold's been odd for a few days."

"Odd?"

"Can't explain it. Just preoccupied. I'm wondering if he's gotten some kind of, you know, biopsy report or something."

"But you have no reason to . . ."

"No. Just conjecturing."

"What about the FBI? Aren't you friendly with . . ."

"Special Agent d'Villafranca. Chip. Yes."

"Confidential inquiry?"

"Normally, I'd ask him. He'd do it for me, you know, a very confidential poking around to see what he could learn."

"But?"

"Something's up with Chip."

"Something's up with Chip. Something's up with Harold. Something's up with Upton."

"Something *is* up with Upton."

"No doubt." He looks at me with his eyes wide. "Anybody else acting strange?"

I consider. Who else is there? Nobody. Dorsey, Isler, Tina. "No. Nobody else. What are you thinking?"

He shrugs.

"What?" I ask.

"You haven't thought of this?"

"What?"

"Have you ever heard the saying that the only thing all your dysfunctional relationships have in common is you?"

"What are you getting at, Kendall?"

"Maybe you're a suspect, Nick."

I laugh derisively.

"Think about it. You tell me that Scud threatened your daughter. You tell me you've said to both Upton Cruthers and Chip d'Villa-franca that you wanted to kill Scud—that you said so on Upton's voice mail, no less. You tell me you've made public cause of these feelings. You tell me you vigorously and openly opposed your boss when the FBI considered using Scud as an informant because you wanted to see him convicted and executed. You tell me you became emotionally connected to both Cassandra Randall and the Phippin boy. You've made public cause of these feelings. And then there's the small matter of your assaulting Scud in his own front yard the day of the search."

"I thought you didn't see that."

"Of course I saw it. Everybody saw it. Given all this, Dorsey and Chip would be in dereliction of their jobs if they didn't suspect you."

"This is insanity," I say. "Everybody knows I wouldn't—"

"Nick," Kendall says, "what's the first thing you look for when identifying suspects in a murder?"

"Motive."

"Have you demonstrated to the entire world that you have motive?"

I don't answer.

"What's the second thing you look for in a murder suspect?"

"Opportunity," I say quietly.

"Yes, and you've told everybody that you spoke with Scud on the phone the night he was killed. You say that Scud previously begged to be taken on as an informant. So tell me, Nick: How easy would it have been for you to set up a secret meeting with him? And of course Scud would agree to meet you if he thought it was about offering him a job as informant."

"Yes, but—"

"And let's talk about access to the murder weapon. If Scud was in fact killed with his own gun . . . You had the run of the house the day you executed the search warrant. Maybe you found it before the agents did: pocketed it."

I try to laugh again, but it won't come. I'm a suspect. Of course. Why wouldn't I be a suspect? At least for Scud's murder. Everyone knew I hated him. But this is ridiculous; I'll just prove . . .

I try to remember where I was, what my alibi would be. It's difficult, because there's no exact time of death. They found Scud in the river midday on a Monday, dead for thirty to forty hours. So where was I on Saturday night? Lizzy and I came back Saturday afternoon from the lake; I dropped her at Flora's. From Saturday night until leaving for work on Monday, I was alone.

I'm still staring at Kendall. My mouth, I realize, is pumping like a grouper's. "Kendall," I say, "I didn't—"

"Of course you didn't," he says, "I know that. I also know the Bureau would be hard-pressed to come up with a more likely suspect. It seems to me, Nick, that you've gone to great lengths to put yourself right in the crosshairs."

I stand up, but then I can't remember why, and I sit back down.

Kendall says, "I know you didn't come to me seeking representation but just to bounce some ideas around. At this time, however, it may be prudent to engage in a more, let's say, formal structure to our conversation. We're still off the clock, so don't worry about that. If you decide you need representation, we'll have a head start. If you're more comfortable with someone else, I'll cooperate in bringing another attorney up to speed."

He's watching me with that intent stare. And without taking his eyes from mine, he finds the legal pad with his right hand and drags it toward him. He looks down at it, picks up his pen, and writes in quick even letters, "Conversation with Asst. U.S. Atty. Davis."

"Now," he says, "let's start back at the beginning."

CHAPTER 36

My office. Where else would I go? Not home, always an unsatisfying place without Lizzy there. What I'd like to do is to hightail it to the lake, lick my wounds, and hide until all this blows over. Office is the next best thing.

Tina is out, so I handwrite a quick note and slip it in her doorjamb. I pass Upton's office; his door is half open and he's at his desk.

"Hi, boss."

"Hi, Upton."

I tell Janice not to put through any calls, then I close the door and settle behind my desk to let in the whoosh of fear that Kendall has set loose.

I don't know if Kendall Vance is completely nuts. Could anyone really believe I killed Scud? What I've learned in the long years of my career is that you can look back at a perpetrator's life and see symptoms and predisposition and secret behavior. Like Upton, for example. I can believe he might have killed Scud *because* I know of his erratic past; his secret addiction, his tangling with bookies and their henchmen, possibly throwing games. It would be consistent. But who would believe it of me—that I could shoot Scud Illman and dump him in the river?

Or have I been erratic, too? I did willy-nilly fall in love with Cassandra as soon as I met her. I did make public cause of my hatred for Scud. I did ill-advisedly snatch the prosecution from the more qualified Upton. And isn't it too convenient that, just when it looked like my case against Scud had fallen apart, when it looked like the only thing we could pin on him was accessory in a deer poaching, he ended up a floater with a hole in his head?

And there was the time some years back, a Friday afternoon at the office, a half rack of beer, all of us talking about cases and crime and criminals. *What is it like to cross the line,* someone wondered aloud, and the discussion spun into confessions. *Have you ever considered . . . did you ever come close . . . can you imagine . . .* Everyone had tiny confessions, nobody wanting to be the goody-goody. And before the afternoon was done, to my unwitting amazement, I'd told them all about wanting to kill Dr. Wallis and of actually obtaining the gun.

Does anyone remember?

Kendall's theory seems far-fetched, because a case needs evidence. And there's no evidence. At most there's suspicion. Has it been talked about, though? Have there been secret meetings? Is Upton part of it? And if he is part of it, is he feeding that fire? Because if Upton is the snitch who sold out Cassandra and Zander, and if he killed Scud, then it's in his interest to divert suspicion from himself and focus it elsewhere. And beyond diverting suspicion, he might want to plant suspicion. Upton might try to set me up. If my suspicion of him is justified, framing me would be consistent. I doubt he'd choose me as his target, but my extraprofessional interest in the case has given him an opportunity. I wonder how he'd go about framing me. If he's the one who killed Scud, he could plant the gun; he might bury it in my yard, or hide it inside the door panel of my car, or take a trip up to the lake and stash it there, then call in an anonymous tip. That's the classic frame-up: Plant the murder weapon, call it in. It would be so easy for him to plant an item with my fingerprints someplace incriminating (that being the other classic frame-up). Maybe he's already done that. Maybe they *have* found the scene and my prints and other evidence incriminating me. Upton is shrewd, he could do it.

No, I'm getting paranoid. Upton isn't involved in anything. He's the true believer. The one who speaks of the urban utopia, the shining city on the hill.

But he also thinks I'm soft. He's told me. He says I'm too ready to go for the plea instead of the hard time. Too willing to let small cases slide. And he's a better trial lawyer than I am. Maybe he thinks that getting rid of me is the collateral damage from keeping himself in the game. I know he wants my job. He wants TMU's job. We're good friends but not close friends. We talk about work, we don't share confidences. So maybe I wouldn't be collateral loss but a necessary loss. Maybe removing me isn't an accident, it *is* the game. I'm the obstacle that has to go.

The only thing for me to do is expose him for the gambling. Get ahead of him. Remove him. Except if he's already planted evidence, already set his trap, it's too late. Maybe the gambling is nothing but rumor. I have no evidence. If I'm wrong—if Kendall is wrong—and if I come out trying to sink Upton with no real evidence, I'll be the one who pays, and if there isn't already suspicion of me, then my reckless accusation will invite it.

These thoughts are a fist buried deep in my gut. I need to strategize, to anticipate what Upton will do and what the others will think. I pick up the phone and dial Kendall, but he's not in, so I leave a long message detailing my fears. When I hang up, I worry that I sounded befuddled and disorganized—unlawyerlike, because being a lawyer, more than the knowledge we possess, is about how we think. It's the linear and considered compilation of ideas. I pride myself on it, but here I was, babbling at Kendall's voice mail like any common criminal. I call Kendall again to try to smooth the message out, but it just gets worse.

Tina knocks at my office door and opens it enough for her voice to snake its way through the crack. "Nick?"

"C'mon in."

We've scarcely spoken since a couple of evenings ago, when I dodged romance. She sits across from me and fixes me in her generous gaze: "You look . . ."

". . . like hell?"

"Preoccupied."

"I am."

"Do tell."

"Usual bullshit," I say. I can hear my voice teetering on hysteria. I wish she'd leave. My predicament engulfs the universe of speech and focus and normal interaction.

"Look," she says. She reaches up and grabs her ears and wiggles them. "I have two; I'd be happy to lend you one."

She looks goofy, pulling her ears forward like that, and her mouth twists into a befuddled smile. When I see beyond the haircut, when I catch sight of the idealistic elementary schoolteacher, I see a pretty young woman who is probably lonely—like so many of us—but manages to contain it inside the chaos of a hectic, high-powered, professional life. For an instant, everything else is gone, and I feel a stab of regret at having simply dropped her at her car several nights ago.

How I'd love to blab, but along with everyone else in this office, she is the government, the people. Even to show her how upset I am is ill advised. Anything I say can and will be used . . .

"How about a drink later?"

She smiles stoically, assuming I'm planning to have the "I like you but not that way" talk. "It'll have to be late," she says. "I've got something right after work."

"Too bad. I've got something late, but I'm free right after work."

"Too bad."

"Maybe tomorrow."

My cell rings. It's Kendall. "I need to take this," I tell Tina. "Hi," I say into the phone.

"Nick, it's Kendall. I got your voice mails. You need to relax."

"Easy for you to say."

"And maybe I'm wrong. Maybe you're not a suspect at all. It's just a theory."

Tina slips out the door.

"Maybe I should go to Harold Schnair and the Bureau with the gambling stuff on Upton," I say into the phone. "I need to protect my position."

"No," Kendall says, "I wouldn't advise it. Think. What have you really got? Accusations from a washed-up bookie who's been at Ellisville for the past six years."

"And the resignation letter."

"You'll make yourself look foolish, paranoid even."

"I am paranoid. But I've got good reason."

"I promise you, you're not going down on this, Nick. Take your lawyer's advice: Do your job, keep the intel on Upton under your hat. Let it play out. Act normal."

"I'm going to keep investigating."

"Fine. Investigate. But promise you'll talk to me before doing anything."

I promise, and we hang up. *Act normal,* Kendall told me, as though such a thing is possible. What is normal? How do I pretend not to know that people might think I killed Scud? Is it different from how I'd act if I *had* killed Scud but was trying to seem like I hadn't?

I can't focus on any real work, so I walk over to Tina's office to finish the conversation. She's standing at her desk putting papers into her briefcase. "Now I'm the one who can't talk," she says. "Got a hearing."

I stand by her door watching her. She stops and looks at me. "You didn't want one of my ears," she says, "but I've got something else you definitely need."

"You do?"

She comes and gives me a hug. It is quick and friendly. Too quick. As she breaks off and walks back to the desk, I follow her, but I resist the impulse to pull her back to me.

"You just look so damn forlorn," she says.

"About the other evening . . ."

"Shhh," she says, and she presses her index finger against my lips. " 'Nother time."

Back in my office, I tidy my desk. Buried under miscellaneous paperwork I find the Leroy Burton file that Janice tracked down for me. Since I don't seem able to do any real work, I open the file and start reading.

Leroy Burton, aka Fuseli, was convicted at seventeen years old on one count of armed robbery of a federally insured institution and two counts of felony murder. He was the driver. His accomplices, in their thirties, went into the bank, and within minutes, three people were dead: a cop, a female customer, and one of the accomplices. The security guard, who had the good sense to hide under his desk, got out of it with a wounded toe.

The slain officer was a popular hometown boy, and the dead customer was rich. The surviving accomplice immediately hanged himself in his cell. This left Leroy as the sole surviving target of public outrage. He was sentenced to consecutive thirty-five-year terms on the felony murder charges and another twenty years on the robbery. One of the accomplices was his cousin, the other a friend of the cousin. Fuseli testified in trial that the cousin said they were going after the drugstore across the street to nab a few fistfuls of pills. Fuseli didn't know anything about the gun or the bank, but he figured it out pretty quick when the shooting started. He stomped the accelerator and peeled away into what would have certainly been most-wanted fame if he hadn't just driven home and hidden under the bed, to be apprehended within the hour.

As he told me that day at Ellisville, nobody ever accused him of killing anyone. Unfortunately for Fuseli, felony murder doesn't distinguish: If you're committing a felony and someone dies, it's murder.

I feel unexpectedly sad for Fuseli. Rarely in this business do I allow myself to empathize with some con whose lousy choices and values have landed him in hot water. But Fuseli impressed me. He is a mentor to young guys who come through the system, helping them get straightened out enough not to bounce right back in when they get released. And his attitude is striking. He has a quiet dignity that makes me want to believe his story. Even if it's a lie, if he knew perfectly well about the gun and the bank, it's easy for me to believe he was a screwed-up kid who has taken his lesson to heart.

I left the prison with the surprising wish that I could help him somehow. It's ridiculous. For some reason, I'm conflating all these lost boys: my Toby who never had a chance, Zander who made a youthful error that cost him his life, Kenny whom I've tried, with questionable success, to steer onto the path of opportunity and responsibility, and now the decrepit Fuseli whose youthful error steered him straight through the gates of hell. This idea of helping Fuseli, I realize, is nuts: Fuseli is nothing to me—just another con.

CHAPTER 37

In Rivertown, a girl barely older than Lizzy steps gingerly over the gutter, clutching her boyfriend's hand. She's thin as a whippet except for her pregnant tummy, which is an organism in itself. Her shirt is tight, and the bump of her outie leads girl and tummy down the road. She is laughing—I assume at herself, her awkwardness, her backward-bending spine, her unapologetic, unembarrassed "predicament." She is in a crowd of relatives: a mom, friends or sibs, maybe aunts or uncles. I thought Rivertown was a slum, but it looks like a community.

In my new reality of living life as a possible suspect, it occurs to me that I might be under surveillance, and that this trip to Rivertown for a nighttime visit to the Elfin Grot might not be a good idea. But the best way to show you're innocent of some crime is always to show that someone else is guilty of it. So I persevere.

The Elfin Grot has come to life. Smoke is thick and feels woven into the smell of beer and sweat. And noise, the blur of liquor-loosened voices. I stand by the door, trying to distinguish smells from sounds from sights. There is no pathway to the back, where Huberly said I'd probably find Platypus, so I wade into the crowd. It's slow going, requiring hands on shoulders, *tap-tap*, " 'Scuse me, buddy" shouted at the ears of strangers whose hips and backsides I find myself pressed against. " 'Scuse me, buddy." A guy in a tank top turns to see who it is as I put a hand on his sweaty shoulder to squeeze past. He studies me a second, then his grin gets wide. He tips his head toward me and says, "*Amigo,*" and his pudgy fingers tap my hand.

I reach the end of the counter where the room widens enough for some small round tables, and at the very back, at a table with two chairs, sits a hunched old guy. His hair is thin and wispy, the exposed scalp an unhealthy pale. The rest of him is an excess of crumpled flesh. His purple lips protrude as though he tried to kiss a wringer washer. Platypus.

I sit in the empty chair. There's a glass in front of him and another at my seat. Platypus points at it. "Chivas instead of Granddad. I took the liberty." He holds up his own glass of something clear and bubbly. I clink, though I'd rather stay away from anything those lips have wrapped themselves around. "What can I do for you, Mr. Davis, Mr. U.S. Attorney?"

"Assistant. Tipper sent me."

"Tipper? I don't know no Tipper."

"We've had some killings, and I'm getting heartburn over a couple of 'em," I say. "I'm beginning to wonder what the hell. You know? So I ask around. And the word is, you're good at information. Maybe you know things other people don't know."

He shrugs. "Hard to say, Mr. Davis. I'm just a guy. But tell me what you've got." He sips his soda and watches me with hopeful eyes.

I sip my Chivas. "Here's what I've got," I say. "I've got two dead hoods and a dead college kid who was selling pot. The Bureau and the troopers aren't coming up with shit. The leaf the kid was selling comes from the main supply, though, you know? That's why we went after him: Use him as the bottom rung and start up the ladder. Only it didn't work out that way. So now we've got four bodies, and nothing leads anywhere."

"Four?"

"A bystander, sort of. Wrong place, wrong time."

He sips his seltzer and I sip my whiskey. There's something likable about him.

"I used to be here a lot," he says. "I lived here, really. But one day . . ."

"Yes?"

"One day, I shit you not, one morning, I woke up in bed like a year after my wife died—and I don't have to tell you what *that* was like for me. Thirty-seven years that woman put up with me, and God knows, if ever a wife had reasons to walk, she did, but no; thirty-seven years. Thirty-seven years. And one night I come home, three sheets as always, and I get right in bed, and it isn't till morning I realize I slept with a corpse and was too drunk to know it, and I don't mind telling you, Mr.—"

"Davis."

"Davis. I don't mind telling you I cried like a baby."

"My sympathies. What I—"

"Well, that was nearly five years ago now, so you know, I'm okay. They got the senior center and I got friends there. And the old gang, well, most of 'em is dead or in jail, like Tipper, but . . . ?"

"I thought you didn't know Tipper."

"'Course I do. But I do okay. My son, he calls. What I'm saying, it was almost a year after Louise died, and one morning I woke up from a drunk, and I shit you not, Jesus Christ Himself is sitting at the end of the bed, and He says . . . Guess what He says."

I shrug.

"He says, 'Do it for Louise.' That's it. End of discussion. And He disappears. So that very week I'm in A.A. And if you have any interest . . ."

"Appreciate it," I say, "but my demons manifest themselves more subtly. So what I was—"

"Three years without a drink," he says.

"Congratulations Mr.— I don't know your name."

"Platypus'll do."

"Listen, Platypus, can you help me?"

He blows a raspberry through those lips, which vibrate like a kazoo, and I wipe my face with a bar napkin. "Like, do I know who's your snitch, who's the shooter? Don't have a fucking clue. Do I know who they're working for? Maybe I got a couple of ideas. What I do know: I know how to find things out. No promises. No money-back guarantee. But I got an expertise that you don't. I live here. I got forty years of who's who, and for thirty-seven of those years, I was pretty good at looking drunker than I was. Me and Tipper. I was the fool, he was the straight. We had us our own information superhighway.

Not like we was informants. I never sold anything that wasn't already in the stream of commerce, so to speak. It's like this: Say a guy goes to the library and learns how to make himself a bomb, blows holy hell out of some bank vault. Do you arrest the library? Whack the librarian? Bullshit. That's me. Me and Tipper. We was the library." He runs an index finger round and round on the rim of his glass. "I never did much business with your gang." His head protrudes from the acres of his overcoat like a mushroom struggling through mulch. "A guy can get hurt that way, you know. I mean, sure, some back scratching now and then, you know. But that's all, and I sure as shit never knew anything firsthand. It's always somebody told somebody told me. Know?"

"Sure."

"So you want help? Let's talk business. I'll need money up front for expenses."

"Bribes?"

"Drinks. Drinks, loans, favors. You come at it sideways, else you pay too much, and you don't get the story. Five hundred to start. If I get something, another five."

He watches for my reaction. I might as well be bargaining for pregnant yaks in Ulan Bator for as much as I know about this. But I've come prepared. My pocket bulges with a fat roll of twenties— my own money; there's no way this is a sanctioned DOJ expense.

"Ain't you got any questions?" Platypus asks.

"Sure," I say, "how come after a career of not working for the feds, you're all eager to help me?"

He blows another raspberry and plays with the rim of his glass. "More back scratching," he says, and he shifts in his seat, and his head moves up and down in the mulch and finally settles low. "See, I got this daughter lives right near here. Never see her."

"How come?"

"She blames me."

"For what?"

"For being in the life. She says that's why what happened, happened."

He's getting close to something. No monologue; he's making me prod.

"What happened?"

He reaches into the big overcoat and brings out a photo: a girl, maybe six years younger than Lizzy. She's laughing, freckles on café au lait cheeks and nose, and hair in small, exotic braids. I feel nauseated, because all I know of this girl at this moment is that something happened, and since I live with this shit every day—true crime—I know it's bad. I didn't see it coming from this lonely, washed-up once-upon-a-timer, but there it is, and my defenses are down and I know, every cell tingling with the knowing, that this pretty girl is dead and the repulsive, spittle-spraying Platypus is trying to resurrect her. I hand the picture back, not meeting his eyes.

"My granddaughter, she went to school one day and never came home," he says, his voice flat.

"Police?"

"Nothing."

"That's that?"

"No. Someone found a photo a few months later. They . . . they . . . the police, they just showed us the face, and truly, she didn't look that bad. Healthy, sort of, you know? But the rest of the picture, what they didn't show us . . ."

"What?"

His hands flap around as he looks for words or maybe gets a handle on himself. Then he pronounces slowly, "Por-nog-ra-phy. Apparently, there was someone else in the picture, but they wouldn't tell us details. Said it's best not to know. The detectives said by the time the photo turned up, she was most likely dead or someplace very, very far away."

"I'm sorry."

He nods.

"I'm not an investigator. I'm sure the police . . ." I trail off. He straightens up some and shifts position. "What do you want?" I ask.

"Just look."

"For her?"

He laughs bitterly. "Look at you. Your idea of blending in is taking off your tie. Know who you remind me of? Mark Trail, remember him?"

"Who?"

"Old comic from the funny pages. Mark Trail. He was a forest ranger or something. Like Lassie on two legs. That's who you look like. Plaid shirt and all."

"Mark Trail? No, I don't—"

"So maybe you can rub two sticks together, but you go out looking for Brittany, only thing you're going to find is a knife in the ribs and your wallet gone. Friendly word of advice, Mr. Davis: At least in a suit, you'd have some respectability."

"So you want what?"

"I just want to know what's happening. Like, are they still working the case, or have they given up and forgotten about her? I got the names of these two dicks. They give me their cards. At first they was real nice when I'd call. Now they don't call me back. Been six months since I've heard a peep."

"If there was news, they'd call."

"I know."

"So what do you want?"

"Attention. And I want to keep reminding them. And I want to know if there are any Jane Does of about the right age but too decomposed to ID. Anything."

He's talked himself through the emotional quicksand, and now he's sitting as straight as his backbone allows. "I'm a realist," he says. "I don't expect much."

"The dicks. Who are they?"

He hands me two business cards from his billfold. I don't know the guys. They're city cops with the JCPTF: Joint Child Protection Task Force. I write down the names and promise to make some calls. "But let me be clear," I say. "I'm just finding out where it stands. I'm not working this. Absolute best you can hope is that my inquiries light a fire under them. More likely, they'll tell me it's over 'cause they could never develop a lead. Agreed?"

"It's something."

"What's her name?"

"Brittany. Brittany Tesoro."

Tesoro. I recognize the name from the list of kids who've gone missing from Rivertown. "I'll read case notes, talk to the detectives," I say, "but that's all."

He nods. We shake. I give him the necessary information to get him started in the right direction, then I hand over the money he asked for and I leave, pushing my way out through the tangle of sweaty drinkers. I wish Platypus had left first. I might have stayed, ordered a beer, let the earthy smells and sounds carry me along, seeing if I could catch the current for a second or two at a time, shedding the moment-by-moment stocktaking of life, and just, for those dreamlike intervals in the beer and smoke and sweat and roar of voices—accented voices, voices in other languages or jargons—for just those moments maybe I could forget about being a murder suspect. Maybe I could forget to think about living life and just live it.

CHAPTER 38

I've done something terrible.
    I killed someone, though the details of who, why, and where are lost in the vaporous otherworld of dreams. I would like to be rid of this crime, but the knowledge of it and the certainty of my capture haunt me from dream to dream and through a dozen awakenings.

Now morning. I'm at the office early, catching up on busywork, and I read the weekly memo from Pleasant Holly, briefing us on cases and investigations over in the civil division. What catches my attention is her summary of litigation by veterans seeking compensation and services for Gulf War syndrome.

Scud was in the Gulf, and so was Seth Coen. In Seth's bathroom cabinet and on his bedside table were dozens of prescription vials. I thought he must be either a hypochondriac or dying of something, but we never followed up on it.

I call Dorsey and ask him to fax over the inventory from Seth Coen's apartment. I need to get to know Seth better. He was already dead when we met him, his only interest to us being through the connection to Scud. Then Scud was dropped from suspicion and got whacked in quick succession, making Seth a complete nonentity, investigation-wise. But I can't shake the idea that it's all connected. With this Gulf War syndrome stuff, he has become interesting in a noncriminal way.

While I wait for a fax, I look through the files on the Phippin/Randall/Illman murders. We don't have a separate file on Seth because, unlike the other three, he wasn't an actual or potential federal witness, so his murder isn't being investigated as a federal crime. Still, I expect to find some background info: probation records, police records, prison records. But there's nothing. Upton must have it all from before I took over the case. For two seconds, I think about devious ways to get these records, but I screw on my courage and walk the ten yards of carpet to Upton's office, doing my best to look like the aggressive and confident administrator I am not.

"Hi, Upton."

"Hi, boss."

"I'm wondering if you have any more materials from the series of murders."

"What murders?"

"Phippin, Randall, Illman, Coen."

"Oh, those murders. Box on the floor there, it says Phippin, but I tossed in a lot of that other stuff."

I pick up the box and start for the door. I stop. "How 'bout coffee?"

I've always liked Upton's face. I wouldn't call him good-looking by any stretch, but he's got an inviting comfortableness, like a favorite slipper. Knobby chin and broken nose and age-softened ruggedness. "How are the girls?" I ask, avoiding using their names—Cicely and Hilary—because one of them always comes out as Celery.

"The girls," Upton says wearily, "are worshippers at the altar of consumerism. How's Lizzy?"

"Good. She's good."

"Good." He takes a noisy sip of coffee.

I take a noisy sip of coffee. "Whatcha working on?"

"The usual. Responding to a pile of suppression motions in the RICO case. They're all bogus."

"Yeah. They're *all* bogus."

"Ain't it the truth."

"Ain't it."

It's true. When a court suppresses evidence, it almost always amounts to guilty people getting away with something. We spend a moment with that irritating thought: how guilty people feel entitled to their acquittals. I feel comforted by how well we understand each other.

"What's your interest?" Upton says, indicating the box I came to get. The question might be innocent, because with no suspects at the moment and the case gone cold, it's in the hands of the Bureau and troopers. We're out of it.

"Tying up loose ends," I say.

He nods. Neither of us hint at the intricacy of the interaction. He and I may both be unofficial suspects in Scud's murder. Upton alone knows whether he's guilty, and only I know whether I am. He doesn't know I suspect him, and while he might know I'm a suspect, he doesn't know that I know it. And since there are several crimes in play, we could both be guilty of something.

Except that I'm not.

And what a waste it will be if Upton is dirty. He always likes to talk about striving to improve our Urban Utopia. Upton's Urban Utopia. I never thought of this before: U^3. I could have had one of those oval Euro stickers made for the bumper of his car, or written it on a congratulatory cake to celebrate a big courtroom victory: "U^3"

"So what's the status with Tina?" he asks with a sideways twist of his lips that indicates, in this instance, the delving into of matters romantic. "Have you closed the sale?"

Another time I would welcome this. I might say, *I like her, but I keep backing off. Don't know why,* and Upton would nod compassionately, and whether or not any more got said, I'd feel better. Not now. Now I just laugh, ignoring the question. I should leave. Kendall Vance would tell me to get the hell out of here. Upton takes our coffee cups out for refills.

"So. The circuit bench," he says when he comes back in.

"Go figure."

"Sounds like you have a shot. The word I hear, everyone else on the short list brings baggage."

"Yeah, but. So much baggage, why are they on the list to begin with?"

"Résumés. It's a trade-off."

"Whatever. I'm trying not to get too invested."

"If I were the president . . ." he says, and this is followed by more coffee drinking. It's a nice thing to say, a vote of confidence from a respected colleague, and it makes me want to believe in his innocence.

"What about you?" I ask, flicking my head sideways in the direction of my office. I'm asking if he hopes to replace me as head of the division if I get the judgeship.

"That'd be great."

"Have you spoken to TMU?"

"Indirectly."

"And?"

"Won't commit."

"I'll put in a word," I say.

He nods gratefully.

I won't ever put in a word. It's all over. This brittle state will shatter. Accusations will be made against Upton or me or both of us—there are plenty of crimes to go around—and the world we've known will end. I look at his face; even when he isn't smiling, you can see the afterimage in pleats of skin around his eyes and mouth. So many times over the years, we've sat here like this, lesser gods, putting people in jail, letting them out, being the government. We were arrogant and charitable and earnest and fierce and strict and lenient. Maybe we should have moved on by now—either of us could have walked into the white-shoe firms in an instant, doubling, tripling, quadrupling our salaries. But we liked it here; we liked the camaraderie, power, public service. Why move?

Now though, I realize I've stayed too long. We've both stayed too long, and all our years in ostensible public service resolve into a simple failure of ambition.

My résumé *is* light. This is all I've done, and it's almost over.

CHAPTER 39

J anice buzzes. "Nick, Special Agent d'Villafranca has been calling and calling. He says you aren't getting back to him.

"Oh, sorry, Janice. I'll call him now."

I have no intention of calling Chip. His urgency to reach me, no
doubt, is because he wants to confront me about Scud's death. The
minute it's out in the open, my wings will be clipped: I'll be ordered
to have nothing more to do with the case. I'll probably be put on
suspension, and that'll be that. Because the moment enforcement
identifies a prime suspect, the system becomes focused on convicting, and all my own investigations will look like nothing more than
the actions of a desperate perp trying to blow smoke over the whole
thing. It's better if I'm able to divert suspicion *before* the idea of me
as a suspect is cemented into Chip's reality.

Janice buzzes again. "Nick, there's a fax for you."

It's the inventory from Seth's apartment. I scan. The list of meds
is daunting. The prescription vials all show the doctors' names. I
could probably get an order for the release of medical records, but
Gulf War syndrome is outside the official thrust of any investigation.
So I take the list of meds to the law library, where Kenny is busy
reshelving books.

"Where you been?" he asks, focusing his affectionate, chip-
toothed grin at me.

"Just busy. Tons going on."

"Don't I know about that."

"Come over for a movie tonight?"

He pretends to yawn.

"I know, I know," I say, "my movies are boring. I'll let you pick
the flick."

"Serious?"

"Sure," I say. I hope he'll come. I feel a wave of love for Kenny, my occasional foster son, as this idea of sitting home with him, downing a few cold ones, and watching a stupid movie momentarily calms my anxiety over this business of being suspected in Scud's murder.

" 'Cept I can't," he says. "Me and Amber's having dinner at her mom's."

"Amber, the one from the pet store? Serious stuff, meeting the parents."

"Just her mom."

"Well, some night we'll chill with a movie. Your pick."

"How's Lizzy?"

"Good."

"Haven't seen her since, like, two weeks. How's Flo? I'm still waiting for my friend with the backhoe to move them rocks."

"Rocks?"

"The patio. Remember?"

"Oh, sure. Listen, I need you to do this. I got a list of pills. Prescriptions. Go get the *PDR* and look up each one. Write it all down. Ignore the technical stuff. Just what it treats."

"Is next week okay?"

"Today, Kenny."

"I don't know, I got all this work from civil, and—"

"Kenny, you're reshelving books, for cripe's sake. Get Penny to help if you need it. Do it now."

"Do it now," he says in falsetto. I take a fake swing at him, he takes a fake swing at me. I have the urge to lock him in a bear hug, this surrogate son, so committed to his life of underachievement.

Back in my office. I sit and rearrange things on the desk. I try the pencil holder on the left side instead of the right. It's a clumpy, ugly ceramic mug Lizzy made in second grade. I LOV YOU DADDY is etched into the bottom.

I file some stray papers. I sip cold coffee. The inventory is in the middle of my desk, and though I'm interested only in the meds, I scan the rest of it. What strikes me is how spare a legacy it is for a man of almost forty. I flip through to see if he owned books. He did: "Twelve books of various subject matter," the list says, no more.

The only thing I know about Seth Coen that makes him interesting is the wild game and fish packed along with his body parts in the freezer. I look at the inventory with this in mind, and I start seeing evidence of his outdoors interest. There is miscellaneous outdoor clothing, a sleeping bag, a camp stove, fishing poles and lures, a tent. He comes a bit more into focus. He was a city rat with country-boy longings. Noticeably absent from the inventory are guns of any kind. How do you hunt deer without a rifle? But since he was a convicted felon, it would be illegal for him to possess a firearm, so was he playing by the rules, or did he keep his guns someplace else?

I wonder if, while he was in prison, the idea of the great outdoors was a comfort or a torment to him. I take a blank file folder and label it COEN, SETH: INVENTORY. I put the inventory inside, but I see something just as I close it. First page, halfway down, it says: "Keys found in apartment, application unknown." On the list of half a dozen keys of unknown usage, this: "Yamaha." Whoever typed the inventory appropriately capitalized the proper noun, which is why I noticed it. Yamaha. But there is no other mention of anything having to do with a motorcycle. I flip to the list of miscellaneous documents, looking for an owner's manual or registration. Nothing. I go to the clothing heading, looking for a helmet or leathers. Nothing. He might have gotten rid of the bike long ago and never thrown out the extra key, but my interest is piqued, so I call Dorsey and leave a message asking if the troopers are aware of Seth Coen having had a motorcycle. Then I file the Coen inventory in the box of miscellaneous documents and try to think of something else to keep my mind off the problem of being a murder suspect.

Janice buzzes. "Nick, you have a call. Lizzy's guidance counselor." I take the call.

"Mr. Davis," she says, "Lizzy tells me you're picking her up after school today. We were wondering if you could come in to talk for a few minutes?"

"About what?"

"Something Lizzy has on her mind. She'll tell you."

"Is Lizzy okay?"

"Of course. She just—"

"Has she *done* something?"

"Nothing like that, she just—"

"Is her mother coming, too?"

"Lizzy prefers to speak just with you."

"This sounds serious. Give me something to go on."

"No, no. Not serious. Not that kind of serious. Will you just come in?"

She's pregnant. What else could it be? I never saw any interest in boys. I'm amazed. I put the phone on speaker so I can start stuffing papers into my briefcase. If I leave immediately, I can get to Lizzy's middle school about lunchtime and . . .

. . . and what? Pull her out of class, out of the lunch hall? She'd never speak to me again. But I want to be with her. *It's okay,* I'll say, *we'll figure it out together, babe, you're not alone.*

"So shall we see you at about three?" the guidance counselor says.

"I could come now," I offer miserably, knowing she's going to say no and I'll just have to wait the four hours till school is out.

"No, no, Mr. Davis, it's no emergency. Just something Lizzy needs to talk about. Three o'clock, then?"

We hang up. I stare at the phone. So now I'm not only a murder suspect, but something terrible is going on with Lizzy.

Dorsey calls. He tells me they have no information about a motorcycle. DMV records show nothing. The puzzle of the Yamaha key feels urgent. I need to unravel these murders, not just because I felt a connection to Cassandra and to Zander and because I'm an assistant U.S. attorney but because Kendall has me convinced that I've been caught in the crosshairs of the investigation. My mission is self-preservation.

I hang up with Dorsey, find a Yamaha dealer in the Yellow Pages, and reach a guy in the service department who says if I bring the key in, they may be able to work backward to get the key-cutting code, and then there might be a record of the model and registered purchaser for that bike.

"Sounds good," I tell him. "I'll do that."

"What's it look like?" he says.

"The key?"

"Yeah, the key, what's it look like?"

"Don't know; I don't actually have it."

"You're sure it's a bike?"

"What else would it be?"

"Four-wheeler," he says.

"Four-wheeler?"

"Yeah. Or a snowmobile, or an outboard, or I don't know, they make lots of stuff."

"Can you tell by the key?"

"Dunno."

"I'll get the key and come over there," I tell him, and we hang up.

The problem is that I don't have the key, and I might not be able to get it. What happens to all a guy's stuff when he ends up in his own freezer? For all I know, it went to his sister, who has already hauled it to the landfill. If the key does exist, Dorsey might be able to get it for me, but I'd need a good reason, and I don't have one.

I scan the inventory again. I remember Seth's freezer—its nonhuman contents: the butcher-paper packages labeled in green marker. Some were venison (perhaps the very deer poached that night at the reservoir), but there were also packages of lake trout, steelhead, rainbow, and maybe others, all the products of Seth's fishing hobby— Seth the outdoorsman . . .

. . . outdoorsman, Yamaha key, fishing . . .

I take out a map of the state and unfold it across my desk. The reservoir area is narrow, stretching roughly north to south. About half a mile west of the reservoir, the map shows the red line of Route 7, and though they're not shown on this map, I know there are lots of spurs from that road to picnic spots by the water. I approximate the location of the one where Seth and Scud poached the deer, and I pencil an X on the map.

The east side is harder. Several miles of wildlife preserve lie against the eastern shore, with only a couple of black threads indicating access roads. With a better map, I could locate the spot more precisely, but for now I triangulate my way to a rough estimate of where Cassandra Randall found Zander Phippin's grave. I draw another X. On this map, where the blue serpentine reservoir extends nearly seventy miles, top to bottom, the two X's lie directly across from each other, separated by under a half mile of water.

Lickety-split, I'm in my Volvo and navigating winding streets to the lowbrow neighborhood that was home to the departed Scud Illman. Scud's yard is tidy, and the flower beds are weeded, though only a few late-blooming mums remain. It is as I remember: an undistinguished, well-kept home in a low-priced neighborhood. The front curtains are open, but nothing of interest is visible. From the road, at least, the master's demise has left the place unchanged.

The car I've come to see, a brown Sentra, is in the driveway—lucky break. With a bit more luck, it would be fronted in instead of backed. I get out and start toward the door of the house to ask permission, but since this isn't an official investigation, screw the niceties of warrants and permission to search. I veer off the path and walk to the rear of the car to find out what I want to know.

And there it is, as expected: a tow ball for a boat trailer. I've got a pretty good idea where to find the trailer. I turn and head back to my Volvo, but before I can get away, Scud's wife comes to the front door. "You want something?" she yells.

"Hello, Mrs. Illman. So sorry about your husband."

She waits.

"We met before. The day your house got searched. I was here."

She waits.

"And so sorry to intrude. I just needed a look at his car."

"Reason being?"

"Just a look. All done. Did you know Seth Coen?"

She blinks at me and doesn't answer. Last time I saw her, she trembled with barely controlled rage. This time she's different—not friendly, just blank.

"Anyhow," I say, "hope you don't mind."

Her son comes to the door to see what's going on. Colin, the kid with the lip scar and the two-tone eye. I'm tempted to greet him by name, but if these people remember me at all, it's not as a friend. I just thank her again and walk toward my Volvo.

"So you ain't going to tell me about the car?"

"Well. No. Not yet. It's okay, though. Nothing to worry about."

"I didn't do nothing."

"Of course. Nobody's implying."

"Son of a bitch," she mutters, meaning Scud, not me. Her face changes. She draws a deep, soulful sigh, probably as close to a sob as this woman gets. "I *didn't* do nothing."

"Look," I say, "this thing with the car, it's not about you. None of this is about you, okay? I'm just tying up loose ends."

"Mom?" Colin says.

"Inside," she orders. He disappears.

"No school?" I ask, making my voice breezy so she won't feel challenged. Colin was home on the day of the search, too, and the day Scud was arrested.

"He ain't feeling well."

"Kids . . ."

"Yeah."

I can't get a fix on this woman. Is she intelligent or not, maternal or not? I can't even say whether she's attractive or not. Her skin is tanned, and she's without makeup of any kind, and her hair, aside from the bangs, is straight and pulled back so tight that her eyebrows are midforehead. But for all her plainness, she has a Sissy Spacek kind of innocence. She has on tight jeans, a loose sweater, deck shoes without socks. "Could I use your bathroom?" I ask on impulse. I need to purge the coffee, but also I want a reason to stay for a minute, poke around, get a sense.

Without answering, she holds open the door and steps aside. "Scram," she says into the house, where, presumably, Colin is hanging around to listen. When I walk inside, he's gone. The house is immaculate, the way it was the day of the search. Everything is nice, though nothing is high-quality. On the wall above the couch is the same triptych by the local artist, Serena, that Tina has in her office. Coffee table has teak legs with a glass top, walls are white, kitchen has mass-manufactured cabinets that give a passable imitation of custom. But the only thing giving any kind of impression, the only statement on the character of the owner, is the absence of character.

It doesn't take a psychologist to figure this out: the extreme unpredictability of life with Scud apparently resulted in hysterical orderliness imposed on the only thing she could control—her home. Even her son, I'm betting, was wrested from her maternal authority by Scud the manipulator. She very well could have killed Scud. Not that she *did* kill him—I'm not letting Upton off the hook that easily—but she *might* have killed him. She *might* have been suffering from such hopelessness . . . She *might* have found herself trapped in the surreal thicket of his psychosis . . . She *might* have feared for her own life . . . She *might* have known that if she tried leaving him, he'd come after her and Colin . . . She *might* have decided there was nothing to lose.

Unfortunately for her, all of those might-haves don't add up to a defense. It's not self-defense, and it's not insanity. It's criminal, and when I'm back at the office, I'll tell Dorsey my suspicion and he'll put his investigators on it, and if they turn up anything, she'll be tried, and if she *is* tried, she'll be convicted. If she's lucky, there'll be leniency in the sentencing, though to judge from this woman's life, luck seems to have kept its distance.

"It's right in there," she says, pointing to the bathroom. I go in, piss, have a look around. I had planned to snoop a bit, but now that I have actual suspicion, I decide to play it by the book; I'd hate to have some juicy evidence suppressed on grounds that I came here and searched without a warrant. But since I've been invited in, anything in plain sight is fair game. Except nothing is in plain sight; the bathroom is like the rest of the house. Sterile. There are no magazines or newspapers, no toothbrushes on the counter, the towels look untouched, the countertop is bare, the porcelain shines, and the toilet paper is folded into a little point just like at a fancy hotel. I have no doubt that when I leave, she'll be in here quick as can be, scrubbing, sweeping, refolding.

I finish and flush. I'd linger longer but can't think of any pretext, so I thank her and quickly walk out toward my Volvo. She calls across the lawn, "What about my other car?"

"I told you, I can't—"

"Not that one," she says. "We had two. Where's the other one?"

"How should I know?"

"He took it that night 'cause we still hadn't got this one back from the police. Took off in my car, then he ends up dead in the river, and I never seen my car again."

"I don't know," I say. "I can make a phone call or two, see what I find out."

She gives me the information on her missing car, then I zoom away to my next stop.

CHAPTER 40

It's after lunchtime. From Illman's place, I beeline through the railroad district, past the auto dealerships and crushing plant, past the strip of titty bars and massage parlors, and I screech up in front of Seymour Apartments. I want to make this as efficient as possible, so I position my Glock in its shiny black holster, where it is seen easily inside my suit jacket, then I walk into the office, where I'm announced by an electronic ding-dong. "One sec," says someone from the back room, then the weasel-faced Mr. Milan appears.

"Help you?" he says in the two seconds before the details of my presence register in his mind. I'm standing back from the counter, feet apart, badge in hand, doing my best to be the stone-faced agent ready to rain down some major federal shit on this transgressor.

"Mr. Milan, isn't it?"

He nods.

"Nick Davis, U.S. Attorney's office. We met the day you discovered Seth Coen's body."

"Oh yes," he says. His ears turn red. One hand comes up to scratch his neck, and the other waves around looking for something to do.

"Mr. Milan, I'm here to ask you one simple question, but before I do, I'm going to explain a few points of law to you, and if there's anything you want to tell me before I get to my question, it might work in your advantage if you speak up. You hear what I'm saying? You just offer some information without me having to ask for it. Okay?"

The hand at his neck moves up to wipe sweat from the shiny bald head and to scratch an imaginary itch at the corner of an eye. The other hand tugs at one of the suspenders. The guy is harmless, except that he's caused untold harm.

"You see, Mr. Milan, what you might not know, and what I'm here to explain to you, is that even if someone is dead, taking his property is still a crime. It can even be a felony, depending on the value of what's taken. See, but it gets better—that's just a state crime, but withholding evidence in a federal investigation is a federal crime, which is why I'm here."

Milan's hands meet under his chin, and the index fingers reach up and work his lips like a lump of bread dough. I wait a few seconds, but he doesn't say anything, so I continue: "Now, here's the kicker, Mr. Milan: If it turns out the misappropriated property— let's say, hypothetically, a small boat—was used in the commission of a crime—let's say the murder and disposal of a body out at the reservoir—and if the person who steals the property is aware of the crime, then concealing that evidence makes you an accessory. Isn't that interesting?"

"Seth Coen owed me rent," Milan blurts with a sob. "And I don't know about any other body."

I wait.

"JesusMaryandJoseph," he says, making his way to a chair, where he slumps into a heap of misery. I knew he'd be easy. I stand in front of him, loading up my glare with the imposing weight of federal power. Normally, I'd have some compassion, but Milan's antic deprived us of the break we needed in this case, dragging it out long enough for Scud to end up dead, so now we might never figure out who pulled all the strings. Scud would have talked. He'd have told us who was responsible—who gave the order or paid the contract. But the weasely, suspender-clad Milan fucked it up.

I let Milan sit there stewing while I call Dorsey, and I wait until he shows up with a couple of troopers. Milan is heaped into the chair. Every couple of minutes, he straightens a bit and says, as if it's something he just thought of, "I can't go to jail."

"You want to arrest him?" Dorsey asks me.

"I haven't decided. You go ahead and take him on the theft

charges, then we'll see what spins out before I decide on the federal charges."

Dorsey reads the Mirandas. Milan wants to talk. He tells us it was a small aluminum boat with an outboard. Yamaha, twenty horsepower, maybe. "Seth didn't have his own car," Milan says. "He'd come and go with other people, or he'd just, like, have some car for a few days, then he'd have another."

"What kind of cars?" I ask.

"I don't know. Like rental cars," he says. Milan admits that when Seth turned up dead and nobody asked about the boat or towed it away, he waited a few weeks until things quieted down, then he put a for sale sign on it and parked it beside the highway. It sold in a couple of days.

"How much did you get?" I ask.

"Forty-five hundred."

"How much rent did he owe you?"

"Around the same," Milan says, his hands in motion again.

"Dammit, Milan," I snap, "do yourself a favor here."

He slumps down and doesn't say anything.

"How much did Seth owe you?"

"About three hundred."

"Who'd you sell the boat to?"

"They gave me cash," he whines. "I don't have a clue who it was."

I have to leave for Turner. Dorsey's team stays with Milan to work on tracking down whoever bought the boat.

It all makes sense. The coincidence was too great that Seth and Scud were out poaching deer on one side of the reservoir the same night someone was burying Zander on the other side. No doubt Seth and Scud thought that by crossing to the untrammeled eastern shore, the chances of anyone discovering Zander's grave were zilch. It was their bad luck (and Cassandra's) that they pulled ashore near the unmapped path along the marsh where some bird-watcher recently claimed to see a yellow rail. I'm betting that when the troopers locate the boat, they'll find traces of Zander—blood, hair, clothing fibers. His body was probably hidden under a tarp in the boat as it was trailered out from town, launched into the cold shallows of the reservoir, and zoomed across to a not so final resting spot.

Two X's on the map. Ninety minutes by road, ten minutes by water. Zander's killers, or at least the body disposers, have been identified: Scud Illman and Seth Coen, both dead.

I should call Chip and tell him, but I don't want to talk to him. So I call Dorsey back: "Nick here. Do me a favor and brief Chip d'Villafranca, would you?"

"Sure, but why don't—"

"Thanks, bye." I end the call.

Stephanie Caplain is the guidance counselor at Lizzy's school. The most noticeable thing about her is that she beams an aura of maternal warmth. Her eyes have a hint of sadness; her voice is firm but entreating; and her smile is . . . well, it's nice. How many rattled adolescents, I wonder, have sobbed their woes into the substantial cushion of her bosom? Has Lizzy?

"Thank you for coming, Mr. Davis," she says sweetly.

I mean to answer, but I'm experiencing a strange bout of lingual paralysis, and all I can do is blink a few times, looking back and forth between her and Lizzy. For a moment this undefined problem wipes away the niggling fear I've had since Kendall deduced that I'm the main suspect in Scud's murder.

"Lizzy needs to tell you something," Stephanie Caplain says once we're settled in her comfy mango-colored office with the door closed. "It's difficult for her, so we thought if she and I met with you together, it might be better. Right, Lizzy?"

Lizzy is sitting on the couch with her hands palm-down on either side of her. She won't meet my eyes.

"Lizzy wasn't sure whether to tell you at all," Stephanie says, "but we decided together that she really needed to tell one of you—you or her mom, right, Liz?"

Lizzy nods.

"So why don't you go ahead, sweetheart," Stephanie says.

"Yes," I add helplessly.

"Okay," Lizzy whispers, but her lip starts quivering, and I feel mine start to quiver in response.

Liz looks up, and her eyes are full of tears, and she looks back down at her lap and says, "Kenny."

"Kenny? Our Kenny? What about him?"

"Bothering me."

"Bothering you? Bothering you how?"

She doesn't answer.

"Did he . . ."

"No, he just . . ."

"What?"

"Wants."

"And he . . ."

"Pesters."

"Oh, geez. And he persists?"

She nods. "It's so gross," she whispers. "He's like my, you know, brother."

"How long?"

"Not too. First I tried to, you know . . . I didn't take him seriously. But now . . ."

I gaze at Liz for a while. She and Stephanie Caplain are waiting for me to say something. Lizzy is in her little-girl getup. She shuns fashion; her outfits are usually T-shirts and jeans, preferably with holes in the knees. Or running clothes. But sometimes she wears a goofy combination of striped kneesocks and a blouse with ruffles. She looks about nine years old right now.

"Daddy?" Lizzy says.

I'm not here to give a legal opinion. I'm here to give fatherly comfort and support. And wisdom. Obviously wisdom, because if she were looking just for comfort, she'd go to Flora. Flora for comfort, me for wisdom. And maybe me for my relationship to Kenny, because though he's close to all of us, it's mainly me. He's my problem child, my wayward son, my project. Naturally, I'm Lizzy's choice; I'm levelheaded and judicious. I'm wise. Father knows best.

"Jesus H.!" I yell. "I'll give him a mouthful of bloody Chiclets, the son of a bitch."

CHAPTER 41

Friday morning. I've decided to do nothing about Kenny until I can talk to Flora.

After leaving the guidance counselor yesterday, Lizzy and I drove home, and she went for a run while I made dinner, then she worked on homework. To my amazement, before sealing herself into the hermetic capsule of her bedroom—there to do who knows what until she went to bed at who knows when—she agreed to a game of Parcheesi with me.

At work now, I skulk from the elevator to my office and get the door closed without having to stop and talk to anyone. I buzz Janice. "Janice, would you inform Ed Cashdan that I'm not able to make it to the weekly wrap-up and I'd appreciate his taking charge?"

"Good morning to you, too."

"Good morning, Janice."

"You usually ask Upton to sit in when you can't make it."

"I'm aware of that."

There are voice messages on my cell phone and voice messages on my office phone and While You Were Outs on my desk. And no coffee in my cup, but if I can hold out till after ten o'clock, the lawyers will be at the wrap-up and I can sneak over to the coffeepot. I work my way through the messages: TMU wants to see me, Kendall Vance wants to see me, Kenny wants to get together for that movie-and-beer night we talked about, Dorsey wants to talk, Platypus wants to talk. The White House called and would like to speak with me, if I'd be so kind as to call back at my earliest convenience. And finally, Chip d'Villafranca called less than eight minutes ago, and he's on his way over right now.

Everything comes into focus. Chip has been trying and trying to reach me, and I've been stiff-arming him. Now, sick of the run-around, he is getting more aggressive. It's obvious. In addition to all the evidence against me—the evidence Kendall itemized—I've apparently increased Chip's suspicions by consistently dodging his attempts to speak with me. I'm certain he wants me for questioning about the murder of Avery "Scud" Illman. Maybe he's already been to the judge and gotten an arrest warrant. He's such a big guy, Chip, but he's gentle. He'll murmur earnest apologies as he takes my wrists in his meaty hands and snaps on the bracelets behind my back. *Is that okay, Nick?* he'll say. *Are they lose enough? Are you comfortable?*

"Why stick around?" I say aloud into the quiet of my office. I'm no match for the FBI if they really want to pick me up, but I could put an extra day or two to good use. I take my briefcase, walk out the office door, and—knowing I might never set foot in the place again but with no time to wax poetic—leave by the back staircase and drive away.

I want to see Platypus because the best way to convince everyone I didn't kill Scud is to prove that someone else, specifically Upton, did. Maybe Platypus has found something. But before I can talk to him, I need to live up to my part of the bargain. I drive over to city police headquarters.

Tony Silva and Bart Curry are the two dicks who worked the case of Platypus's missing granddaughter. Silva isn't in, Curry is. Curry invites me into his office (a real office, surprisingly; I expected a cu-bicle or maybe just a desk). He studies my business card. "Not too often you guys come down from your mountaintop," he says.

"No, you're thinking of the FBI," I tell him. "They're the stuck-up ones; us guys in the U.S. Attorney's office, we drink Bud."

"Settle for coffee?"

"Music to my ears."

He gets the coffee. I tell him about Platypus's granddaughter and how I promised the guy I'd make some inquiries.

"Platypus," Curry says, "poor schmuck. He's desperate. They're all desperate: parents, grandparents, aunts, uncles. Living hell. It's cold, though, that case, and Platty just won't hear what we're telling him."

"Which is?"

"Missing kids like that, generally speaking, you get 'em back quick or you don't get 'em. That one though, Brittany Tesoro, we found those pics of her on the Internet, which at least told us something."

"Told you what?"

"There're only a few reasons kids go missing: There're the runaways, but we pretty much ruled that out. After that, kidnapping by a noncustodial parent is most common, but it's not a factor here. Then there's kidnapping by some screwball with an empty nest they're trying to fill, but those are rare, and they go after infants and toddlers. Brittany's too old. That leaves the pervs and entrepreneurs."

"Entrepreneurs?"

"Sex trade, kiddie porn, baby sellers. Those pics of Brittany; they tell us she was with an entrepreneur, and the entrepreneurs aren't exactly sentimental people. It ain't easy keeping a girl Brittany's age hidden, if you hear what I'm saying."

"I see."

"Is it cold in here?" he asks. He points at my coffee cup, which, I hadn't realized, I'm pressing against my cheek, creating a little spot of warmth in a cold, shitty world.

"Are you still working it?" I ask.

"Yes and no. You know how it is."

I do know how it is. There are newer cases that still have the possibility of saving a life.

"How did you find the pics?" I ask.

"One-in-a-million chance," Curry says. "We found her in the national database. The Bureau has a team that works this stuff, mostly Internet, but some in print. They search it out, catalog it, crop it for the face shots so we can search by age, gender, race. We found her there, but the Bureau didn't have any leads. They pulled the image off the Internet, but it dead-ended. They couldn't trace it."

"How long ago?"

"At least a year. Maybe more."

A year. We both know the truth.

"Fucking A," Curry says quietly.

"Fucking A," I agree. I like him. He's a bland-looking guy, a little doughy, but with the crusty edge cops need to have. His face is kind, though, and while he's built walls against the tragedies of his daily fare, he doesn't pretend it's not all tragic. "Have you looked in the database again for another picture of Brittany?"

"Not specifically. We've looked for others, but you know, you generally have to search for one at a time. You need to have a good eye. Some people can really pick them out. Not me. You want to try?"

"Yes."

I didn't plan to get involved. I'm just here to get an update for Platypus, but strangely, I want to see all those lost children. I want to be their witness, as if, by descending into that catalog of unfathomable heartbreak, I might help bring them home.

Curry tries to put me on the site. He enters his personal authorization code, except it turns out the database is offline for updating. "Come back in a couple of hours," he says, "we'll try again."

I tell him I'll be back in the afternoon. I hope Chip won't have found me yet and I'll still be at large. From city police headquarters, I drive toward Rivertown to see Platypus, and from the car, I dial one of the calls on my list.

"This is the White House, how may I direct your call?"

I ask for the deputy chief of staff, and I'm transferred to another receptionist, who asks my name and the purpose of my call. I'm put on hold, then a man picks up, and in a voice sounding as warm and intimate as if he knows me, he says, "Nick! Hi, Vinny Sherman here. Glad you called. I suppose you've heard?"

"No," I say, "I've been kind of incommunicado the past day or two."

"Yes, we've been trying to reach you. The president hates to release his decision until we've spoken to the others. You know how it is. But we had to go ahead because, you know, we don't want to get accused of foot dragging. So listen, I'm sorry it didn't work out this time. The president appreciates your willingness to serve, though, and I tell you what, Nick: Next time we're out in your neck of the woods, whatever we have going on, we'll get you involved in it, whatsay?"

"That would be nice," I say. "I'd love to meet the president."

"And I know he's eager to meet you, Nick. Okay?"

"Okay."

"Listen, I've got this other call, but it's been great talking with you and—"

"Wait," I say, "who got the seat?"

"Oh, I thought you heard. The president picked Leslie Herstgood."

"A fine choice," I say.

We hang up. For a few preposterous minutes, I allow myself to enjoy the comfort I got from the man's soothing bluster. Maybe the president really will call sometime; maybe it really *was* a tough decision, and after making it, the president and his advisers talked about how regrettable it is to pass up a good prospect like Nick Davis, and they ought to find me a position where my talents would shine.

Good thing they didn't pick me. I can imagine the embarrassment to the president (and to me) if the nominee for a seat on the U.S. Circuit Court of Appeals turned out to be the suspect in a murder investigation.

I should call TMU, my champion in this misbegotten quest, but I can't face him right now, so I call the switchboard and ask for his voice mail. I say that I'm out of the office for the day, and I hear in my voice the strain of pretending that all is well. I tell him that Leslie got the seat, and damned if my voice doesn't collapse into a sound like . . . well, the sound a mouse might make as a tabby's needle teeth bisect its spine: *You should know that Leslie (squeak) Herstgood got the seat.*

Leslie Herstgood. TMU's predecessor, my erstwhile boss. She's not evil, merely without passion. She is capable of sympathy but not empathy, generosity but not compassion, sadness but not anguish.

She is clever, ruthless, and smart, and I wonder how she could have been picked to sit in judgment.

"So sad," I whisper at the phone. It is no longer connected to TMU's voice mail, but I'm still gripping it as I steer the Volvo toward Rivertown. *So sad.* The words were out before I knew what I felt sad about. But I do know: It is sad that Leslie got the nod instead of me. Sad, because what I realize is that I'm the right one for the job and she's the wrong one. I didn't know it until this very moment.

Platty's house is a narrow over/under duplex with porches on both levels. It sits eave to eave with houses on either side. I'm sitting at a chipped Formica kitchen table, where I give Platypus the news—or nonnews—of Brittany. He rises from his chair, and with a hand on the table, then on the doorframe, then against the wall, he disappears into the dark living room and returns with a framed photograph. It is Brittany, a school photo of her at about eight years old. She is in a pretty yellow dress, sitting in front of the photographer's backdrop of palms on a tropical beach. She's smiling radiantly. Her eyes, re-touched perhaps, glisten with childish exuberance.

"That cross," Platty says, pointing at her pendant with his trembling finger, "I gave her that."

"Beautiful girl."

He sits down. The house stinks of cats, though I'm not sure if it's from droppings or open cans of cat food. I spot two cans on the floor and one right here on the table: LIVER DINNER IN GRAVY, it says.

"Sorry I don't have more for you," I say. "I'm going back this afternoon to see if I can spot her in the database of photos." *Don't get your hopes up,* I want to add, but I let dangle the desperate notion that we might find another intercepted pic.

Platypus stands up and goes about fixing tea. I put the liver dinner on the floor and nudge it away with my shoe while Platty gets cups and saucers from the cupboard. I can see into the living room, which is dark. Dusty lace curtains hang in front of shades pulled most of the way down. Lampshades have dangles of fringe; end tables are cluttered with picture frames and doilies. The wallpaper is dark and floral. I wonder what Platty does with himself now that he doesn't drink; goes to A.A. and to the senior center, he told me. Anything else?

He brings tea in gilt-edged cups and settles back in the chair. The stink of the place seems to be getting worse. I nudge the liver dinner farther away with my foot.

"I've had some luck," Platty says, and he stops to sip his tea. "First about your man Uptown. What I hear, he's definitely known on the street. Not *known* known, but known of. Known by rep. Like Tipper told you: There was a time Uptown Cruthers would go odds on anything. Anything! Got in trouble a time or two. Had to get visited once. I talked to a guy claims he was the visitor but says he didn't actually *do* nothing, just smacked him a time or two and the problem got cleared up. That's what I got on that. But I couldn't get any word if Scud Illman was working him. You know? It's possible, but either nobody knew or nobody's talking."

He lifts his cup, and those lips vacuum off a couple drops of tea. I lift my cup and then I put it down. No way I'm drinking this.

"Who told you?" I ask.

A soggy blast of air explodes from Platty's livery lips. "Jesus H., Mark Trail," he says, referencing again my having shown up at the Elfin Grot in a Woolrich shirt, "you really don't understand how this works, do you? Lucky fucking thing you got book smarts, 'cause you sure as shit don't got street smarts. 'Course, you can get away with poking and prodding like that, 'cause nobody's going to mess with you, federal agent. Don't none of us need that kind of grief."

"Lucky for me," I say. I'm warming up to the guy. "Is there any hope of finding out whether Scud was working Upton?"

"Always a chance," Platty says, "but it's pretty slim. See, Scud Illman had moved up. He wasn't a street hood no more, so he didn't brag on the streets; learned to play his cards close. So the only guys who knew for sure if Scud was working Uptown is Scud and Uptown. One of 'em's dead and the other ain't talking."

"Boy-shucks. What about who killed Scud? Any word on that?"

"Mark Trail," Platty says, blowing in his tea. He looks up with an amused frown. "How 'bout this, Mark Trail: How 'bout I go downtown and sit at your big fancy desk like Mr. Big-dick while Miss January buffs my toenails? I'll do that, and now you take a cab over to the Grot and warm a barstool for the next three days and get all your answers that way. Okay?"

Understood. I get a roll of cash from my pocket and start peeling off twenties. At fifteen of them, I look up at Platty, but he's staring at the roll in my hand, so I keep going until I reach twenty of them.

He nods and leans sideways until his ass clears the seat, then he stuffs the cash into a back pocket. "Okay," he says, "this is pretty fucked up. See, most of us, we just figured whoever Scud was working for didn't trust him. Somebody didn't want him going all witness protection. And maybe that's it. 'Cept there's this rumor out there." He stops. I make a move to go for my roll of bills, but he holds up a hand to stop me. "No," he says, "it ain't that. It's too fucked up even to talk about, but it's your money, so here it is: There's a guy out there."

"A guy?"

"A guy some of us used to know. A loose cannon, if you know what I mean. He played by different rules. All these guys he did business with kept ending up dead. Decent guys. I knew some. And everybody figures it was him making 'em dead. At first it was nobody's business, then it *was* people's business, but everyone was afraid to hurt him. Word was, he was connected."

"Connected how?"

"Yeah, exactly. 'Cause none of the big boys would own him. So who the hell was he connected to? Right?"

A cat jumps up on the table and turns circles, rubbing her haunches against Platty's chest and her tail across Platty's jowls. "Puss puss puss," he says. He takes the saucer from under his teacup, pours in cream from the pitcher on the table, and sets it on the floor. The cat jumps down. Platty watches her lap the cream. His prodigious lips slacken, and his bent back bends farther, and for a second I think he's going to tumble from the chair. But no. He's just slouching as he watches the cat. It's a tired slouch; more than tired, it is a slouch of utter exhaustion, and he exhales a long breath from a hundred miles inside of him. What I know at this moment is that the cat was Brittany's.

"I'm sorry," I say.

He nods. "Anyhow," he says, "anyhow, we figured someone finally hit him, this guy, 'cause he disappears and nobody hears nothing from him ever again. Except now. Suddenly, rumor is he's back. Settling some old scores, maybe, or doing some new business. Who knows. And maybe I don't believe it, but that's what I hear. And what I hear is that this guy is maybe the one who did Scud Illman, and what I hear is maybe this is the guy who did Seth Coen. It's what I hear."

"And I suppose," I say, "if I want to know who this guy is, you're going to call me Mark Trail again?"

Platty laughs, but I'm beyond range of the spray. "Shit, no," he says, "you're missing the nuances. What the hell good am I if I can't even give you the guy's name? Right?"

I shrug.

"The guy's name," he says, "is Maxy."

CHAPTER 42

Maxy? But there is no Maxy. Maxy was the alias of an informant who either got whacked or went into hiding. Platypus is correct that nobody has heard from him in a decade. He's a mythic figure; he's the bogeyman, Sasquatch, or D.B. Cooper. He is smoke. He's a figment.

It's not the first time I've heard his name come up in matters felonious and mysterious, but never from a serious source, which makes me wonder if I've just wasted nine hundred dollars on a kook. (Though considering I'm trying to solve a murder that has baffled the FBI and troopers, and I'm hiding out from the FBI and trying to pin a murder on my friend and colleague, I may not be the best judge of kookiness.)

When I fled Platypus's house, desperate to get out of his fetid kitchen, I scooted back across town, and now here I am at Kendall Vance's office, sunk deep into the umber Naugahyde of his easy chair. It is the perfect place to be. The stink of Platypus's depressing rooms followed me here in the Volvo, but it is replaced by the coffee fragrance wafting up from the mug between my palms. Last time I was here, Kendall gave me a paper cup. This time it's ceramic, and as in Bart Curry's office, I find myself soaking up the comfort of it.

I look at the documents and certificates on his wall of fame, and I feel a surprising fondness for Kendall, for his obvious commitment to charity and good works. I like it here, embraced in the protective wraps of our attorney/client relationship, and I am tempted to allow myself a metaphorical prance in the sunshine of that comfort. Prancing, I suppose, would amount to confessing all my festering secrets. Except that I have nothing to confess. I briefly consider confiding to him about Kenny's illicit interest in Lizzy, but it's just a momentary urge, and I recognize that it springs from this feeling of reaching a place of safety.

I do have one other thing I'm itching to confess, but it's the one thing I can't tell my lawyer, because it involves him. It is that I snooped in his cell phone log to see who Scud had called.

Beside Kendall's desk is a wall safe, and I wonder what secrets he must keep in there: all the secrets of his criminal clients. "You must hear astonishing things," I say to Kendall. We're sitting at right angles, with our feet on the same hassock.

He shrugs.

"Confessions, I mean. Criminals unburdening themselves here in the unconditional . . . what? I guess you could actually call it a kind of love: attorney/client confidence. Love of an impersonal and unaffectionate sort. Am I right?"

"You're kind of weird, Nick," Kendall says, but he's smiling, and he looks comfortable, and he's holding his cup as cozily as I'm holding mine.

"You're like a mini-god," I say. "We come to you for absolution."

"I've been called lots of things, but this . . ."

"So do you?" I ask. "Do you hear amazing things? Do you peek into the convoluted darkness of the human soul?"

"No," Kendall says, "most crooks are just crooks. There isn't a lot of convoluting going on. They're simple. Boring. A guy wants money, he goes and robs a store or mugs somebody or embezzles from his employer. He's angry or inconvenienced by someone; he shoots them or bludgeons them or kicks them in the face. Nothing Shakespearean about it. Truth is, Nick, I *wish* you or Upton had killed Scud Illman. That would at least be interesting. That would have convolutions."

"How do you know we didn't?"

He sips his coffee slowly and doesn't answer for several seconds, then says, "You get a feel for things, sitting here," and he looks around his office in self-important reference to the loftiness of being a defense lawyer. (But how can I criticize him for this? I'm the one who called him godlike.)

"Anyhow, you're right about me," I say, "I didn't kill Scud. You might be wrong about Upton. And I've got a third suspect, but it's my own private theory."

Kendall takes his feet off the hassock and sits forward, watching me intently.

"I'm the only one who suspects her," I say.

"Her?" He sits back and puts his feet up again.

"His wife."

"Christ, Nick, you're shooting in the dark," he says, spitting the words in an instantaneous change of mood that has me sitting up on alert with my feet off the hassock. "These are people's lives. Do *you* like being a suspect? Look at you, you can't go back to your office; you're sleuthing around and trying to get the goods on one friend, Upton, while your other friend, Chip, is supposedly trying to arrest you."

"Just trying to do my job, Kendall."

"No, you're goddamn not doing your job," he snaps, "you're just spreading the misery. If you and the Keystone Cops were doing your jobs, you'd have solved this by now. What's so goddamn wrong with the simple theory that the drug organization killed Scud? The meth makers, the heroin dealers. He knew too much, and they whacked him. End of story."

"That's fine, except—"

"He was my client," Kendall says. "Maybe I knew a few things about him."

"We have no leads," I say. "Nothing to tie anybody Mob-like to this. But they've got circumstantial against me, and I've got motive up the wazoo against Upton. Scud was blackmailing Upton, for cripe's sake, and if I could find one shred of physical or circumstantial evidence against Upton, I'd go to the grand jury in an instant and convict his ass. As for Scud's wife, why not her? The woman makes Morticia Addams seem like Mr. Rogers. And she's the only person alive with more motive than Upton: namely, that she had to live with Scud, the sociopathic, murdering son of a bitch. And she had opportunity, just like Upton had motive. She lived with him, and who else could have had access to that gun? Remember, he was killed with his own gun, or at least with the same gun that killed Seth Coen."

"It's all bullshit," Kendall says. "Haven't you guys got anything? What did forensics turn up?"

"Zilch."

"Zilch from the body and the scene both?"

"You know I can't discuss that, Kendall."

"Oh, for Christ's sake, Nick, this is real life happening here. Get over yourself."

"Go to hell."

"You go to hell."

"You go to hell." After a second to consider the ridiculousness of this I lift my feet back onto the hassock. "Zilch from the body," I tell him. "And we've never actually figured out where he was killed."

He looks at me, confused.

"That's right," I say. "Scud was a floater at the dam, but we've never found where he got whacked."

"Geez. I just assumed . . . No wonder you're groping in the dark. Let's think it through. I can put my own investigator on it, I suppose, but let's think first." He gets up and goes to his desk and takes out a legal pad. "Okay, the body was found when?"

"For pity's sake. If the FBI can't—"

"Work with me, Nick."

"And the state troopers. I'm on borrowed time here, Kendall."

"My hands are tied," he says. "I'm working blind here, just like you. Let's at least pool what we know. We know he was found at the dam on a Monday at—"

"You pool it," I tell him. "Pool it right where the sun don't shine. You want to chase the Mob, then chase the Mob. I'm chasing Upton and the dolorous Mrs. Scud. See which of us passes Go first."

"You goddamn idiot," he says, resorting to his steely-eyed stare. "I'm trying to help you."

He seems desperate. So much for that comforting moment between attorney and client. Kendall, I realize, is my second kook of the day, thinking he can theorize his way to the crime scene. "I'm a man on the run," I say, "so I have to run. Forgive me. I see how earnestly you want to help, and that is a great comfort to me. Let's talk this evening, okay? You do your investigating, and I'll do mine, and we'll pool. I promise."

He nods and I head for the door, but before I'm out, he says, "Wait. About Lizzy. Kaylee keeps asking me if she can see her again."

"Of course," I say. "Lizzy would like that. We'll do it as soon as things settle down a bit, okay?"

"Okay," he says, and I wonder if it is hard for Kendall, the father of a girl with special needs, to remind me, the father of a girl with a million things going for her, that we talked about getting them together. I promise myself I won't forget again. Someday soon we'll get the girls together. But talking about Lizzy brings to mind this other problem I've been avoiding thinking about: One day soon I need to have it out with Kenny over his atrocious overtures to Lizzy. I leave Kendall's office and call Bart Curry to tell him I won't make it back over this afternoon. It'll have to wait until tomorrow, assuming I'm not in prison.

I wasn't exactly honest with Kendall when I told him there was zilch evidence from Scud's body. Truth is, I haven't followed up. All I know is that Scud was shot with the gun that killed Seth Coen. I've never looked at the medical examiner's report. Now, though, since I have two suspects of my own—Upton Cruthers and Mrs. Illman—it's possible there's some orphaned bit of evidence that would mean everything to me but mean nothing to the investigators because they don't have the right suspects in mind.

I drive to the trooper headquarters. It's a risk, but a small risk. I don't know many people over here, and since I doubt the Bureau considers me a fugitive, they won't have spread the word to be on the lookout. Dorsey probably knows, but so long as I avoid him, I'm okay.

At the front desk, I show my ID and explain my interest in seeing the medical examiner's report from the Scud Illman murder.

"Have a seat," the desk clerk says, "it will be a few minutes."

I sit. She types. I wait.

"Nick," says a familiar voice behind me, "thanks for stopping in. Let's go to my office."

I follow Dorsey toward his office, and I have the silly notion to bolt out a side exit as we walk down the corridor.

"How you been, Dorsey?" I say stupidly, because it's all I can think of. I feel light-headed. If I had to stand still for a few seconds, my knees would give out. I expect that any moment, someone will step up behind me and snap on the cuffs, or Dorsey will do it himself.

He steers me into his office.

"You've spoken with Chip?" I ask, my voice strange to me.

"Sit down," Dorsey says. "You feel okay? You look green around the gills."

"I'm fine."

"Forensic report right here," he says, turning the computer screen for me to see. "Not much to go on. The river washed away most of the trace. We pulled a few fibers, but nothing unique."

"What about the ME's report?"

Dorsey clicks some tabs, and the medical examiner's report comes up on the screen. *Gunshot wound to the head . . . entry at left temple,* the report says.

Dorsey is probably enjoying studying my reactions as he leads me, like a bull with a ring in its nose, into the slaughter of self-incriminatory behavior.

(How did Mr. Davis react on reading the medical examiner's report? the prosecutor will ask, and Dorsey will answer: *He was cold and detached and showed no emotion.* Or else Dorsey will say, *He was sweating and panicky. I'm sure he knew we were on to him.)* Whatever I do, I'm fucked.

What I find, though, is that the details of the report create an eye-of-the-storm calm inside me, and I'm more at peace than I've felt in days. I'm not faking it. I'm here and focused. I continue reading: The report describes the region of the brain the bullet traveled through, then concludes, *exited through the right occipital region.*

"So if the bullet exited and he was dumped in the river, how did they match it to the gun that killed Seth?"

"Keep reading."

The next paragraph is headed *Gunshot wound #2*. This one entered in the left shoulder, traveled down through the chest region, and lodged in the lower-right rib cage. That's where the slug was recovered and later identified.

"Odd that both bullets entered from the left side," I say.

"And did you notice the angle?" Dorsey says. "Both of them traveled downward through the body."

"What does it mean?"

"Well I kind of tricked you," Dorsey says. "I didn't show you the cover sheet. Look." He scrolls up to page one. The page is a form: victim's name, identifiers, height, weight data, and location of body. The fourth line is cause of death. The ME has typed in, *Suffocation.*

"Are you kidding me? He was strangled?"

Dorsey pages forward. "Read."

I read: *Victim's larynx and cricoid cartilage are crushed with some tearing of the pharynx, and with a submucosal hematoma . . .*

I skip forward.

. . . indicating the probable cause of death was suffocation from loss of airway, consistent with a prodigious blunt trauma directly to throat, which conclusion is born out by the above-mentioned bruising and subcutaneous hemorrhage with the region . . .

"He was slammed in the throat? What do you think he was hit with?"

"Beats us," Dorsey says. "A fist, a stick, a bat. Who knows?"

"Did you know all this?"

"Of course. Why didn't you?"

"I, um . . ."

"You lawyers," he says, "we've sent you all this."

"You sure?"

"Positive." He gives a self-satisfied twitch of the bear rug. He's a very cool customer, Dorsey, giving no hint of the drama playing out here. I'm a fly caught in his web, he's the spider, not especially hungry and in no particular hurry to suck out the juice of my existence, because he knows I can't escape. So we engage in this discourse. He is in a quietly giddy state of anticipation; I'm in the preternatural calm of inevitability.

"The reports aren't in my file," I say, "which means either we never received them, which is unlikely, or Janice misfiled them, which is impossible, or the other attorney working this case diverted them."

"And which attorney would that be?" Dorsey asks. It's a strange question, because as a state cop, he doesn't know any of the assistant U.S. attorneys except Upton.

"Upton Cruthers," I say.

We lock eyes for a second.

"Dollars to doughnuts," Dorsey says, "it's a clerical error. I'll print you a copy right here."

"But if Scud died of asphyxiation . . . I thought you told me he was killed with the same gun that killed Seth."

"Yes, sorry about that. I got the ballistics report before the ME's report. I assumed. Turns out he was merely *shot* with the gun that killed Seth."

"And you've never found the scene?"

"No," he says, "officers searched for miles upriver, both sides, never found a thing. For all we know, he was killed elsewhere, then driven to the river for a quick dumping."

"Which reminds me," I say. "Apparently, Scud's wife hasn't seen their car since that night."

He squints at me. "You know this how?"

"I talked to her."

"Really? She's been unhelpful with my people."

"She's scared. Maybe she's scared that he's not really dead. We talked a bit."

"And no car, eh? We'll look into it."

Dorsey retrieves a new copy of the ME's report from his printer and hands it to me. I look at the cover sheet. The body was found at about one-fifteen P.M. on that Monday afternoon when Tina and I were eating lunch at the Rain Tree. The medical examiner estimated Scud had been dead for thirty to forty hours. That makes time of death late at night on Saturday evening/Sunday morning.

"What does it all mean?" I ask Dorsey.

He holds up his hands helplessly. "Someone smashed him in the throat, then shot him twice for insurance as he lay on the ground dead or dying, then dumped him in the river."

"Yes, but . . ."

"What?"

"Well . . ." Something occurred to me, but I don't want to voice it until I've had a chance to think it through, so I switch directions. "Who killed him?" I ask innocently, naively.

"That's the sixty-four-dollar question," Dorsey says with a wise and weary nod.

"Thousand," I say. "Sixty-four-thousand-dollar question."

Dorsey stands and points at the reports. "Hope those help," he says. He takes his gun and shoulder holster from a coat tree and puts them on, then his jacket. "Sorry to be rude. Gotta run."

Then he's gone, and I'm back in the Volvo, driving out the highway toward Turner, wondering what the hell just happened and why I'm free without so much of a mention of what I thought was my imminent arrest.

I love my car. I love driving. The expression "happy as a clam" makes sense to me. A clam lives inside the walls of its bio-home, the tide bringing along something new a couple of times a day, all necessities close by, safe, familiar. The Volvo is safe and familiar, with necessities close at hand, climate adjustable for my comfort, while outside, the landscape continuously renews itself to keep my interest. Regardless of what I need to do back in the world, I can't do anything until I get wherever I'm going.

Driving the highway to Turner, I notice that the gold and rust of autumn have spread like a contagion across distant hills. I revel in the contemplative opportunity of the thirty-minute drive. I slow down and pull into the slow lane, hoping to stretch it to forty minutes.

If I get charged . . . If I get tried . . . If I get convicted.

I've never had thoughts like this. I've been focusing on trying to solve Scud's murder to avoid getting charged with it myself. It's the best strategy, but I should at least give a nod to how I leave the table if I actually do get sent away; how does it leave Lizzy, Kenny, Flora? Maybe even Tina.

A horn blasts. A pickup swerves around me. The driver is a wiry kid with a cig stuck in his face. NO FEAR, his bumper sticker boasts as he roars away. I'd slowed to thirty-five without intending to. I'm a hazard.

I think about the ME's report. Scud went down with a brutal blow to the throat, then he was shot twice as he lay on the ground. Odd. If it were a gangland killing, then neither the blow to the throat nor the bullet in the chest makes sense. Mobsters like one-bullet execution-type jobs, like we saw with Zander. And since Scud died of asphyxiation, he was pretty well on his way to dead, if not completely there, when he was shot. Why shoot him? Dorsey called it insurance. I can think of at least one other possibility: rage. If someone killed Scud not as a business proposition but out of hatred, maybe the killer couldn't help adding those final shots following the perverse pleasure of watching him die on the ground.

I size up this new theory against the current suspects. I can well imagine Mrs. Illman being enraged enough to shoot up her husband's corpse, but could such a small woman inflict a vicious blow to the throat? Even if she used a bat, her small stature and meek demeanor make it unlikely.

As for Upton Cruthers, he isn't the kind of guy who loses control of emotions. He's whip-smart and levelheaded. If he were being blackmailed, I could believe him capable of making the considered decision to remove Scud Illman. But unless he has demons I've never had a peek at, it would be a well-planned and businesslike action. Upton might want to buy two bullets' worth of insurance, but then why bother with the blow to the throat? The only way for Upton to be the killer is if, in committing the crime, he had the foresight and composure to execute it in a way nobody would believe him capable of.

Now it *does* make sense. He's a meticulous man, fully capable of thinking through the subtle assumptions of an investigation. He would anticipate our reasoning that the viciousness and petty cruelty of the attack places him above suspicion. Drawing the rationale one step further, if Upton were trying to make the killing look like someone else's handiwork, who might he have in mind? Who is less in control of emotions and more passionate? Who is impulsive? Who else has a motive?

It is diabolical. If Upton is the killer, then all of this is intentional. The killing looks professional but, on closer inspection, not professional. It was committed with brutality, like a vengeance killing, but not with the torturous or sadistic brutality of a real sicko. It was personal and impersonal, bold and timid, emotional and clinical. Yes, if Upton committed this act, he tailored it perfectly to fit the third suspect: me.

I have slowed down again. Cars are speeding past, and I'm late picking up Lizzy. I call Flora on my cell phone.

"Hello, Nick," she says, "were you trying to call me? I've been out in the yard."

"No. I'm just calling now. I'll be there in about fifteen minutes—didn't want you thinking I forgot."

"We're just starting dinner. No hurry."

"Listen," I say, "would you mind if I had dinner with the two of you but then left Lizzy there? I need to be at my office most of the night."

"Of course."

"And there's something we need to talk about, you and me, in private."

"Is everything okay?"

"Maybe," I say, thinking about the problem between Lizzy and Kenny.

"Sounds mysterious," she says, but she's missed the note of significance in my voice. "Oh, and you should park on the street. There's equipment in the driveway."

"Equipment?"

"A truck and trailer with a steam shovel on it."

"I think you mean a backhoe, Flo."

"Backhoe." She laughs, delighted with herself for this error. I laugh, too. I'm happy to be going there for dinner. "Finally, Kenny got his friend with the backhoe to show up."

"Did they move the rocks?"

"In the morning. They just dropped if off a little while ago."

"Is Kenny there?"

"No, just that equipment."

"See you in a minute, Flo."

The idea of going back to the office hadn't occurred to me until I got Flora on the phone. I realized that if Chip is trying to find me, he'll probably go to my house, maybe even to Flora's, but I doubt he'll look for me in my office in the middle of the night. More important, the details of Scud's murder and everything I overlooked make me want to sit down with the evidence and go through it all again, item by item. Maybe I'm sitting on info that would have let the real investigators crack it open weeks ago. I'm the only one who knows that Scud snatched Kendall's cell phone and used it to call Upton Cruthers and those other two numbers that I haven't figured out yet. One call was to a cell phone that the Bureau traced to an alias: Maxfield Parrish. The other was to a construction firm: Bernier Construction. Chip told me that Bernier Construction is thought to have Mob involvement.

I should take this info to Dorsey and Chip, though it will mean coming clean with Kendall Vance about my bit of snooping. He'll be livid, but he'll get over it.

I exit at Turner and drive through the maple-lined rural roads. The leaves are still brilliant in the dim light of late afternoon. Flo's kitchen is always welcoming, and it always smells good, and despite the unconventional relationship between us, she's family. Right now I'm craving that comfort. I won't tell them about losing out for the circuit court seat today, and I won't tell them I'm apparently wanted by the FBI for a murder committed by my friend and colleague, and I won't tell them I recently looked love in the face, Tina's face, and fled. The problem between Lizzy and Kenny is plenty for one night. I will guzzle up the warmth and comfort of this home that is always open to me; I'll guzzle like a desert wanderer at an oasis. Even now, as I pull alongside Flo's split-rail fence and get out of the Volvo and walk toward the house, my eyes fill with the emotions of having reached, however briefly, this place of comfort and safety.

I see the dark form of the truck in the driveway and the robotic form of the backhoe on a trailer behind.

This mess with Kenny is so sad. Emotionally, he's a kid, so it makes sense that he might go for girls like the developmentally delayed Amber, or like Lizzy, who, though years ahead of him emotionally and intellectually, is only fourteen to his twenty-five. I've always known that Kenny has a blind spot. He is infantile in his refusal to take responsibility and to anticipate consequences, infantile in his selfishness. It has been explained to me that the dehumanizing abuse of his childhood caused his emotional limitations. I guess I didn't fully appreciate the implications.

I'll put the fear of God in him: threaten to banish him from our lives. Then I'll get him into counseling and help him through. He'll be compliant, because the one thing Kenny can't risk is being cut out of our lives. Back in the early years, when he was a kid and we'd have him to the lake for a weekend or a Sunday together at my house, every time I'd drive him back to whichever foster home he was in at the time, he'd ply me for some reassurance that I wasn't done with him and that we'd be together again soon. Eventually, I started ending our visits by locking him in my earnest stare: *Flora and I love you*, I'd tell him, *you're one of us now. That won't change.*

At his core, Kenny is a sweet, mixed-up kid. He loves doing favors like this one, getting a buddy of his to come out here with a backhoe to move the boulders for Flora's patio.

As for Lizzy, I'm amazed at how maturely she handled it. Hopefully, that means it isn't too traumatic for her. But just to be sure, we'll get her in with a shrink to talk it through. And of course we'll never let the two of them be alone together again. The problem will change things in our ad hoc family, but it probably won't ruin things.

I walk into the driveway alongside the truck, and I see the gilt lettering stenciled on the driver's door. In the dimming light, it takes a moment for my eyes to read it and another for it to register. It is a nicely lettered, professional-looking sign. Obviously, a high-class operation. BERNIER CONSTRUCTION, it says. GENERAL CONTRACTING.

CHAPTER 43

Lizzy is inside doing homework. Flora and I stand in the yard on a lawn of pine needles. I've just told her about Kenny's amorous advances. Flo's right hand is pressed against her chest. This is how she listens to serious things, as though her fingertips reconnect old circuits, bypassing the flaky Flora and bringing back from her numbed-out la-la land the Flora of all those years ago.

"The bastard," she says. "I'll cut his frigging dick off."

This makes me smile, because it is so characteristic of the former Flora; it is honest and packed with complex layers of love and contempt and exasperation. I hear in it that she loves Kenny but loves him less than Lizzy, and if this problem turns into anything, she won't spend a second anguishing over conflicting loyalties.

"I'll talk to him," I say. "Till then, we'll make sure he stays away."

"Kenny," she says. Again, this is a conversation in itself: the recognition of his childishly underdeveloped sense of responsibility and consequence. What she is saying is that though she never would have expected this from him, it makes perfect sense.

"Kenny is Kenny," I say.

She sighs and says, "I just don't know." What she means now is that, hope though we may for the return of normalcy, Kenny *is* Kenny, and that even if he can be made to behave, he can't be made to understand. He won't feel contrite or ashamed; he'll merely feel caught.

Flora walks me to my car, past the truck. This glimpse of old Flora makes me sentimental, and with everything else going on—Kenny, the circuit bench, Upton, Chip, and the threat of prison—Bernier Construction is a drop too much. I grab Flora's arm, maybe to stabilize myself or to hold on to this better Flora of yesteryear.

"Nicky," she says, patting my hand, "are you okay?"

Good question.

At about ten P.M., I park in my designated spot and ride the elevator to the criminal division of the U.S. attorney's office. The floor is quiet, but I see a sliver of light from one of the office doors. I consider stopping, backstepping quietly toward the elevator and driving off into the night. Or I could tiptoe into my own office, where, without turning on a lamp, I could stretch out on my couch and maybe catch some snooze before skulking away in the early morning.

I could, but I don't. I stand in the hallway, struck dumb for the second time tonight. The first was that unhappy surprise in Flora's driveway. This time it is a good surprise. A wonderful surprise. Tina is here, and the surprise is that the light from her door enters me like breath, and where a second ago, I was mentally writing out lists of evidence, I'm now just placidly watching the cinema-verité scene as my feet transport me and knuckles rap and the sound track seems to skip at her startled scream. I see my hand push the door open and hear a voice, mine, apologize for scaring her.

We eye each other.

"Your hairdo is growing out," I say.

"Thank goodness," she says. "Whatever possessed me?"

"Just different ways of being. You keep trying till you find one that fits."

She nods. Smiles. Then the smile is gone, and she studies me. She sees something, though I don't know whether it's exhaustion, fear, or most likely, the tremulous surfacing of these new emotions. "Nick," she says, and pauses a moment before finishing. "What's going on?"

"Nothing." But it's too late; my long list of woes has muddled my mind. Where is my lawyerly, clearheaded objectivity that I take such pride in? I stand here gaping. I'm stunned by how happy I feel to see her.

* * *

Six A.M. Friday morning. Tina is going home to change and shower. I walk her to the elevator, where, before stepping in, she tugs at the two points of my shirt collar to focus my attention. "Be careful," she says, then pulls me toward her and kisses me quickly on the lips. Our first.

I spent last night telling her everything, including peeking at Kendall's phone and about my being a suspect, which she said she hadn't heard anything about in the office. My frequent absences were noticed, she said, but everyone thought it was about my circuit bench nomination. She said she'd see what she could learn today. We slept together on my office couch, fully clothed and with her head at one end and mine at the other.

I return to my office and start packing my briefcase for the day. I've promised Tina that if nothing changes by the end of the day, I'll call Chip and turn myself in. But she's back. "Forgot something," she says, and I wonder if she's about to put her arms around me for a real smooch, or to say something bigger than "Be careful." Her hair is messy and her blouse is untucked and wrinkled. She's lovely the way women you want to sleep with are.

"Forgot what?"

"I saw Fuseli yesterday. He wants you to know he's pissed."

"The tattoo guy?"

"You promised him you'd come back and tell more of the story."

"Story isn't over."

She shrugs. "Just telling you what he told me. Poor guy."

"Poor guy?"

"Yeah, you know," she says, "he's been inside a long time. And his MS got worse in the past month. He's in a wheelchair now."

"Poor guy," I say, affectionately mocking her.

She smiles sadly at me.

It's uncommon for a prosecutor like Tina to express sympathy for an inmate. As prosecutors, we apply the laws as they are handed down. If one guy gets the raw deal, there'll be another along any minute who gets the sweet deal. It averages out. Let the politicians deal with the morality of it all; I'll take the cookbook approach, thank you very much. I go where evidence leads, follow the rules, apply the law. That's what goes into the oven, and what comes out is, by definition, justice.

"Poor guy" Fuseli is doing sixty to ninety on an armed robbery and two felony murder convictions, and the wheelchair doesn't change a thing. The chair exists in the context of the prison, which exists in the context of a life. He made his choices.

"Poor guy," Tina says again.

Then I'm stroking her cheek without having actually decided to. "Compassion," I say.

She reaches up and holds my fingers in hers.

"I'll go see him soon," I tell her, and before I lose this thought, I take the notepad where Tina and I spent the night summarizing all the evidence in all these murders, and at the top, in big letters, I write, "Fuseli—compassion."

Then Tina is on her way home, and I'm packing up to leave.

CHAPTER 44

B usy day ahead. I can't do anything until the working world comes to life, so I find an espresso shop and settle in with biscotti and a latte, and read the summary of evidence I wrote with Tina's help. It was a good exercise, going back through everything, because there are details I overlooked: There was the white "rental car" someone noticed on Cassandra Randall's street the night she was killed, and the bloody shoe print—visible only with luminol—in the bathroom of Seth Coen's apartment. And there were the frustratingly unsolved questions of who the hell is Maxfield Parrish and what Bernier Construction's role is. And now the question of how Kenny knows someone at Bernier.

About nine in the morning, once I'm sure Kenny has left for work, I drive to his apartment. I have a key.

And I have rubber gloves. I work systematically, starting at the glass-top dining table, which is covered with mail and breakfast dishes and bills. I search through all the paperwork, putting old phone bills into a box I brought along. I scrutinize credit-card statements and bank statements. The bank statements show several unaccountably large deposits. There are copies of *Popular Mechanics* and *Consumer Reports,* and there is the sales literature for the Jet Ski he's so excited about. There are old newspapers—sports sections and funny pages, mostly—with geometric doodles in the margins because Kenny always doodles when he reads the paper. The glass terrarium with his motionless snake is on a bookshelf.

I found him this apartment seven years ago when he aged out of the foster care system, abruptly cut loose at eighteen. I shudder to think what would have happened to him if he hadn't had Flora and me to help out. When he first moved in here, I came over a lot to keep him company. He used to call me in the evening and talk endlessly, trying to keep me on the phone as long as he could. Sometimes I think I should have had him live with me a year or two until he was mature enough to better fend for himself. But Kenny got his footing in time. He has his own life.

When I'm done going through the papers, I make a quick check of cupboards and fridge, then I move to the bathroom, where I empty the wastebasket on the floor and rummage through old Kleenexes and dental floss and pocket litter. I look in the medicine cabinet. I look in the cabinet under the sink where cleaning rags hang from the plumbing. What I notice is that the bottom of the cabinet is a few inches above the bathroom floor. I poke it with my pocketknife, and sure enough, it seems loose, so I remove the Drano and plunger and toilet brush and everything else down there and try to lift out the plywood panel, but it won't come. It's dark, but I identify one empty screw hole and another that seems to have a screw in place. I get a screwdriver from the kitchen and am able to get the screw out. The panel won't come out entirely because of the plumbing in the way, but I peek in and don't see anything. I forgot to bring a flashlight, but I have a lighter, and lying on my stomach, I get a pretty good look. I see nothing. I pat around with my hand, just in case, but all I come out with is a sprinkling of mouse poop on the palm of my rubber glove.

I move along to the bedroom. Dresser, closet, bedside table. Next, the spare room where Kenny has his desk, which is piled with dirty laundry. There is also a bookshelf—he likes fantasy and mystery and is actually a faster reader than I am. On the wall are some framed pictures that Flora gave him: there is one of all of us at his high school graduation eight years ago (we all look so much younger); some pictures of us at the lake; and Lizzy's eighth-grade school portrait. I add more bank statements and some paper scraps to the box I'm carrying with me from room to room.

Before I leave the bedroom, I upend his wastebasket on a sheet of newspaper. And there in the bottom, I find one chilling scrap of crumpled paper. I recognize it immediately; it was in my possession for several hours one day last June, and during those brief hours, I consulted it many times because it seemed, in my besotted state of mind, to have meanings deeper than simple numbers and letters. It made me think of the flutelike *tinga tinga tinga tinga ting* of a hermit thrush, and of spring growth in rain-washed woods. It is the note, Cassandra's contact information, written in Dorsey's sharply slanted, no-nonsense writing, that he handed me in the Drowntown Café when I coyly offered to follow up with her.

Done searching now, I have found nothing that tells me who killed Scud or Zander or Cassandra, but while I was struggling an hour ago against the awful suspicion of Kenny's involvement, I'm now dazed by the awful certainty of it. Kenny is the snitch who sold Cassandra to her assassins. I am going to lose another son. I set my box by the door and go through the apartment again, putting things back the way I found them. In the bathroom, I screw the cabinet floor down and replace the cleaning supplies, then I prop myself over the toilet for the several minutes it takes the pit of nausea I'm feeling to rise almost to eruption and then subside. But it doesn't fade entirely. I straighten up, get my box, and leave the apartment.

CHAPTER 45

From Kenny's place, I drive to the city police headquarters to search again for recent pictures of Brittany Tesoro.

Screen after screen of children. The pictures are redacted so that witnesses and relatives can search the faces without becoming complicit in the atrocious intent of the photos. Bart Curry shows me how to restrict my search: We can scan by gender, approximate age, the date the images were intercepted, hair color, or race. We punch in the particulars for Brittany.

"All these missing kids," I say.

"No, most aren't missing," Bart says, "just exploited. The missing ones . . . at least someone's looking for them. But these kids, it's just intercepted kiddie porn. They never get recognized because most of them *aren't* missing, and decent folk who might recognize them and alert authorities . . . Decent people aren't looking at this shit."

Bart watches over my shoulder a few minutes, then goes back to his desk. I keep searching, wishing I could step into the screen, slipping across rifts of time and space, to deliver the kids to safety. I go back to the setup screen and remove the age and gender parameters. I want to see them all. Screen after screen after screen. Sometimes as I click from one to the next, the images hang up a few extra seconds, and I stare at a child's face—this particular one is a puzzled African-American boy, about nine years old—I imagine he is hanging on, trying to squeeze through the time/space bars to reveal his secret; *almost there, almost there,* but before he makes it, the computer screen fades him into nothing.

What would a shrink say? That I'm searching this hellish catalog in hopes that, by rescuing one of these kids, I can redeem my own failure to stand between my innocent Toby and Dr. Wallis's fascistic eugenics?

Goddamn him. Goddamn Doctor Wallis.

Maybe I'm looking for Toby himself. Screen after screen of these children. Screen after screen. I have the strange sensation of Flora here beside me. Two searchers trying to get themselves unstuck.

I don't find Toby, of course, but who I do find—and when I see him, it's no surprise at all, almost as if he is exactly the person I expected to find here—is a serious-looking, sandy-haired boy, about seven. He has the lip scar of a repaired cleft palate, and his left iris is brown with a splotch of green. It is Colin, Scud's stepson, posed in front of an old tie-dyed bedspread. Maybe if I keep searching, I'll find more pictures of him, perhaps posed with other kids, but I have no stomach for any more. The queasiness that almost got me at Kenny's apartment explodes with the grotesque suddenness of a lily blossoming in time-lapse. I barf most of it in the wastebasket, and immediately, Bart is behind me with his hand on my shoulder. He stays there as I blow out the pipes and sinuses.

"Bathroom's that way," he says when I'm done.

When I return, the garbage bag has been replaced and the floor toweled off.

"It's pretty rough shit," he says. "You okay?"

I nod, then I say, "In the old photos of Brittany: Is the tie-dyed bedspread the same?" I point at Colin's picture on the screen.

"I don't know," Curry says. "I'll pull the file to look."

"Call me," I say, and I head for the door. Outside, I pause, getting my bearings, remembering where I left the car, then I speed across town, blue and reds flashing.

It is afternoon. My phone chirps with messages: Chip, TMU, Tina, Kendall. I listen to Chip's first. "Nick," he says, and his voice is strained to the point of hysteria. "This is deadly serious. I need you to—"

I delete it. I don't want to hear him say he's out hunting for me.

Whether I find something within the next couple of days or not, I'll surrender myself.

I go to Dorsey's message. "Nick, it's me," he says. "We found Scud Illman's wife's car. Some pretty weird shit. Call."

I will, but later. Right now I call Bart Curry.

"How you feeling?" he asks.

"Better. Did you . . . ?"

"Yes. I pulled the pictures of Brittany Tesoro. You're right: same tie-dyed bedspread. How did you know?"

"Police work," I say. "Here's the address."

"What address?"

"Where the pictures were taken. Where the perv lives. Except he doesn't live there anymore, he's dead."

"You know this?" Curry shouts. "You know this guy?"

"Of course."

"Oh my God. Oh my God," and now he shouts it, yelling it to the whole office full of cops. "Oh my God, we finally friggin' found one. Oh, sweet Jesus."

I give him the address. It is possible Scud was doing the camera work someplace else, but I'm betting it was right there in his basement. We'll know soon.

"Come back to the station," Curry says. "We'll need you to swear for the warrant."

"You won't need a warrant," I tell him, "just meet me there. And bring protective services. There's probably a minor on the premises."

I had waited until I was almost at Scud's house to call Curry. I didn't want cops beating me to the scene. Now I pull up in front of the small house with the tidy yard and the old fifties-era front door with its three stair-step windows. Such a humble place. It's odd that a guy like Scud could go around ruining lives for profit but profited so meagerly.

Mrs. Illman is home and comes to the door when I pound. Her hair is pulled back tight, as always; same jeans, same sweater, same shoes. We stare at each other a couple of seconds. She knows something has changed.

"We found dirty pictures," I say.

The effect is almost imperceptible. This woman has survived by making herself impervious to hope and despair, but something slackens in her by a millimeter.

"The police will be here any moment," I say. "Get a lawyer and tell him you want to cooperate as much as possible. If you aren't involved in the pornography, you can probably stay out of jail."

She nods.

"And I'll need your shoes," I say.

"My shoes?"

"A shoe print found in Seth Coen's apartment," I say, "it was invisible to the naked eye. I'm betting it matches these deck shoes you always wear. Am I right?"

She shrugs.

"That makes you an accessory to murder," I say, "but you've got your hands full enough as it is. I'm guessing that when Scud told you he needed help cleaning up because he got a little carried away, telling him no wasn't exactly an option. I'm also betting he wasn't squeamish about threatening Colin, am I right?"

"How?" she whispers.

"Toilet paper. You must have been a chambermaid, Mrs. Illman. Sheraton? Hilton?"

"Milltown Square."

"Old habits," I say. "In Seth's bathroom, you left the TP folded into a point."

"Scud," she says. "We met when I was at the hotel. I showed him how we do it. He says to me he's as good as all those rich scumbags. So at home, I always did it in a point like that."

Her bottom lip is quivering. She takes her shoes off and is about to hand them to me but stops. Shoes are personal things. "Would you like a bag?" she asks.

"Please."

She retreats into the house, then returns with the shoes in a plastic shopping bag.

Two city police cars pull up outside.

"These guys are going to want to search your house. I think you should let them."

Bart Curry comes toward me across the lawn. I hold up a hand to stop him. He waits.

"One question, Mrs. Illman. Just between you and me, scout's honor, did you kill your husband?"

She finally meets my eyes. Hers are watery. The rigidity that has served her all these years is back in force. But her mouth spreads a millimeter in a pale shadow of a wistful smile. "I wish I had," she says.

I nod at Curry, and he approaches. "She has requested a lawyer," I tell him, "but I think you'll find her cooperative in other respects."

I walk to the Volvo and lift the spare-tire well and toss in this bag I'm holding. For the first time in my life, I have committed a major crime: I am withholding evidence and interfering with an official investigation. But human affairs are minute and intricate things, and the law is a blunt instrument. It is too blunt to re-solve the tricky problems of domestic violence and psychological imprisonment in Scud Illman's home. This is what I believe, and by resolving it myself, by removing the evidence of Mrs. Illman's complicity in cleaning up Seth Coen's murder, maybe Colin won't have to go into foster care for so long. Kenny was in foster care for years, and he didn't fare too well. So I have decided that Mrs. Ill-man had nothing to do with Seth Coen's murder, and Colin might get to keep his mother.

I slam the Volvo shut and return to the house, where I hand Ken-dall Vance's business card to Bart Curry. "If she doesn't have a lawyer of her own, give this guy a call," I say.

From where I stand, I can see into a bedroom. The protective-services woman is sitting on the bed talking to Colin.

"Geez," I say to Curry, "too much coffee again." I walk into the bathroom, close the door, then tear off and flush away the end of the toilet paper, which was folded neatly into a point.

* * *

It is almost time to give myself up. I'll have Chip meet me in TMU's office. Kendall Vance will be there as my attorney and Tina as my friend. I'll tell them my theory about Upton. I'll tell them about the gambling problem of his younger years, the suspicious call Scud made to him on Kendall's phone, and the letter of resignation I found in Upton's desk, written the day of Scud's murder. It is pretty obvious that Scud was blackmailing Upton. Upton will be ruined, but I'll have to wait and see whether the Bureau has more luck than I did with building the case that Upton Cruthers killed Scud Illman.

I'm driving out to Flora's in Turner. I need someplace safe to stash Mrs. Illman's shoes and my box of evidence from Kenny's apartment. I thought of asking Kendall to take them, but that's preposterous. No ethical lawyer would think of hiding evidence for a client.

Dorsey calls. "Talk to me," I say. I'm impatient to settle deep into TMU's sofa for that long, cathartic surrender. I'm tired.

"Are you sitting down?" Dorsey asks. "I've got good news and weird news."

Again he waits for me to answer. It's an annoying habit. "Yes, I'm sitting down, Dorsey."

"We found Seth Coen's boat. Milan gave us a description of the car that hauled it off. Since the buyer saw it for sale right there beside the road, we figured maybe he works in the area, so we put some cops on that road to pull over every brown and white Blazer driving past. Found him quick."

"And?"

"Tarps were still in the boat. Blood residue. We've matched some of the blood to Zander Phippin."

"Good work," I say, still in my cop-speak voice. The theory was right: Zander took his final ride in the bottom of Seth Coen's boat.

"There was blood from several other sources."

"Able to ID any of it?"

"Negative."

"Okay, listen," I say, "there's an open missing persons case, juvenile female named Brittany Tesoro. Talk to Bart Curry in city police. See if she's a match. I'll fill you in later."

"You're a mysterious bastard, counselor. You ready for the weird?"

"Dorsey, I don't believe it can get any weirder."

"Oh yeah? Well, we followed up on Scud Illman's other car. Get this: It was parked for like a week at the Rainbow Bend picnic area. The state finally towed it and sent a certified letter to the registered owner."

"Who never answered because he was inconveniently dead at the time?"

"Right."

"Where is Rainbow Bend?"

"Like thirty miles out of town. We never searched that far. Figured how far can a guy float downriver in two days? Turns out farther than we thought."

"The rains," I say. "Remember how it rained that week? The river was probably raging."

"And rising," Dorsey says. "We searched the site, and can't be sure because it's been too long, but the reconstruction guys say the body might not have been dumped in the river. Just left by the edge. The river came up and got him."

"Interesting," I say. "But not too weird."

"I haven't gotten to weird yet. Here's the weird: We've worked the car for trace, okay? And we found something usable, maybe. Some fingerprints, the only ones not from Scud or his wife or son. They were on a coffee cup that had spilled all over the floor. We've ID'd them. Want to guess?"

"Upton Cruthers," I say without hesitation.

"No," Dorsey says in a perplexed voice.

I've blown it. I tipped my hand and he's suspicious. I realize it's not sudden, he's been suspicious all along, and now he's toying with me, setting his trap. I see it, but I can't help myself, and I know it has all been leading up to this. *Don't say it,* my decades of training scream to me. *Remain silent, remain silent,* but even if Kendall Vance were here with a choke hold around my neck, I couldn't stop the words as they flow out with effortless certainty. "The prints," I say, though I don't know how I know, and I have no clue how they got there. (Or yes, I do know how they got there: Upton Cruthers must have done it. Upton planted my prints at the scene of a murder that he committed.) "The prints are mine."

The phone is silent; just the fuzz of static tells me we're still connected. I hear the sharp intake of breath. Then an explosion of breath.

"Oh, sweet Jesus, Nick, that was beautiful. You had me for a second." He laughs. "But seriously, you're sucking all the air out of my punch line. Can you guess whose prints they were?"

I hold the phone away again and steady my breathing, steady my voice. "No, Dorsey, I can't guess."

"Then I'll tell you. Did you ever hear of a guy named Maxy?"

CHAPTER 46

TMU is out sick, and Tina is in court. So much for those plans of surrender.

I stash the box of Kenny's stuff in Flora's garage, and I'm about to send Mrs. Illman's shoes flying out the car window into the Aponak River, but I change my mind. What if I've been conned? Maybe she isn't just the abused spouse of a sociopath but a sociopath in her own right.

I call Kendall Vance. "Can I meet with Agent d'Villafranca at your office?" I ask. "I'm tired. I need to turn myself in."

"You know, Nick, you might be taking this idea of being a suspect a bit too far."

"No, you were right about it, Kendall, I'm sure."

". . . because I'd suggested it merely as a possibility. I didn't mean—"

"All I know is that Chip has been calling and calling, and I've been dodging and dodging, and then he was on his way over to my office. He never comes to my office. And now, in his latest message, he's saying it's urgent."

"Nick, calm down."

"And everybody knew I hated Scud. It was all I talked about. When Scud called me that time, I said I'd kill him if he ever mentioned Lizzy again. I've told everybody about it. I wrote it in my report of the incident—that I threatened him. And I've told everybody how I wanted to murder Dr. Wallis . . ."

"Murder who? You haven't told me—"

"Never mind. Thing is, of course I'm a suspect. Think about it. I thought he'd murdered two people I cared about, Zander and Cassandra, then I have this long conversation with him on the phone, he threatens my daughter, and that's the last known contact anybody ever has with him before he turns up dead in the river. I have motive. And I could have had opportunity: Who's to say I didn't arrange a meeting when we were on the phone that very night? And I've proved myself unstable, haven't I? Haven't I, Kendall? I've admitted to wanting to kill Doc Wallis, I've admitted to threatening to kill Scud . . ."

"Okay, calm down, Nick. Take a few deep breaths."

"Oh Jesus, Kendall, I've really screwed myself."

"Let me see what I can find out. Let me make some calls. Don't do anything yet. Can you calm down? Take a moment, I'll stay on the phone."

I do as he says. I even pull into the breakdown lane and stop and close my eyes, taking some steadying breaths.

"Still there?" Kendall asks after a minute.

"I'm sorry," I say. "I guess I started to panic."

"Okay, I'm going to see what I can find out. Don't do anything before you hear back from me. Promise?"

"Okay. Promise."

We hang up. I pull back on the highway. He's a good guy, Kendall, and I feel lucky to have him. Just a few weeks ago I thought he was a Neanderthal, but now I get the feeling his concern for me goes beyond his professional obligation. I want to spend more time around him. He makes me feel safe. So I call him right back to say that if I'm not in prison, why don't he and Kaylee drive up to join Lizzy and me for an afternoon at the lake Saturday. Kendall says they might like that.

As soon as I end the call with Kendall, Chip calls. I deliberate whether to answer. I just promised Kendall I wouldn't do anything. But when I see Chip's name on caller ID, that little island of calm is blown. I start trembling. There is a rest area a few miles ahead. I'll pull over there and breathe some breaths of the cool fall air. I'll smell that sweet humus-y scent of how life is supposed to be. *Free* is how it's supposed to be; follow rules, do your best, think good thoughts, and shouldn't that be enough to steer you clear of all the Dr. Wallises and Scud Illmans and this bad dream of getting set up for a murder rap by the diabolical likes of Upton Cruthers?

Ah, but I remember the new evidence. Maxy's prints found in Scud's car. Maybe it wasn't Upton.

In the rearview, I see a trooper barreling up behind, lights flashing. I pull over to let him pass. He pulls in behind me. I flash my blues and reds to let him know I'm someone. He responds with a burp of his siren and stays on my bumper. Damned if I'll pull over before the rest area, but as a show of compliance, I put my blinker on. Then I continue three more miles to the rest area with Johnny Law burping the siren every few seconds.

At the rest area, I get out of the Volvo (cops hate it when you do that) and walk over onto the grass. My legs are trembling. My voice sounds like it's coming through a long hollow cylinder. "Doesn't it smell good?" I say to the cop, who has already maneuvered himself in front of me. "Autumn leaves. Don't you love them, Officer? Think of all the things you'd miss in jail. Ever thought of that?"

"Assistant U.S. Attorney Davis?"

"The very same."

"Do you know we've got an APB on you?"

"Are you arresting me?"

"No, sir. I'm escorting you."

"Escorting where?"

"FBI."

"Why?"

"I wouldn't know the answer to that, sir."

"Can I refuse?"

"No, sir."

"It sounds like an arrest to me."

"No cuffs or anything. Protective custody. There's a wrecker on its way to take your car."

"Really sounds like an arrest."

The officer opens the front passenger door of his car. "You can ride in front with me."

"Okay," I say. "That isn't very arrest-like, is it?"

* * *

"Oh, thank God," Chip says when I appear in the doorway of his office. He gets up from his desk and hugs me.

"What's the deal, Chip? Sorry I haven't gotten back to you sooner."

Isler is in the office with Chip. "We've got an intercept," he says. "It sounds serious, Nick. We think you're a target."

"Whose target?"

"Nobody's sure. It was just by chance, see. We're interested in this guy for some unrelated bullshit. We've been following him around, so this morning an agent followed him into a coffee shop and sets up at the next table, and the guy gets on his cell and starts blabbing, and our guy records the whole thing. And damned if your name doesn't come up. We're taking it seriously, Nick."

Chip isn't looking so good. The flesh under his eyes has gone back to a mustard color. It must be harder on him than I thought, investigating me.

"We only caught half the conversation. And we're just into street level, so we only get the trickle-down, you know? We don't have principals. . . ."

"Of course you do, Chip, you're the most ethical guy I know."

It's gallows humor, but it fails. Upton would have gotten it; Tina, too; Lizzy for sure. But my friend Chip, new-age guy with analytical smarts, bovine wit, and rudimentary human insight, just says, "Thanks, Nick," and he hands me the printout to read:

> . . . *cocksucker knows too much . . . we gotta assume Scud*
> *spilled everything, miserable pussy . . . wants to nip this one . . .*
> *keep the rest of the cats in the fucking bag . . . Uptown ain't*
> *running it, and he never played ball anyway . . . they pulled*
> *him off . . . Davis is the one, Nick Davis . . . no leverage . . .*
> *can't take the chance . . . yeah, but if it goes south . . . you*
> *and me, asshole . . . he does good work . . . saved your ass ten*
> *years . . . okay, but then he goes all Boy Scout . . . can't listen*

*to that shit . . . too hot for local . . . transponded him is all I
had to do . . . keep the rest of the cats in the fucking bag . . . it's
all set up, the talent does the rest . . . (laughter) . . . blow his
lawyer ass away . . . all the better. Your secrets will be safe, too,
right? . . . (laughter) . . .*

"Who is this?" I ask.

"He goes by Spawner. Real name is Milton Roe, or Milt, another
nobody, but he—"

"From my perspective, Chip, he's trying to kill me, which makes
him a very definite somebody."

Chip settles into his desk chair like a sack of grain, except grain
doesn't emit a long soul-weary sigh. "Dorsey's people gave him to
me. He's got a rap sheet of petty shit, brought in for questioning
a hundred times, but no big convictions. We never connected him
to the Randall/Phippin matter. He seems to be connected to Percy
Mashburn."

"Mashburn? I thought Mashburn was small potatoes."

"We all did. We were wrong. Mashburn franchises these little
meth labs, but he's somehow involved in the overall flow of goods."

"Shit, Chip, you never told us."

"Just now figuring it out."

"My God, you know we just gave Mashburn a walk on meth
charges for cooperating?"

"Oops."

"What do you know about him?"

"Almost nothing. He's got money. He lives in a big house in the
hills with big south-facing windows."

"So in this conversation," I say, holding up the transcript, "who
is Spawner talking to?"

"We don't know."

"What's it all mean?"

"It sounds like they think Scud spilled his guts to you, so someone wants to kill you to nip any prosecution. But since you're a federal agent, it's a hot job, so they've got someone from out of town."

"What's it mean, 'transpond him'?"

"Weird shit," Isler says. "There have been some suspicious deaths around the country. Car plunged off a bridge someplace out west—"

"San Jose," Chip says.

"No, someplace else. Terrible accident; whole family killed. Witnesses say the car was sideswiped by an SUV. Turns out the guy was a hot property."

"A naughty businessman who'd agreed to cooperate," Chip says.

"And a house fire," Isler says. "Everyone killed. The strange thing is, the guy somebody might have wanted whacked, another hot property, was just an overnight guest. It was his sister's place. He'd stopped in for the night on his way someplace else."

"Yeah, but—"

"And a few others. Guys with troubles," Isler says.

"Big guys," Chip says.

"Big in terms of the trouble they've gotten themselves into. Risk takers, and one day they just kill themselves. Nobody thinks too much about it because, you know, they were under so much stress, until one of these deaths doesn't sit right. So this city cop in . . . Where was it, Chip, Texas?"

"Right. Texas."

"He smells a rat, so he has the guy's car taken apart piece by piece."

"Piece by piece."

"And they find this transponder. It's an electronic gizmo, sends out a blip. You enter it into your GPS, and you can see where the guy is, twenty-four/seven. Or where his car is, anyhow. Easy to make it look like an accident or a suicide when you can follow a guy's every move," Isler says.

"Take your time; wait your chance."

"So after this Texas cop figures it out, cops all over the country start looking at the cars of guys who were big and died in accidents or fires or suicides, and damned if these transponders didn't show up in a handful of cases."

"Thing is," Chip says, "every one they've found has been in a different part of the car. One was tossed under the backseat, one was welded inside the frame. And everything between."

"Suggesting," Isler says, "whoever is doing the hits has some local schmuck plant the thing ahead of time."

Chip and Isler stop. Their narrative is spent, leaving me blinking in the newly constructed reality that someone not only wants me dead but is taking pains to get me there. Maybe if I'd been in a war, like Upton and Kendall and, yes, even Scud and Seth, the idea wouldn't be so hard to swallow. Or if I'd been a real cop, like Chip and Dorsey, who've probably been in standoffs with bullets zinging. But I haven't.

"When did you get this?" I ask, holding up the transcript.

"This morning."

"So all this week, when you've been trying to reach me?"

"Other matters," Chip says, moving his eyes uncomfortably toward Isler.

Oh yes, I forgot. Being a murder target temporarily drove from my mind that I am also a murder suspect. Everything is relative.

"Now what?" I ask.

"We're moving your car to a remote location out of town. Hopefully, this guy will find it a promising place to make his move. Then we'll take him."

"Right now," Isler says, "we'd rather you not go home or back to your office. If you need anything, we'll send a guy in as a furnace repairman to get it."

"What about this Spawner guy?"

"We're looking for him, and when we find him again, we'll bring him in for questioning. He ought to be a useful source. To put it, you know, understatedly."

There is a knock on Chip's door, and a scrawny red-haired man stands there holding a big file box. "Hi, Mr. Davis, I have personal items from your car. How you doing?"

"Fine, um . . ."

"Sparky."

"Of course. Sparky. Sorry, I've got things on my mind."

He puts down the box and leaves. Sparky the AV nerd. I suspected him as our snitch for a while.

Isler leaves. Chip looks sorrowful. I should be a good friend (especially since he seems to have saved my life) and make this easier for him. But I can't. I don't want to be arrested. I don't want to be a suspect. I don't want to go to prison. In my briefcase, I have a handwritten summary of all my evidence against Upton. I planned to deliver it to TMU, but with Chip about to bring the hammer down on me, I'll give it to him. Maybe it will change his mind.

"I've been trying to reach you," Chip says. He looks miserable.

"I apologize. I've been evasive."

"You figured out why?"

"Yes."

"Sorry," he says. "If there was anyone else . . ."

"But there is," I say. I take the summary from my briefcase.

"Not really, Nick. You're thinking of my men's group, right? All nice guys. But."

I stare at him.

"I know you held my hand all through the divorce," he says. "Now this. Can't really blame you."

I'm wondering if he's lost his mind. He was staring at his own fidgeting hands, but now he looks at me, and he sees that I don't have any idea in hell what he's talking about. "Sylvia," he blurts.

I stare.

"The woman I'm seeing. Was seeing. She broke it off." His voice cracks. "I'd even bought the ring."

"Chip, Chip," I say in my most soothing voice, "you should have called."

But he did call—a dozen times, at least. Poor Chip. He never used to be this way. Or rather, he hid it deep inside his imposing six-two, 240 pounds of badass, gun-carrying, frown-wearing, Miranda-reading, family-neglecting, conservative-voting, football-watching federal-agent persona. We've been friends for a decade. I remember a briefing on Medicare fraud. Half a dozen agents and four attorneys in the Bureau's conference room. When business was finished, everyone started talking about the most recent high school shooting in some distant state, where an apparently normal kid from a good home brought in a gun and opened fire. And this big bland agent I'd never met said, "Poor parents." And we all started talking about the victims' parents. And this agent says, "Yes, them, too. I meant the shooter's parents."

This guy was clearly outside the norm.

Several days after that, I saw him testifying in trial. When he was done, I caught up with him on his way out of the building. "Agent d'Villafranca," I said. "Let me buy you a cup of coffee." We hit it off, became friends. But now, poor guy, he sometimes seems lost. Did his divorce make him weird or the other way around?

"And I'm not even a suspect, am I?" I say quietly, thinking aloud.

But Chip hears me and scrunches his brow, and his composure surges back. "Nick," he says in an angry voice, but he's not angry, he's just overcompensating for that moment of emotion, "what in the hell are you talking about? A suspect in what?"

CHAPTER 47

Across darkness, I hear the rhythm of Lizzy's breathing. So many times I've lain here listening to her. When she was young, she'd sleep snuggled beside me. Now she's across the room, but I still tend to wake up in the night whenever we're at the cabin to hear her breathe—to experience the pleasure of lying here like this, inhaling the darkness and cautiously swapping workaday cares for this peacefulness. I assess things, and they usually balance out to the positive.

Tonight is different. Now the darkness is an unbounded landscape for the anxiety and sorrow at play in my head. The crimes have mostly resolved themselves, but I don't like all the answers. Scud Illman and Seth Coen buried Zander Phippin, of course: Zander's blood in Seth's boat gives us proof. But with Seth and Scud both dead, we have no evidence that they were the ones who tortured and killed him, and no leads to whomever else might have done it. As for the other crimes, I thought Upton was our snitch, and I thought he killed Scud. But now there's Maxy. He is the key. His prints in Scud's car tie it all together. Maxy is no doubt Maxfield Parrish of the mysterious calls Scud made on Kendall's cell phone. Maxy, who has had a decade to work his contacts and build his organization. A decade to whack anyone who got in his way. I'm sure Maxy was the go-between for the hit on Zander. The most significant thing about Maxy is that ten years ago, back before he disappeared, he was undercover for the troopers. He knows who's who; he knows who's dirty. He worked both sides. Who better than Maxy to recruit a snitch from within the troopers? Maxy is the key. With Scud and Seth dead, he's the last thread for us to bring the whole thing down. We need to find him.

I'm wide awake. Falling back to sleep is out of the question, so

I get up and grope for a sleeping bag, get a beer from the cooler, and slip outside as quietly as possible. It's very dark, but I find my way to the dock and walk haltingly out to the end, feeling along the edge with one foot so I don't get disoriented and walk right off into the lake. I settle into my Adirondack chair, arrange the sleeping bag over me, open my beer, and surrender to the sorrows, regrets, and self-recriminations dished out by my unleashed angst.

It is late Saturday night. Just yesterday I searched Kenny's apartment, though nobody knows I was there. Just yesterday I found Colin's picture on the exploited-child database. Just yesterday Dorsey told me they found traces of Zander Phippin in Seth Coen's boat. Just yesterday he told me that the new suspect in Scud Illman's murder is a ghost named Maxy; yesterday Chip told me that a professional killer, whose specialty is making high-profile deaths look accidental, wants to kill me. Just yesterday Chip told me I was never a suspect in Scud's death.

It is quiet on the lake but not silent. I hear occasional watery plinks when fish surface or bugs submerge. An owl hoots, but it is far away, and the sound has only now separated itself from all the subliminal things you hear without hearing. A deer or a skunk or a raccoon moves through leaves over near the driveway.

My Volvo is spending its weekend in a garage at a rural retreat a hundred miles from here, which, the Bureau believes, is just the sort of place the killer likes. An agent in sunglasses, a guy my size and hair color, and accompanied by an unmarked escort, drove the Volvo there directly from the FBI building. I last spoke with Chip at about four this afternoon; the killer hadn't struck yet, they hadn't found the transponder, and the guy, Spawner, who planted the device, seems to have vanished.

Something huge splashes across the lake.

The Bureau loaned me a car. It has tinted windows with reinforced everything. I drove it out the gate of the FBI garage and straight to the lake. I spent last night here alone, then this morning, Kendall and Kaylee picked Lizzy up in Turner and drove up to spend the day.

The girls did great. Kendall and I did okay. Our relationship has gone, in quick order, from that of wary opposing counsels, to attorney and client, and now to two guys whose daughters are friends. The haughty Kendall, whose sanctimony is reassuring when discussing my legal woes, is pretty irksome as a social companion. Kendall remains, alas, Kendall. I like him better than I did before, but I still can't say I enjoy his company outside the office. He adores his daughter, Kaylee, though, and is obviously enchanted with Lizzy for befriending her. So long as Kendall and I focused on the girls today, we got along fine.

Kendall and Kaylee were planning to leave after dinner, but the girls were writing an adventure story. Lizzy would feed ideas to Kaylee, who'd add a twist of her own, and Lizzy would write it down.

Maybe the sisters entered the dragon's cave, Lizzy suggested.

Yes, Kaylee yells. *They went into the cave, and there were mushrooms everywhere.*

Edible mushrooms?

No! Poisonous mushrooms. You die from just even touching them.

So Lizzy wrote: *Hand in hand, the sisters tiptoed into the cave where Goreyclaw the dragon lovingly dusted off the skulls of everyone who ever brushed against the beautiful turquoise caps of his deadly mushrooms.*

Perfect, Kaylee said, and she tipped over sideways, laughing.

Kaylee didn't want to leave. Lizzy suggested Kendall and Kaylee stay in Flora's cabin for the night. It was agreed. I set them up with bedding.

Thinking of Kendall and Kaylee reminds me of Platypus, for some reason: how bereaved he is for his granddaughter. If Dorsey's people find any trace of Brittany in Seth Coen's boat, I'd like to tell Platty myself. Give it the personal touch. If Scud was pimping his own stepson for kiddie porn, and if he also shot pics of Brittany, that makes him a pretty compelling suspect in Brittany's disappearance. I think of Mrs. Illman's answer when I asked if she killed Scud: *I wish I had.* Right now that's how I feel, too.

I wonder if the Bureau has sprung their trap on my would-be assassin.

The animal in the leaves is moving across the gravel of the driveway.

Criminals are such assholes. I'm thinking about whoever hired someone to try and kill me. Sheer stupidity. I remember Platty telling me, *Nobody's going to mess with you, federal agent. Don't none of us need that kind of grief.*

How come someone is willing to take that on?

What was it Spawner said in that transcript? *Gotta assume Scud spilled everything . . . Uptown ain't running it . . . Davis is the one, Nick Davis . . .*

And later:

. . . blow his lawyer ass away . . .

It sounded like they were talking about the possibility of applying pressure to Upton, but since he wasn't running the case, and he *never played ball anyway,* he was an unlikely prospect.

It's chilly. I pull the sleeping bag tighter. The woods are getting noisier. This happens; the rustling sounds of my walking from the cabin out to the dock suspended all dramas of nature playing out around the cabin. The predators froze in place; unsuspecting prey got a stay. But the tiny dramas have resumed. I hear things.

. . . he does good work . . .

. . . saved your ass ten years . . .

. . . okay, but then he goes all Boy Scout . . .

Wait. This doesn't sound like it's about me. It doesn't make sense.

. . . keep the rest of the cats in the fucking bag . . .

They're not worried about what I know.

. . . assume Scud spilled everything . . .

They don't care what Scud spilled to me; those cats are out. The concern is what someone might know that hasn't yet come out.

. . . he does good work . . .

They're worried about what Scud spilled to someone else.

. . . saved your ass ten years . . .

The only other person Scud might have spilled to.

. . . he does good work . . .

The person who, when Scud got whacked, was left with all this inside information and no client to be loyal to.

. . . he goes all Boy Scout . . .

Kendall Vance.

It makes sense. Scud's death has left an unknown. Whether it's accurate or not, some of the players fear that Scud got overly talkative, and now Kendall, with no client to protect and too much information in his head, creates an unacceptable hazard.

. . . blow his lawyer ass away . . .

Kendall is the target.

. . . transponded him, is all I had to do . . .

And Kendall's car is parked a few hundred feet away, beside the cabin where Lizzy is sound asleep.

I might not have figured this out so quickly another time. But here I sit in the blackness of night, no moon, no city lights. It is the blackest of nights, and the absence of anything to see has left my mind free. The blackness of night may also make my hearing more acute, and what I hear, I realize, doesn't fit in. The noises—crunching gravel, crackling leaves—don't sound quite right. There is no deer. No raccoon. The footsteps continue, suspending the tiny dramas. Everything is on alert. Someone is walking down my driveway.

Ridiculous, I think. I'm getting paranoid.

Then I hear, ever so faintly, a throat being cleared. Or did I imagine it?

My breathing becomes jagged. I try to hold my breath to listen.

More footsteps.

Someone is approaching, there's no question. I almost moan aloud. I am paralyzed. This is terror.

The footsteps keep coming.

There are two cabins, Flora's and mine. The driveway is between them. Flora's is less visible, but maybe he'll see it and choose that one. Lizzy will escape. Kendall and Kaylee will die, but Lizzy will escape.

Kaylee will die.

Dr. Wallis would like that.

Kaylee: How happily she laughed this evening, working on the story with Lizzy. We all laughed.

I overcome my paralysis. I am on hands and knees, feeling along the edge of the dock toward shore.

I reach the shore. The grass is wet, but I stay on all fours and crawl toward the cars. Certainly by now he's heard the thunder of my breathing, and any moment he'll walk up and put a bullet in my head. I go down on my stomach in the grass and try to get control. I feel cold from the dew in my shirt.

I lie still. My breathing slows. Lifting my head from the grass, a tiny window opens in the blackness. It is bluish, whitish, a light that spreads out to reveal a man. The light is his GPS screen, I realize. He's checking to see that he has traced the electronic blip to its source. Kendall's car. The light goes off, and the darkness is blacker than before.

In my cabin, in my briefcase, there is a gun. My Glock service handgun. If the assassin goes first toward Flora's, I can crawl inside and get it. I've hardly ever fired the thing. It isn't loaded, but there's a clip in the briefcase. I think of trying to do all this: getting to the cabin, finding the briefcase, loading the gun. Aiming. Shooting. It's too much. Impossible.

The man moves. It sounds as though he has stopped a few feet in front of Kendall's car. I hear him set something down in the gravel. He is rummaging. Then I see another light, this time a red beam. It plays across the lawn and out along the dock into the woods. It finds my cabin. It fails to find Flora's cabin, which is hidden in the trees from where he stands. If the man were standing a few feet one way or the other, it would have found me, and I'd be dead, but it leaves me flattened into the grass between the alleys of its thin red glow.

There are two cars: Kendall's car, which, with its hidden transponder, has lured this man to us; and to the left, "my" car. The Bureau's. The assassin is doing something, preparing something, just in front of Kendall's car. I rise up on all fours and crawl until I'm hidden behind my car, then I move alongside it so I'll be shielded as

I head toward the cabin. But there, on the far side of my car, I stop. There is something. Blackness within blackness. It blocks my path. Another car. The killer's? Probably. But he walked down the driveway; I heard him. An accomplice? Maybe. Wherever it came from, it is one obstacle too many.

The man clears his throat. "Blow them fucking up," he whispers. He laughs. Putting my head to the ground, looking under the car, I see the glow of a lamp he's using to illuminate his work.

Now he's moving. I press myself into the grass alongside this mystery car. He walks a few steps and stops where, if he looked, he would see me. If I had hidden in a crouch instead of flat on the grass, I could lunge from here. My breathing is so ragged, it will give me away, so I'm holding my breath, but I can't hold it long. If I have to gasp, I'm done for, so I might as well try a lunge, though I'll probably be dead before I make it to my feet. He's a trained killer; I'm an administrator.

No. I'm a father. I'm a father. I'm a father. I feel this idea spread through me. It is a drug. It settles the clamp on my throat and the tension in my chest, so I can take a silent breath, and I feel the blessed air feed muscles in my back and legs and arms. I'm a father, and this man will hurt my Lizzy if I let him. I am electric. I will spring.

But he steps away before I move. In my ears, I hear the pounding of my heart, and with him farther away, the swishing of his steps on the grass. I get a huge intake of breath, and all my muscles quiver with expectancy.

He walks toward my cabin. Toward Lizzy. I have to move now. I charge around the back of the mystery car, full speed, rage coming up from my throat in a scream; a scream to wake Lizzy so maybe she'll escape even though I will die. A scream to wake Kendall—Kendall the warrior—so he can come out and slay my slayer. It is a scream of death, of predator and prey, of fury and sorrow. It is me. It is instinct.

I catch him in the open. I'm aware of something wrong, an anomaly, but I catch him, taking him down from behind; taking him down as he's turning toward my scream. In a rage unhinged, I go all at once for eyes and throat and mouth and ears. The intruder doesn't fight. I don't give up my grasp on him.

Now, in brilliant light, I can see him: the man I sit astride. One eye is opened and unmoving, the other is a pool of slime and blood. His hair is dark and short. His neck is held in my hands, head twisted around to lie cheek down on the grass. My hands are red and shiny. And the anomaly I felt—the sense of something wrong—as I slammed into this man: It is the intruder's partner, and he stands above us, his mouth twisted in rage. I see his foot come at me in a pendulum arc, ending its travel where it meets my face. I roll backward and then I'm sitting in the grass. For a moment I curiously eye the white light shining at me from the direction of the mystery car. The man who kicked me is silhouetted in the beam. He holds a gun at me. I hear the shot. But it is he who falls. He sinks to his knees and tips forward, lying across my lap.

And now I lie down, too.

CHAPTER 48

The doctor removes the gauze from my unaffected eye. I had heard that there were flowers in my hospital room, but geez, there are *really* flowers. Lizzy sits beside the bed reading.

"Whatcha reading, Liz?"

"*Mansfield Park.*"

"Haven't you read that already?"

"Only about eighteen times, Daddy."

"Why—"

"It's comforting," she says in her irritated voice.

She reads. I stare at the ceiling with one eye.

I say, "So, I've been out of it for a couple of days."

"Duh."

". . . but have you gone to school at all this week?"

"I'm a traumatized child, Daddy. I don't go to school."

"Oh. Who's been here, Liz?"

"I already told you. If I tell you again, you'll just forget again."

"No. I'm clearer now."

"Yeah, right. Mom has been here a lot. A real lot. Captain Dorsey came once, and Chip came, and Kaylee and her mom and dad. And Kenny, and—"

"How'd Kenny seem?"

"I left while he was here. And Tina came. You know she's in love with you, Daddy, right?"

"No, she's not."

"Fine, have it your way. And Upton came." She goes back to reading her book.

TMU comes in. I lift a hand, and he grabs it and gives a squeeze. I say, "How you doing, boss?"

"How *you* doing? Jesus, have you looked in a mirror?"

"No."

"Don't."

TMU looks terrible, too, but I can't put a finger on it. "This ought to be good," he says, tipping his head at the TV, which is on a bracket bolted to the wall.

"What oughta be good?"

"Daddy, I told you," Lizzy says, and she explains again that C-SPAN is covering Leslie Herstgood's confirmation hearing in the Senate Judiciary Committee.

"Harold," I say to TMU, "I don't remember much of what happened the other night."

Lizzy slams her book and leaves the room without a word.

"What happened," TMU says, "is you killed a trained assassin with your bare hands. Snapped his neck, gouged an eye, tore his cheek half off, and generally left him looking like he walked into a meat grinder. But there were two of them, and the other kicked you in the head."

"How'd I get here?"

"Your hillbilly hospital up north took one look and had you medevac'ed. Apparently, you had a shattered eye socket, and they were worried about brain swelling."

I have a memory of a man falling onto my lap and the crimson blossom of his shirt. "The one who kicked me," I say. "Kendall shot him?"

"Kendall? Not hardly. Agent d'Villafranca shot him."

"Chip," I whisper. Chip. Now I remember someone telling me. Chip was there. He got concerned when they couldn't find the transponder in my Volvo. It didn't settle right. So he drove to the lake to watch over us for the night. He dozed in his car. This is a side of Chip I've never seen. The hunch-playing, lightning-reflexed, vigilant agent. My excellent protector.

"Chip," I say again, and this time my voice cracks at the idea of the quirky new-agey guardian angel—or guardian agent—watching over me.

TMU spots the threatening tsunami of my emotion and wants none of it. "Professionals," he says loudly, "paid assassins from out of town."

"But who—"

Lizzy comes back. Then Tina and Upton walk in. They're here to watch the hearing. It is all professional. Everybody sits upright on folding chairs; nobody sits on the bed. I watch Upton. He's pretending to be normal. He sits there looking at me with the kind of grin a guy like Upton gives you when you've had a brush with death. He has his usual jaw-thrusted, stubbly-chin look, and his eyes glow with affection. I know it's all bullshit because I remember from before my injury that Upton killed Scud and was trying to pin it on me. I can see it in him. He looks terrible. The stress is getting to him.

But something . . . what is it? It's a feeling; something less bad than all this badness. A lightness, and it has to do with Upton, and it's a memory from before but lost for now in the jumble of concussive and pharmaceutical confusion.

The hearing starts. On television, Leslie looks just like herself. She sits at the table in front of a microphone, looking as composed and confident as she did every day of the three long years I worked under her. Her hair is shorter than the last time I saw her, but she looks not a day older.

"Beneath that bosom," TMU says, "there lies a heart of stone."

I don't know why he dislikes her so. For that matter, I don't know why *I* dislike her so.

The chairman gavels the hearing to order. Leslie is sworn in, and some introductory comments are made by the chairman, who, along with a dozen or so other senators, sits magisterially at his bench above the room. Questioning begins. The first speaker is a young, slick-looking senator with hair like Barbie's boyfriend, Ken. He is from the president's party, and I expect him to toss a few softballs for the nominee to smack over the fence. He doesn't. He takes from his jacket a newspaper article, unfolds it, and studies it a few seconds, then peers over the top of his reading glasses at Leslie. "Ms. Herstgood, as you're no doubt aware, *The Washington Post* printed an article yesterday alleging that, in your position as partner in the Graham and Rush law firm, you undertook the representation of Coral Sand Fashions, which is an Indonesian clothing manufacturer. Is that correct?"

"What the hell?" I say.

"I have provided limited representation on their behalf," Leslie says.

"Tina," I say, "come snuggle with me on the bed?"

TMU chuckles, and Lizzy says, "Daddy, you're not normal yet, you know. As if you ever were."

The senator continues, "And that Coral Sand hired you as part of their public relations and legal effort to overcome a consumer boycott of their products."

"I can't speak to those issues," Leslie says with a pleasant tilt of her head. "I was merely working on import compliance regulations."

"Just another friggin' lawyer," Tina says. She is beside me with her feet on the bed, holding my hand.

"And that Coral Sand is mentioned in a State Department report about the slavelike employment conditions among some overseas clothing manufacturers."

"Well," Tina says in a squeaky imitation of Leslie, "don't believe everything you read, Senator."

"And even *The Wall Street Journal* has called Coral Sand, quote, 'the putrid scum at the bottom of the noxious barrel that is overseas outsourcing.'"

"But, Senator," Tina squeaks, "I'm just their *lawyer*, I'm not getting paid to *judge* them."

TMU chuckles.

"And that up until a couple of weeks ago, you were listed as chief counsel for Fashions International, Inc., which is the sole U.S. importer of Coral Sand products?"

"Daddy," Lizzy says, "you actually worked for this woman?"

"Senator, a lot of this is out of context," Leslie says.

"She wasn't as bad as all that," I say.

Upton clears his throat.

"Bullshit," Tina says, turning to glower at me. "If you didn't have those holes in your skull, I'd swat you."

"My skull?"

"Daddy, I already told you," Lizzy says. "They drilled holes in your head to let the fluid out, and you're on drugs to reduce brain swelling. As if you didn't have a fat enough head already."

"Heehee."

"As corporate counsel, I had a fiduciary obligation to see that . . ."

"Corporate hack is more like it," Tina says to Leslie on the television screen.

TMU gently punches my leg. "Hold on tight to that tail, boy," he says. "You've got a tiger."

"Tiger," I say, but it comes out garbled, and the television blurs.

When I wake up, the television is off and the room is dark and I'm alone, but I have the dreamy memory of Upton coming in and speaking to me long after the others left. And more than that, he keeps popping up in my disjointed memories of the past few days.

CHAPTER 49

There is a buzz. Maxy is back. This is what I couldn't remember last week in the hospital: Maxy's fingerprints in Scud's car. Maybe it wasn't Upton.

Not that it proves anything, because with Upton's underworld connections, he could have hired Maxy for the job. Or maybe Upton somehow planted the evidence. The important thing is that even if it was Upton, at least he wasn't trying to frame me.

I'm back at work. It feels good to be here. People are nice to me. My office has lots of cards and flowers. This morning Pleasant Holly, my equivalent in the civil division, came down and brought some cheesecake, which was considerate, because it doesn't need chewing. We talked for an hour, and it made me wonder if I've made a mistake, focusing on criminal law all these years. There are interesting things about civil law: disability rights, tenants' rights, economic equality, environmental regulation, land use; it goes on and on. It helps that Pleasant is so damn pleasant. She has a smile you can see a mile, and she has that rosy-cheeked exuberance. Stand her up beside Leslie Herstgood, and what do you have? Ambition without integrity in one, and integrity without ambition (at least not venal ambition) in the other. They should have tapped Pleasant for the circuit court.

Midafternoon: I have a meeting with Dorsey at the Rain Tree. Kenny, my chauffeur until I'm driving again, meets me in the parking garage. Just looking at him—sideways cock of the head, boyish grin—I know he's itching to tell me about some new excitement in his life. His eyes are bright and lively today. If I didn't know him so well, I might think he's in love. But he's not; if he were in love, he'd show it differently. He'd be evasive, embarrassed, or fearful. Whatever he has up his sleeve, it's something less terrifying to him.

Kenny opens the door of his Toyota pickup for me. "How long till you can drive again?"

"Probably drive now, except I don't have a car."

"So what happened to your friggin' car?" This is Kenny's affectionate jab. I smile, and smiling makes me sad because I love Kenny and I love his pretend grouchiness. He always teased me about the Volvo, which, to his thinking, is as boring as a car can be.

What happened to the Volvo is that the Bureau searched it for the transponder. Sparky drove me to the garage outside of town yesterday in case I wanted to claim anything. The dissected Volvo reminded me of Seth Coen in his freezer. There was a chassis sitting on the concrete. Its doors and upholstery were removed and the frame cut into pieces. "It was a well-built car," said the man standing there with welding goggles on his forehead and an acetylene torch in his hand.

"The Bureau kept it," I tell Kenny.

"I finally bought my Jet Ski," he says.

"You bought a truck. You bought a Jet Ski. Where the hell . . . ?"

"Been saving."

"Apparently." We pull up in front of Rokeby Mills.

"Really nice," he says. "It's got a-hundred-and-thirty horse, four-cylinder, four-stroke—"

I never got the chance to confront Kenny about his amorous interest in Lizzy before my injury. Now, blocking traffic in front of the Rain Tree, I can't wait any longer. "Shut up, Kenny," I blurt.

He stops and looks over at me. He's stunned.

"You know how old Lizzy is?" I ask.

"Well, she's—"

"—a minor," I say. "And make no mistake: If anybody messes with her—any adult at all, whether it's consensual or otherwise—I won't hesitate a second to put his ass in jail and keep it there as long as possible."

"Well, I—"

"And let me educate you a little about the law, Kenny, since you're too lazy to do it yourself. We have enhanced sentences for statutory rapists who are in a position of influence over their victims, like teachers, clergy, or family members."

"But Nick, I—"

"Shut up, Kenny. The only thing I want to hear from you about this is 'I'm sorry.' And right now I don't even want to hear that. I'll have Dorsey take me back to the office. I'm getting out. You're driving away."

I step out of the truck. Kenny sits there pale and speechless. Cars behind us are blasting horns. I take out my badge and hold it up, showing it to honking drivers as I walk around behind Kenny's truck. "Shut the hell up!" I scream at them, surprising myself with the fury of my voice. Then I take a few minutes, collecting myself before going inside.

The Rain Tree is thick with its usual smell of steamed clams and beer. I notice some of the guys at the veterans' table eyeing me as I cross the room. I give them a sloppy salute, and one salutes back. Dorsey is already here, and when I see him, I remember how bandaged and bruised I look.

"Look at you," Dorsey says, grabbing my hand for an affectionate two-handed shake. Then he's pulling out a chair for me and grabbing a menu. We order clams.

Steve glides over in his wheelchair, and we're doing the thumb-grip handshake and he's studying my head with unapologetic curiosity. "Reminds me of 'Nam," he says. "All kinds of fucked-uppedness there."

My head is almost entirely bandaged except for the left eye and cheek and my mouth. Those exposed parts are blue and purple. Steve and I punch fists, and he leaves.

"So. About Maxy," Dorsey says.

"Yes, about Maxy," I say. "He's the missing link. He connects the street hoods to the big boys."

"That's my thinking," Dorsey says. "Maxy is the big enchilada. Scud Illman was just doing Maxy's bidding. Then Scud became a liability. This is huge, Nick. We track this bastard down, it'll be huge. Dollars to doughnuts, we've got him dead to rights on the Illman murder, and I'm betting we can trace him to Phippin. But that's nothing, because a guy like Maxy, he isn't afraid of the big boys. *He* is a big boy. He's on the inside. He knows where the bodies are buried. He calls the shots, and mark my words, this is a guy who'd sell his granny to take off a single day of prison time. He'll tell us everything."

"Do you have any leads on where to find him?"

"We'll get some, believe you me. This boy has played it cool for ten years, but he's finally shown his hand."

"About Cassandra Randall . . ."

"I'm sure he was involved in that one, too," Dorsey says. "Of course we don't know . . ."

"I have a theory," I say. "You might want to ask the nefarious Mr. Milan about the cars that Seth Coen drove. Particularly a white rental-looking job like the one reportedly seen on Cassandra's street that night."

"You think Seth—"

"It was a difficult shot that killed Cassandra. But someone did it cleanly. One shot through the window. I read Seth Coen's service file. He was a sniper in the Gulf. Scud had the balls-to-the-wall audacity, and Seth had the talent and composure to pull it off without leaving calling cards."

Dorsey eyes me with his head cocked. "It looks like we have perps for four out of four murders, plus an airtight theory of who the puppet master is. We just have to find him."

"That's the hard part."

"You think Kendall Vance really knows anything? Someone was awfully eager to keep him quiet."

I shrug. "If he does, we'll never get it out of him. He takes his client confidentiality a bit too seriously."

"Is he in hiding?"

"Kendall? Hiding out isn't his style. The Bureau thinks the danger is over because he's too hot a property and they wouldn't dare make another go at him. If he was going to squawk, he'd have done it by now. The reward isn't worth the risk."

"I guess that's about it," Dorsey says. His big black mustache is in motion as he masticates one clam after another. Just swallow, I want to tell him. The clams are perfect for me, because they're small and slide down without chewing.

"We'll go national for info on locating Maxy." Dorsey adds, "I bet we can get him on the Bureau's ten most wanted. Then we sit back and let the Bureau reel him in, right?"

"I guess," I say. But I'm not ready to sit back. This new evidence of Maxy's involvement could be even more damning to Upton. He needed Scud dead; Scud wound up dead, and it looks like Maxy played a part. So maybe Upton is connected to Maxy, which could connect him to the murders of Zander and Cassandra, and to all the associated crimes brought upon this city by those purveyors of misery. Upton's urban utopia: what a grotesque joke. I've decided to summarize my suspicions in a confidential memo to TMU. Let him decide Upton's fate. I can't handle it.

Dorsey grabs the bill. "My treat today."

He drives me back to my office. It takes a few minutes, and I wish it would take an hour, a week, a month. I'm enjoying his company, though we haven't said a word since leaving the Rain Tree. More significantly, I dread everything waiting for me up in the criminal division of the U.S. attorney's office. I don't like that I'll spend the afternoon polishing a memo to TMU that could end the career, and maybe the freedom, of my former friend Upton. I don't like that the Circuit Court of Appeals nomination was handed to the less deserving Leslie Herstgood (forcing me to find the where-withal to continue in this job for the rest of my career), and I don't like that Lizzy is camped out in my office and refuses to go back to school.

"I hear Cicely is doing well," Dorsey says.

This makes no sense. I look at him, confused.

"Upton's younger daughter."

I shake my head.

"She OD'd. Crystal meth. Almost died. She was in the hospital same time you were. Upton never left her side except to visit you sometimes. She pulled through fine, but they're unsure if she's affected."

"Affected?"

"Mentally."

So Upton was at the hospital. This explains his appearance in my shadowy memory.

The Upton memo isn't letting me write it. I outlined it earlier, so it's just a matter of putting it into whole sentences, writing an introduction, writing a conclusion, writing regrets. But I can't get it written.

Lizzy lies on the couch. Looking at her, I remember something. No. It's not a memory, it's a feeling. I feel something, the same something I felt that night. It should be horrible and terrifying, but it's not. It's thrilling, and it leaves this sensation jingling in my chest, in my arms and legs, my fingers. The primal thrill when your mind slips beyond the reach of fear and rationality. Beyond governance and reason. I feel the slipperiness of his blood and his sweat and the tremors of his dying resistance as I kneel astride him. I was the predator and he the prey, and I ran him to the ground. I grew claws and fangs. I tore and slashed with animal rage, and when Chip turned the spotlight on us and I saw the opened flesh and ruined eye and twisted neck, I pressed dripping hands to my face and roared again in what might have been anguish or might have been conquest. And now, thinking of this again, I have my hands against my cheeks—one palm on cool and whiskered flesh, the other on bandages. I do this subconsciously, painting my face in the blood of my enemy, which seems to coat my hands in its wet warmness. He was a threat to my Lizzy, and I killed him. I'd do it again. I'd do it every day for eternity.

CHAPTER 50

TMU's office: He called me upstairs for a meeting even before I had my memo ready. I have a rough draft in my briefcase. It will have to do. Neidemeyer, the FBI section chief, is in TMU's office. He always strikes me as having the personality of a sack of concrete.

TMU looks terrible. He suddenly has become old, with pallid cheeks on a face from which energy and enthusiasm have fled. He doesn't get up when I come in. "Harold," I say, "you look tired."

"Yeah, yeah, yeah," he says, "let's talk about who looks worse, shall we?" To Neidemeyer, he says, "Our boy Nick got into a tussle."

"I heard."

"We're proud of him," TMU says, then bends toward his intercom and calls, "Coffee!"

Neidemeyer opens his briefcase and takes out some documents.

I open my briefcase and take out my memo about Upton.

A guy comes in with three coffees on a tray. We each take one. I smell raspberries, and I hold my cup to my nose and sniff.

"You like it?" TMU says. "I think it's refreshing."

Neidemeyer puts his cup down on TMU's desk with a thunk of finality, but I take a sip of mine. I like it. "Harold," I say, "that's nice."

"Got to live it up, eh, boy?" He sips his raspberry-flavored coffee and smiles. "I'll start. We've got a problem: Some fingerprints were recently found at a crime scene where an underworld figure named Avery Illman was murdered."

"I'm aware."

"The prints belonged to a guy who went by the name of Maxy. Full name: Maxwell Patterson."

Neidemeyer hands me one of the documents from his briefcase.

It is a photocopy of a newspaper clipping. At the top of the page, someone has written, "From *Helena Daily Record*," and it is dated about six years ago. It's an obit for a guy named James Donaldson, resident of Helena, age forty-nine, who died at home following a brief illness. Mr. Donaldson, the article said, was a retired building contractor who moved to the Helena area from Los Angeles four years before. He enjoyed downhill skiing and horseback riding. He leaves a wife but no other immediate relatives.

"What's the connection?"

"How much do you know about Maxy?" Neidemeyer asks.

"He was an informant," I say. "He worked his way into the heart of the beast, and then he disappeared. But every now and then someone claims to have seen him, and some people think he's active again."

"He was a scammer," Neidemeyer says. "A born actor but a fraud. He had a knack for getting people to trust him, getting himself into positions of responsibility. He moved around a lot to stay under the radar. We nabbed him, and our handwriting analysts tied him to some impressive jobs. We put together a very tight case. Lots of charges. Serious time inside, but it was all property crimes, nothing violent. So his lawyer cooks up this idea. Maxy buys himself a walk by going to work for us. He'll use his talents and get right into the middle of things, then he'll draw us a road map of who's who and what's what. So we agree to try it out for a while."

I'm watching Neidemeyer speak. He has a gentle, phlegmy voice and disinterested eyes. "It worked out," Neidemeyer says. "Best undercover we've ever had in this city. But after we work him for a year, we catch wind of something wrong. There's chatter. He's suspected. Any moment he might end up dead, so we have to move quick. We invent this big meet-up and put him at the center of it, and we put out rumors on the street so it takes some weeks before anybody figures out that he's gone, and by then everybody's pointing at everyone else, and we're pounding on doors pretending to look for him, and word gets out that he's screwed us. So he becomes an underworld folk hero."

"Everybody likes myth better than truth," TMU says. "The myth is that he beat the system. He screwed the feds and he screwed the bosses. He's living it up in some tropical paradise, flitting back to stir up trouble and then gone again."

"And the truth?"

"Truth is that witness protection sent him to Helena with a new name and enough money to buy a couple of acres and a horse."

"And this obit . . ."

"Pancreatic cancer," TMU says. "It's a bitchingly fast death sentence."

"It's true?"

"It's true," Neidemeyer says. "Mr. Donaldson, formerly Maxwell Patterson, alias Maxy, has been unquestionably dead for the past six years."

"Who knows this?"

"Nobody," Neidemeyer says. "Other than the three of us and maybe a couple guys running the witness protection program."

"Hmmm," I say. "I guess not even Maxy himself knows it, because despite being dead, he somehow got his prints at a murder scene just two weeks ago."

In my office, I lie on the couch, waiting for the Percocet to take effect. I've got another of the blinding headaches that my doctor said I should expect.

So there is no Maxy. Does this mean there is no unifying source of evil to these crimes, no puppet master, or is it simply that we haven't located him yet? I lie there on the couch with my palms over my eyes. I'm glad for the pain. It feels appropriate.

Believing in Maxy was a way out for me. If Maxy killed Scud, then I had one avenue of hope that Upton was innocent. And if Maxy recruited the snitch from among his old contacts at the troopers, then it got everyone in my office off the hook, specifically Kenny.

But how do a man's fingerprints show up at a crime scene six years after his death?

I yell for Janice. She comes in. I say, "I need a file. Immediately. Sooner. If you can't get cooperation from whoever controls the archives, tell me, and I'll kick some ass down there myself. Name is Maxwell Patterson. It was about eleven years ago. If you can't find anything, call the Bureau and have them run the name. Get me whatever you can find."

I return to my couch and doze for an hour until I'm awakened by Janice coming in with a file she got from the FBI: Maxwell Patterson.

"Love ya, Janice," I say.

"Watch it, buster, that's harassment. Prepare to be sued."

It doesn't take long to read. There was never a prosecution, just an investigation, an interview, and a conference with the suspect's lawyer present. The Bureau never sought an indictment. The case seems to have dropped off a cliff. In effect, it did. Maxy went to work for us as an informant, and we closed the investigation.

I take more Percocet and lie back down on the couch, trying to control the pain in my head. Then I'm up. I need to go have a look at the cup from Scud Illman's car where Maxy supposedly left his fingerprints.

Kenny drives me to trooper headquarters. He is quiet and clearly nervous. We don't speak. I write out my request and show my shield, and the officer retrieves a small brown bag from the rows of steel shelves. It's stapled at the top. I open it. Inside is a plain white paper cup, stained with coffee and dusted in fingerprint powder. I study the cup and the prints, walking a few steps to see it more clearly under a bulb in the poorly lit basement room. Suddenly, I get a wave of pain. I press both hands over my eyes. Kenny is right there. He has an arm around me and walks me to a chair. "Jesus, Nick, should I call someone?"

"Comes in stabs," I say. "Gone now. Doctor says it's not unusual."

"You okay," he says, not as a question but as an expression of caring.

"Think so." I sit with my face in my hands and with Kenny's arm around my shoulders. After several seconds, he goes and picks up the cup, which I dropped, and I put it back in its paper bag. We return it to the evidence clerk. Kenny walks me back to the truck, holding on to my arm the whole way. He drives to the office and stops in front to let me out. As I open the door, he says, "Um . . ."

I wait.

In a barely audible voice, eyes staring straight out the windshield, he says, "I'm sorry." He means about Lizzy.

"Noted," I answer.

I go up to my office and lie down again.

There is no Maxy, meaning the crimes might add up to nothing more than small criminal acts by small criminal minds. This is what Kendall Vance said: *There's nothing Shakespearean about it. They're all kind of boring.* Kendall is wise. I wanted to believe in the syndicate, though, the idea of a single thread to pull and the whole thing comes apart. Maybe I liked the idea because it feels less threatening. It's more containable, less spread out among us all.

The central question is how Maxy's fingerprints showed up in Scud's car. A white paper cup with the fingerprints of a man who has been dead for the past six years . . .

With this thought, I'm asleep.

Then I'm awake, and I know the answer. I know who killed Scud Illman. Before I do anything, I drive over to see Kendall Vance. He's still my lawyer, and I trust him. In the car loaned to me by the Bureau, I drive myself out of the parking garage and slowly through town. I have one good eye, and my palm is cupped around my forehead. When I arrive in front of Kendall's office, there is a wood chipper by the curb. The noise of screaming blades feels like it will split my skull.

"Jesus, you look awful, Nick," Kendall says.

"I just needed to get away from the office. Talk things through," I answer. He guides me to a chair and I start talking. I tell him how the troopers found Maxy's prints on the cup. I tell him about Kenny and my awful suspicions. I tell him what I've discovered about Scud's exploitation of Colin, and what I learned about Brittany and how

I'm finally convinced Upton had nothing to do with Scud's death. I tell him all of my suspicions. He has new respect for me, because with Chip's help, I probably saved his and Kaylee's lives ten days ago.

"Are you okay to drive?" he asks after I've talked myself out and headed for the door. "Do you need my help?"

I wave the question away and make it out of his office. I feel like throwing up again, but I'm able to stifle it.

How sad Kendall looks by the time I leave.

The wood chipper is gone. I get in the car and drive. I don't want to go home. I don't want to go to my office. I don't want to go anyplace. Where I do go is to Kenny's. I walk around the apartment looking at things, touching things. His bed is unmade, and I lie down with my head on his pillow, breathing in the scent of this man I love like a son. I bury my bandaged face in the pillow and let it come. Sobs. It comes and comes and comes, and every time I think it has stopped, it comes again, this wellspring of sorrow that seems without a bottom. My boy. My Kenny.

When I finally stand up, the pillow is wet. I go into the bathroom and come out. Then I call Kenny and catch him at work before he leaves. "I'm at your place," I say. "I just needed to get away from everything. Why don't you pick up Chinese takeout and a movie? Your choice. I'll pay you back."

Kenny says he'd like that, watching a movie together.

CHAPTER 51

There are so many things I wish. I wish that Flora and I offered Kenny the stability of a permanent home instead of leaving him in foster care. One or both of us probably could have gotten licensed as a foster home and had him live with us. Maybe we could have adopted him, but we were both busy with careers, and his existing foster family didn't seem so bad, and he was a handful. I wish I'd been better at loving him. It wasn't easy, because I think we got him too late. He cared about us and enjoyed being with us, but maybe the traumas of his younger years left him too impervious, and he never soaked in the idea of being loved. Or—since he wasn't our son and he didn't live with us, and since he was a difficult boy, maybe the love we offered him was more watered down than we knew.

We had a good time together two nights ago. The movie was awful, but he loved it. I drank a couple of beers, which, with the Percocet, knocked me for a loop. Kenny brought me a pillow and blanket for the couch. In my imperfect recollection of that drug-and-alcohol-induced fogginess, as we high-graded shrimp out of the stir-fry and then downed a quart of mint-chip ice cream, I see Kenny's boyish grin unleashed from its constantly niggling awareness of his lesser status in my life. "How come we don't do this more often, Nick?" he asked.

How come, indeed?

In my office, I have the shades closed and the light off. I'm lying on the couch with a towel over my eyes. I yell for Janice a few times, but she doesn't hear me through the office door, and getting off the couch feels impossible right now. I use my cell phone, peeking from under the towel long enough to dial, and call the office number.

"Nick Davis's office," Janice says.

"It's me. Would you tell Upton I need him in my office for a few minutes?"

A minute later, Upton comes in. "You wanted me, boss?"

"Close the door."

He does. I don't sit up, and I don't take the towel off my eyes. I like it better here in the blackness.

"You okay?" Upton asks.

"I was sure you killed Scud," I say.

Silence.

"I've concluded you didn't. But you must have considered it."

Silence.

"Did you take any actions to impede the investigation of Scud Illman, Upton?"

"No."

"I'm inclined to believe you."

"Thank you."

"You need to come clean about the gambling. The next blackmailer might not get so conveniently murdered. Do it in a letter to Harold, and do it soon. He's not well, you know—could step down or check out at any moment, and who knows what the next TMU will be like. Leslie Herstgood would have cut your balls off. But Harold will go to the mat for you. Write out your story; go heavy on the stuff about your sad childhood and the culture of moral chaos in professional athletics. The letter will go in your file, and nobody will ever see it again."

There's a knock on the door.

"I'm busy, go away," I say. I hear the door open.

"Nick," Tina says, "it's important."

I take the towel off my face. Tina's eyes are full and red. She looks from me to Upton. She says, "Captain Dorsey just called. They got a tip on the Scud Illman murder." She walks to the couch, bends down, and takes my hand between hers. "It sounds authoritative,

Nick. They claim that our own Kenny was the shooter. Apparently it was a drug transaction of some kind, and it went bad."

"An anonymous caller?"

"Yes."

I sit up. "Are there inidit . . . indy . . . innoc . . ." This word I know so well, this word I use daily in my job, has fled my mind.

"Indicia," Tina says. "Yes, there are indicia of reliability. The caller gave motive—the drug deal—and he described where to find the gun, and he told them how he knows about it. It was a pretty complete narrative. Captain Dorsey's people are getting the warrant."

I know that what I'm being told is true, that the case against Kenny will be tight, and that he will be convicted. I squeeze the hands that are so warm in mine. "I might as well go over to the apartment. Maybe there's something I can do."

"What about Kenny?" Tina asks.

"He's still here?"

"Yes."

"Glue yourself to him this second," I say. "He's impulsive. Make sure nobody talks to him till I get back." It feels good to be giving orders, taking some responsibility. We leave Tina to keep an eye on Kenny. Upton drives me over to the apartment. The police are just arriving. They have the signed search warrant. I stand outside and watch. It's very quick. They have the gun in minutes. It is a small, deadly looking thing that, I have no doubt, will test out as the gun that shot Scud Illman, which means it is the same gun that killed Seth Coen.

PART III

CHAPTER 52

Friday afternoon. Spring has returned. From my office window, I see the highways leading out of town. Already they are clogged with urbanites making an early break on this Memorial Day weekend. They will go to lakes and mountains and rivers. They will fish and drink and boat and make love and fight; some will commit crimes or cause accidents, and others will be the victims of crimes or accidents. And on Monday evening, the survivors will stream back into town to resume the pace of life in this struggling urban utopia.

I'm in my office, but in a few hours, Tina and I will join the throng. We're going to the lake for the long weekend, and on Sunday we're having a barbecue there, and we're hoping many people will come to enjoy the day with us. Flora and Chip will be there, and they're bringing Lizzy and her friend Homa. Upton says he'll be there with his family; Kendall and his wife are coming with Kaylee.

From here I can see the highways, and far on the horizon the mountains, and just across the river Rokeby and the other decrepit redbrick mill buildings built here because of the river, which provided cheap power and easy transportation. The mills are the womb from which this city grew, and those jobs were the teats on which it suckled and from which, when money dried up and jobs went overseas, it was rudely weaned.

It was a rough quarter century.

I will soon have a better view than I used to. Leslie Herstgood, facing a bitter confirmation battle in the U.S. Senate, withdrew her name as nominee for the seat on the appeals court. I didn't appreciate the irony until Tina pointed it out: Leslie, former U.S. attorney from this city of shuttered textile mills, met her downfall as a lawyer for the overseas child-exploiting, worker-killing sweatshops that put our city on the economic skids. Good riddance, Leslie Herstgood. She remains employed at her old law firm, but Herstgood has been removed from the firm's name.

This time, the president selected me for the vacant seat on the circuit court. Assuming I make it through the confirmation process— and why shouldn't I?—I'll be moving to the office three floors above this one. Below me will be Two Rivers; below him, Pleasant Holly, who has been designated the acting U.S. attorney following TMU's resignation for health reasons two months ago. A floor below Pleasant, I expect, will be my good friend Upton Cruthers, whom Holly has selected to replace me as head of the criminal division.

Five murders. The killing of the innocent and lovely Cassandra Randall has been officially attributed to Seth Coen. The Bureau's investigation of the white rental car has turned up a renter who, on further investigation, is revealed to have died in Iraq twenty years ago. It's an alias that Seth probably acquired while he was in Iraq, probably lifting identification papers from a dead compatriot. The name has followed him around for years; it shows up on some miscellaneous documents taken from the apartment where Seth was found in the freezer. Seth, as a hunter and an army sharpshooter, had the skill to make the shot that killed Cassandra. His motive was that he and Scud believed Cassandra had seen them burying Zander Phippin.

It was determined almost immediately that Lizzy's ill-advised blab on the day we found Zander's body was innocuous. She never spoke Cassandra's name, and everything that she told my staff deadended at the office doors. There must have been a more malevolent snitch. Someone revealed Cassandra's identity from within one of the agencies, someone who was present at the reservoir, or who had access to proprietary information. The identity of the snitch has not been officially determined.

Another murder, the killing of Seth, is attributed solely to Scud.

What I alone know is that Scud's accomplice in concealing the murder and destroying the evidence was his wife. I've decided that for this unintentional felon, time served as Scud's wife is sentence enough. Her debt is paid. Case dismissed.

The disappearance and presumed murder of Brittany Tesoro, and the similar disappearance of two other kids from Rivertown, also remain unsolved. Carrion-sniffing dogs have been working the area where Zander Phippin was buried, but we haven't found anything, and we found no trace of these kids in Seth's boat. Though we know Scud was involved, we don't know whether he worked alone.

Regarding Zander Phippin, the Bureau believes that the new drug boss in the city had him abducted. He was interrogated and tortured, held for a few days without food or water—probably in a storage closet of some kind—and in his efforts to escape, he got oil paints all over his hands. Scud was given the body for disposal. This new drug boss is Percy Mashburn, whose ascent has been meteoric. He is thirty-five but looks younger. He has spiky hair and black-frame-glasses, and he is said to read new-age poetry and to dabble in painting landscapes. He has a penchant for buying art prints. Those who have been inside his house say he especially likes the surreal and oddly sentimental work of the early-twentieth-century artist named Maxfield Parrish; it appears Percy Mashburn occasionally used that name as an alias. But Percy has disappeared.

As for the murder of Scud Illman, my friend and foster son Kenny has confessed. To be precise, I shouldn't call it a murder, because what Kenny pleaded to (twenty years in prison, eligible for parole in twelve) is involuntary manslaughter.

Kenny was arrested in the law library downstairs. It was very formal; Tina and I stood on either side of him as the young trooper with cuffs dangling from one hand nervously read Kenny his rights, as Kenny sat staring in bewilderment.

"You should probably stand up, Kenny," I said.

The trooper cuffed him behind his back.

"I never killed anybody," Kenny said.

I walked with them into the hallway. "Remember," I told him before the elevator door closed, "the only words you speak are 'I want my lawyer.'"

He stared at me in terror and confusion. I stared back, but who knows what he saw in my one unbandaged eye in those last seconds before the elevator door closed.

Kendall refused to have anything to do with the case, so five weeks after Kenny's arrest, I convinced him to fire his public defender and I breached propriety by representing him myself at one informal plea negotiation. I caught up with the assistant DA in a hallway of the state court building. He is a sullen young guy I recognized from bar functions. He takes himself way too seriously.

"You don't want to try this case, David," I said, "it's full of holes. What are you offering?"

"I don't see any holes," he said. "Best I can do is second-degree murder with a recommendation of thirty years."

I knew he'd be this kind: the kind who starts off with the absolute most he can possibly charge, and he offers it up like it's a great deal. I know this lawyer. I've seen him a thousand times in a thousand cases over the thousand years of my career. He is a workman but one without passion or creativity. He is unmoved by my relationship with Kenny, as he is always unmoved by any defendant. In court, he might harp on and on about the horror visited upon a victim, but he's probably inured to that as well. I've read a thousand résumés he's written and turned him down for jobs a thousand times. Have I been him?

I think I have.

"David," I said, "I can see you're a shrewd bargainer. But we both know you haven't got a chance in hell of convicting on first degree, so second degree is no offer at all, it's your baseline, and I'm insulted by it because I'm not some snot-nosed public defender coming in here with hat in hand begging for a bit of slack. You want to go, we'll go. But consider that, right from the start, we've got a strong argument for insufficient probable cause on the warrant, and a pretty strong case for acquittal because nothing in the world besides that gun ties our guy to this murder."

"Untrue," David said in a voice of singsongy petulance. "We can show that Kenny Teague and Avery Illman knew each other. They had *dealings*." The word comes out the way a twelve-year-old says "sex."

"Knowing someone and killing him aren't synonymous, counselor," I said. "The only thing you have is a weapon. Consider how easily someone could have planted that gun in Kenny's apartment, then called in the tip."

"Juries don't buy that Machiavellian shit," David said with an angry curl of his top lip. He's the kind of prosecutor who hates defense lawyers, and the fact that I've prosecuted for twenty-five years earns me no cred.

"And the victim was killed with his own gun," I said. "Doesn't that kind of scream self-defense, especially seeing as your vic was a very bad motherfucker and my defendant was an employee of the U.S. attorney's office with no adult record at all?"

"No, counselor, it doesn't scream self-defense."

"David," I said, "you take this to trial and you'll be flogging a losing case against me, with the city's best defense lawyer, Kendall Vance, advising me. Win or lose, we'll tie this up for months and miss no chance at making you look like an asshole. Or else you can get realistic. Save us all some grief. I have a proposal."

He looked at me warily. No doubt he knew of me and wanted to make a good impression, but at the same time, the idea of going up against me and winning was delicious for him to contemplate. It was a career game of chicken. I didn't wait for him to answer. "Here it is," I said. "I can get Kenny to plead to involuntary manslaughter. Twenty years, eligible for parole at twelve."

David tried to conceal his surprise. He wasn't expecting anything even close to twenty. It was a good offer; it would give him bragging rights that he had squeezed so harsh a plea out of the former assistant U.S. attorney on a loser of a case.

"Twenty-five and fifteen," he said.

"This isn't a negotiation, David. Twenty and twelve. Take it or leave it."

He didn't want to seem too eager. It was a gift to him, but he was wary. He checked his watch as if it might have an answer for him. He cleared his throat. David is a young guy with a few extra pounds that he's probably had all his life; he wears a wedding band and a frown. I had the strange inclination to ask Upton to hire him; to play Henry Higgins, molding him into a less obtuse, less adversarial version of himself. "Twenty and twelve," I repeated.

He accepted.

Kendall would have gotten it lower, shaving years off the plea. Or maybe he would have taken it to trial and kicked some ass, getting it thrown out for insufficient probable cause on the warrant, or winning acquittal on the weakness of the case. Kendall would have done better, but he wanted nothing to do with the whole mess. Besides, Kenny deserves every day of those twelve years.

David and I shook on the agreement. He turned and hurried toward his next case in a courtroom down the hall. I watched him go. His suit jacket was short in the cuffs, but otherwise, he could disappear flawlessly into any crowd of young lawyers. A few seconds before he reached his doorway, in a baffling surge of *something*—call it desperation to mark the momentousness of our brief exchange, or call it hope, or call it sorrow—I yelled for him to stop, and I ran after him. People turned to see what was going on.

"Listen," I said, "why don't you come over to the U.S. attorney's office for a visit sometime. Bring your résumé."

CHAPTER 53

My nomination to the U.S. Circuit Court is stalled. Midterm elections are coming up in the fall. The Senate and the White House are controlled by different parties; partisanship is out of control. The chairman of the Senate Judiciary Committee has made it clear that he has no intention of moving on judicial nominations until November at the soonest. Depending on the outcome of the elections, the standoff could easily go another two years.

I hope I do get confirmed someday. As a judge of the circuit court, it would be my job to determine, with perfect objectivity, how laws and legal precedents apply to every twist of every sorry set of facts.

But is that not madness?

Because if you look at the facts from over here, the case resolves one way. You look at the laws from over there, it turns the other. Objectivity? There is no objectivity. Do you think I couldn't find a legal argument for affirming a zillion-dollar jury award against, let's say, a toy manufacturer whose carelessness has caused empty cribs and ruined families? Do you think I couldn't find grounds for overturning the conviction of—I'm just imagining here—a confused, dyslexic, gay pot pusher like Zander Phippin?

It all depends on where you stand. Or more to the point, where you're stuck. Except I don't feel stuck anymore. I used to cringe at the idea of judging. Now I crave it.

Last fall, after my brief negotiation with the assistant DA, I had to talk Kenny into accepting the plea bargain. He was brought to me in gray prison pajamas. His eyes were red-rimmed, though I doubt it was from crying so much as sleeplessness. Already he walked with a timorous shuffle. I could see the first bits of eye-shifting, shoulder-bending decay of his natural self. Kenny is not a conqueror. He has gotten along in life by keeping his head down and mouth closed. It's how he survived in the violent home of his childhood, and it's how he slipped past the well-intentioned but overworked teachers all through school who, if he ever made himself more conspicuous, might have found a way to bring the grindstone up to Kenny's nose. Does invisibility work in prison? We'll see, but already, as we sat down in the private cubicle reserved for lawyers and clients, I had the sense that if Kenny sat between me and a bright light, I'd see the glow right through him.

"You'll plead guilty," I told him.

"I never killed anyone."

"I'm doing you a favor here, Kenny. It's a good deal for you."

"But . . ." he said. Then a tsunami of grief poured from him.

We spent several hours, just Kenny and me, inside that small cement room. With animal panic in his eyes, Kenny sometimes looked like he was about to go for me or the reinforced window that looked out over guards and prisoners who wandered past like hollow extras in a nightmare. *Breathe, Kenny, breathe,* I'd say with my hands on his knees, and together we'd take deep, controlled breaths until I saw the panic drain away. Twenty years, maybe to be released on parole as soon as twelve.

I got him to agree. He'd take the plea bargain. Then we went to work on his story. It helps to have a story. Something to repeat to himself so that, in time, maybe he'd come to believe it:

What happened, Kenny?

I was buying drugs.

What drugs?

Pot. Just pot.

To sell?

No. Just for me.

And you were where?

Rainbow Bend picnic area.

Why? That seems a long way to go just to buy some pot.

That's where Mr. Illman said.

Had you met before?

Couple of times.

To buy pot?

Yes.

Any other business between you?

No.

What happened that night?

I don't know.

You goddamn better know, Kenny.

Okay. He gets out of his car and I get out of mine, and he asks, have I got the money, and I say I do, and I give it to him. And then I say, "Where's the stuff," then he says, "Here's the stuff," and he opens his jacket, and there's the gun in his belt. He calls me a fucking retard, and he's got the gun in his hand, and I swing at him with everything I've got, but I miss his face and catch him in the throat. He goes down and drops the gun, and I, like, I try to find it. He was going to kill me, I think. Finally, I find the gun and jump up and shoot him.

How many times?

I don't know.

Did you mean to kill him?

All I meant was for him not to kill me.

Seems like a lot of fuss over a few hundred bucks.

For sure.

What did you do then?

I just left him there.

Where?

Right at the edge of the river.

What was the weather?

Rainy.

What did you do with the gun?

I wiped it off.

Right then?

No. I mean I took it home and wiped it off. Then I hid it.

Why did you keep it?
I don't know.
Did you touch his car? Get in his car?
No.
Did you tell anybody?
No.
No?
I mean yes. I told some guys I know. I showed a couple of them the gun; they must be who called it in.
What are their names?
Silence.
Kenny, what are their names?
Silence.
Kenny, are you refusing to give their names?
Yes.
Why?
I'm scared of them.

Kenny pleaded guilty to this crime he didn't commit, explaining it with a story that never took place. He took the twenty years, eligible for parole at twelve.

Kenny's confession to this murder, in addition to having been caught with the gun, is all the proof anybody needs that Kenny is, in fact, guilty of killing Scud Illman. The remaining matter of Maxy's prints on the paper cup is easily explained: Maxy *is* back, and Scud was connected to him in some nefarious way. Maxy must have left a paper cup in Scud's car. But given the confession by Kenny, there's nothing linking Maxy to that killing.

As for the FBI Bureau chief, Neidemeyer, and the few others who know that Maxy has been dead for years, the appearance of his fingerprints probably looks like exactly what it is: a shady character who had an old paper cup for some reason, must have wanted to spread confusion. It is not in law enforcement's interest to challenge cases that have been resolved with a confession and a sentence.

CHAPTER 54

Flora and I met one afternoon at Kenny's apartment. We had put it off for weeks, but now we were out of time, and the new tenant was ready to move in. I had already done my crying over this wayward boy. I'd already been to the apartment and brushed fingers over the photos, which, taken so many years ago, had promised better things. I had considered his crimes; I'd prosecuted him, defended him, judged him, and sentenced him. For me, this trip was the sad errand of cleaning out the apartment. Though the events were poignant, even tragic, I had confronted the realities and moved from short-term shock into long-term acceptance. Not so Flora. It was newer to her. She cried, as I had the day I came here alone to wait for Kenny, the day we watched a video and ate Chinese takeout. Now Flora lay on Kenny's bed, and I sat beside her.

"But he didn't even smoke pot," she said in reference to Kenny's explanation that his shooting Scud was the result of the botched purchase of some pot.

"Go figure," I said. She was right. Kenny had no interest in drugs, pot or otherwise. He liked his beer, he was continually quitting smoking, but he claimed to have an allergic reaction to pot.

"And he's a coward," she said with a tragic laugh. "I can't see him wrestling that man's gun away."

"People surprise you."

"Twelve years."

"Twelve years."

"Seems you could have done more," she said.

"More how?"

"To keep him out of jail. Or not as long."

The front door opened. Flora sat up, startled, and rubbed her puffy eyes.

"It's just me," yelled a man. He was one of the carpenters. "Bathroom break." He unhooked his tool belt, peeking in at us unapologetically. It was the younger of two brothers I had hired to build the wheelchair ramp. Mrs. Kapucinski, the landlord, vetoed the ramp at first, but when I offered to pay for it myself—and then mentioned a housing discrimination action if she refused—she relented. Kenny has moved out. Fuseli, the tat man of Ellisville Max, has been released from prison and will move in as soon as the ramp is completed.

Flora is right, I could have done much more to lessen Kenny's sentence, but I wasn't about to tell her so. I shrugged and said, "I don't know, babe. They wanted to charge him with first degree. I think we did okay getting him twenty and twelve on manslaughter."

"Well, we've lost another one," she said, her eyes red and swollen, her cheeks wet. "We don't do so well with boys."

CHAPTER 55

Last fall, when it looked like I'd be the new judge on the circuit court, Tina and I drove to Ellisville Maximum Security Prison for a meeting with the warden. I had an idea that arose after the night we spent in forehead-scrunching analysis of all the evidence in all the murders.

Fuseli, the tat man of Ellisville Max, was doing sixty to eighty. His appeals had been used up decades ago, and the only way to reopen a case all these years later, was if new evidence is uncovered. Even then, it's far from a sure thing. No, there isn't a defense lawyer on earth who could have gotten Fuseli out of prison now.

But what about a prosecutor? What came to mind when Tina told me about Fuseli's wheelchair was a little-known provision of federal law called "compassionate release." It allows the Bureau of Prisons, in extraordinary circumstances, to ask the court for permission to release a prisoner before his term is up. The circumstances usually involve a terminal or chronically debilitating illness.

The warden at Ellisville is a reasonable and uneffusive man who courteously congratulated me on my nomination to the circuit court. He and Tina and I spoke for perhaps an hour. A week later, Judge Two Rivers received and approved a request from the Bureau of Prisons for the compassionate release of one Leroy Burton, aka Fuseli, after thirty-two years served of a sixty-to-ninety sentence. We moved him into Kenny's newly vacated apartment. I'm not sure why I went to this trouble for Fuseli. I like him, but it's more than that. Maybe I'm investing in the hope that sometime down the road, Kenny, too, will catch a lucky break.

* * *

Now it is springtime, the Saturday morning of Memorial Day weekend. I'm in my Adirondack chair, coffee cup between my palms. Mist rises off the black and golden surface of the lake. The birds are raucous. I'll never be a serious birder, but I'm learning to identify a few of them, and to start thinking of them in groupings: sparrows, warblers, flycatchers, and thrushes. I hear one now, my favorite bird: *tinga tinga tinga tinga ting.* The hermit thrush.

Last summer I made a promise to the memories of Cassandra Randall and Zander Phippin that I'd catch their killers. Have I succeeded? Yes and no. Scud and Seth are dead, but they were mere accessories. The real killer, Percy Mashburn, has disappeared. And the snitch within law enforcement who handed Cassandra (and probably Zander) over to her assassins has never been identified.

Lizzy and her friend Homa come out of the cabin in running shoes and shorts, and with barely a glance in my direction, they're off around the lake. They slept in my cabin last night instead of bunking next door with Chip and Flora. Tonight Tina will be here with me, and Chip is heading back to town, so the girls will probably move over to Flora's cabin.

Chip and Flora are "together." I'd never have predicted it in a million years. They're both oddballs who were flung from their established orbits by the woes of life. What were the chances, as they hurdled randomly into the future, that their courses would line up so well? But I'm not complaining. It's the happiest I've ever seen either of them.

Knowing comes in stages. I think the first stage for me was the day last fall when I went to Scud's widow and asked for her shoes. I was committing a crime, but instead of being remorseful, I felt unleashed. Giddy. I was unsure what to do with the shoes. If I threw them out, the crime would be solidified, whereas if I kept them, the crime could almost be undone later on. So I had the preposterous idea of taking them to Kendall, my lawyer. Because isn't it his job to protect me, to hear my confession and keep me safe? Except lawyers aren't in the business of concealing physical evidence. He could lose his license to practice, go to jail. Ultimately, I took them to Flora's and hid them there.

It was about two weeks later, the day before the police, responding to an anonymous tip, raided Kenny's apartment, just over a week after I got out of the hospital, with my head still bandaged and the revelations that Maxy had been dead for the past six years newly entered into the equation, when I violated doctor's orders by driving myself over to Kendall's office. Out in the street, a couple of city workers were feeding brush into a wood chipper, and the screaming of it felt like it would split my skull. I made it to Kendall's door with my hands pressed against my ears.

"Jesus, you look awful, Nick," he said.

"I just needed to get away from my office, talk things through."

"Of course," he said. "Make yourself comfortable. What can I get you?"

"Coffee, please. For here."

"For here?"

"Yeah," I said, "like when you get it at a coffee shop. As in: 'For here or to go?' Then they bring it in either a ceramic cup or a paper cup. I'll take ceramic. I like the warmth. It feels good against my cheek."

Kendall looked at me, bemused, then he got the coffee. When we were sitting as before, with our feet on the hassock and my cup warming me through the bandages over my right eye, I said, "You know, Kendall, your client Scud was a real sociopath."

"Was he?"

"He was. He pimped his stepson into kiddie porn."

Kendall made a helpless gesture. *I can't talk about it,* he seemed to be saying.

The warmth of the coffee felt good against my head. I said, "I think he also acquired a ten-year-old girl named Brittany Tesoro, took pictures of her, then sold her or murdered her. Have you heard about any of this?"

Kendall held both hands in front of his face as if shielding himself from the wretchedness.

"Oh God," I moaned. A bolt of pain passed through my head. It seemed to appear and disappear with purpose, like a snake crossing a path, emerging from and disappearing into the grass on either side.

"You okay, Nick?"

"Sorry," I said. "It's quite intense."

"Can I do anything for you?"

I waved him away and sat motionless until it was completely gone.

Kendall sat impassively, staring into his own cup.

"Killed her," I whispered. "A little girl."

"But do you have evidence?"

"What the hell do I need evidence for? Scud's dead. I can call him a perverted, child-murdering wart on the asshole of humanity, and if that offends your loyalty to your dead client, then go ahead and cry into your coffee, because I don't give a good goddamn."

Kendall swallowed and was about to say something but apparently decided not to. My head felt better for the moment. I got up and walked over to his wall of fame and looked at the plaques. Most of his charitable and service work was with organizations focused on children; I recalled that he wouldn't represent defendants in crimes against children.

I said, "What would you do, Kendall, if you knew someone who'd done shit like that? Who snatched a kid like that? And let's say you're the only one in the world who knows it."

I turned to look at him. He was staring at the floor and he looked ashen.

"What would you do?" I said again.

"Go away, Nick," he said in a barely audible voice.

"Can't," I said. "I'm not fit to drive."

I went back to the comfy chair and put my feet on the hassock and held the warm cup against my head. Then the pain came back. I closed my eyes and tried to massage it away with my fingertips. I said, "You want to know what's always confused me about defense lawyers? It's how you can defend scumbags like Scud Illman. I mean, you said it yourself last time I was here. You said you don't defend criminals, you defend principles. And it's unfortunate that some pretty unsavory characters are the vehicles of those principles. Right, Kendall?"

He didn't answer.

"You're an ethical person, and you're expected to keep the secrets of monsters."

He straightened up in his chair. He had faltered for a moment. I saw it—his pale features, the quiet terror in his eyes—but he'd conquered it. His eyes were back to icy and fierce, his hands on the arms of his chair. He was the commando, ready to grapple with my threat, but able to sit still and let it come to him.

"I mean, what's a man like you supposed to do? Every client you've represented, every cause you've served, every stand you've taken . . ." I waved my hand at the plaques on the wall. "Everything you stand for is about adherence to a code. Am I right?"

I could see him deliberating how to respond. He was becoming a coiled spring of explosive energy, just waiting for the go.

"Military code, personal code, the legal code. Remember the oath we swore to all those years ago? 'I will maintain the confidences and hold inviolate my clients' secrets.' You said it yourself that night you invited me to address your law school class. You said you'd sooner die than turn traitor on a client. Remember?"

"What do you want, Nick?"

"So what do you do as a defense attorney if you know the most heinous secrets? The kind of shit that wakes you up at night in a cold sweat. The shit that separates humans from beasts . . ."

He stood up and opened his office door, trying to get me to leave.

I met his eyes and pointed at the wall of fame. "I'm talking about the shit you've gone to war to fight against, and here it is in your own backyard, and you're expected to actually *defend* these perps. And nobody knows but you. Nobody. Maybe it doesn't even have anything to do with what the guy is charged with."

I stood and met him face-to-face. I said, "So some client comes in and sits here, all cozy in this chair, and he's smart enough to know that whatever he tells you can't be breathed to anyone, and he's fucked up enough that he wants to boast about it to someone, and he's cruel enough not to care what the knowing of it does to a guy like you. What can you do, Kendall? You can't tell anyone, because that violates your oath as a lawyer. You can't let the bastard go down on a flimsy murder charge, because that violates your oath, too. But you can't do nothing, because that violates everything you're about, doesn't it?"

Kendall moved toward me, and I worried that I'd overplayed my hand. Even at my best, I was no match for him. In my current state, I might as well be shackled in place. But after glowering at me a second, he turned and collapsed back in the chair. He watched me and waited. I held him steady in my one good eye.

"What do you want?" he whispered.

"Never mind," I said. "I'm just enjoying conversing with you about the difficulties of legal defense. Actually, I've come to tell you some sad news: Did you know that Maxy is dead?"

"What are you talking about?"

"Maxy."

"Maxy disappeared years ago."

"Yes. And he's been dead for six years. Confirmed. Trust me on this one. Maxy is long gone. Which is what every thinking person assumed, but since there was no actual record of his death, he makes a great and mysterious suspect, don't you think? Other than the few federal cops who set him up in witness protection, nobody knew what happened to him. I'm betting even his lawyer never knew what happened to him or that there was proof he'd died: natural causes, by the way. So just for kicks, I looked up Maxy's old criminal file at the Bureau. And do you know who his lawyer was? Can you guess?"

Finally, I saw real, focused concern in Kendall's eyes.

"You," I said. "You were his lawyer. Then he up and disappeared, and you, along with every crook in the city, figured he got whacked. So now, if a perp was somehow able to focus suspicion on this ghost named Maxy, the crime would go unsolved, right?"

He didn't answer.

"But dead guys don't leave fingerprints, do they, Kendall?"

He moved so quickly that by the time I had my hands instinctively protecting my face, my collar was bunched in his fists and my face was inches from his. He held me there a second.

"Down, boy," I said in a strangled voice, my shirt choking me.

He released me. I thought of going for the door, but the situation felt brittle. I worried that if I flinched, he'd pounce. I sat down slowly, trying to look calm and controlled. For a few seconds, neither of us spoke, each waiting to see what the other would do.

"What do you want, Nick?"

"I want you to open your safe."

This took him by surprise. He studied me, calculating.

"Or wait," I said. "Give me a copy of your standard representation agreement first."

He didn't move. I put my hands out to either side in a submissive gesture. "Do it, Kendall," I said gently.

He stepped to the computer, pushed a few keys, and the printer spat out a blank client contract. I picked it up and bent over his desk with it. Every place it gave Kendall's name, I crossed it out and wrote in my name. Wherever there was a space for the client's name, I wrote in Kendall Vance. Where it discussed his fee, I changed the hourly rate to one dollar. I signed it on the line titled "Attorney," and I handed it back to him. "You can sign as client if you want. Doesn't matter, I'm bound either way."

He didn't take it, so I tossed it on his desk. Kendall turned to face me and ran both hands over the shiny knob of his head, and though his eyes still had that downturn, his mouth, the line of his lips as he waited, lengthened the meagerest, dreamlike fraction of a millimeter. Not a smile—certainly not a smile—but the settling of something; a grain of sand that had tumbled ocean depths to settle in a perfectly sized hollow of the ocean floor. He was peaceful. He could be the condemned prisoner eyeing his executioner, or he could be the king standing on a parapet to oversee his lands.

I said, "I'm your lawyer now. I will hold inviolate my client's secrets."

CHAPTER 56

I could have gotten a warrant to open the safe. I could have advised Kendall of his rights. I could have arrested him and tried him and jailed him. It was not my job to make laws. *If you want to make laws, go into politics.* My job was to enforce laws. Years ago, I gave up judging for myself; life is too complicated, better to pick a side and hold tight. But then came Mrs. Illman's shoes. With Mrs. Illman's shoes, I relaxed my grip.

"Now open your safe," I ordered.

"About the paper cups," Kendall said, looking like he was standing at attention. "I was trained as special forces; we never knew where and how the enemy was going to hit us. So when I started my practice . . . I deal with some merciless bastards in this business . . ."

"Like the ones who tried to kill you."

He was silent a long time, then he said in a softer voice, "Will your eye be okay?"

"Focusing-wise, it'll be fine, but they're not sure whether it will move okay."

"The headaches?"

"Temporary, they think."

Silence.

"You were talking about fingerprints, Kendall."

"Yes. Guarding against a surprise attack. Plus, my dad was framed on extortion charges. So I'm a suspicious bastard. The paper cups are something I started doing when I opened my practice."

"Do you print everyone?"

"Everyone. Nothing personal."

"You must have hundreds."

"Two hundred eighty-seven."

"Have you ever used one before?"

"What do you want, Nick?"

"I already told you."

With that, Kendall spun the dial on his wall safe, then swung it open and stepped to the side.

Perps are always trying to get lawyers to hide evidence. I imagined Scud asking Kendall to hold on to his gun: *This bad boy's a little too hot for me, counselor, how 'bout I keep it here till things cool down?*

The gun that killed Seth Coen. Had Scud already bragged to Kendall about his photography business? Maybe he bared his soul about snuffing life from the blameless young Brittany Tesoro? Had he trumpeted to the ethically pure and duty-bound Kendall Vance his utter lack of remorse—or never mind remorse, had he chuckled about how he was just getting started? *I got big plans, counselor.* I imagine Scud, with his perpetually amused eyes and malevolent smirk, telling Kendall Vance, *Big plans. Stick with me, counselor. Keep me out of jail, and I'll keep you in the gravy.*

What else could Kendall do—a man of his moral rigidity? He couldn't violate his oath to protect his client's secrets. But with the knowledge of whatever happened to Brittany Tesoro—and perhaps to other children like her—he couldn't ignore the moral imperative of ending Scud's activities.

The conflict must have caused a psychological battle for Kendall's soul, threatening everything he believed in. As a commando and a trial attorney, Kendall responded to the threat by attacking. He lured Scud Illman out to Rainbow Bend picnic area. Barehanded, he crushed Scud's throat, then shot him twice. The gunshots were so we'd link the killing to Seth's murder, assume it was all gangland, and let it go. But just to be sure, Kendall brought along a paper cup from his collection, a decade-old cup that had the prints of the mythic Maxy. No doubt Kendall figured that bit of misdirection would send the investigation spinning far off in the wrong direction.

I reached into the opened safe and picked up the small black handgun. "I'll be needing this," I said. It had a textured grip and fit comfortably in my hand. I released the clip into my palm and put it in one pocket, then I dropped the gun in the other. I'd known Kendall had kept the gun—he wouldn't destroy or dispose of such critical evidence, even if it was against himself. It would violate his code of ethics.

In the seconds before I left Kendall's office, I considered and rejected many parting comments, but in the end, there was nothing to say. The lawyer had killed his client.

The pain came back. I pressed both palms against my eyes and moaned.

CHAPTER 57

Flora will always suspect that, because I was angry about Kenny's inappropriate attention toward Lizzy, I didn't work as hard for him as I could have. She's half right. I didn't work as hard as I could have, but it wasn't about Lizzy—though maybe my suspicions started there. It was the problem over Lizzy that made me stop seeing Kenny as a harmless, overgrown kid. The knowing of difficult things comes in stages: Would you casually pry boulders from the stone foundation where you live? Of course not. If they have to go, you shore up; you reinforce. Call it denial if you want, but I'll call it self-preservation; I'd had the roof and walls of life tumble down on me once already. I wasn't taking chances. With regard to Kenny, my knowledge came in stages, and the first stage was in the counselor's office at Turner Middle School. Maybe he wasn't just a rambunctious kid but, rather, a rationalizer, a self-dealer, a damaged soul whose seeping psychic wound, like those of so many criminals I've jailed, would someday put at risk whatever healthy life it comes in contact with. So yes, the problem with Lizzy changed my thinking enough that everything fell into place when I saw the Bernier Construction truck in Flora's yard. He'd made too many big-ticket purchases for his income. When I searched his apartment that day, I didn't know what it would be, but I had a pretty good idea I'd find something.

I did: I found the bank statements with several unaccountably large deposits. I found the phone records with calls to Bernier Construction, and I found the note, torn from Dorsey's spiral-bound pad, with Cassandra Randall's name and address. Kenny must have gone into my house when Lizzy and I were at the lake that weekend and snatched the note from my shirt pocket.

* * *

Almost everyone is here at the lake. Children are jumping off the dock; Bill-the-Dog is chasing Chip's black Lab, while Upton's wife's Pomeranian hides under the picnic table. Chip and Flora, in love and wanting to show it to the world, are strutting around, hand in hand. Dink Sammel, my neighbor up the lake, has trapped Ed Cashdan, one of the assistant U.S. attorneys, in an endless monologue of how the IRS exists in violation of the U.S. Constitution. Seamus, Dink's cousin's stepson, the boy with leukemia who stays at Dink's cabin, is here. He had a bone marrow transplant this winter, and though he looks emaciated and pale, his prognosis is good. He sits in a folding chair watching other kids play in the water, and Lizzy, I notice, checks in with him every few minutes.

And me, I'm on edge because Tina is late.

It would have been easier to let Kenny go down on the charges stemming from being a snitch. It was Kenny who delivered Cassandra Randall's name to his contact at Bernier Construction, a Mob-owned, quasi-legitimate business. But there would have been problems with prosecuting Kenny for that crime. For one thing, I had searched his apartment without a warrant, so all the incriminating things I found that day, as the fruits of an illegal search, might have been suppressed. Without that evidence, there was no case at all. A good prosecutor would argue that my having Kenny's key gave me an implied consent to search, but who knows how a court would rule on the question.

A second problem with letting Kenny be the snitch was that, besides being charged with obstruction of justice, he might also get charged as an accessory in Cassandra's murder. (Probably Zander's as well; I assume it was Kenny who let it be known that Zander was cooperating.) As an accessory in these murders, Kenny could have gotten life in prison.

And the biggest problem was that, if he went to federal prison, he'd be dead within a year. The lower-echelon criminals would hate him for working with the U.S. attorney's office, and the big boys of organized crime might see him as a threat because maybe he really did know something damaging. And of course everyone would worry that he was snitching for us, feeding info back to his old employers. So I couldn't let him go in on federal charges.

But I couldn't let him off, either. So I did the equation: the severity of his crime versus his prospects for rehabilitation, his good character versus his denial of responsibility, the likelihood of his reoffending versus his potential for becoming a productive member of society. My compassion for the difficulties of his childhood versus my anger over the choices of his adulthood. The contempt I felt toward him for Cassandra's death. And finally, the equation that only I, as judge and jury, could calculate: my grief over his betrayal and the deaths of Cassandra and Zander versus my grief at the prospect of losing another son.

You can't put numbers on these things. No meter measures loss and sorrow. No blood test shows the level of remorse. I was on my own. And in the weeks before my talk with David, the assistant DA, I thought over every prison sentence I'd ever seen handed down in my long career. Some were raw deals, some were sweet.

The mystery of who was selling information from inside the official offices of the federal criminal justice system remains unsolved. Naturally, Kenny has incurred suspicion, but I've taken pains to cover his tracks. Among other things, I filed a tax form this year, declaring several cash gifts to Kenny that coincided with the large deposits made to his bank account. If any official investigation should trend too heavily in Kenny's direction, I believe I can use my influence to steer it away.

Last fall, I walked out of Kendall Vance's office with the gun in my pocket and that searing pain in my head. I staggered to the car loaned to me by the FBI and slumped in the front seat. The wood chipper had left while I was inside, so I sat there a few minutes.

Kendall had done what he believed was right, and that belief would make whatever followed tolerable.

I drove from Kendall's office to Kenny's apartment. I let myself in with my key, got the screwdriver from his kitchen drawer, removed all the cleaning supplies from under the bathroom sink, unscrewed and lifted up the bottom panel, and then, after wiping it clean of any prints, I put Scud Illman's gun there, then replaced everything as I'd found it.

I took more Percocet, then I lay on the bed and sobbed. I called Kenny and told him to pick up a video and some Chinese takeout on his way home.

We had a nice time, and by the end of the evening, I saw Kenny's boyish grin unleashed for once from its constantly niggling awareness of his lesser status in my life. "How come we don't do this more often, Nick?" he asked.

How come, indeed?

In the morning I called in the anonymous tip of where to find the gun that had killed Scud Illman.

Chapter 58

A t the urging of my new-agey friend Chip, I was briefly involved in a men's group, though we didn't beat drums and dance in the woods. Our mission was practical, not psychological. There are only a few members in the club, and we were chosen with intention. It was Hollis Phippin's idea. Hollis, bereaved father of a murdered boy, has lots of money and lots of connections. Hollis needed someone in the U.S. attorney's office, so he approached Upton Cruthers (bad boy for the prosecution and dreamer of the urban utopia), whose daughter spent a week in ICU and suffers permanent cognitive impairment from a drug overdose. Hollis and Upton needed a judge, so they asked me, thinking I was about to be installed on the circuit court.

As I say, Percy Mashburn has disappeared. He had reached that point in the career of a kingpin where he never traveled without his entourage and bodyguards, so it's unlikely that anybody could have gotten to him. What we know is that he was brought in on a federal warrant for questioning. The entourage wasn't invited. True, the grounds for the warrant were flimsy and would have been deemed insufficient probable cause by the cautious Two Rivers. But Upton requested the warrant from Judge Washington, not Two Rivers. We were unsure whether he'd sign it, but with it stuck into a small stack of other petitions, the tired and overworked Washington didn't hesitate.

Nothing was left to chance. A certain result was desired, so the necessary information flowed outward from our little group to those whose participation was needed. Percy was brought into the FBI for a fruitless Q and A and then released. For his own protection, he was released secretly out the rear entrance. And yes, we have the security footage of him leaving the building, this scrawny purveyor of misery walking from the building without the safety of his henchmen. Percy walked away beyond the range of the video and has never been seen since.

And my little men's group has now disbanded.

CHAPTER 59

Kendall and his family finally arrive. Kaylee jumps from the car and runs to Lizzy, who hugs her like a sister and takes her into the cabin to change into their swimsuits. Kendall introduces me to his wife, whom I introduce to Flora and Chip and everyone else. Then Kendall and I, by unspoken agreement, stroll away from the crowd along the edge of the lake. We stop and face each other, and Kendall asks how I'm doing and about my confirmation by the senate. I tell him I'm doing okay, but that the confirmation is stalled.

There isn't much to say. We could talk about Kaylee and Lizzy, but we don't. Maybe if we weren't such guys, we'd put our arms around each other and get weepy. But Kendall is a commando and a hard-bit defense lawyer, and I'm an assistant U.S. attorney and a nominee to the U.S. Circuit Court of Appeals. Naturally, I told Kendall all about Kenny so he, Kendall, wouldn't worry about somebody else doing his time for Scud's murder. Kendall and I are pretty balled up in mutual confidences. To pull any thread would unravel the whole.

After too much awkward silence, Kendall and I walk back toward the group.

In my nearly thirty years as a criminal lawyer, only twice did I sign on as defense counsel, but those cases have left me with secrets to keep: for my client Kendall, I keep the secret that he killed Scud Illman. For my client Kenny, I keep the secret that he didn't.

Finally, I hear the rumble of tires on the gravel, and I turn to see Tina pull up in the line of cars. I trot over to meet her. Colin, the boy with the two-tone eye, gets out of the back and stands embarrassed, the way kids do in new environments. It turned out that

Colin's mom, Scud's wife, was an accessory in some of Scud's less contemptible crimes. She's doing a few years inside, and Colin is in foster care. Tina and I take him out sometimes, trying to show him life from the other side. Call it another attempt to redeem my failures with Kenny.

As Colin stands there, our three-month-old mutt from the pound hurls herself from the car and runs barking toward the other dogs. Colin runs after them. I close the car door, noticing as I do that the backseat is a mess of muddy puppy prints and kids' books and soda bottles and spilled bags of chips.

I take the wheelchair from the trunk, but Fuseli is already out. "I'll try it myself," he says, waving the chair away as I wheel it over to him, and he starts his faltering journey to the picnic table.

"Wow," Tina says, "I really have to pee. Again. And I think I'm going to barf. Again." With one hand supporting her swollen belly, she hurries toward the cabin. Her hair has grown out, and she has tied it in back. It's beautiful.